I0527836

ALEXEI

(Her Russian Protector #8)

Roxie Rivera

Night Works Books
3515-B Longmire Drive #103
College Station, Texas 77845
www.roxierivera.com

Publisher's Note: This is a work of fiction. Names, characters, places, and incidents are a product of the author's imagination. Locales and public names are sometimes used for atmospheric purposes. Any resemblance to actual people, living or dead, or to businesses, companies, events, institutions, or locales is completely coincidental.

Alexei/Roxie Rivera—1st ed.

CHAPTER ONE

"**S**HAY, WILL YOU cover my shift tonight?"

I glanced up from the small workstation in my bedroom where I made the leather goods I sold online and frowned at my older sister. "It's my one night off this week, Shannon. I'm trying to catch up on orders before the Christmas rush hits."

"I know it's your night off." Wearing a slim-fitting sleeveless halter dress, Shannon leaned against the door frame and blew on her freshly painted nails. Her blonde hair was piled atop her head in fat hot rollers. "And I hate to ask…"

"But?"

"But Ruben called and there's a last minute thing he can't miss tonight. He needs me with him." She did that batting her eyes thing that drove me crazy. "*Please*?"

I didn't want to ask what event couldn't be missed. Knowing what I did of Shannon's drug dealer boyfriend, he had probably received an invite to some athlete or hip-hop wannabe's mansion as a supplier of their recreational fun. "Shannon, I hate it when you go to these parties. You know I worry about you all night."

"We aren't going to a party. It's a concert at the Arena. And Shay?" She rolled her eyes at me and huffed. "Seriously, you are going to give yourself an ulcer. You don't need to sit up all night waiting for me. I'm a big girl. I know what I'm doing."

"Do you?" I put down the metal punch and the leather strip I had been working. "Shannon, you just got popped for being a dog fight! It's been less than two weeks since I bailed you out of jail. Ruben is on the hook for a felony!"

"They can't prove anything against him. We were just there to watch the fights. That's it."

"You can pull that bullshit with your lawyer, Shannon, but I know better." Shaking my head, I expelled a frustrated breath. "If you get pulled over or picked up with Ruben and he's carrying again, you could go to prison. Okay? Like *for real* prison and not the county lockup."

"That won't happen." She said it so quickly and easily, brushing off my concerns without a second thought. "He never carries weight on him. That's what the slingers are for obviously." She preened proudly. "He's *very* careful with me."

"But are *you* being careful?"

"What are you talking about?"

"Shannon," I said her name in my no-bullshit tone. "I found your stash in your purse."

Her stance turned aggressive. "Why were you digging around in my purse?"

"I wasn't! Your purse fell out of our locker at work and I was picking up everything that spilled on the floor. I found a rolled up twenty and that dinged up credit card, Shannon." My tightened and my stomach pitched with anxiety. "Are you snorting coke or molly?"

"Both. Sometimes." She swallowed nervously but held my

gaze almost daringly. "Look, it's just a little bump here and there, Shay. I like to roll when we party. It's not a big deal. I know what I'm doing."

I had to give her credit for not lying to me but her nonchalance drove me crazy. "It is a big deal, Shannon. That's how it starts. A little *llelo* at a party, a bump on a long night at work and then the next thing you know you're a total junkie selling her ass on some dirty street corner for a fix."

"Oh my God!" She snorted as if I were the most ridiculous person in the world. "Do you always have to be so dramatic?"

"I'm not being dramatic!"

"You are such a drama queen, and you're so out of touch with reality. So what if I like to cut loose on the weekends? I know what I'm doing, Shay. I know how to control it."

Irritated by the easy way she justified her use of drugs, insisted, "You promised me that you wouldn't use Ruben's product. You promised," I repeated, my eyes burning as my fear for my sister's life hit me hard.

Her jaw hardened and her eyes went cold. "You're not a little girl anymore, Shay, and I'm allowed to have a life. I'm allowed to party with my boyfriend and have a good time. We aren't hurting anyone."

"You're not hurting anyone?" I repeated incredulously. "Do you even watch the news, Shannon? Two months ago, there were cartel pushers dead in the streets, okay? Do you think that you're safe from that? If Ruben screws up a deal, you could be collateral damage."

She scoffed loudly. "You watch too much TV, Shay. That's not the way it works. Ruben is protected. We're safe."

"Even after the dog fighting?"

She glared at me. "You just have to keep bringing that up, don't you? You just have to rub it in my face that Ruben made a mistake."

"A mistake?" I scoffed. "Shannon, he got busted and now the DA and the cops are digging around in his boss's business. Lalo thinks he's a kingpin. He thinks he's some hotshot mob boss—and one of his soldiers just embarrassed him in front of the whole city."

"Shut up, Shay. Just shut your mouth," Shannon snarled. "Enough!"

I didn't know what else I could say. She wasn't going to listen to me. She believed that Ruben's connections to the cartel's top man in Houston would protect her. I wanted to believe it because I loved my sister and wanted her safe but I wasn't naïve. I knew the score—and I suspected she did too.

Exhaling slowly, I counted back from four. "Just promise me that you aren't carrying anything in your purse. If you get popped with drugs in your possession, you are screwed. They will hit you with every charge they can to make your arrest painful, Shan. They'll hurt you so you'll turn on Ruben—"

"I would *never* turn on Ruben. I fucking *love* him. He's my bae, and I'll go do my time before I betray him."

"Lord," I grumbled and sat back in a huff. I couldn't stand it when she called Ruben her *bae* and her *boo*. "Will you listen to yourself, Shannon?"

"You know what, Shay? I didn't come in here for a lecture from my baby sister that I raised through junior high and high school. I came in here to ask you to work my damn cleaning shift. That's it."

I scowled. "Why do you always do that?"

"Do what?"

"Why do you always have to throw it in my face that you had to raise me after Mom bailed?"

"I don't!"

"Yes, you do." I hated fighting with Shannon, but I was getting tired of hearing how much she had sacrificed to keep me out of foster homes. "I love you, Shannon, and I will never forget what you did for me, but I would really, *really* appreciate it if you would stop using it as a stick to beat me with whenever you're pissed or frustrated with me."

She swallowed and glanced away from me. "I don't mean to do it, Shay. Sometimes it just comes out before I can stop it. I don't regret any of the choices I've made." For a moment, she met my gaze, and I could see the sincerity reflected in her eyes. "You fought like hell to get into college. You started this business on no debt and you've done it your way. I'm proud of you, Shay. Even when I'm a jerk," she added with a lopsided smile.

My frustration with her faded. I reached out and touched her hand. "You're not a jerk."

"Softie," she murmured and poked my arm. "Does this mean you're going to work for me?"

I rolled my eyes and poked right back at her. "Yes, I'll work for you."

"Thank you." She squeezed my fingers as if to let me know that all was forgiven and bent down to noisily peck my cheek. "Kylee is working tonight. At least you get to work with your best friend, right?"

She had a point. "Be careful, okay?"

"I will. I'm going to be late so don't wait up for me."

"Okay."

She took one step out the door before turning back toward me. "Can you spot me a few hundred bucks?" She pressed her hands together. "Please?"

"You just got paid on Monday!"

"And I've got bills!"

"So do I, Shan."

She rolled her eyes at me again. "Oh please! What bills do you have?"

"Rent, utilities, groceries, cell phone, car insurance, health insurance," I said and ticked them off on my fingers. I didn't add that I had had to cover her half of the household bills for the last four months. She was going to snap at me, I was sure, but I still said, "The diner is hiring for the morning shift. The tips are good there."

"Not happening," she replied and shot me a withering look. "I'm done cleaning offices and waiting tables."

"What does that mean?"

"It means I'm put in my notice yesterday."

That was the first I had heard of this so I sagged with shock. "When did you get a different job?"

"I didn't."

I bit my lip to stop myself from shouting at her. *What the hell are you thinking?* "Shannon, don't you think you should have had a better job lined up before you quit?"

"Shay," she said with an exasperated exhale. "I've got this figured out, okay? Now are you going to loan me the money or not? I'll pay you back next week."

Experience had taught me that she wasn't going to listen to anything I had to say. I rose out of my chair, crossed my room to my purse and retrieved my wallet. I tugged the three crisply folded hundred dollar bills I kept tucked into a card slot and handed it to her. "Here."

"Thank you." She took the money but held onto my hand a moment longer than I had expected. "I love you, Shay."

Bewildered by her unexpected show of emotion, I smiled at her. "I love you, too, Shan."

She stepped back and hovered in the doorway. "It's going to be okay, Shay. Things are going to change for us in a big way. A really big and wonderful way."

Before I could ask her what that meant, she flitted away and disappeared. I decided not to chase after her for more information. Knowing her history, whatever scheme for fast cash she had planned would fizzle and burn. I just hoped that she wouldn't drag me into this one.

I cleaned up my workstation and tried not to think about how far behind I was going to be on getting this purse and wallet order finished. Although I wanted nothing more than to focus on growing my handbag and wallet business from its online presence to a real brick-and-mortar store, I had to focus on paying the bills and saving up for a proper expansion first. I probably could have gotten a small business loan or tried to shoestring my plans on credit cards but the idea of debt had always made me nervous.

While I was pulling on a clean uniform for the janitorial company where we worked, I heard the front door open and close. The loud thumping bass of reggaeton music from our short driveway rattled the windows as Ruben's new and very shiny SUV idled in front of our single-wide mobile home. I tried not to think about all the danger Shannon was in every time she went somewhere with Ruben but I couldn't just flip off that switch from caring to not caring. She was my big sister and I loved her and desperately wanted her to make better choices.

But I also had to acknowledge that what I considered a simple, black and white decision wasn't so simple for Shannon. She had been in love with Ruben since they were both young teenagers. I could still remember the giggly fourteen-year-old version of my sister confessing to me that she loved Ruben after sneaking back into our house from a party.

Back then, he had been flirting with the idea of jumping into the Hermanos street gang. It wasn't long before he made the commitment and started rising through the ranks of dealers who helped push the cartel's products onto Houston's streets. Shannon had walked away from Ruben for a short time after our mom bailed on us but that separation hadn't lasted long. Four months later, they were back together.

Convincing her to give up on the man she had loved for twelve years? It wasn't going to happen. For better or worse, she had committed herself to Ruben and the dangerous life he lived. I loved my sister and didn't want to lose her so I had been forced to accept Ruben wasn't going anywhere. I didn't like it, and I worried that he was going to get her in so much trouble, but she was an adult who could make her own choices.

Dressed in my pink scrub-style uniform and comfortable but ugly white shoes, I grabbed a light jacket and my purse before locking up and leaving the house. I had some time before I needed to leave so I decided to check the mail. It was a short walk across the trailer park to the community center where the mailboxes were located. I slipped into my jacket as I crossed the street, careful to avoid the puddles filling the potholes in the craggy pavement.

"Hey, Shay!" Little Homer Rodriguez peddled his short, chubby legs as fast as they would go as he whizzed toward me on the hand-me-down bike that had once been belonged to his older brothers. He rode his bike dangerously close to the middle of the road, and it made me nervous. It was getting dark, and the street lights in our park were so dim. The oilfield guys who lived along this street would start racing down this street soon. Tired from long shifts, they might not see him until it was too late.

"Homer! Dude, get out of the street!" I waved him over to the broken sidewalk. "Your mom is going to flip her lid if she sees you riding in the road like that."

He took my warning to heart and angled his bike toward the side of the road. His heavy backpack sagged down too low and threw off his balance as he hit a pothole. He splashed my pants with muddy water. "Oh man! I'm sorry, Shay."

"It's okay." I smiled at him and didn't dwell on the stains. By the end of my cleaning shift, my pants would look much worse anyway. "Here. Let me fix your backpack."

He sat still while I adjusted the straps on his bag. "Hey, Shay?"

"Yeah?" I fought with the too-tight buckle on the strap.

"Do you need wrapping paper or cookie dough?"

Not really, I thought, but I had a feeling I knew where this was going. "Maybe. Why?"

"We're selling things for school. It starts on Monday. If I sell the most stuff in my grade, I get to ride in a limo and go to a pizza party!"

I was glad he couldn't see my face as I fixed his backpack. The memories of being the only kid in school who had to explain why my fundraiser sheet had lots of entries but no money in the envelope made my stomach churn violently. The humiliation of having to admit that my mother had stolen the money to gamble still made my cheeks burn and my chest tighten.

"So do you want to see the order form?"

"Sure, but not tonight," I replied, pushing aside those ugly memories of my dysfunctional childhood. "I'm headed to work. Why don't you come see me tomorrow?"

"Okay."

I finished adjusting his backpack and stepped away from him. "Stay on the sidewalk until you get home. Say hello to your mom for me."

"I will." He smiled that boyish gap-toothed grin of his and pedaled away down the sidewalk.

I watched him for a few seconds, just to make sure he kept off the street, and then turned toward the small building that housed the mailboxes and a community laundry room. I found only a handful of bills and the weekly batch of coupons and ads. I quickly sorted out the coupons I would use from the ones I wouldn't and left the rest in the stack of glossy sheets on top of the mailboxes for someone else to use.

While ripping into the electricity bill, I headed out of the building and back toward our house. I grimaced at the amount due and wondered if Shannon would be able to help with her half this month. If I had to cover the entire amount, it was going to eat into my Christmas savings. It was hard not to be irritated with her about the bill when she was the one who left lights on and ran the ceiling fan in her bedroom when we weren't home and kept the television in her room blaring all night long.

I glanced down at my pants and decided the muddy splotches were just too big to ignore. Even though I really didn't have the time, I ran back inside the house and switched to a clean pair of uniform pants. While I locked the front door, I heard a vehicle pull up behind me but didn't think much of it.

This was a busy street, especially with Mrs. Rodriguez and her big family a few houses down. Her older boys had friends over for dinner every single day. How she could afford to feed a dozen hungry mouths every night I would never understand but she did it and always with smile on her face. There had been many, many times over the years when my hungry belly had been filled by her kindness.

"Shannon Mitchell?"

I whirled around at the unknown male voice that called my sister's name. Three men I had never seen before were standing in front of a double cab black truck. I didn't like the look of them—or the tattoos I could see from this distance. I gulped nervously at the sight of all that ugly white supremacist ink. There weren't many things that scared me but as a dark-skinned Latina girl? Facing off with these three monsters had my knees knocking together.

The tallest of the three stepped forward. He had meaty arms and massive hands that I was sure had done a lot of dirty, mean things. "Are you Shannon Mitchell?"

I managed not to jump when he barked at me. "No."

"So you're the little sister then, huh? Shay, right?"

I nodded silently. What the hell were these men doing here? Why were they looking for my sister? *Shannon, what have you done now?*

Before I could muster the courage to ask what these guys wanted with my sister, the roar of motorcycles barreling down our street drew my attention. Normally, I tried to steer clear of the motorcycle gang that our landlord, Spider, ran with but today? Today I wanted to drop to my knees and thank the heavens for the small crew of rough, leather-clad men riding to my rescue.

Spider killed his bike first, popped the kickstand and slowly slung his leg over the seat. He had recently cut his hair and somehow it made the Calaveras MC Vice-President look even scarier. The neighborhood had become so quiet as people watched the faceoff in my front yard. I could hear the leather of his vest creaking as he moved. His heavy boots crunched grass as he took deliberate steps between me and those terrifying men. "You boys lost?"

"We have business here, Spider."

"If you have business on my property and in my territory, your boss needs to lift the white sheet off his head, pick up a phone and ask me for permission."

"I'll make sure to pass that message on," the man said. "But since we're already here, Mueller wants to talk to her. I'm just here to pick her up for a little chat."

A little chat? A cold spear of terror lanced my chest. If I got into that vehicle with those men, I wasn't going to come back whole or alive.

Spider glanced at me. "Shay, do you know these men?"

Feeling braver now, I shook my head. "No, sir."

"Do you want to go with them to meet with their boss?"

"No."

"Do you want these men to leave?"

"Yes, sir. Very much," I added forcefully.

He gestured to the truck. "You heard the lady. Get in your truck and get the hell off my property. You tell your boss that he needs to respect the boundaries—or else my boys and I are going to start making some visits of our own on your territory." Spider pointed to the truck again. "Go."

The three men glanced at Spider's backup, smartly ran the odds and retreated to their vehicle. The tall one shot me a warning smile before sliding behind the wheel. "We'll be seeing you around, sugar."

His threat struck me cold. I gripped the handle of my purse and watched the truck disappear down the street. Two of Spider's men, the ones who hadn't dismounted from their bikes, followed the truck. I was relieved to lose sight of the tail lights but what would happen once I left my driveway? There was no way I could ask Spider or his men to tail me around Houston.

As soon as the truck disappeared from view, the VP turned toward me. Hands on hips, Spider stared at me and shook his head. He had always been something of a father figure to me. I had gone to school with his daughter Marley so it had been a natural role for him to assume after my own dad had been killed in a car accident. When the apartment I had shared with Shannon had been robbed, he had packed us up and moved us into this park so we would be safe.

"Well, hon, it looks like you've got some explaining to do."

Spider waved his tattooed hand in the direction the truck of white supremacists had taken. My gaze lingered on the heavy silver rings adorning his fingers. The skulls and letters were a language I didn't speak. "How do you know those men?"

"I don't."

"You're sure?" He narrowed his eyes in a way that warned me not to hide anything from him.

"Positive."

"What about your sister?" When I waited too long to answer, Spider exhaled roughly. "Were they here looking for Shannon?"

Reluctantly, I nodded. "I don't know why."

"Considering the company she keeps, I can think of ten different reasons they might show up here and none of them are good." He glanced toward the street and then back at me. "Those men won't bother you again, not here at least, but you need to be careful, Shay. You tell your sister to clean up whatever mess she's made and to do it fast. I'm not about to get tangled up in some nonsense with Mueller's boys."

Mueller? The name was familiar but I couldn't think why. Whoever Mueller was, it was clear that he was powerful and dangerous, maybe even more powerful and dangerous than Spider and his club. That didn't bode well for me or Shannon.

Spider stepped closer and dropped his voice so only I could hear him. "I'm about to give you some fatherly advice, Shay. I would highly suggest you listen close and do what I tell you."

I swallowed nervously. "All right."

"Get out of here."

The words weren't spoken meanly or aggressively but I

still shrank back with shock. "What?"

"Pack up your things and get out of here, Shay. It's time for you to cut ties with your sister and start your own life. Away from here," he added forcefully. "You're a smart girl. You've got drive and ambition. You need to get out of here and make something of yourself. Cut the dead weight, sugar." He made a snipping gesture with his fingers. "Go be somebody."

It was probably good advice, but how was I supposed to just walk away from my sister? From the only person who had always been there for me? From the woman who had given up her dreams of cosmetology school and her own salon to raise me after Mom left?

"You stay safe, Shay." Spider backed away slowly. "Be smart, honey."

His advice given, he returned to his bike and left the street as quickly as he had appeared. I hurried to my car and fished my cell phone out of my purse as I unlocked the door on my dinged-up white sedan. The car was nearly fourteen years old but I had paid cash for it in high school and planned to drive it into the ground.

As I waited for my sister to answer, I slid behind the wheel and tried not to freak out totally. "Come on, Shan. Pick up."

But she didn't.

My call went to voicemail and I drummed my fingers on my thigh as I waited for her greeting to end. "Shannon, call me. Like right now. It's important. Some skinhead creeps were looking for you. I think you should get out of town with Ruben." I rubbed my forehead and hoped the swirling pit in my stomach would stop spinning. "I don't know what you've done, and I don't really care. Just call me, okay? I'm really worried about you."

I dropped my phone in the cup holder and tossed my purse onto the passenger seat. I cranked the engine. It turned over with a little whine. How many times would this old beast light up for me? If I made it through the end of the year, it would be a miracle.

Seatbelt secured, I backed out of the driveway and headed out of our neighborhood. I didn't miss the nosy neighbors watching my car creep along the road or the way they pointed and shook their heads. There was always some sort of trouble in the park but Shannon and I had never been the source of it. I could only imagine what wild stories would be circulating the neighborhood by sunrise.

As I headed for I-10, I kept checking my rearview mirror and expected to see that truck following me but it never appeared. Where were they? I didn't believe for one second that they weren't keeping an eye on me. Those men had come to my house to rattle me—and they had succeeded. I suspected they expected me to head straight for Shannon but the joke was on them. I was going straight to work, just as planned.

What had Shannon done to gain their attention? My thoughts rolled back to her parting words to me. Yeah, things were changing all right but not for the better. I thought of all the little scams she used to run with Ruben when I was still in high school. Stolen credit cards, fake lotteries, fake collection calls…

"Jesus, Shannon," I murmured as panic rolled through me again. "What have you done now?"

When I arrived in the small parking lot outside the commercial cleaning company where I had worked since graduating high school, I called my sister one more time and sent her a series of texts in all caps.

CALL ME. NOW. 911!

She probably had her cell phone on silent or shoved down in the bottom of her handbag. I could practically hear her response once she did see my missed calls. She would probably laugh and tell me I was overreacting. She would insist that Ruben would fix it.

"You had better fix this, Ruben," I muttered while gathering up my things and leaving my car. By now, the sun had fully set and the early November chill had me shivering even with my jacket. I scurried inside the small, unremarkable building that served as the headquarters for CleanRite and quickly shut the heavy door behind me.

Even before I reached the main room that served as a meeting and locker room, I could hear the brassy wail and growling *ba-da-ba-dum* of *banda* music. When I walked into the room, I spotted a dozen or so of my fellow coworkers grabbing their assignment sheets from the night manager and co-owner Juan.

Pushing aside my concern for Shannon, I smiled and waved at the friendly faces that greeted me. I was just about to swipe my ID to clock in when Juan stopped me with a gentle tap on my shoulder and a confused expression. "Shay?"

"Hey, Juan."

"Hey," he replied and started flipping through the sheets of paper on his clipboard. "You're not on the schedule tonight, Shay."

"I'm covering for Shannon." I held my ID ready to swipe but didn't finish the motion. Something in his voice made me nervous.

His eyebrows arched toward his forehead. "Shannon? She was fired yesterday. She doesn't work here anymore."

Now I was the one frowning with confusion. "She told me that she gave notice that she was going to quit."

Juan's expression turned stony. "I'm sure she tells you all sorts of things, *mi'ja*. That doesn't mean that they're true." He shook his head. "After I split you two up and put you on different crews, there were too many complaints from our clients—and not just about her lax cleaning standards."

"What do you mean?"

He shot me an exasperated look. "What do you think I mean?"

There were all sorts of things I was thinking but I didn't want to believe any of them, especially not about my sister. Worried about my own position with the company that I had faithfully served for years, I asked, "Do I need to start looking for a new job, Juan?"

He seemed surprised by the question. "You're one of my best employees. If I didn't know about your plans to start your own business, I would push you into managerial training. No," he said emphatically. "Your job here is yours until you don't want it anymore."

Relief rushed through me. "Thank you, Juan."

He waved away my gratitude and tapped his fingers on his clipboard. "Since you're here, would you like a few hours of overtime? I'm having hell filling a last minute cleaning call because of that concert tonight. No one is answering their phones."

You have no idea, I thought crossly while thinking of the way Shannon was dodging my calls.

"Sure, I'll take it." Happy for some extra cash on my paycheck, I swiped my ID and clocked in for work. "Where am I going?"

"Sarnov Luxury Autos."

The mere mention of the high-end dealership that sold outrageously expensive cars to Houston's movers and shakers sent a zip of delight down my spine. An excited, tingling feeling settled in my lower belly. I couldn't help myself. I wanted to see *him* again.

Him.

Alexei Sarnov.

Last Christmas, the dangerously sexy and overwhelmingly alpha businessman had rescued me from a run-in with Houston's most notorious drug dealer, Lalo Contreras. Alexei had faced off with Ruben, his crew and my sister to save me from what had promised to be a forced double-date from hell. He had offered me his protection that night and a promise of safe harbor.

If you ever need anything, Shay, you come to me first. I'll take care of you.

His gruff, deep voice echoed in my ears, even all these months later. Since that cold, wet night, we had developed an odd sort of friendship. We never interacted outside of his car dealership and my weekly cleaning visits, but I knew, without a shadow of a doubt, that if I asked for his help, Alexei would come through on that promise he had made to me.

"Hey, girl!" Kylee, my best friend, greeted me by bumping

her hip against mine. She flashed me one of her bubbly, sweet smiles while gathering her honey blonde hair into a high ponytail. "You want to borrow some perfume and makeup from my kit? Because I know you want to look good for that sexy Russian fox you like to make eyes at," she mercilessly teased.

"Hush!" I laughed it off but my cheeks were burning hot. "I do *not* make eyes at him."

"Girl, please." She rolled her eyes at me. "You're over there blinking all pretty at him, and he's standing there brooding and staring at you like he wants to just eat you right up."

I squeezed my thighs together at the images her words evoked. Sometimes I let myself imagine that maybe, just maybe, Alexei was as infatuated with me as I had become with him. But those hopes died quickly when I considered how rich and powerful he was compared to me. He lived in a world that I would never understand. There was nothing good to come from crushing on a man who would never notice me.

"Do you want to come over tomorrow and see the new dresses I've designed?" Kylee adjusted her employee lanyard. "I'm trying to decide which two or three I'm going to include in my end of year portfolio. I could use your help choosing."

"Sure."

"And maybe you could loan me some of your purses and accessories for the photos?"

"I still owe you big time for loaning me the outfits for my graduation project earlier this year so consider it done. You can have whatever you want."

"What I want is for us to finally scrape together enough money to open our own boutique," she said before giving me a rib-cracking hug. "Because I've had it up to here with scrubbing urinals and mopping floors!"

"Two more years," I reminded her. "We need two more years to save our capital, Kylee."

She made a face but didn't argue. Like me, she was conservative with money and terrified of debt. After watching her parents go through a humiliating and painful bankruptcy, foreclosure and an SEC investigation that had driven her father to take his own life, she pinched her pennies so hard that poor ol' Abe Lincoln begged for mercy.

"Kylee! Let's go!" Judy, one of the shift supervisors, stood in the doorway and waved her hand. "We've got a lot of stops to make before sunrise."

"I'll see you around, chica." Kylee playfully tugged my ponytail. "Make sure you bat those thick eyelashes of yours when you tell that Russian fox *do svedaniya.*"

She was too quick for me to whack as she scampered toward the door, her giggling lighting up the room. I stuck my tongue out at her back. There was no way in the world I was going to flirt with Alexei. The odds of embarrassing myself were too high, and I valued our friendship too much.

But as I climbed into the front seat of the work van Manny was driving, I wondered if tonight was the night I would finally break down and ask Alexei for help.

CHAPTER TWO

ALEXEI SARNOV BLEW out a noisy breath of frustration and flopped back in his desk chair. He wiped his hands down his face and rubbed at his tired eyes. His irritated gaze landed on the computer screens on his desk. His stomach swirled like a pit of black despair as he took in the evidence of what he was beginning to fear might be an attempt at full-blown theft of his clients' financial information.

All that money he had spent hiring Kostya's little hacker to set up his computer system seemed to finally be paying off for him. He hadn't been sure that investing in that blue-haired tattooed pixie was a good idea but now he thanked his lucky fucking stars he had taken Kostya's advice. The former spy could be overly paranoid at times, but he had been right about this.

But who would be stupid enough to try to steal from me?

That question perplexed him the most. Although he had left Nikolai Kalasnikov's mafia family and created a new, clean life for himself, Alexei still had a reputation as a brutal street enforcer and a businessman willing to cut his rivals off at the knees. When he discovered the identities of the people who had tried to compromise his clients and ruin his business? He was going to make them hurt.

For now, though, he was reassured that no client information had been stolen from the finance department. And thank God for that! He had built a solid name for himself among Houston's elite and moneyed crowd as *the* go-to guy for high-end luxury vehicles. If people lost their trust in him, he would lose everything. Thinking of all the hard work he had put into growing his business empire, he experienced a wave of nausea.

He refused to lose *anything*. He had fought and clawed his way off the streets of Solntsevo and into the Prokhorov crime family. He had proven his loyalty and his worth and earned a spot on Nikolai's hand-picked crew.

Later, he has used his fists and cunning to buy his way into a better life here in Houston. From one dealership, he had grown to a string of them up and down I-45 as well a trucking company, a couple of automotive parts stores and a small fleet of tow trucks and tire service shops. He had built something *real* and successful. He would fight to the last breath to protect that.

Still seething with fury that some stupid bastard had dared to steal from him, Alexei ignored the soft knock at his closed office door. More than an hour after closing, there were only a handful of employees remaining and he had given them explicit instructions to leave him alone. When the knock grew louder and more insistent, he shoved out of his chair and stormed across his office with forceful strides. He jerked open the door and shouted, "What?"

He instantly regretted his snarled outburst when he spotted Shay Sandoval standing in the hallway. The discovery that he had just yelled at the sweet soft-spoken beauty hit him like a punch to the gut. Those dark eyes of hers, the ones that tormented his dreams, were now wide with fear. Her luscious pout wasn't curved with its usual smile either.

"I'm sorry," she stammered out quickly. Seemingly shocked by his angry greeting, she shrank back and quickly retreated from his doorway. She gulped as if suddenly nervous and tightly gripped the small plastic tote packed with cleaning supplies and a microfiber duster. "I'm really sorry."

Her gaze dropped to the gang tattoos visible on his forearms and hands. Not expecting to be bothered for the rest of the night, he had rolled up his sleeves. The inked evidence of his history in the Russian mafia were now on full display, and he was painfully aware of her reaction to them. Remembering what he knew of the men who had knocked her around when she was a little girl, he felt instantly shamed at scaring her.

"*Blin*," he muttered under his breath and took a careful step forward. Thankfully, she didn't flinch when he touched her shoulder. It was the first time he had dared to touch her so intimately. A quicksilver spark of need burned his fingertips, and he had to fight down the urge to slide his hand toward the sleek curve of her neck where he could stroke her silky brown skin. "I'm sorry, Shay. I didn't realize it was you."

"It's fine." Her voice was quiet and tense. "I shouldn't have bothered you while you were working."

"It's not fine, and you are not bothering me. I enjoy your company. Always," he said, the dark intensity of his voice drawing her attention. A curious expression played upon her gorgeous face. For the briefest of moments, he considered finally being honest with her and telling her the truth about the feelings that had been tormenting him since last Christmas.

How would she react if he told her that he purposely stayed late on Wednesday evenings just because he wanted an excuse to talk to her? What would she say if he told her that his heart was thumping against his ribcage right now because he was getting to see her a second time in the same week? Because he was close enough that he could breathe in the tantalizing scent of that barely-there hint of beach and sunshine from the perfume she wore?

Clearing his throat and abandoning *that* line of thought, he asked, "Why is your crew here again?"

"Your manager called and asked for us to come back because of all the mud and rainwater that got tracked onto your showroom floor. Apparently you had a busy day," she said with a timid smile. "She wanted everything to be bright and shiny for the weekend."

Happy to talk about something positive, he nodded. "Fridays are always good for business, but today was one of our best Fridays ever. I have a good feeling about this weekend." Despite the knowledge that his office was perfectly clean and tidy, he still moved aside and waved toward his desk. "Come in, please."

She tried to slip by him, but he purposely angled his body to force her to brush against his chest. It was a provocative move but he couldn't stop himself. As soon as they made contact, he noticed the flush that deepened the color of her face and neck. She never wore makeup when working so he could easily see the blush spreading. His entire body thrummed as he imagined having Shay in his bed, naked and writhing under his greedy hands, and watching that sweep of pink spread from the very tips of her toes to the top of her head.

Shay whacked his arm with the duster. "Behave or else I'll send Manny up here to tackle your office."

There it was. That sweet, flirty smile that he sometimes managed to draw from her. It was the smile that brightened his whole day. Playing her game, he drew a little cross over his heart. "I swear I'll be on my best behavior."

She laughed. "I'll believe that when I see it."

He didn't follow her into the office. Tempted to overstep the line of friendship that existed between them, he remained near the door because he truly didn't trust himself to behave. On edge with the discovery of the attempted theft from his business, it would be too easy to give in to the walking temptation that began to dust and polish his furniture. He respected Shay all the more for the way she never allowed their friendship to get in the way of her job. She had a work ethic that he wished he could bottle up and force feed to the new employees who tried to make the cut on the showroom floor.

"Looks like you've been busy." She eyed the mess of paperwork on his desk before glancing at him with obvious concern. "You shouldn't work so late, Alexei." Her gaze drifted to the gym bag in the corner of his office. "Were you training this morning, too?"

"It was just a workout."

"At what time?"

"Six."

"So you were up at five?" When he nodded, she said his name in a censorious tone. "Alexei! You're going to run yourself ragged!" She looked at his trash can and surely noticed the containers from his uneaten lunch. "Have you eaten today?"

"I had breakfast."

She shot him a look of consternation. "Do you remember two months ago when you got onto me about my schedule? About how I needed to drop one of my jobs and take better care of myself?"

He remembered it clearly. He had discovered her damn near dead on her feet with her stomach growling so loudly he could hear it all the way down the hall. He had forced her into his office, closed the door and ordered her to sit on the couch. He had leaned against his desk and watched her eat an apple and Cliff Bar from the snack basket in the employee lounge.

It was the night he had nearly broken the rule he had created for his friendship with Shay. He had sworn to himself that he wouldn't get involved with her but that night? Christ, that night he had wanted to smash that wall he had built between them, sweep her up in his arms and smuggle her away to some place private where he could keep her safe and protected and pampered.

But Shay was proud and independent. If he offered her the same sort of arrangement he had given the other women in his past? She would smack the shit out of him. Even now, he could feel the phantom sting of her small hand slapping his cheek. He couldn't decide if such a hit would anger or arouse him.

"I thought you stopped working Fridays and weekends." He needed to steer his thoughts and the conversation into safer waters.

"I did but my sister needed me to cover her shift." She rose on tiptoes to drag the edge of the duster along the top of a bookshelf. The undershirt she wore prevented him from getting a peek at that smooth plane of stomach he hadn't glimpsed since the weather turned colder. He wanted to rip that damned shirt to shreds. "But it turned out that Shannon got fired yesterday so she wasn't on the schedule. Juan offered me a couple of hours of overtime to come here and take this job so—"

"Wait." He held up a hand and tried to follow what she had just said. "Your sister was fired? For what?"

She shrugged. "I have no idea."

He had a few of his own. From what he had seen of Shannon's attitude during her weekly stops at his dealership, he could only imagine the long list of complaints CleanRite had on file for her.

But something else she had said had piqued his interest. "If she was fired yesterday, why did she ask you to work for her today?"

Shay didn't answer immediately. Instead, she seemed very interested in a corner of his desk. She wiped and swirled a microfiber cloth over the already polished wood. "I think she wanted me out of the house tonight."

There were only a few reasons he could think of for such a thing. None of them were very good. "Why?" Again she hesitated. "Shay?"

She stopped cleaning and lifted worried eyes toward him. "Some guys came by the house looking for her as I was leaving."

"Guys? What guys?" His protective instinct raged to life. He shot off the door frame he had been leaning against and crossed the office with purposeful strides. His mind raced as he tried to figure out who might have come after Shay. Knowing what he did of the underworld's recent and very violent power shifts, he worried it might have been Nikolai's men. "Who was it, Shay?"

"Those crazy skinheads," she said, her dark eyes flashing with fear. "There were three of them in a truck. They had tattoos all over them. *Ugly* ones, if you know what I mean."

He did. Her body language confirmed his worst suspicions. "Did they threaten you?"

Reluctantly, she nodded. "If Spider and his crew hadn't rolled up, I'm not sure what would have happened."

Alexei bit his tongue rather than unleash the stream of expletives that burned his mouth. He had always feared that Shannon and her drug dealing boyfriend would put Shay in danger. "What did they want?"

"I don't know. We didn't get that far before Spider tossed them off his property."

He made a mental note to send the motorcycle club vice president a bottle of Dalmore from his private collection. He and Spider had done business over the years and had run in the same underworld circle back in the day. He was a complicated man but a mostly good one. Right now, Spider was the best chance Shay had at staying safe when at home. Alexei wasn't above bribing the man to keep a close eye on her.

"Alexei?"

The sound of his name coming from that sweet mouth of hers was nearly his undoing. "Yes?"

"They wanted me to go with them. They said their boss wanted to have a chat with me." She wrung the microfiber cloth between her hands now. "What do I do if they find me again?"

Chat my fucking ass, he thought crossly. Mueller played the role of upstanding citizen and successful real estate developer but Alexei knew *exactly* what sort of man he was.

That massacre out in eastern Montgomery County a few weeks earlier had been reported as meth dealer on meth cooker violence, but Alexei and everyone with connections to the murky undercurrent of crime running through Houston knew the truth. Mueller and his men had ambushed that meth den with shotguns blazing.

There were whispers that Mueller and his men had let some young black kid go but he didn't believe that. Not unless there was big money involved or some sort of favor that had been traded for the kid's safe return.

If they got their hands on Shay? *Blyad*. He couldn't bear to even *think* about what those hateful thugs would do to such a beautiful Latina girl. The image of her supple skin marked by bruises or worse made him want to hurt someone. His tattooed fingers curled into fists at his sides. He would beat those men bloody if they put one fucking hand on Shay.

"Do you have your phone on you?"

Her brow furrowed at his question. "Yes."

"Give it to me. *Now.*"

She slipped her hand into the front pocket of her smock and retrieved her iPhone. The device was encased in a buttery yellow leather case. He could see the fine stitching and embossed initials and knew that it was one of her creations. Why she hadn't made the jump to expand her business he would never understand. Her products screamed luxury and would fly off the shelves but something was holding her back.

When this mess with her sister was tidied up, he intended to figure out what that was.

Her thumb danced over the screen, unlocking it with her chosen code, and then she handed it to him. Their fingers touched, and he let them linger there. It didn't escape his notice that she didn't pull her hand back either.

Taking the phone from her, he punched in his phone number and saved it as a new contact. "If you see those men again, you call me." He stared down at her and made sure she was looking right into his eyes when he said, "If you have any trouble with anyone, you call me. If someone tries to hassle you, I want you to use my name."

"Alexei," she hurriedly interjected, "I don't want to drag you into this. It's not your problem."

"I'm making it my problem."

"But—"

"This isn't up for discussion." *Why is she fighting me on this?* "Shay, you're a very smart girl. You know what sort of men your sister hangs out with and you know what people in that world are capable of doing. I'm your best chance at staying safe."

She wrapped her slim fingers around his thick wrist and a jolt of something powerful traveled up his arm and into his chest. Her anxious expression surprised him. "I don't want you to get hurt. Not for me," she added quietly.

He couldn't remember the last time someone had been worried about him. Maybe Ivan when his friend had cornered that final bare knuckle fight? The realization that Shay was more concerned about his welfare than her own made him want to take care of her even more. She was the sort of person who would put everyone else first without stopping to think about her own needs.

"I'm not afraid to get hurt." *Not for you*, he silently amended.

"I don't want you to feel as if I'm taking advantage of our friendship."

He damn near laughed upon hearing her voice that fear. If anyone was trying to take advantage of their friendship…

"It's not a concern. We're fine." He pressed the phone into her hand and curled her fingers around it. "If I find out that you didn't call me when you needed me, I'm going to be very upset, Shay."

It was said with a teasing smile but she seemed to understand that he was serious. If she let her pride get in the way of her safety, he would introduce her to a side of himself she might not like. The side of himself that would think nothing of heating up that perfect little ass of hers to teach her a lesson…

"Shay?" Manny ducked his head into the office and startled Shay. She tried to pull back but he held tight to her hand and the phone, keeping her right there. They were doing nothing wrong, and he didn't want her to feel as if she had anything to hide.

"Yes?" She avoided his intense gaze and focused solely on her coworker. He could feel her fragile fingers flexing beneath his as she tried to free her hand from his but he was stronger and she soon abandoned her attempt to escape.

"We need some help down on the floor when you're done in here."

"I'm finished. I'll be right down."

Manny glanced at their entwined hand but didn't say anything. Whatever he was thinking he kept to himself and retreated from the office.

Alexei held fast to Shay's hand even after Manny disappeared. She stared at their clenched hands and slowly rotated hers until she was able to touch one of the tattoos decorating the first joint of his finger. Her touch burned his skin as she traced the solid black rectangle. Without lifting her eyes, she asked, "What does this one mean?"

He considered making something up but then she glanced up at him with that curious, sincere expression. "It means I served my full sentence. I did my time without early release."

"And what about this beetle?" She outlined the scarab there.

"It's a talisman. For thieves," he explained, all the while wondering what she was thinking.

"And these?" She touched the five dots marking the web of space between his thumb and pointer finger.

"It means I served time in prison." Before she could ask, he said, "The white cross on the field of black? It means I served time in solitary."

"That must have been hard." She slid her finger to the small black birds flying along the curved space below his thumb. "These are pretty."

He let loose a sharp breath. "Don't let Vanya hear you say that. We both had these done when we met in a juvenile labor camp. They say the birds are supposed to remind you of freedom." He considered the small black shapes. "After a few months, they mock you."

Her finger returned to the solid back rectangle. "How many years?"

His throat tightened as memories he had set fire to and buried and encapsulated in the far corners of his mind tried to burst free. "Six."

She slackened with shock. Her dark eyes searched his face. "How old were you—"

"When I went inside?" he finished her question. "Fourteen when I was sent to the juvenile camp and seventeen when they shipped me to a men's prison to finish out my sentence."

"You were just a kid!"

He laughed harshly. "I stopped being a kid around seven or eight. I was a grown man when I made the choices I did—and I paid for them."

"Still…"

"It was a long time ago." He shut her down carefully but forcefully. Her kindness and horror on his behalf threatened to turn him inside out. He didn't deserve her concern. He had been a miserable, mean little bastard as a kid. He had deserved all six years of that sentence and probably more.

"I need to go." She carefully extricated her hand. "Manny and the rest of the team have more stops to make tonight after they drop me off."

"Where are you going after work?" He was riding right up against the wall he had built between them now and searching for any weakness or opening that might let him through.

She eyed him with uncertainty. "I'm headed home. I have a couple of handbags that need to be finished."

"Drive straight home," he instructed. "Don't make any stops, Shay. Just go home and get inside as quickly as possible." The million ways her drive home could go wrong flashed before his eyes. "Is there someone you can stay with tonight?"

"Well… I mean, I guess I could see if Kylee wouldn't mind if I crash at her apartment."

Two young women alone in an apartment were just as vulnerable. He didn't like that option at all. "Let me drive you."

"What? No." She waved the duster side to side. "That's way over the top, Alexei. I'll be fine. I'm going to get in my car, drive home and go inside. It will be fine."

"Shay—"

"I appreciate the offer, Alexei, but I don't need a babysitter. I'm a grown woman. I can handle this."

He didn't want to fight with her so he simply nodded. "All right. Be safe, Shay."

"I will." She smiled at him. "Thank you, Alexei. For everything."

He understood she meant his offer of help and his phone number. He waited until she was out of sight to turn back toward his desk. He picked up his cell phone and scrolled through his contacts until he found Boychenko's number. It was time to collect on a favor.

While he waited for the young enforcer to answer, he moved to the wall of glass that allowed him to overlook the showroom and sales desks. He watched Shay trading out the mats along the entrance doors. Down on her hands and knees, she used tight circular motions to wipe away the smudges left behind. The sight of her working like that bothered him. It was honest work, and he respected her for that, but she deserved a fucking break from hard labor.

I could take care of her. I could take her to the apartment and give her everything she wants and needs.

But not everything, he silently admitted. He couldn't give her a commitment. He couldn't give her love and marriage and all the things a woman like Shay wanted and needed. He wasn't that kind of man. He liked to keep his relationships neatly compartmentalized. He enjoyed the mistress arrangements that had served him well over the last few years.

She's better than that, he conceded. *She's too good for that.*

"Hello?"

"Roman? It's Alexei. You remember that favor you owe me?"

Boychenko laughed. "A guy gets one discount on a new car…"

"Discount?" Now it was Alexei's turn to laugh. "I practically let you walk off the lot with that new A7."

"Fair enough. What do you need?"

He watched Shay trailing her crew out of the dealership. When she reached the doorway, she paused and looked over her shoulder and up at his office. Their gazes met across the distance. She lifted her hand and waved at him. He wasn't the waving type but for her? He made an exception tonight. Her lips curved with amusement and then she was gliding out the door and into the cold, dark night.

"I need you to get over to the CleanRite headquarters. I'll text you the address. You're going to follow someone for me. I want you to sit on her house until I can get there."

"I know where that is. We do business down there." Boychenko paused. "Anything I should know?"

"She's in trouble but it's not her fault. It's a family matter."

"Uh-huh." Boychenko didn't seem very enthusiastic about this favor but he would do as asked. "Our family?"

"No."

Boychenko sighed. "I'm not going to ask questions, okay? But you need to get this cleared from the top. The boss won't be happy if I step in dog shit and drag it back to his front door.

"I'll take care of it. As soon as I get the answers I need, I'll find you." He ended the call, shut down his desktop, locked the files on his desk in his safe and left his office with his gym bag strap draped over his shoulder. He stopped just long enough to give the last manager on shift his orders for the night.

Once in his SUV, he quickly triaged his priorities. Shay had him all twisted up inside. The discovery that she was in serious trouble had him more on edge than the discovery that someone had tried to hack into his financial department and steal client information. He could deal with the people who had tried to steal from him. No one could hide from him, not in this city and not with his connections, but Shay could be badly hurt by the men who were after her sister. The old rules that used to govern the underworld were no longer respected. He didn't trust Mueller and his racist crew as far as he could throw them.

There were two places he could go for information. Kostya had been out of pocket for a few weeks, and Alexei was smart enough not to ask too many questions about that. So that left only one man in Houston who had the answers he needed.

Alexei lifted up in his seat and retrieved his wallet from his back pocket. He checked to see how many twenties and fifties he had for tips. Besian Beciraj, the Albanian mob boss, was a friend, but the bastard was stingy as hell with his information unless his dancing girls were getting their cut. Tonight, he would have to make it rain to pry the answers he wanted from Besian.

Backing out of his reserved spot, Alexei caught sight of the dark tattoos covering his forearms and hands. For the first time in a long time, the calling card of his criminal history was going to be useful.

CHAPTER THREE

I KNEW SOMETHING was wrong even before the van rolled to a stop behind CleanRite. Manny inhaled sharply and Jake cursed softly. I had a bad feeling so I leaned toward the rear passenger window to get a better look at what the two guys in the front seats had seen.

Shit.

My stomach lurched as I took in the slashed tires and smashed windshield on my car. It looked as if someone had taken a sledgehammer to it. Juan, my boss, stood next to the car. He ran his fingers through his hair and shook his head as he stared at the destruction in front of him.

Manny slowed to a stop and I bailed quickly. My two coworkers started to follow me but I put my hand up to halt them. "You guys need to get to those other jobs. I'll be fine here."

Showing his paternal instincts, Manny hesitated. "Are you sure?"

"Juan is here. I'll call the police and then grab a taxi or hang around until Kylee is back."

"All right." He eased out of the parking lot and turned onto the street.

Juan strode toward me, his face showing complete shock.

"Shay, I am so sorry."

"What happened?" I stood next to my car and tried to take in all the damage. It was even worse up close. There wasn't a piece of solid glass left on the vehicle. The dents in the doors and the hood were so deep I could sit in them. I spotted the note on the driver's seat and carefully reached into the car to grab it.

"I was doing inventory in the stock room," Juan explained. "The music was loud so I didn't realize what was happening out here until I heard the glass shattering. It sounded like a damn bomb had gone off. By the time I got out the back door, the truck was driving off."

I brushed the bits of glass from the folded note and opened it with trembling fingers. Inside I found a meanly scrawled message.

We want it back.
Sunrise.
Or you're all dead.

I swallowed hard as I folded up the note and tucked it into my pocket. I realized Juan was staring at me and waiting for me to say something, but I didn't know what the hell I was supposed to say.

"Should I call the police?" he asked quietly but I could tell he already knew the answer.

"No." My cell phone started to vibrate in my pocket and momentarily distracted me from the terrifying thoughts racing through my head. These guys were the sort of people who wouldn't be afraid of the police. For that matter, I didn't know what Shannon had done to anger them. The last thing I wanted was for her to be arrested. I didn't know a lot about county lockup but I didn't think it would be very hard for the skinheads to find someone to hurt her on the inside.

I grabbed my phone and glanced at the screen. Shannon's face greeted me, and I expelled a relieved breath. "Shannon! Where the hell are you?"

"Shay? Can you hear me?" Loud music, heavy on the accordion and brass, covered her voice. "Shay?"

"Shannon?" I spoke louder. "You're in trouble. I need to see you!"

"Shay? You there? Listen, if you can hear me, come to the Arena. Just use Lalo's name. They'll let you inside. Text me and I'll come find you."

"Are you freaking kidding me? Shannon, this is serious! I am not coming to the Arena. You need to—"

The call dropped, and I swore with frustration. I looked up from my phone and stared at my surroundings. A ripple of fear rolled through my stomach. We were so exposed here. If those guys came back…

"Shay, tell me how to help you." Juan seemed to share my fear about hanging around here too long.

"The Arena is a couple of blocks from here. Can you drop me off?"

He didn't look very excited by that idea but nodded nonetheless. "Get your stuff. We'll get out of here."

I hurried inside the building, grabbed my purse and jacket from my locker and raced back outside to find Juan waiting to lock the door behind me. Once the building was secure, I followed him to his idling truck and slid into the front passenger seat. As we were pulling onto Fondren, I remembered I had forgotten to clock out. "I forgot to swipe my ID."

Juan shot me a strange look. "We've got bigger problems than you staying on the clock."

He had a point. I sensed he wanted to ask me what the hell was going on, but he probably understood that was dangerous. Sometimes it was better not to know all the facts, especially when dealing with a situation like this one. He didn't need that kind of trouble, and I didn't blame him for staying quiet.

I gripped my phone in both hands and questioned my decision to meet Shannon at the Arena. On one hand, I doubted those jerks who had trashed my car and threatened me at the house were stupid enough to get anywhere near that concert. Considering the bands that were playing, the place was going to be crawling with gangs and dealers and all of those enforcers loyal to Lalo Contreras. There would be a battle royale if those two groups of enemies met.

On the other hand, I really, *really* didn't want to see Lalo. Shannon had tried to get us together so many times, but my list of wants from a man and a relationship didn't match hers. She viewed a guy like Lalo as the ultimate catch. He was good-looking and had lots of money and power.

But he scared me.

He had a bad reputation for being ruthless and cruel. He was the reason Shannon had gone to that awful, horrible dog fight last month. Ruben had wanted to get in good with his boss and fighting dogs was something Lalo loved so she had gone to support him. It just sickened me to think about people standing around those cages while starved and beaten dogs chewed each other to pieces. It was so barbaric.

A man who enjoyed something so violent and brutal was a

man who would think nothing of hurting a girl like me. So I definitely did not want to see Lalo tonight, but there was little chance of avoiding him if I wanted to speak to Shannon. I hated that my sister was putting me in this position. If I was being brutally honest, I sort of hated myself for always letting her have her way and not pushing back and enforcing boundaries.

You've got to grow up and put a stop to this crap. Never again, I swore silently. *Never again will I find myself in a situation like this.*

Running my finger along the edge of my phone, I remembered the way Alexei had taken it from me and entered his phone number in my contacts. The way he had shoved off that door frame and rushed toward me had filled my stomach with a swarm of butterflies. Even now, I experienced a fresh flutter in my lower belly.

That protective streak of his did crazy things to my heart. It made me want something I had never dared to chase. It gave me a glimpse of what it would be like to belong to someone who wanted to take care of me.

Call him. He'll come for you.

I turned the phone over and ran my finger over the screen. If I called Alexei right now, he would insist that I come back to the dealership or he would want Juan to drive me somewhere other than the Arena. If I didn't go find Shannon right now, she could get hurt. Those men might ambush her and Ruben after the concert. I needed to get to her quickly.

And then I would call Alexei. This was one time I wasn't going to let my pride get in the way of my safety. He had offered his help, and I was going to grab hold with both hands and hang on tight while he dragged me out of this mess. He knew this world better than me, and I trusted him to get me out of this alive and whole.

Before I was ready, we neared the Arena. Juan turned down Bellaire and looped around the freeway. He glanced at me as we sat in traffic. "Do you want me to take you up to the parking garage? There's that covered walkway between the garage and the entrance. It'll be warmer."

"I've got my jacket. Just let me out here," I decided, already shrugging into it.

"Be careful, Shay." Concern filled his voice. "Just find your sister and then lay low. If you need help getting out of town, call me. My brother drives out to San Antonio to see his kids on the weekend. He could take you with him in the morning. You could hide out in a hotel there."

"I'll think about it." Dread swirled in my stomach as I slid out of the truck and scurried along the sidewalk toward the Arena. I fell into a crowd that included concert latecomers and couples leaving early. There was a heavy police presence outside that made me feel marginally better about my decision.

I squeezed between two small groups and entered the lobby. I drew some strange looks in my work clothes and jacket. Oh well. I wasn't here to find a date or have a good time. I was here to find my sister. That's it.

As I glanced down to type in a quick text to Shannon to ask her to come meet me, I heard my name being called by a male voice I really, really didn't want to hear. *Shit.*

"Shay! Baby! You made it!" Lalo Contreras called out to me, and I tried not to flinch. The last thing I wanted to do was make him mad. From the stories I had heard straight from Shannon's mouth, I knew he had a mean streak in him.

Schooling my features, I tightly gripped my phone and turned to find Lalo walking toward me. Flanked by his inner circle of enforcers, Lalo commanded the attention of every person standing in the lobby. With that snow white blazer layered over a black shirt, he looked slick and like a flush entrepreneur out for a night on the town. Over the summer, he had toned down his usual jewelry choices to diamond studs, an outrageously expensive watch and a single gold chain with a simple crucifix. He could almost pass for an upstanding citizen. Almost.

Lalo swooped in and curved his arm around my shoulder. I had to muscle down the urge to shrug him off. His cologne was too heavy, and I couldn't stand the scent of it. He dipped down until his mouth was close to my ear. I shivered but he misread it as encouragement. "Come with me, *mami*. Your sister sent me to get you. We're in the back."

The arm curved around my shoulders tightened and pressed me forward. Every instinct in my body screamed to push him away and run out the main entrance and back into the cold, dark night, but I had to find Shannon. She would believe anything Ruben told her, but I prayed she would listen to me and maybe even agree to come with me.

Lalo dropped his arm from my shoulders, grasped my hand and dragged me along behind him. Immediately, I compared his possessive grip to the way Alexei had held my hand in his office. His fingers had been strong and warm, his grip firm but gentle and reassuring. I still couldn't believe I had been so bold and traced that black rectangle tattoo on his skin. I might have imagined it, but I could have sworn his breath hitched in his throat when I touched him.

But my breath wasn't hitching in my throat as Lalo led me through the thick crowd. The blaring live music momentarily disoriented me. A driving beat of brassy bass and drums pushed a lively accordion tune as a pair of singers wailed lyrics that had the entire arena up on their feet. The band on stage was somewhat infamous for their *narcocorridos* so I wasn't surprised by the violent imagery on the posters lining the walls or on the merchandise displayed at the first table we passed.

As the singer crooned, he caught my attention with one of his lyrics about a Russian. I looked toward the stage and listened more intently as he sang about an ice cold Russian king who had had his heart melted by the blue-eyed machete princess. He sang of the way the Russian was made immortal and untouchable because of the love of his wife and of a night when new blood washed away the old and new kings were crowned by the Russian.

I wasn't the only one listening to the music now. Lalo had stopped and glared at the stage, the darkness inside the building hiding eyes that I was sure were shining with fury. I didn't know everything that had happened over the summer and early fall, but between Shannon and the news reports, I had been able to piece together the power shift in the cartel and in Houston's underworld. The fact that the band had the balls to stand up there and sing about the bloody coup Lalo had perpetrated both impressed and horrified me.

Lalo said something to one of his enforcers before jerking on my hand and dragging me along more forcefully. That band was probably going to have a rough end to their night as the enforcer left the group with a couple of other men.

That's not my problem. Worry about yourself. Find Shannon and get her out of here.

I tried to keep my head down and my eyes averted as I reluctantly followed Lalo around the outer rim of the seating area. Even so, I didn't miss the way people deferred to him or the way his enforcers cut a wide swath through the crowd. Seeing the street respect he had earned helped me understand why Shannon had gotten swept up in Ruben's lifestyle. To be treated like someone important? She must have found it utterly addicting.

As we neared the backstage entrance, I quickly glanced around to get my bearings. Back behind me, there was an emergency exit near the bar. Up ahead, I could see a flash of light as a pair of doors opened to the loading dock. If I needed to get out of here quickly, I had two good options.

Clutching my phone in my hand and hiking my purse strap higher on my shoulder, I let Lalo lead me into the backstage area and down a dimly lit hall. His enforcers peeled away in groups of two until we were alone outside a closed door. Instantly, my heart leapt into my throat. This wasn't right. This wasn't right at all.

Pulling back on his hand, I managed to free myself from his grasp. "Where is Shannon?"

He opened the door without looking at me. "She's gone."

"Gone?"

If Shannon was gone, why was he taking me into this room? Into a room that was at the very end of a long, dark hallway and guarded by his enforcers. A room so isolated that no one would be able to hear me scream over the loud music from the onstage band.

Before I could fully process the sudden danger I was in, Lalo grabbed the back of my neck and shoved me into the room. I stumbled forward and right into a desk. My phone and purse skidded across the surface and onto the floor. I had barely regained my balance when Lalo fisted the collar of my jacket and spun my around until my back slammed into the now closed and locked door. My teeth rattled as my head whacked into the metal slab behind me.

In the next instant, Lalo's mean face was right up in mine. The scent of peppermint and his cologne overwhelmed me. I put both hands on his chest and tried to push him off of me, but he used his hip to pin me in place before grabbing my ponytail and yanking my head back. I cried out in pain and shock but he didn't loosen his grip. "Stop!"

"Stop?" He laughed and used his other hand to grab my throat. His fingers bit into my skin, marking me and threatening to choke the air right out of my lungs. "No, Shay. We are so far beyond that now."

He released my hair but kept that cruel hand of his on my throat, all but immobilizing me. Tears sprang to my eyes when he unzipped my jacket and shoved it off my shoulders. He grabbed a handful of the pink fabric of my work uniform and sneered. "You need my help, and this is the way you present yourself to me?" He clicked his tongue against his teeth. "You're going to have to learn quick how my girl is supposed to look."

"Your girl?" I sputtered in gasping breaths.

He nodded slowly. "Your sister and Ruben fucked off and left a huge pile of shit right on my doorstep. I'm going to clean up their mess but your little ass is going to be my payment."

Horrified by the quid pro quo he was describing, I scratched at his hands and tried to force them away from my throat. "No! *No!*"

He winced as I clawed at his skin and drew blood. With a slap to my face, he knocked the fight right out of me. His hand tightened around my throat as he surveyed the damage I had inflicted. "*Ay, mami.* You are really going to have to work for it now."

"Please." I coughed out the word. "Please, Lalo. *Don't.*"

"I don't want to hurt you." The fingers around my throat eased some but he roughly hissed, "You played your little game with me too long. I can't let your family get away with this disrespect."

"Please, Lalo," I begged futilely. "I don't know what Shannon or Ruben did. This isn't my fault."

He dragged his fingers along the hot strip of skin he had just slapped. "It doesn't matter. People will talk. They have to know I'm in control. Do you understand what that means?"

Oh, God. I did. I did understand—and it terrified me.

I bit back a sob and tried to keep my eyes lowered demurely. Those old painful lessons from a childhood of being knocked around by my mother and the angry men she brought home told me the only way I was getting out of this without major damage was to show him that he was in charge and that I would do whatever he wanted.

Lalo started dragging my work smock and undershirt up my torso and over my head. I wanted to fight him. I wanted to kick and scream and punch but I remained motionless like a doll, letting him undress and fondle me. My face still burned from the smack he had given me. Bile rose in my throat. The fingers on my neck were a constant reminder that with one good squeeze he could put me down for the count.

"I know you're a good girl, Shay." He ran his fingertips along my exposed flesh. "So I'm going to go easy on you tonight. I'm going to let you earn my protection and show me your loyalty."

When his hand drifted from my throat, I stifled a cry of panic. Of all the ways I had imagined my first sexual experience, this wasn't it. I didn't want this. I didn't want him touching me. I sure as hell didn't want to put my mouth or hands anywhere on his body either.

But I didn't want to die and I didn't want to get beaten bloody for something I hadn't done.

His hand moved back to my throat, and he pushed me back against the door. His hard gaze turned my insides cold. "I want you to remember why I'm doing this, Shay. This is to teach that *puta* sister of yours what happens to the people we love when we do stupid, stupid things."

Looking into his sadistic and dark eyes, I lost all hope. I didn't want to die. I didn't want to get beaten bloody. I didn't want to be sexually assaulted. But what I wanted no longer mattered.

He was going to hurt me here in this office, in a building where we were surrounded by thousands of people, to prove a point to everyone on the street that he wasn't a man to be fucked with and that no one could touch him. He was going to show the underworld that he could commit a heinous crime right under the nose of HPD and nothing would happen to him. By tomorrow night, everyone in town would be talking about what happened to me. I was going to be the cautionary tale they used to keep their street crews in line.

"Tell me you're sorry, Shay."

I swallowed anxiously and found the courage to stare into his eyes. "I'm sorry."

He tilted his head to the side as if to study me. "You aren't sorry. Not yet," he added quietly. "But you will be."

His promise of pain and humiliation sent a cold spear into my heart. He pushed down the cup of my bra and bared my breast. He cruelly pinched my nipple and drew a pained cry from my throat. "Shh," he murmured. "It will be easier if you relax."

He gripped my face in his hand, pinching my chin and cheek between his thumb and fingers, and forced a kiss on me. I sobbed pitifully and tried to push him away but he stabbed his tongue into my mouth uninvited. I recoiled with disgust but he wouldn't stop. His hard erection jabbed against my stomach. He was getting excited over the power struggle.

Proving my suspicion, he laughed acidly. "You can fight all you like, Shay. You aren't getting out of here until I say you can. Tonight I'm getting my first payment on the big fucking bill your sister just rang up."

Desperate now, I cried, "I have money. I can pay you."

"I don't want your money." He used his thumb to trace my mouth. "I want the one thing no other man in Houston has ever gotten to touch." His hand slid down my stomach and between my thighs. "This." His hand moved from between my legs back up to my mouth. He jammed two fingers between my lips, and I gagged at the intrusion. "And this."

Drawing back his hand, he retreated a few steps and started to loosen his tie. "We'll see how fucking uppity you are once you're on your knees with your lips wrapped around my cock." He pointed at my bra and then my pants. "Take off your clothes."

I shuddered inside at the horror of what awaited me. In the throes of panic unlike any I had ever know, I made a decision. I had to get out of here. I had to get out of here *now*.

My panicked gaze jumped to the small window behind the desk. There was a short bookcase and filing cabinet underneath it. I scanned the room for anything I could use as a weapon. A heavy crystal paperweight shaped like a teardrop caught my eye. Did I have the courage or the strength to use it?

Lalo made the biggest mistake of his night by turning his back on me while shrugging out of his blazer. I didn't hesitate. With two quick steps, I reached the desk and swiped the paperweight. I had to use both hands to lift it high overhead. I thanked my lucky stars that Lalo wasn't much taller than me.

I embraced that primitive survival instinct to do whatever was necessary to get out of here. Inhaling a sharp breath, I slammed the paperweight onto the back of Lalo's shaved head. He grunted and stumbled forward but didn't fall. Panicked that he might spin around and hit me, I struck him again.

This time, he dropped like a sack of rocks. Shocked by what I had done, I dropped the paperweight and stumbled away from the sight of the cartel's top man bleeding and knocked out on the dirty cement floor. Had I killed him? No, no. He was breathing. But there was so much blood…

You have to get out of here. Run. Now.

I snatched up my jacket, my purse and my phone and jumped up onto the filing cabinet. I didn't even bother trying to put on my shirt or work smock. I wasn't sure how long Lalo's enforcers would leave us alone in here or how long he would be unconscious. I needed to disappear. Fast.

The window opened but it wasn't a very big space. I stuffed my phone into my purse and wrapped them both up in my jacket before shoving them out of the window. I slipped one leg through and then managed to shimmy the rest of my body out of the small slot.

Out in the shockingly cold night, I hurriedly jammed my bare arms through my jacket sleeves and tried to figure out where the hell I was. I could see the loading dock to the right and decided to run toward the left instead. Regretting every decision I had made since finding my vandalized car, I retrieved my phone from my purse, unlocked the screen with trembling fingers and found the newest contact that had been programmed into my phone.

While I prayed Alexei would answer, I clutched my handbag to my chest and ran. I didn't know where I was going, but I just kept moving away from the Arena. I had to find a place to hide.

"Hello?" Alexei's confident, strong voice glided across the airwaves.

"Alexei!" His name burst from my lips in a sob of relief.

"Shay?"

"Oh my god! Alexei! I need your help." I began to weep uncontrollably. "They trashed my car and then Lalo tried to—" I couldn't bring myself to say the word rape. "And I hit him and he's bleeding everywhere. God, I'm so scared."

"Shay! Calm down." He spoke firmly. His stern, commanding voice calmed my rapid heartbeat. "Where are you?"

"I'm behind the Arena? I think?" I glanced left and right and then straight ahead. In my panicked sprint, I had somehow run around the edge of the parking garage. "I don't know what to do."

"Can you get to one of the restaurants on Fondren? There's a couple of fast food joints there."

"I don't know." Could I make it? I had to try.

"I'll stay on the phone with you. I'm only a few minutes away on Hillcroft. I've been looking for you."

Find me, I pleaded silently. *Please find me.*

Holding tight to my phone, I hurried across a short piece of paved road where a couple of buses were parked and squeezed between them. They were wrapped in band and sponsor logos so I tried to be as quiet and inconspicuous as possible. I could hear raucous male voices and got nervous. The band's road crew was probably tucked away in Lalo's pocket. I could just imagine the price on my head now.

As I made it through that obstacle, I noticed how strangely quiet my surroundings were. Where were the police? Where was security?

You can't trust them. You can't trust anyone except Alexei. Lalo can buy and bribe anyone he wants.

"Shay? Are you there?" Worry edged into Alexei's voice.

I waited until I was well clear of the band buses to answer him. "Yes."

"Can you see those restaurants?"

"I think so." There were bright lights up ahead, just through a line of trees. "Yes. I'm almost there."

"Good. Keep moving. I'm coming for you."

Grateful for my Russian knight in shining armor, I burst

through the tree line and experienced a wave of elation—but it was quickly dashed by the sight of small groups of men hanging around SUVs and cars. I recognized the white gleaming SUV as one that belonged to Lalo. Four of his guys stood next to it and bullshitted the night away with a circle of Hermanos gang members, their neck tattoos boldly displayed for all to see.

Shit. I quickly flitted back into the shadows of the trees and ran back toward the parking garage. There was no way in hell I was getting anywhere near those guys. The mix of Hermanos gang members and cartel enforcers on Lalo's payroll meant certain death if I was caught.

"Shay? Is something wrong?"

"Lalo's guys are in the parking lot. I can't go there."

He cursed in Russian. "There's that dim sum restaurant on the other side of the parking garage. If you can't get there, stay hidden. I'll find you."

When I rounded the back edge of the long parking garage, I came out between a parked police cruiser and a long line of cargo vans. For a split-second, I considered trying to find the police officer who drove that cruiser but then I caught sight of the blood on my hands. Almost naked under my jacket, I didn't want to explain what had happened back in the Arena. If I got the police involved? I was a dead girl.

I scurried across the street and made it to the strip of parking lot behind Fung's Kitchen. I skirted along the edge of a massive dumpster and hurried toward the main parking area that had much better lighting. As I walked fast, I noticed the bounce of headlights to my left. I glanced back to see if there was a vehicle turning into the parking lot and nearly had a heart attack.

"Oh, God. Oh, God! Oh, God!" I started running even before my brain could piece together what my eyes were seeing.

"Shay? *Shay!* What is it?"

"It's the truck that was at my house earlier! Shit. *Shit.*" I was sprinting now, my strides tearing up the parking lot as fast as my legs would take me. I didn't know where I was running or why. In a full-fledged panic, I had gone straight to flight mode. I didn't want to stick around to fight.

"I'm on Southwest Freeway. I'm almost there. Just keep moving, Shay."

I hooked a quick left across the next parking lot and slipped between cars. The truck revved its engines as those skinhead goons chased me. Barely able to breathe, I raced forward on wobbly legs. Somehow I managed to make it to the car stereo place. I swung around the side of the building and found myself in a large rectangular space between commercial buildings.

Up ahead, I could see a narrow outlet to the front of the shopping strip. That area nudged right up against the road Alexei was traveling down right now. If I could just get there…

Brakes squealed and car doors slammed closed behind me. I whirled around and tried to gulp down the dry ball of terror lodged in my throat. Four men advanced on me. One of them had a long piece of rope dangling from his hand. The other held a baseball bat.

"Oh, God." My hand started to drop, and I could just barely make out the sound of Alexei shouting at me, telling me he was almost there.

But he wasn't going to make it.

It was too late.

CHAPTER FOUR

One Hour Earlier

ALEXEI SLIPPED HIS SUV into a parking space along the outer edge of the lot in front of the strip club. Besian Beciraj owned a string of adult entertainment spots around the city and this was one of his newest acquisitions. By the looks of it, the place needed a shitload of renovations. The club had a reputation as the place tired and rundown dancers found work at the end of their careers. Besian would have to sink a ton of money into revamping the business and discovering new talent to turn this sinking ship around, but if anyone could pull it off, it was the Albanian enforcer turned loan shark and mob boss.

Glancing around the parking lot, Alexei made sure his alarm engaged before crossing the pavement to the entrance. A pair of bouncers waited by the doors. They took one look and waved him inside. What would Shay say if she knew that he got VIP treatment in establishments like these? She'd probably wrinkle that dainty little nose of hers and shoot him a disappointed look. The thought of her reaction made his chest tighten with shame.

That girl has you wound right around that pinky finger of hers!

Shoving aside that troubling discovery, he passed the hostess station and angled toward the rear of the club where Besian had told him he would be waiting. The heat inside the club slapped him in the face, especially after that brisk walk across the parking lot. The scent of musky, spicy perfumes saturated the air.

Every now and then, he caught a lungful of that awful smelling body spray so many of the young male patrons were overusing. It was a product he forbid the employees at any of his dealerships. He glanced at the clueless twentysomethings doused in that ungodly scent who tossed wrinkled dollar bills onto the main stage in a disrespectful display.

As he passed the stage, he reached into his jacket and retrieved a pair of crisp twenties that he had tucked away there. He slid them onto the stage and winked up at the blonde who smiled down at him. In a club like this, forty dollars would probably cover the stage fees and tips she would be expected to pay at the end of her shift. At least she would be able to leave tonight with some cash in her pocket.

His good deed done, Alexei weaved around the tables and kept his gaze straight forward when he walked by the lap dance booths. He doubted the men hidden away there with dancers were only getting a private show for their thirty or forty bucks. It was an ugly side of the business but it was a reality, especially in a place like this.

When his cell phone began to vibrate, he answered it. "Yes?"

"Hey, it's Boychenko. Can you hear me? The music is loud!"

"Yes, I can hear you." He pressed his finger to his other ear and turned away from the DJ stand. "What's wrong?"

"Look, there was a wreck so it took me longer than expected to get to this cleaning place. Your lady? She's not here."

"Has she gone home?"

"I don't know, man. Does she drive a white car?"

"Yes." His stomach knotted with worry. "Why?"

"It's been beat to shit, Alexei. The windshield and windows are busted out. Someone took a sledgehammer to the side panels and the hood."

"Is there blood?" He held his breath as he waited for an answer he didn't want to hear.

"No. I checked. I think it was a message to her. Wait. Hang on. There's a truck pulling into the parking lot."

"What kind of truck?" He remembered the vehicle Shay had described. Had they come back looking for her?

"I think it's the owner. He has decals on his doors and hood. Fuck it!" Boychenko said suddenly. "I'm going to go ask him where she is."

"He might not talk to you, not after her car was just vandalized in his parking lot."

"He'll talk," Boychenko murmured darkly. "I'll call you back."

The line went dead, and Alexei tried not to entertain the worst possibilities. Hopefully she had been at his dealership when the vandalism occurred. She could either be hiding out in the company headquarters or safe at home or with one of her friends. Knowing how much everyone liked Shay, she had probably gotten a ride somewhere with one of her coworkers or her boss. Roman would get the information they needed.

He checked his phone to make sure he hadn't missed a

text or phone call from Shay. *Why didn't she call me?* He tried not to get aggravated with her for not asking for his help after discovering her beaten up car but it was difficult. Hopefully she would understand now that this wasn't a game. Her sister had obviously pissed off the wrong people. Shay needed his help if she was going to get out of this unscathed.

Pocketing his phone, he spotted Besian sitting on a couch in the VIP area. The Albanian boss had one arm slung along the back of the leather seat and his legs extended in front of him as he watched four women dancing. He wasn't there for the show. No, he was scrutinizing each movement they made as if they were race horses or greyhounds. Judging by the tight line of his mouth, one or more of those girls wasn't going to make the cut tonight.

As Alexei slid onto the opposite end of the couch, he noticed the absentminded way Besian rubbed his chest. After taking a cartel sniper's bullet earlier in the summer, the mob boss had bounced back remarkably fast. Or maybe he was just damned good at hiding the physical struggle.

Besian glanced at him and grinned. "Been a long time since you've slummed it like this, huh?"

Alexei frowned. "That's a nice fucking way to talk about your own club."

"Have you looked at this place?" Besian angled his upper body so they were talking face-to-face. "I had to toss half of the dancers here because they had prostitution convictions or were on pimp payrolls. I'll be lucky if I see a profit in the next year."

"So why the hell did you buy it?"

"It's all part of the master plan," he replied with a mysterious smile. "So what favor does Alexei Sarnov want from his old friend?" He gestured to the women gyrating to a slow Trey Songz track. "Is it time for a Marissa replacement?"

"No." The hard edge to his voice seemed to rouse Besian's attention.

"Oh. I *see*." The Albanian sat back and chuckled softly. "You fucking Russians are falling one by one, huh? Ivan, Nikolai, Dimitri, Yuri, Sergei… It's like popping cans lined up on a fence. So? Who is the lucky girl?"

"That's none of your fucking business." He wasn't about to start spilling his secrets in a strip club.

Besian held up his hands. "Calm down."

"Look, I came to talk about something that is your business."

"Talk isn't free or cheap here."

Alexei reached under the lapel of his jacket and retrieved the money clip tucked away in his pocket. He started peeling off twenties and dropping them on the small, low stage for the women dancing there. Besian nodded after the first four hundred dollars and then switched to Albanian, "What do you want to know?"

Sliding easily into Besian's mother tongue, Alexei asked, "What business does the AB have with one of Lalo's street slingers?"

"Ruben?"

So Besian did know something. "Yes."

Besian made a face and shook his head. "That's bad fucking business, Alexei. You sure you want to get involved?"

"Yes." *I'll do anything to protect her.*

Besian blew out a breath and then leaned closer. "Ruben

and his girlfriend cooked up some identify theft scam. The girlfriend is a cleaning lady, right? So she goes into these commercial buildings—real estate firms, financial planning offices, clinics—and she plugs in a flash drive when no one is looking. She infects the computers with some virus or whatever." He moved his fingers like a big spider. "It crawls around in the company's network and gathers up all the information they need to steal identities and open up credit cards and take out loans and mortgages and buy cars."

Alexei swore nastily and ran both of his hands over his head. He tugged on his hair and gritted his teeth in frustration. Was Shannon the culprit behind the attempted hack at his company?

"What is it?"

He leaned forward and peeled off ten crisp fifties for the dancers to encourage Besian to keep talking. "She cleaned two of my dealerships, the luxury flagship store and the Toyota lot. My network people isolated the threat earlier today. They managed to keep the virus from stealing information from my clients but it was a close call. Too close."

"You're lucky. Other business owners? They got screwed. Bad," Besian emphasized. "What's worse? Those two idiots packaged up that information to sell it but they got greedy. They figured out a two-way split was better than three. So they planned to screw the hacker guy who helped them, but he found out Ruben was going to—"—Besian made a cutting motion in front of his neck—"—so he ran."

"Where?"

Besian eyed the stage again, and Alexei sat forward to toss more cash onto it. Seemingly satisfied, the boss said, "He ran right to Mueller and told him all about the scam."

"And?"

"And Mueller realized those three stupid fucks had stolen some *sensitive* information, if you know what I mean."

"I do." He could only imagine what awful, twisted secrets Mueller had hidden in the books for his business. Money laundering was a dirty necessity for the underworld bosses ruling this city. "Where is he? The hacker who ran?"

Besian tapped the floor beneath his feet.

Alexei stared at the highly polished concrete. It was no secret that Mueller was developing a major strip of retail space uptown. There were plenty of places to hide bodies there. Strictly speaking, it wasn't the best way to get rid of evidence. Kostya would blow a pupil if he found out one of his men had taken such an amateur route, but Mueller and his crew weren't playing on the same level as the professional cleaner.

"Alexei, you should know that this went up for a council vote this morning. We agreed to let Lalo and Mueller clean house. Some of your people were hurt by this scam. Some of mine were, too. Lalo didn't speak up for them or offer to settle it. From what I understand, he made arrangements for it to happen tonight."

His gut churned violently. "Who was green lit? Just the girlfriend and Ruben? What about family?"

"Just those two, but you know how it goes with collateral damage…"

An invisible vise squeezed his heart. For a moment, he thought he really was having a heart attack. "Shit. *Fuck*."

Besian tapped his shoulder. "What's this about, *bratan*?" Dark eyes studied him intently. "Were you fucking the cleaning lady?"

"No!" Alexei slashed his hand through the air. "She has…" He stopped but had already said too much. There was no use in hiding it now. "There's a younger sister."

"I see." Besian exhaled loudly and shook his head. "Alexei…"

"I know. Believe me. I fucking know." This was the whole reason he preferred keeping a mistress. There was no emotional entanglement. It was clean and simple and there were rules.

Rules that he was about to blow up by doing whatever the hell was necessary to save Shay.

"Alexei, you better be damned sure this girl is *the one.* You're talking about getting between Lalo and Mueller. And you might not have your old boss' support on this one," he warned. "He's battle fatigued, you know? Some of his best men are still recovering from that awful shit that went down last month. And what if this blows up in your face? If your friends on the Chamber of Commerce and all those country club assholes you run with find out that you had to cross the line to save this girl? You can fucking kiss the reputation you've built as a successful, legitimate businessman goodbye."

Everything Besian said was true but…

"She's worth it." He leaned forward and dropped the last of his cash, fifties and hundreds, on the stage for the women who had been dancing for them. Standing up, he straightened his cuffs. "You better put the word on the street. I won't let anyone touch her."

"No, I don't think you will." Besian regarded him carefully before rising to his feet and extending his hand. As they shook on it, Besian dragged him in closer. Staring him in the eye, he promised, "I've got your back. You do what needs to be done. I'll smooth it over if Nikolai won't."

Alexei narrowed his eyes. "Why?"

"You have connections I need if I'm going to make legitimate moves. That means you're more useful to me alive and whole than chopped up and buried under concrete."

He snorted and clapped Besian on the arm. "Thanks."

"Anytime." Besian stepped back. "Good luck."

"Yeah." Almost two thousand dollars lighter but armed with much needed information, Alexei left the strip club. He checked his phone on the way out and noticed a text from Boychenko.

Boss man says he took her to the Arena to find her sister. Headed that way.

Alexei considered the situation he had unknowingly put Boychenko in and experienced a wave of guilt. If the kid tangled with Lalo or any of his enforcers, there would be hell to pay with Nikolai. Not wanting Boychenko to get into any unnecessary trouble, he shot him back a quick message.

Hang back. I'm on my way.

He slid into his seat and fastened his seatbelt. His mind raced as he drove down Richmond Avenue. He could think of a dozen different ways to save Shay and get her out of this mess her sister had created, but he couldn't think of one viable option for saving Shannon. He had no leverage and nothing to trade for her. She was complicit and guilty and the underworld dons would want her to pay the price for her crime.

How the hell was he supposed to tell Shay that he couldn't save her sister? She would hate him for failing her. She would despise him for breaking her trust in their friendship. Before he had even had a chance to find the courage to pursue her properly, the possibility of building something *real* with her would be snuffed out like a candle flame.

He had just turned onto Hillcroft when his phone started to ring. The Bluetooth connection in his vehicle answered the call. Hard, panicked breaths poured out of the speakers. Instantly on alert, he answered, "Hello?"

"Alexei!" A woman sobbed his name. It took him a moment to realize that was Shay's voice all twisted up with fear and panic.

"Shay?"

"Oh my god! Alexei! I need your help." She began to cry. "They trashed my car and then Lalo tried to—" She broke off for a moment before continuing, "And I hit him and he's bleeding everywhere. God, I'm so scared."

Lalo tried to what? He wanted to scream the question, to demand she tell him what that son of a bitch had done to make her cry, but then he zeroed in on what she had said. *He's bleeding everywhere.*

Had she attacked Lalo in self-defense? Was the cartel's golden boy dead? Were his men chasing her?

"Shay! Calm down." He used his most commanding voice with her, hoping it would calm her down and help her think straight. "Where are you?"

"I'm behind the Arena? I think? I don't know what to do."

The fear in her voice cut him deep. He squashed the pet names burning the tip of his tongue. This wasn't the time to coddle her. He needed to keep her from panicking. He needed to be firm and give her quick instructions that would keep her safe and alive until he could find her.

"Can you get to one of the restaurants on Fondren? There's a couple of fast food joints there."

"I don't know."

"I'll stay on the phone with you. I'm only a few minutes away on Hillcroft. I've been looking for you."

I'll find you, he silently swore.

Navigating the late night traffic proved tricky. He kept his ears perked and focused on the sounds coming from his speakers while his eyes were trained on the busy road in front of him. Every single intersection was agony. He just had to make one left onto the freeway and then he would be so close to her.

"Shay? Are you there?" She was being unnaturally quiet, and it worried him.

"Yes."

"Can you see those restaurants?"

"I think so. Yes. I'm almost there."

"Good. Keep moving. I'm coming for you."

Every muscle in his body tensed as he raced toward the Arena. Flashes of violent memories from his time as an enforcer taunted him. All of the awful, terrible shit he had done haunted him now. Was Shay about to pay the price for his misdeeds? Was the universe going to settle that score by hurting the only woman who had ever tempted him to lower his defenses?

A sharp intake of breath and a rustle of clothing heightened his concern. "Shay? Is something wrong?"

"Lalo's guys are in the parking lot. I can't go there."

He swore rudely and tried to think of a better option than asking her to hide. His mind recreated the surroundings of the Arena Theater. "There's that dim sum restaurant on the other side of the parking garage. If you can't get there, stay hidden. I'll find you."

As the sounds of her staccato breaths and the swish of her jacket echoed in his SUV, he gauged the traffic in front of him. The vehicles were creeping along the freeway as the backup of cars entering and leaving the concert venue caused a backup.

"Oh, God. Oh, God! Oh, God!" Terror drove her voice into a higher octave.

His fingers tightened on the steering wheel. "Shay? *Shay!* What is it?"

"It's the truck that was at my house earlier! Shit. *Shit.*"

Judging by her hard breaths and the *whoosh* of fabric, she was racing now, sprinting like an Olympian toward the finish line. He couldn't even imagine how scared she was. He had faced men with guns and knives and crowbars and worse during his many years in the mob, but he had never been afraid. He had been an arrogant prick and a man who enjoyed the explosion of adrenaline that came with brutal bloodshed.

He thought he had left that man behind—but he was wrong.

Listening to Shay running for her life? It had unleashed the monster inside him. With each terrified sob, the shackles chaining down the violent man he had tried to lockup and forget busted free. He was going to hurt someone tonight. He was going to hurt them *badly.*

"I'm on Southwest Freeway. I'm almost there. Just keep

moving, Shay."

She didn't answer. She just kept running and panting and panicking. He heard the whine of brakes and car doors opening and closing. She whimpered like a cornered puppy, and his damn heart shattered in his chest.

"Oh, God."

"Hold on, Shay!" He made a last minute decision to get off the freeway. Pressing on the accelerator, he beat the yellow light at the intersection and made a squealing right turn onto Bellaire. He had a vague idea of where she must have ended up and hoped his instincts were right.

Another call beeped in the background. Hoping it was Boychenko, he slapped at the touchscreen. "Roman?"

"Yeah?"

"Get over to the parking lots next to the Arena. The ones behind the dim sum place and that car stereo store," he clarified. "Shay's cornered. I'm on Bellaire. I may need your help."

"I'm there."

The call ended, and Shay's picked right back up but he could only hear faraway sounds. Had she dropped the phone? Had it been taken from her?

There was suddenly a cry of pain ricocheting around the cab of his SUV. Shay began to beg and plead for her life. He couldn't breathe. Was this it? Was he going to hear the end of her young and promising life?

The universe gave him a lucky break when he needed to make a left turn across three lanes of traffic. There were no cars to be seen as he floored his accelerator and entered the parking lot of a Mexican restaurant. He went straight through the parking lot and started weaving his way through the rabbit's warren of intersecting lots and loading and delivery docks for the businesses on that block.

Just when he started to despair, he spotted a truck parked at an angle in a dead end space between two buildings. He quickly slammed the brakes, reversed and then threw his SUV into drive. With his gas pedal jammed to the floorboard, he clenched his jaw and unlatched his seat belt. The bright lights of his SUV lit up the scene before him, and the blood pumping through his veins started to boil.

He was reduced to his most primitive state as he took in Shay on her knees and half naked in only her bra. There was a man standing behind her and two standing off to the side. The one in front of her held a baseball bat up to her cheek.

Beat. Hurt. Kill.

His brain stopped forming complete thoughts. The primal male instincts to protect and defend overwhelmed him. He was out of his SUV before it had even come to a full stop. Hell bent on destruction, he stormed across the pavement and headed right for that stupid bastard with the baseball bat. The other man was taller by an inch or two and well-built but he seemed startled to see someone rushing him.

Jaw clenched, neck tight and scowling, Alexei titled his forward and slammed his forehead into the man's nose. The man cried out in pain but Alexei wasn't done yet. Ignoring the ache spreading through his own head, he wrenched free the bat and cracked the man across the stomach before landing another blow to his ribs. The man dropped to the pavement in a bloody, gasping heap.

Armed and dangerous, Alexei turned his attention on the

next closest target. One well-aimed strike to the ribs and a blow to the front of that one's knees sent him down. Out of the corner of his eye, he saw the third man shake free from his stupor and run. Alexei let him go before turning his attention to the man standing behind Shay.

This close, he could finally see why the man was standing there. He had tied Shay's elbows and wrists together in a brutal knot that contorted her slim shoulders into an unnatural and painful position and then had looped a length of the rope around her neck. The fucker held onto the other end and pulled it tight like a leash. Blood trickled from Shay's nose and soaked into the piece of cloth—a man's handkerchief—that had been shoved into her mouth to gag her.

Growling with fury, he unleashed hell on that bastard. A blow to the shoulder sent the man stumbling to the side. Alexei followed him as he staggered away from Shay and then cracked him across the chest with the bat. The man had tried to block the blow but succeeded only in breaking his hand. It took another two hits, one to his knees and one to the middle of his back to drop him for good.

Panting for air and high on adrenaline, Alexei whirled around to search for the fourth man. He was taken aback to see Boychenko striding toward him with the other man at gunpoint. Hands in the air, the man marched forward as if heading toward the gallows. For a moment, Alexei considered taking the bat to him but then he decided Shay had seen enough violence tonight.

Turning back toward Shay, his heart beat erratically as he watched her shoulders shake with silenced sobs. He crossed the distance between them and crouched down in front of her.

Headlight beams illuminated her beautiful face. She gazed up at him with wet lashes and leaned into his touch when he cupped her cheek. That simple movement of seeking his warmth and reassurance threatened to break him.

Very carefully, he pulled the gag from her mouth and tossed it aside. He didn't bother trying to undo the knots in the rope. He pulled a small but razor sharp knife from his pocket and used it to cut her free. When the knife was safely back in his pocket, he shrugged out of his suit jacket and draped it around her bare shoulders.

"Are you hurt? Do you need me to take you to the hospital?" He looked her over as quickly as possible but it was difficult to tell in the dark. She shook her head, and he decided to wait until he got her some place safe to check her more closely. He quickly gathered her small body in his arms, cradling her close to his chest, and carried her to the front seat of his idling SUV. He fastened her seatbelt and turned up the heater before closing the door and returning to Boychenko.

"You need to get out of here, Alexei. *Now*," the kid added forcefully. "You don't want to be here if the police show up."

Nodding, Alexei gathered up Shay's things. Her jacket was ruined with the blood splatter from the beatings he had given those men. He grabbed the bat, rope and handkerchief because he didn't want to leave behind his fingerprints or her DNA. As he picked up the personal items that had tumbled out of her purse, he spotted a folded up note. He didn't mean to read it but his eyes flicked over it before he could stop himself.

The threatening words scribbled on the paper sent a new flash of rage burning through his body. Note in hand, he strode back to Boychenko and placed the dented, bloodied end of the bat right against the skinny man's jaw. The man shook with fear as Alexei pressed the weight of the wooden implement into his skin. He made sure that nervous gaze was on him as he laid it all on the line.

"You go back to Mueller, and you tell him that my girl is off-limits." He balled up the note and roughly shoved it into the man's mouth, scraping his knuckles on crooked teeth but barely registering the pain. "You tell him he knows where to find me if he wants to settle this."

And then, just because he was so angry, Alexei sucker punched the man right in the stomach. He kept his fist buried in the man's soft belly and brought his mouth close to the man's ear. "I'm going to gut the next one of you skinhead fucks that gets within five hundred feet of Shay. Do you understand?"

The man coughed and nodded enthusiastically. "Ye-yes," he stuttered out a raspy reply around the paper jammed in his mouth.

"Good." Drawing back his hand, Alexei glanced at Boychenko. The young enforcer jerked his head, silently telling Alexei to beat it and fast. He didn't waste time apologizing to the kid for dragging him into this mess. There would be time for that later.

He opened the passenger door behind the driver's seat and placed Shay's purse and jacket there along with the bat and the other items he had collected. He slipped into his seat, fastened his seatbelt and quickly backed out of the narrow rectangle between the two buildings. Glancing left and right, he chose a path out of the interconnected parking lots and headed for Bellaire.

The sight of flashing lights up ahead and the blare of police and fire sirens rattled him. He exhaled a breath of relief when he realized they were responding to a collision up ahead. As he navigated the slow crawl of traffic, he could feel Shay staring at him. Thinking of what he had just done back there and of the violent way she had seen him react, he feared what he would see if he finally found the courage to look at her.

When he slowed to a stop behind a line of vehicles waiting for the minor accident to be cleared from the intersection, he glanced at Shay. Her bruised and bloodied face saddened him more than anything in the world ever had. He leaned over to retrieve the extra monogrammed handkerchief he kept tucked away in the glove box and wet it with the bottle of water sitting in the center console.

Very gently, he dabbed away the blood drying under her nose and trickling along the curve of her chin. When she was clean, he dropped the folded up handkerchief in a cup holder. Her long dark hair was such a mess. He carefully uncurled the lime green elastic that held her tresses in a ponytail and combed his fingers through the messy strands. He had no fucking idea what he was doing but he couldn't stop gliding his fingers through the silky waves. The scent of her shampoo filled the air and inspired thoughts that were better suited to another time and place.

Gathering up her hair, he managed to tame it into a simple, low ponytail. "It's not very pretty," he apologized, "but it will do."

Her sweet mouth slanted with a timid smile. In a voice that was raw and thick from crying and fear, she whispered, "Thank you."

Marveling at her reaction, he held tight to the ends of her hair. "How is it that you can still smile after all that?"

She slowly reached for his hand. The tips of her fingers peeked out from the too long sleeves of his suit jacket as she shyly and uncertainly grasped his wrist. He swallowed hard as she tugged his arm down and slid her hand on top of his. "You came for me, Alexei."

That quietly spoken statement struck him with the full weight of the responsibility it carried. For most of her life, Shay had been on her own. Her father had been killed in a car wreck. Her mother had run off and left her in Shannon's care. Though her older sister had done her best, Shay seemed to have been the more responsible one in that household. So how many times had she needed help and been on her own? How many times had promises been broken?

Burrowed deep in his jacket, with her knees pulled up to her chest, she reminded him of a little wounded bird desperate to take flight and escape. Not to escape him but to escape the hard life of poverty and heartbreak she had known since birth. In so many ways, she reminded him of a younger version of himself. Her drive and ambition matched his, but she was infinitely more talented and kind-hearted and good than he ever would be.

Suddenly, he understood what needed to be done. There was no use in fighting the inevitable. He was going to give her the chance that no one ever gave him. He was going to give her the break that she so desperately deserved.

Still holding her hand, he shifted out of park as the traffic began to move. He had a destination in mind. It was the one place he had always told himself he would never take her, but it was also the one place where she would be safe, safe from Lalo and Mueller.

And me…

He was honest enough to admit to himself that that he wouldn't be able to keep his hands off of her if he took her into his home. She was temptation on two legs, and he refused to put her in a situation where she felt pressured to say yes. A little distance between them was the perfect solution.

"*Ptichka.*" *Little bird.*

"Yes?"

Interlacing their fingers, he lifted her hand and placed a tender kiss on her soft, warm skin. "Do you trust me?"

"Yes."

One word.

No hesitation.

No question.

It was all the permission he needed to keep her.

CHAPTER FIVE

D AZED AND STILL in shock, I clung tightly to Alexei's hand as he drove through the city. I tried to get my bearings but my brain was so fuzzy I finally gave up. Wherever we were going, I would be safe. Not even the faintest glimmer of doubt existed in my mind now.

The bat rolled around on the floorboard behind the driver's seat. When I closed my eyes, I could see Alexei storming right up to the leader of that crew and slamming his forehead into that jerk's nose. I could hear the crunch of bone and the shocked curses from the men who knew they were next. The thud of wood slamming into bellies and knees echoed in my ears.

I was no stranger to violence. A childhood of loser boyfriends trailing my mother into our home had taught me more about cruelty and meanness than any one person needed to know. Even with all that ugly history behind me, I still couldn't quite believe what I had just witnessed. One single man taking out four others without a gun or a knife? With just his bare hands and a bat? It was breathtaking and terrifying.

I glanced at my hand clutched in his. Those hands that had just committed such brutal violence had also tended to me with such tenderness. Alexei swiped his thumb side to side along my skin, the small gesture soothing my raw nerves. The two sides of this complicated man intrigued and unsettled me. Until tonight, it had been easy to categorize our friendship. There were lines and boundaries, and everything fit neatly in a friendship box.

But now? After watching him unleash hell on those men? After witnessing what he was capable of doing to protect me? After the way he had just cleaned my face and fixed my hair and now held my hand? That box had just been obliterated.

What does he want with me? A different question, one that made my stomach pitch with anxiety clamored right on the tail end of that one. *What does he want* from *me?*

Because that was the real question, wasn't it? Nothing in this life was free. A man like Alexei, a man who had survived prison and escaped the mafia to become a successful, wealthy businessman wasn't going to stick his neck out for me without expecting something in return. Would I be able to meet his price?

He's not Lalo. He won't make you trade your body for his protection. He's not a monster. He's a good man.

"Are you all right?"

"Yes." My voice was still dry and rough after all that crying and running. "I'm fine."

"You're not dizzy? Are you hurting anywhere? Bleeding?" He gave my hand a light squeeze. "I can take you to an emergency room if you need one, Shay." His grip tightened. "If they hurt you…"

"You got there in time," I said quietly. "They were just getting started when you showed up."

He muttered something in Russian, something angry and

harsh. His grip changed and he threaded our fingers together again. "And before those skinheads found you? When you called, you said Lalo was bleeding." He paused, and I could see the profile of his Adam's apple bobbing up and down as he kept his gaze fixed on the windshield. "Your shirt is missing. You were crying. Did he—?"

"He tried," I cut him off before he got more worked up about it. "But he didn't get very far."

Alexei's teeth grinded together so hard I expected his jaw to snap. "Did he hit you?"

I touched my still aching cheek. "Yes."

Alexei snarled angrily in Russian before switching to English. "I'll fucking kill him for touching you."

That wasn't hyperbole. He wasn't saying outlandish things to impress me. He meant it.

Remembering the bloody scene I had left behind, I whispered, "You may not get the chance."

"Why?" The lines in his forehead were prominent when he glanced at me. "What did you do?"

"I didn't have a choice." I started to bite my lower lip with worry but hissed when I experienced the sharp sting of pain.

Alexei must have realized what I had done because in the next instant he gently chided, "Be careful. You have a busted lip. We'll get some ice on it soon." He stared at me as we waited for a red light to turn green. "How badly was Lalo hurt?"

"I slammed a crystal paperweight into his head," I admitted somberly. "Twice."

He didn't even blink at the revelation that I had done something so violent. "Was he breathing when you left him?"

"Yes, but there was so much blood."

"Head wounds gush. If he was breathing, he'll probably survive."

Fearful of the answer, I asked, "Is that a good thing or a bad thing?"

He eased on the gas and flicked on his blinker. "It's good for you and bad for me."

That didn't make sense to me. "Why would you say that?"

"It's good for you because you won't have Lalo's crew or their friends in the Hermanos street gang hunting you down to win a bounty."

"Why is it bad for you?"

"You don't need to worry about that." He guided his SUV through the intersection. "You're safe now. That's all that matters."

Alexei's voice had that edge of finality to it so I didn't protest. And honestly? I was so tired. I sagged in the seat and leaned my head back against it. As if sensing my exhaustion, Alexei said, "We're almost there. We'll get you cleaned up and find something for you to eat. It will help you feel better."

A thousand questions raced through my mind. *Where are you taking me? When can I go home? What about my sister? Where am I going to find clothes? What's going to happen tomorrow?*

I didn't ask any of them. I had a sinking feeling I wouldn't like any of the answers.

When Alexei slowed down and flicked his blinker to enter a private parking garage, I perked up a bit. A sticker with an RFID tag allowed Alexei to pass through the guarded entrance to the garage attached to the soaring building that housed million dollar hi-rise condos and penthouses.

"What is it?" he asked as he began the looping climb to his assigned spot in the garage.

"I just never figured you for the type that would live in a condo."

He cast an approving smile my way. "You're right. I don't."

His reply confused me. "But if you don't live here—"

"This is the apartment I keep for…" His voice trailed off as he swung his SUV wide and backed into his slot.

"For?" I prompted nervously.

Alexei shut down the engine and turned in his seat. With his hand still clamped between both of mine, he explained, "This is the home I keep for my mistress."

Tense seconds of silence stretched between us. "Your mistress?" A horrifying thought struck me, and I tried to jerk my hands away. Faster and stronger, he placed his other hand on mine and held me in place. "Alexei! Are you married?"

"What?" He laughed as if that was the most outlandish thing imaginable. "No. Never."

"Then why—"

"Girlfriend is a teenager's word but mistress? That suits me just fine."

"Because?"

"Because it's an arrangement," he said matter-of-factly. "There are clear rules from the first day. It doesn't get messy or uncomfortable. It's as simple as outlining a business transaction."

The cold, distant way he described his romantic relationships saddened me. I tried to mesh together everything I knew about him with this new discovery. It didn't jell. "You're happy with that, Alexei?"

There was a brief moment of hesitation before he nodded. "Yes, I'm perfectly happy with it."

I didn't believe him. He might be able to fool other people but that subtle shift of his eyes spoke volumes.

It's none of your business, Shay. Don't push.

Was his mistress upstairs in bed right now? Had he left her to come find me? Was she going to be super pissed off when I walked into her home?

Worried that I might be walking into a minefield of awkwardness, I said, "I don't think this is such a good idea. I don't want to cause any problems for you with your mistress."

"It's no problem." He untangled our hands and reached down to unbuckle my seatbelt. "The apartment is empty." He pushed the seatbelt away from my shoulder and hip and tugged his jacket closed around my naked torso. He tipped my chin with two fingers and met my questioning gaze with a steady one of his own. "It has been since February."

"Oh." What was he trying to tell me? Not wanting to read more into that statement than he intended, I let it go.

"Let's get you inside." Alexei left the SUV. He grabbed his gym bag from the backseat before coming to my door. Before I could move, he had slipped one arm around my shoulders. In the next instant, he scooped me right up and out of the SUV.

I gripped two handfuls of his shirt. "What are you doing? I can walk!"

"I'm sure you can." He pushed the door closed with his foot. "But I'm not taking any chances."

I started to tell him that he was going to hurt his back carrying me and his gym bag but he moved effortlessly. When we reached the elevator, I could feel his hard, well-honed muscles rippling beneath my thighs and across my back as he shifted me in his arms. His hand dipped under the borrowed jacket I was wearing and into the pocket hidden away there. I tried not to think about the brush of his warm skin against mine as he retrieved his wallet and presented it to me.

"Can you open this and find the keycard?"

"Sure." I took the wallet from him and pried it open. There weren't enough slots for all of the items he kept in there so it bulged in places. "You need a new wallet."

"I just bought that two months ago." He gestured with his chin toward the cards jammed in the slots. "It's the white one with the gold lettering. Yes. That one. Swipe it, please."

Seconds later, we were in the elevator and zooming up eleven floors. Alexei stepped into a beautifully decorated hall and carried me to a door at the far end of the hall. "Will you grab the keys from my pants pocket?"

I swallowed nervously and carefully dipped my hand into the front pocket of his trousers. I refused to meet his heated gaze as I retrieved them and did my very best not to touch anything except for the cold metal and plastic. Though I had dated a lot of nice guys, I had never stuck my hand in one of their pockets or gotten that close to…well…*you know.*

"You keep that up, and I'm going to make you buy me dinner."

Mortified by his teasing, I quickly retrieved the keys and studiously avoided his sinful grin. "Which one?"

"The silver key with the red dot on it." I held it up to be sure, and he confirmed it. "Yes."

After I unlocked and opened the door, he carried me inside and slapped the light switch in the foyer. A warm light illuminated the entryway and part of the living area. Floor to ceiling windows lined the exterior wall of the unit. I suspected the downtown views would be breathtakingly perfect come morning.

"Sit still," he ordered as he placed me on the marble slab covering the oversized kitchen island. His gym bag was dropped on the floor, and he started rifling through the cabinets and refrigerator. He found ice, a bowl, a dish towel and a small first aid kit under the sink but he wasn't satisfied with that. He placed a call down to the building's concierge and gave him a short list of groceries he wanted delivered as quickly as possible.

I waited until he had returned the phone to its cradle on the counter before pointing out the obvious. "It's, like, one in the morning, Alexei."

"And?" He turned on the faucet and wet one end of the dish towel.

Incredulous, I waved my hands. "And you're asking that poor guy to go buy groceries?"

"That's his job." Alexei wrung out the fluffy cloth and brought an armload of supplies to the island. "This building has round-the-clock staff for a reason."

"Still…"

Alexei moved to stand in front of me. For the first time ever, we were the same height. A small bruise had already formed from the contact his forehead had made with that man's nose. This close, I could see that his eyes were actually a mix of green and brown. The fine lines around them were crinkled with the hint of a smile. I wanted to reach up and run my fingers along them, to trace the line of his strong jaw to the barely visible cleft in his chin. "Will you feel better if I give him a big tip?

"Yes."

"Fine. That's settled." He unbuttoned his cuffs and rolled up his sleeves. I tried not to stare at the new swaths of Russian mafia tattoos revealed to me. Under this brighter light, the blood spatter on his shirt was clearly visible. Following my gaze, he frowned. "We've got to get rid of all this. Everything you're wearing tonight has to be destroyed. As soon as I'm done getting you cleaned up and in bed, I'll take care of everything."

It was such a sordid, dirty thing but I understood he was just being practical. He seemed so calm about it though. "Have you done this a lot?"

To his credit, Alexei didn't lie. "What you saw tonight? That was my old job. I was a street soldier and an enforcer."

"Oh." I tried to wrap my head around the idea of Alexei beating the crap out of people to make them pay protection money or to force them to toe the family line.

His peered down at me, his jaw tight and his eyes slightly narrowed. "Are you afraid of me now?"

"No!"

"You probably should be," he grumbled. "I'm not a very nice man, not when you get right down to it."

"I don't believe that."

He expelled a harsh breath. "Then you are more naïve than I ever imagined."

His remark pissed me right off. After everything I had

been through tonight, I wasn't going to take that kind of crap from a friend. "Don't talk to me like that!"

Taken aback by my outburst, he dropped his gaze and seemed instantly chastised. He leaned forward and shocked me by pressing his forehead to mine. With that bruise there, it must have hurt him but he didn't flinch. "I'm sorry, Shay." He pulled back slowly. "That was a dick thing for me to say."

"Then why did you say it?"

"I don't know." He rubbed the back of his neck and shook his head. "I could say that I'm tired but that's just an excuse. Maybe I said it because I know what a shit person I was ten years ago and what an incredibly good and kind person you are and I know that eventually I'm going to hurt or disappoint you."

The self-loathing filling his voice surprised. Gone was the powerful, confident man who ruled in business. Here was the man with the wounded soul who tried so hard to distance himself from feeling anything close to love. His insistence on keeping a mistress suddenly made sense to me. He didn't want to expose himself to anything that might make him vulnerable.

"Maybe you were a terrible person ten years ago, Alexei, but you aren't that terrible person tonight." I reached for his closest hand. The mob ink decorating his skin no longer seemed as menacing as it once had. "You've never been anything but kind to me. Kind and generous and good. That's the man I know. That's the man I trust." I squeezed his fingers and smiled up at him. "That's the man who would die before he hurt me."

"I won't hurt you," he promised. "I could never hurt you like this." He brushed his hand along the bruise blossoming on my cheek. "But I will disappoint you."

"All friendships have disappointing moments, Alexei. That's just part of the deal." I found myself leaning into his touch and wondered if it was simply the shock of the night causing me to seek out human contact or the feelings for this complicated Russian finally coming to a head. "Just be honest with me. Tell me the truth, Alexei. Always."

He nodded stiffly and then carefully prodded the edges of the bruise forming on my cheek. "It's not broken but you're going to be swollen tomorrow."

"I've had worse," I muttered without thinking. Alexei visibly stiffened at the comment. Was he remembering what I had confessed to him last Christmas?

"I still think you should tell me the names of your mother's old boyfriends so I can kick their asses for you."

I quirked a smile at that. "Don't tempt me."

He murmured something in Russian, and I decided right then and there that I was going to have to track down some books and videos so I could learn his language.

"May I take this off?" He gestured to the jacket draped around my shoulders.

In any other setting, the question would have been followed by the promise of erotic possibilities. Right now, though, it was Alexei's way of proving that he wasn't going to hurt or take advantage of me. "Yes."

He peeled the jacket off my bare shoulders and let it pool around my waist. The second I heard his sharp intake of breath, I knew that he had seen the bruises on my throat. Stepping forward, he insinuated his trim hips between my knees and gently clasped my chin in one big hand. He carefully tilted my face to the side and examined the marks that Lalo's mean hand had left behind. When he snarled in his mother tongue, I decided it was a good thing I couldn't understand him. He was furious.

"Shay, did you lose consciousness when he choked you?" Alexei's eyes were dark with worry and anger.

"No." I inhaled a shuddery breath when Alexei's fingertips ghosted over the sore spots developing on my throat. "He didn't squeeze that hard. He…"

"He what?" Alexei asked when my voice trailed off to nothing. "Tell me what happened, Shay." He cupped my face between his palms and brushed his thumbs across my cheeks. "You'll feel better if you get it out."

My eyes prickled with hot tears as I tearfully told everything. He didn't interrupt or comment as I described arriving at the Arena and the harrowing moments inside that office when Lalo had tried to rape me. When I was finished, Alexei wrapped his powerful arms around me and pulled me into a comforting, secure embrace. I closed my eyes and found comfort in the strength surrounding me.

"You're all right now." He rubbed my back with languid circles. "No one will ever touch you again, Shay. I swear it."

I didn't know how he was going to pull off that promise but if anyone could do it? Alexei was that man.

A long time later, Alexei finally unwound his arms. Wordlessly, he picked up the damp cloth and cleaned my face. He bundled up some ice and pressed the cold pack against my swollen cheek. "Hold this."

I held the ice pack in place while Alexei tugged the jacket he had given me back up around my shoulders. He pulled it tightly closed in front before crouching down to dig through his gym bag. He retrieved a folded shirt and put it on the counter next to me. The logo for Ivan Markovic's acclaimed MMA fighting gym was emblazoned on the front.

"You can wear this after your shower. It's clean," he added with a smile.

"Thank you."

"Let's check out your arms, okay? They had you tied up so tight." Very gently, he grasped my right wrist and lifted my arm. He rotated my hand and checked my fingers before meticulously working his way to my shoulder. After I switched hands holding the ice pack, he repeated the process on my left arm. He asked me to take deep breaths and watched my face for any sign of pain. "How does your back feel?"

"Fine." Thinking of the old scars crisscrossing my back, I was glad there was no reason for him to investigate. If he had felt them earlier when he was hugging me, he hadn't mentioned it. After talking about what Lalo had tried to do to me, I really didn't want to unearth old, buried history from my childhood.

"And here?" He touched my thighs. "Did you get kicked? Did you trip?"

"No." I tried to concentrate on my limbs instead of the unbelievable body heat that radiated from his larger frame or that incredible scent that followed him everywhere. "I might have bruised them a little when they made me kneel."

"I'll put some antibiotic ointment in the bathroom. If you need it after your shower, use it."

"I will."

"Can you walk?"

Even though the prospect of having him carry me again sent a bright frisson of excitement through my body, I nodded. "I can walk. Just point me in the right direction."

Alexei eased me off the kitchen island and gave me a short tour of the apartment. No longer dazed, I took in the sleek, modern furnishings and the art adorning the walls. The place was much bigger than I had realized with three bedrooms and two bathrooms plus a separate office and a generously sized balcony off the master suite.

But as I walked through the rooms with Alexei at my side, I sensed that he spent very little time in this place. Though it was beautifully and professionally decorated, it wasn't a home. Eyeing the massive bed and the sumptuous linens, I couldn't help but wonder how many women had tumbled onto it with him.

Jealousy and sadness dueled inside me. The type of women who would be comfortable in a place like this were women I couldn't compete with in a million years. It was easy enough to imagine the richly dressed, ultra-classy women with perfect manners Alexei chose to play the role of his mistress. They were the types of women who moved easily in the social circles he inhabited. They were the types of women who were confident and sexy and knew how to please a man.

And that isn't you, I thought sadly.

Alexei stepped ahead of me and switched on the lights to the master bathroom. After placing the gym shirt on the counter, he moved back outside the door and waved me inside. "There are towels and travel-sized toiletries in the cabinet. I'll be in the living room if you need me."

Grasping his jacket tightly to my nearly-naked body, I

grew insanely aware of how close we were standing. "Okay."

"Bring your clothes to me when you're done. I'll get rid of them." He started to back away but stopped. "Where are your keys?"

"To the house? In my purse. Why?"

"I'll need you to give them to me so I can stop by your place to get your things."

The idea of Alexei going through my bedroom and picking through my drawer of boring undies wasn't one that I relished. "I can pack my own things."

"That's not happening."

"But—"

"Shay, you aren't leaving this apartment until I've secured your safety. Whatever you need? It comes through me." He must have sensed that I wanted to argue with him because he quickly changed the subject. "Come find me when you're done."

Left alone in the master suite, I walked into the bathroom and closed the door. After stripping out of my clothes and his jacket, I stood in front of the marble vanity and stared at my reflection. My face wasn't as badly bruised as I had feared it would be but my throat would bear Lalo's marks for days.

I ran my fingers over the marred skin but it wasn't the phantom sensation of Lalo's ugly hands that caused goose bumps to rise on my flesh. No, it was the memory of the way Alexei's hands had felt on me. A part of me despaired at the notion he might not ever touch me like that again.

"So what happens now?" My whispered question barely registered in my ears.

What would happen with Shannon? Would Lalo's men

come after me? What about those skinheads who had tied me up and planned to leave me beaten and bloodied in that parking lot as a message to my sister?

My reflection didn't have the answers I wanted but I had no doubt Alexei would. If I wanted to get out of this mess alive, I had to trust him.

He'll take care of you.

If you let him…

CHAPTER SIX

A LEXEI CLOSED HIS eyes and leaned his head back against the closed bedroom door. All that separated him from Shay, from the woman that had turned him inside out and left him craving the one thing he could never have, were two thin slabs of wood. Two simple, unlocked doors kept him from the woman he wanted more than anything in the whole wide world.

Leaving her alone in that bathroom had taken every ounce of his self-control. If it had been any other night, he would have stripped her bare and pulled her into a shower with him. He would have lathered up his palms and glided them over her supple curves and then carried her to bed. The very idea of learning every secret, ticklish place on her body with a swipe of his tongue left him lightheaded and aching.

But not tonight.

Tonight she had been through so much. She needed space to decompress. She needed to cleanse away the horror she had experienced. His only goal tonight was to make sure that Shay felt safe and secure. Whatever the cost, he would give that to her.

He pushed off the door and made his way to the office where he opened the safe hidden in the credenza and removed an envelope of cash. He tucked it into his back pocket, closed and locked the safe and left the office. Back in the kitchen, he washed his hands and treated the scrapes on his knuckles from that bastard's teeth. As he rubbed in the ointment, he thought of all the ways his actions tonight might play out. Mueller might be a racist but he wasn't stupid. He would try to leverage his threat against Shay to make a deal.

But Lalo? Lalo was the real problem. Newly anointed as the cartel's top man in Houston, he had a taste for power and the added pressure to prove his worth as a boss. He wanted respect, and if it got out that a tiny little thing like Shay had knocked him the fuck out while his entire crew of thugs and enforcers stood outside? He was going to be a laughingstock.

Alexei placed both palms on the counter and leaned hard against it, dropping his head and closing his eyes as he tried to work out the angles. There was something else about Lalo that was even more dangerous. He wanted Shay. He wanted her in the most primal way a man could want a woman.

She's mine. She belongs to me.

Shaking his head, Alexei let loose a dark laugh. Shay didn't belong to him. She wasn't his. She didn't belong to any man. She was her own person, independent and strong and ready to fight the world to find her own success.

But as much as he admired that tenacity, Alexei knew better than anyone that it made her vulnerable. She was alone in this world. She had no one to back her up and give her support when she needed it most.

I could be that support. I could have her back. I could be the man who—

"Alexei?"

The sound of Shay's voice snapped him out of his thoughts. She stood just inside the living area and clutched her dirty clothes to her chest in a neatly tied bundle. His jacket was draped across her shoulders and her shoes dangled from her fingers. The long damp strands of her coffee-colored hair had been combed back and left to air dry, but it was the sight of her in just his shirt that drove the air out of his lungs and made his blood run even hotter.

"Alexei, your phone is ringing." Still standing there, she tilted her head to the side. "Are you going to answer it?"

He patted his pocket and felt the vibrating, chirping block hidden away there. He quickly answered it. "Hello?"

"We have a problem." Mob boss Nikolai Kalasnikov didn't sound happy. "I need to see you. *Now.*"

Glad that Shay didn't understand a word of Russian, he cast a brief glance in her direction. He couldn't leave her here alone, not right now and not even for his old boss. "I can't get away from here."

Nikolai sighed. "I'll come to you."

"I'm at the other place."

"Yeah. I figured." He paused. "Do you need anything?"

"Maid service would be nice." He thought of the evidence that needed to be destroyed. The services of a cleaner like Kostya would come in handy right now.

"Our maid is out on sick leave, but I'll put in a call with the company."

The line went dead, and Alexei pocketed his phone. Getting into an argument with Nikolai was the last fucking thing he wanted to do tonight, but it was better to just get the ass chewing over with, pay whatever fee the boss demanded and move forward.

"Is everything okay?"

Shay's anxious expression spurred him into action. He walked around the long kitchen island separating them and took the bundle of clothing and shoes from her arms. When they were out of the way on the counter, he placed his hands on her shoulders. She had asked him for honesty, and he was going to give it to her.

"Nikolai Kalsnikov is coming over. Do I need to tell you what that means?"

Her eyes widened, and her lower lip actually wobbled. On the verge of tears, she asked, "Is he going to kill me?"

"What? God no!" Alexei hauled her into his arms and crushed her tight to his chest. Dipping his head, he touched his cheek to the unbruised side of her face. The mere mention of Nikolai's name had scared her so much she was shaking. "I told you, Shay. No one is going to hurt you."

She tried to pull back so he let her. It wasn't until that moment that he realized she had grabbed hold of him in her fear. She still gripped his shirt on either side of his hips as she gazed up at him with watery eyes. "But he's *the* mob boss in Houston."

"Yes, he is." There was no point in denying what she knew. "But he's my friend. We go back. *Way* back," he emphasized. "We have history, and he owes me. If he can't provide the coverage we need, there are other men who will for the right price."

Shay slowly released her hold on him but she didn't attempt to step out of his loose embrace. "What if the price is too high?"

Didn't she understand? Leaning down, he kissed the top of her head. He allowed his lips to linger there for a moment longer than necessary. "There is no price too high, not for you."

"Alexei," she breathed his name, and his control wavered. Maybe one little kiss wouldn't hurt...

A knock at the door startled them both out of that unexpected moment of romantic tension.

"It's probably just Carlos," he murmured. "The concierge."

"Oh. Um." She glanced around nervously. "I'll go hide in the bedroom."

Before he could ask her why she thought she needed to hide, she was already scampering away like a little rabbit. It occurred to him as he tucked away the bloody clothes in a cabinet and headed for the door that she might be embarrassed to be caught wearing only his shirt. Her sense of modesty amused him.

A quick peek through the peephole confirmed his suspicions. As he let Carlos inside, Alexei felt uncomfortably prepared for an ambush or a fight. *I need to start carrying a piece again.*

After the groceries were stowed on the counter, he walked Carlos back to the door and handed him the envelope of cash. "No one comes up to the eleventh floor without my approval. I want it locked down. Understand?"

Carlos slipped the envelope inside his suit jacket. "As you wish, Mr. Sarnov."

Owning every unit on the floor and keeping them all empty save for this one had its perks. Chief among them the fact that Carlos and his friend in the maintenance department could shut down elevator access to the floor. It wasn't a perfect solution for keeping Shay safe but it was the best option he had right now.

"I'm expecting a visitor soon. He'll come through the trade entrance. Make sure he gets up as quickly as possible and without being seen."

"Done." Carlos left the apartment, and Alexei locked the door behind him.

When he made it back to the kitchen, he found Shay putting away the groceries. It was a domestic vision that rattled him. For a moment, he could almost believe they were like any other couple. There she was with her wet hair, wearing his shirt and putting away groceries as if this were something they did every night. It was such a simple thing to witness, but fuck. It made him *want* something simple and normal and real.

"Do you want some coffee? I could make you something to eat," Shay offered.

"Sit." He pointed to one of the tall leather barstools on the other side of the island. "You fed me once. Now *I'll* make *you* something to eat." He caught her disbelieving smile as she slid onto a seat. "What?"

"I just never figured you for the cooking type."

"And how do you think I feed myself?"

"Takeout? Restaurants?"

He had to give her that one. "All right. Most days, yes. But I do know how to cook eggs. You'll see."

Before he started on their eggs and toast, he poured a glass of orange juice for her. "Drink this."

She dutifully sipped the cold liquid. When she licked her upper lip, he had to avert his eyes and suppress a needful groan. Did she have any idea how damned alluring she was? If she did, she played the game superbly and better than any woman he had ever known. But he sincerely doubted that was the case.

He had just finished plating their scrambled eggs and toast when a knock interrupted his work. He thrust a fork into her hand. "Eat."

She accepted the fork but her scared gaze darted toward the doorway. While he understood her fear of Nikolai, it was misplaced. The boss was a hard man, ruthless when necessary and not afraid to get his hands dirty, but he never hurt women. In some ways, he was the dark champion of the innocent.

Alexei smiled encouragingly and gently pushed her hand toward the plate. "Eat."

Shay took a small bite. Satisfied that she was going to get some food into her stomach, he left the kitchen and answered the door. Instead of his customary bespoke suit, Nikolai wore jeans and a black hoodie that obscured most of his face, but those Ferragamo boots gave him away. Alexei stepped aside and gestured for the boss to enter.

Once inside, Nikolai lowered his hood. His green-eyed glare warned Alexei to tread carefully. "I had to leave my home and my bed and my pregnant wife, Alexei. After everything that's happened this year, how do you think I feel leaving Vee with her guards at night?"

To say the boss was unhappy was an understatement. He was so incredibly protective of his wife. It was no secret that Nikolai worshipped Vivian, and now that she was giving him a son and heir? He was utterly devoted to her. Dragging the boss out of bed and entangling him in this mess? *Blin.*

"If I could have avoided this—"

"You are not a street soldier anymore," Nikolai hissed. "If you want to make a move, you clear this shit with me first." The boss stepped forward and invaded his personal space. "This," Nikolai lifted his hand and pointed to the tattoo on the underside of his wrist that every member of his crime family was given, "is the only reason Ten and Danny aren't dragging you out of here and down to the warehouse."

Alexei rubbed the tattoo branding his own wrist. Guilt soured his stomach as he considered the impossible position he had put Nikolai in tonight. "Boss—"

"Where is she?" Nikolai turned his back and started toward the kitchen. "What's this one's name? Treasure? Satin? Dynasty?"

It was a mean barb that hit its mark. His preference for dancing girls was part of the underworld legend. "Her name is Shay. She cleans my office. Part-time," he clarified. "She's an entrepreneur with a college degree."

Nikolai stopped and turned. His discerning gaze made Alexei uncomfortable. The man had a gift for seeing right through people. What was he seeing now?

As if trying to figure out a puzzle, Nikolai asked, "Are you serious about her? Because if you are, I need to know now."

"I'm serious about her." Whether or not Shay was serious about him remained to be seen.

"You should have told me about this woman when things got serious. I should have been made aware of her connections so I had a complete picture of our family's underworld ties." Nikolai exhaled a long breath. "You won't get out of this cheaply, not after you put three of Mueller's men in the hospital."

"I know," he gravely answered. "I know."

The boss nodded. "So long as you know…"

Alexei trailed Nikolai into the kitchen where Shay anxiously stabbed her fork into the small mound of scrambled eggs left on her plate. Half of her toast had been eaten and her glass of juice was empty. Glad that she had gotten something in her belly, he flashed her a reassuring smile.

Without a word of introduction, Nikolai walked right up to Shay and carefully clasped her chin. He gently turned her face left and then right before tilting her head back to get a better look at the fingertip bruises on her neck. The marks had really blossomed now and provided a clear picture of what had happened to her earlier in the night.

The tic in Nikolai's jaw eased the tension in Alexei's chest. He trusted Nikolai to be fair with Shay, but after seeing her battered face, the boss would make sure she was protected.

Nikolai gave Shay's shoulder a squeeze and then stepped back. Her grip on the fork loosened, and she visibly relaxed. Hoping to set her at ease, Alexei traded her empty glass of juice for the full, untouched glass sitting next to his plate. She took the juice with a thankful smile and sipped it.

"Shay, this is Mr. Kalasnikov."

She wrapped both hands around the glass. "Hello."

"You don't need to be afraid of me, Shay. So long as you're honest with me," Nikolai added as he slid onto the closest barstool. "I don't tolerate lying."

"I understand," she said softly.

"Good." He tapped the countertop with tattooed fingers. "Do you know why I am here?"

Alexei made Nikolai a cup of tea while Shay cooperated with this mini-interrogation. It kept his hands busy, and his stress levels in check while he waited to see how this would play out.

"You're here because my sister and her boyfriend did something really stupid, and now we're all in trouble." She swallowed nervously. "You're here because Lalo tried to rape me and I nearly killed him with a paperweight."

That last piece of information caused Nikolai's eyes to widen. The boss's irritated glare landed on Alexei. In Russian, he asked, "What the fuck is this?"

Surprised the boss hadn't heard that piece of information yet, he said, "I thought you must have known."

"No, I didn't. I thought the damage to her face was caused by Mueller's men."

"No, it was Lalo."

"Fucking little prick," he swore nastily. Switching back to English, he addressed Shay. "Tell me what happened with Lalo."

She cleared her throat. "I went to the Arena to find my sister, to warn her after those awful men trashed my car. When I got there, Lalo was waiting. He took me into an office, and he tried to…" Still traumatized, she lowered her gaze. "He wanted me to pay for my life and for my sister's life with my body. He hurt me…so I hurt him." She ran her thumbs up and down the glass. "And then I ran."

Nikolai placed a cautious hand on her arm. Shay's gaze flicked to the mob boss' face. "You were defending yourself. Whatever happened in that room, whatever you did to get out of there, it was the right thing. Do not ever apologize for protecting yourself. Do you understand?"

"Yes, sir."

Taking back his hand, Nikolai said, "Considering I haven't heard this story yet, it's clear Lalo wants it quiet. I'm sure he'll put a spin on it. Whatever story hits the streets will be one that makes him into a hero or a martyr. If your name isn't mentioned, then keep your mouth shut about your involvement, Shay. If he can save face, it may save your life."

"Duly noted," she whispered.

"Now tell me about this identify theft scam your sister and that street slinger were running."

"What?" Shay couldn't fake that confused expression. "What identify theft scam?"

"Why do you think Mueller and his men want your sister?"

"I don't know. I just sort of assumed this was another one of her dumb counterfeit scams. You know, like purses and DVDs. She and Ruben got into a scrape earlier this year when they were selling that stuff in someone else's territory."

"This isn't about territory. It's not about counterfeit goods. It's about your sister and Ruben stealing financial information so they can sell it on the black market."

Alexei placed the cup of tea in front of Nikolai and offered him milk and sugar. Shay seemed to be trying to wrap her head around this new revelation.

"Look, I love my sister, and she's everything to me, but she is not smart enough to run a scam like that. Okay? She's not detail-oriented. She never follows through on anything. She can barely work her freaking iPhone! There is no way she did this."

Nikolai stirred his tea. "Ruben outsourced the tech side. All your sister had to do was plug in a little flash drive and hit a couple of keys. She used her access to all those offices she cleaned to infect as many networks as possible. The information they compiled? It's worth millions and millions of dollars on the black market. Word on the street is that they have a buyer ready and waiting."

Alexei filed away that piece of information. There weren't many buyers with that kind of cash on hand. He needed to nail down the buyer and fast.

"Your sister and Ruben have some information in their possession that is extremely sensitive. Mr. Mueller wants it back. He's not going to stop until he gets it." Nikolai put down his spoon. "Do you understand what that means, Shay?"

"Yes," she whispered.

"Mr. Mueller and Mr. Contreras reached a compromise on this matter. The terms were all worked out very neatly, and I raised no objection because I had no reason to interfere in business that didn't concern me. Had I known that you belonged to Alexei, I would have made sure you were protected from this." He gestured to her bruises. "Now that I understand the situation more clearly, I'll make sure that you can walk the streets of Houston safely."

When Nikolai leveled a serious stare in his direction, Alexei didn't have to ask what the boss was thinking. Alexei was already cataloguing the assets he controlled. There wasn't a damn thing he owned that he wouldn't gladly give away to ensure Shay would reach old age.

"Mr. Kalasnikov?" she asked in a soft voice.

"Yes?"

"What's going to happen to my sister?"

Nikolai took a slow sip of his tea, lowered his cup and met her tearful gaze with that cold, distant stare he had perfected. "You'll find it easier to move on with your life if you learn to stop asking questions that have answers you don't want to hear."

Shay's lip trembled pitifully, and she blinked rapidly. She couldn't manage an answer, only a shaky nod.

Alexei hated Nikolai for being so callous with her. Aching for Shay as she realized that her sister was marked for death, he crossed the small distance between them and stood behind her. He placed a hand on her hip and another on her shoulder. He needed her to know that she wasn't alone. Whatever happened, he would help her through this.

"Do you know where your sister is? Where she would hide?" Nikolai might have felt some compassion for Shay but he wasn't going to let it get in the way of business. "The sooner this matter is cleared up, the better for everyone."

"I don't know where she is. Really," she insisted. "We had one short phone conversation earlier tonight. Lalo said Shannon and Ruben had run off and disappeared."

Nikolai drained the last of his tea. "When your sister contacts you, I need to know about it. You will tell Alexei, and he'll take care of it."

Shay agreed sadly. "Okay."

The boss stood up and carried his empty cup and spoon to the sink. "A few days hiding out here is your best option."

Alexei patted her hip before following Nikolai to the door. Alone in the hallway, they drifted back into Russian.

"You're going to need someone to sit on her while you're

at work." Nikolai stated the obvious. "I have the perfect man."

"I bet you do," Alexei grumbled. "Which soldier? Danny? Boychenko?"

"Stas."

"I don't know him."

"He's a new guy, down from Brighton Beach. We're transferring in some new blood. Loyal blood," he added. "We need to grow but I need men with experience. He's a good enforcer. He's done bodyguard work. I trust him."

Because Nikolai trusted him, Alexei was expected to do the same. "I'll give him a try, but if he makes Shay uncomfortable…"

"You can throw him back to me," Nikolai promised.

"Fine."

"He'll be up in a few minutes. I brought him with me."

Alexei frowned. "I see."

"And he's going to need a salary."

Alexei snorted roughly. "Why do I get the feeling you had this planned even before this mess with Shay happened?"

"Because I did," Nikolai answered honestly. "Your companies are clean. You have plenty of job openings for a man like Stas. Just give him a job title and put him on your payroll."

"It's not that easy, and you know it. Fuck. I hate it when you do this. I've worked hard to keep the businesses legit."

"And you have those legit businesses because I gave you the first dealership," Nikolai reminded him.

"I haven't forgotten." *Because Christ knows you aren't ever going to let me forget.*

Nikolai glanced away and grimaced. "I sound like Maksim when I say shit like that."

Alexei didn't know why that was so surprising or why it seemed to bother Nikolai so much. Maksim had been his mentor, after all. "He's the big boss. You learned everything you know from him."

Nikolai made a throaty humming sound before running his fingers through his hair as if exasperated with himself. "You're my friend. You gave years to the family, and you helped me take this city one street at a time. You bled for me. Everything you've built? You earned that through hard work, and it's bullshit for me to simply assume you'll do what I tell you, even when it puts your legitimate holdings at risk."

"I am grateful for every opportunity you gave me. Our brotherhood? The blood we've spilled? That binds us forever." Accepting Nikolai's apology, he decided, "I'll hire Stas because I need him."

"Thank you. Now, listen, I'll set up a meeting with Mueller. It shouldn't be too difficult to iron out your issues with him. He'll want payments for the soldiers you've put out of commission." Nikolai glanced back toward the kitchen. "What's the story between Shay and Lalo?"

"He's wanted her for a long time, but she doesn't want him."

"Were they involved?"

"From what I know of their history, she's done everything possible to stay away from him. She's not like her sister. She doesn't have a taste for the gangster life."

"Smart girl." Nikolai unlocked the door. "I'll be in touch soon. Whatever evidence you have can be dropped off at the new warehouse. Boychenko is waiting for you. He'll ride escort for any other business you need to handle tonight."

"I have to go by Shay's place to get some things she needs."

"Where does she live?"

"In one of Spider's parks."

Nikolai's eyes widened fractionally. Was the boss trying to work out why Shay was still living on her own? It wasn't his usual arrangement with the women in his life. In fact, it was more similar to Nikolai's and Vivian's.

From what Alexei knew of Vivian, she had lived on her own, paying her own bills and taking very little from Nikolai, until she had been kidnapped. Only then did she move under Nikolai's roof. Vivian was the virginal matriarch of the family, untouched and unknown by any man except her husband. The men who guarded her day and night would swear on their mothers that the couple never shared a bed or were alone until the night *after* they were married.

It was too old-fashioned for Alexei's tastes, but he understood why it had to be that way for Nikolai and Vivian. Even if the boss's wife wasn't known for her religious devotion and her conservative values, she would have been held to a higher standard. Nikolai simply couldn't have a wife with a complicated history of lovers. His position within the family wouldn't allow it.

The thought of lovers and histories unsettled Alexei. Had Shay known true love? Was there a man out there somewhere who still owned her heart? Was he competing for her affection against ghosts he could never best? As beautiful and interesting and intelligent as she was, Shay must have had no problem attracting good men. *Better men than me*, he thought crossly.

"I'll talk to Spider and square things. You two were friends back when you handled all the gun runs from Liam. I assume that friendship still stands?"

"It does."

"Good. That will be useful to you. There's one more thing."

"What?"

"I want the balance of Boychenko's debt to you wiped."

"Done." With a sigh, he said, "Kolya, this wasn't supposed to happen. Not like this."

Nikolai actually grinned. "You? Me? Two gangs who want to take us out? It's like old times, huh?"

"Yeah," Alexei replied with a wry smile. "Except this time we're too old for this shit and have too much on the line to lose."

Nikolai's gaze softened. "Sometimes too much to lose gives us a better reason to fight." He angled his head toward the kitchen. "I like her. She reminds me of Vee."

Alexei figured that was the highest compliment the boss could pay.

"She's a good choice. She suits you." Nikolai whacked his back with a series of hard claps. "But, Lyosha, get her the hell out of this apartment. This is the place you fucked your strippers. Your future wife shouldn't have stepped foot in this apartment."

The comment was a stark reminder that Nikolai was one of those old school gangsters who still had very black and white ideas. There were women you fucked, and there were women you married. Period. Full stop. The two pools were never supposed to overlap.

Nikolai opened the door and stepped into the hall. He adjusted his hood to make sure his face was covered. Alexei waited until Nikolai disappeared from view to step back into the apartment and lock the door.

When he returned to the kitchen, he found Shay slumped forward, her shoulders rounded with defeat, as she sobbed helplessly. The heartbroken weeping cut him deeply. Moved by the sadness engulfing her, he quickly ate up the floor with long strides.

Wrapping his arms around her, he lifted her off the chair and onto the counter. He tucked her wet cheek against his shirt and combed his fingers through her damp hair. She clung to his shoulders and sobbed.

"*Ptichka.*" Kissing the top of her head, he closed his eyes. He wasn't sure what she needed or how to help her. Nothing he could say would make any of this easier. "Shay, it's all right. It's okay."

"It's not okay. God, I'm so sorry," she cried. "I'm so sorry for getting you in trouble and dragging you into this. I shouldn't have—"

"Hush," he whispered gently. "Don't apologize to me about this. We're fine."

She exhaled a shuddery breath and burrowed in closer. The move sent his heartbeat into overdrive. She needed love and comfort tonight. It would be so easy to seduce her but he refused to take the choice from her. Shay's life was unraveling, and right now, she needed to have control over the most important decisions.

The apartment phone rang. With an irritated sigh, Alexei kissed Shay's temple and left her on the counter so he could answer it. "Yes?"

"Sir, there's a man in the lobby who says he's one of your

guests. His name is Stas."

"Send him up, Carlos."

"Yes, sir."

The call finished, he turned back to find Shay sitting there with her hands clamped between her knees. He plucked a napkin from a drawer and used it to dab away the shiny streaks on her face. "No more crying tonight."

She sniffled and nodded meekly. "All right."

He placed the napkin on the counter and then cupped the back of her head, tangling his fingers in her hair. With every intimate touch she allowed, his craving for her increased in potency. Much more of this and he was going to spontaneously combust.

"A friend of mine is going to watch you while I go take care of some things."

"A friend?"

"His name is Stas. He's trusted and safe, but I know you've been through hell tonight so I'll make sure he gives you some space." Wanting her to feel comfortable, he picked up his bag and dug through it until he found the red hooded sweatshirt showcasing the Ivan's logo. "Here. Put this on. You're so short it will reach your knees."

"Thank you." She lifted her arms and let him glide it into place over her head. He reached into the open neck and pulled free her hair. The floral scent of the shampoo from the toiletry basket wafted from her hair, and it momentarily confused him. She was supposed to smell of beaches and sunshine, not generic flowers.

A knock at the door announced Stas' arrival. The man he let into the apartment looked like a street brawler with his stocky build. He had a scruffy beard and the coldest gray eyes Alexei had ever seen. There were no tattoos on his fingers or hands but intricate sleeves covered his arms. The ink that peeked out from the collar of his shirt and curled along the side of his neck gave Alexei a brief rundown of the man's history.

"Alexei Romanovich," Stas greeted respectfully.

Alexei shook the street soldier's hand but didn't let go immediately. He held tight and tugged the man off-balance. "Nikolai vouches for you, but I don't know you. So here's the deal. If I come back here and Shay is upset or you've done anything that makes her uncomfortable, I start breaking fingers. When I'm done with fingers, I move to bigger bones. Understand?"

"Perfectly," Stas assured him. "I'm not here to cause problems. I'm here to work. I'm here to earn my place. You tell me what you want—and it's done. No questions asked."

Thinking of how much Stas reminded him of his younger days, Alexei let go of the street soldier's hand. He had been hungry to prove himself once. Hungry men were loyal men, and Alexei knew exactly how to ensure Stas did what was necessary to keep Shay safe. "If you keep her happy and out of trouble, I'll pay you a bonus at the end of each day. Cash," he clarified. "Under the table and off the books."

"Deal." Stas glanced around the luxurious apartment. "The boss didn't mention what sort of arrangement you have with your…mistress."

"You don't need to worry about the arrangement I have with Shay. You just need to worry about how you'll keep her safe when I'm not here."

Stas held up a hand. "Hey, I'm not trying to get into your business. I just wanted to know if I need to worry about being ambushed by a pissed off wife or another girlfriend."

Wondering what sort of men Stas had worked for back in Brighton Beach, he shook his head. "There is no one else. There is only Shay."

"Well that makes this job a hell of a lot easier. I know how to deal with hostile crews and hit squads but wives and girlfriends?" He whistled low. "That shit gets real fast."

Alexei could only imagine. He gestured for Stas to follow him into the apartment. Shay stood next to the kitchen island and warily eyed the new face trailing him. He didn't blame her. She had probably had quite enough of big, tattooed men for one night. Fuck. She had probably had enough of big, tattooed men for a lifetime.

"Shay, this is Stas. He's going to stay here while I take care of some things."

"Hello." She greeted Stas with a tremulous smile.

Stas stopped at the other end of the granite slab and stuffed his hands in his pockets. "Hi."

Alexei grasped Shay's hand and led her into the living area. "Would you like to go to bed or—"

"I can't sleep," she hastily interjected. "I just can't."

"That's all right." He rubbed her shoulder and guided her into the corner seat of the large sofa. The stone-colored cashmere throw artfully draped over the back caught his eye. He tugged it free and tucked it around Shay's legs and lap so she would stay warm.

"Alexei," she said in an almost pleading tone while clutching his hand. "Please be careful."

Her fear and concern for his safety detonated a wild burst of emotion in his chest. Bending down, he pressed a chaste kiss to her forehead. "Don't worry about me. I'll be fine." He lowered his mouth until his lips were touching the shell of her ear. "They think we've been involved for a long time, and it's best if you play along with that."

She turned toward him, seeking out his gaze with one of understanding. She knew the stakes here. She wouldn't do anything to put either of them at risk. Embracing the role he had foisted upon her, she leaned over and kissed him properly. The shock of her soft, warm lips upon his nearly took him out at the damned knees. It was an innocent kiss, the type he had first tried on a girl when he was eleven or twelve, but this one made is heart race and his lungs ache.

Unable to help himself, Alexei brushed loose strands of hair behind her ear and cupped the back of her head, holding her in place a moment longer just so he could enjoy her mouth on his. When he found the strength to break the kiss, it was all he could do to straighten up and walk away from her.

After ducking into the master bedroom to grab the emergency set of clothing he kept stowed there, he gathered up their bloody clothes and stuffed them in his gym bag. Stas followed him to the door. "She's in good hands."

"See that those good hands of yours stay away from her, yeah?" Alexei warned before shutting the door. He waited to hear the lock engage and went straight to the elevator. After punching the button for the parking garage level, he leaned back against the wall of the box and closed his eyes. He lifted his hand to his mouth and traced his lips. He felt like an overeager teenager as he relived that simple kiss. With one unexpected and wholly innocent move, Shay had fucking shattered him.

When he stepped out into the garage, he inhaled a deep, invigorating lungful of cold air. It was going to be a hell of a long and dangerous night, but he had a damn good reason to get back here as quickly and as safely possible curled up in the corner of his couch.

CHAPTER SEVEN

I KISSED HIM.

I kissed Alexei.

What the hell was I thinking?

What was *he* thinking now?

My lips were still warm from the contact of his hard, sinful mouth. All I could think about was when I might have the chance to kiss him again.

"Do you want some coffee or tea?"

I popped up a little higher so I could see over the top of the lush, comfy sofa. Stas banged around in the kitchen, opening drawers and cabinets as he surveyed the food situation.

Not quite as tall as Alexei but heavier and with a more solid build, he had shucked his leather jacket. The navy blue polo he wore was stretched tight across his shoulders. His full sleeve tattoos looked nothing like Alexei's mafia ink. Here and there, I picked out symbols that were similar to the ones on Alexei's skin but it seemed as though Stas had chosen to decorate his arms for different reasons that Alexei had.

"How about some hot cocoa?" He held up two of the small cups that fit into the coffee maker reservoir. "There aren't any marshmallows but I bet it's sweet."

The idea that this intimidating gangster was going to make me hot cocoa brought a surprised smile to my face. "That sounds nice."

"All right." He turned back toward the coffee maker, and I reached for the television remote on the glass coffee table. I clicked through the channels in search of something mindless to watch. Eventually I found re-runs of one of those reality cooking shows to keep us entertained.

"What are you watching?" Stas handed me a cup wrapped in a cloth napkin. "Careful," he warned. "It's really hot."

I blew across the top of the steaming liquid, creating little ripples in the chocolate drink. "Some reality show about bankrupt restaurants."

"Have you ever worked in a restaurant?" He went back to the kitchen and returned to the living room with a cup of coffee and Alexei's abandoned plate of cold eggs and toast.

"I waited tables and washed dishes in a couple of different places when I was in high school, but eventually, I switched to cleaning offices and homes. What about you?"

"I was a dishwasher and did some cooking before I shifted to this line of work." He placed his food on the coffee table and dragged the table closer to the sofa. After plopping down on the opposite end, he dug into the cold eggs and toast.

"And what exactly is this line of work?" I took a tiny sip of the hot cocoa and waited for him to answer.

Stas shot me a funny look. "I would have a thought a woman in your position would know not to ask questions like that."

"A woman in my position? And what the hell does that mean?"

"You know what it means." He gestured around the apartment with the half-eaten slice of toast. "It means that the tradeoff for all this is that you don't ask questions about where the money comes from. This is a nice step up for you." He took another bite of his toast. "You went from cleaning toilets to playing private maid for a man like Alexei. Don't fuck that up by asking about things that are none of your business."

I couldn't decide if I was more angry or humiliated by the way he had spoken to me. "Maybe you should take some of your advice and mind *your* business. I sure hope you didn't have plans for that bonus Alexei promised you."

Frozen like a deer in headlights, he had that piece of toast clamped between his teeth as he watched me.

"Yeah. That's right. I heard you two talking back there. And let me tell you something, Stas. The second Alexei finds out you just spoke to me like that? He's going to kick your ass all the way out the door and down eleven flights of stairs."

Because he would. One thing this wild and crazy night had taught me was that Alexei wasn't going to let anyone treat me badly. He wouldn't stand for it—and I wasn't going to stand for it either.

Stas put down his toast and swallowed loudly. "I'm sorry, Shay. You're right. I should mind my own business."

"Your damn right you should," I muttered grumpily. "For your information, I've never taken a penny from Alexei. I work hard. I have a college degree. I'm saving to start my own business. Everything that I own is *mine*."

"I didn't mean to upset you. I can see that I did, but that wasn't my intention." He drank some coffee and shook his head. "I was just trying to warn you, to remind you that asking questions about men like me and men with a history like Alexei's can get you in a lot of trouble."

"I'm not stupid, Stas. I know that."

"So why did you ask about my line of work?"

"Because I'm curious? Because I was trying to be nice? There were other ways to answer that question without being a jerk, you know?"

"Yeah. I know," he glumly replied. "Maybe I'm just an asshole. Did you think about that?"

"You made me hot cocoa. An asshole wouldn't have done that."

He actually smiled. "I really am sorry for the way I behaved."

I wiggled back into the corner of the sofa and curled my knees up tight. "I really am sorry that you aren't getting your bonus for tonight."

Stas laughed and picked up the plate of cold eggs. "That's fair." He leaned back and ate quietly while I tried to figure out what was happening on the television screen. During a commercial, he said, "My mom and I came to the States when I was four. I was a good kid. I stayed out of trouble. I went to school. Hell, I even played football and ran track. I thought I would go to college and be a stock broker or some shit like that."

"So how does a good kid with aspirations for the American Dream end up working for someone like Nikolai?"

Stas rubbed his fingers together in a universal symbol I recognized. "Money."

"Gambling?" I asked, thinking of all the families in my neighborhood who had been ruined by gambling debts and playing the lottery.

"No. Much worse." He put down the empty plate and picked up his coffee cup. "Medical debt." He took a drink and seemed almost hesitant to delve into memories that I suspected were painful and sad. "Mom had cancer. Ovarian," he said, "but by the time they caught it, she was all eaten up inside. The treatment was expensive, and she didn't have health insurance. A friend of mine? His uncle was the boss back home so I asked him for work, and nine years later, here I am."

"Here you are," I murmured. "What are you? Twenty-six?"

"Twenty-seven." He took a long drink of coffee. "And before you ask… No, my mother didn't survive. She died but she died in the best hospice program available. She was at home, and she was comfortable and she didn't have to worry about anything."

"She worried about you," I said without thinking.

Stas glanced at me and smiled sadly. "That's what mamas do. I bet your mother is up right now, pacing her house and wondering what's happening to you and your sister."

"I bet she's not." Bitterness crept into my voice. "Mom bailed when we were younger. She just walked right out of the house and never came back."

For a man who seemed so hard and wise, he looked shocked by the discovery that my mother had abandoned me. "Where is she now?"

I shrugged and pretended as if I didn't care. "No idea."

"Why did she leave?"

I ran my finger around the rim of my cup. "I don't know. I mean, now that I'm older and I understand what it's like to sacrifice and to put dreams on hold? I think maybe she was just tired of being a parent. I think maybe she just wanted out."

"Like your sister?" he asked quietly.

My head snapped up at that. "What do you mean?"

His shoulders inched higher in a defensive shrug. "I heard some things tonight about your sister."

"What sort of things?"

"She strikes me as the type of woman who wants things she hasn't earned. She craves the kind of life other people have but she isn't willing to work for it. She wants money and nice things, designer handbags and jewelry and five-hundred-dollar shoes." He drained his cup and set it aside. "She put her baby sister's life at risk for some money. She decided that your life was worth less than whatever some guy out of Tirana was willing to pay for a block of stolen financial information."

The blunt description of the situation made my chest ache. Was that true? Had Shannon ever framed the situation in that way or had she just blithely gone along with Ruben's scheme? Had she been so blinded by dollar signs and the promise of riches that she hadn't even considered what would happen if her scam was uncovered?

"Shay?" Stas touched my arm and startled me.

"Don't touch me!" Gasping and in a blind panic, I practically flew off the couch, spilling what was left of my hot cocoa all over the blanket. My feet got tangled up in the blanket, and I tumbled forward. Stas caught me and settled me back on the couch.

"Are you okay?" He quickly took his hands away from me and stood up straight, putting space between us and showing me his palms like a perp in the a police officer's spotlight. "Shit! I'm sorry. I didn't mean to scare you."

"I'm sorry," I apologized in a breathless rush. "It's been a long night for me. I'm still on edge."

"Don't apologize. This is all on me." He cautiously pulled the wet, stained blanket away from me. "Let me put this in the laundry, okay? We'll find you another blanket."

"Don't put that in the washing machine," I warned, thinking of how lovely and soft the cashmere was against my skin. "It has to be hand-washed with special soap, rolled in a towel to squeeze out the water and then left to air dry."

Stas blinked. "Yeah, so I'm just going to put this in the laundry room for the housekeeper to handle. I'll be right back."

Housekeeper? I wanted to laugh at the idea that I had a housekeeper to tackle chores but then I remembered that Alexei most certainly did have a full staff at his home. I assumed his mistresses all benefited from the perks of his wealth. As spotless as this apartment was, it was clear that someone was maintaining the space even when unoccupied.

"Here," Stas said as he unfurled a light, fluffy comforter in the palest gray. "I found this in one of the bedrooms."

"Thanks." I tucked it in tight and got comfortable again.

"How about we agree that we don't talk about family any more tonight?" Stas dropped down on his end of the sofa again. "You and I have enough baggage to sink a ship. Let's just find something really stupid to watch and hang out, okay?"

"I like that idea." I tossed the remote at him. "Your choice this time."

Stas flicked through the channels until he landed on the one of those shows about repo men. "Is this okay?"

"It's fine."

He toed off his sneakers and got comfortable, propping his feet on the coffee table. I let it slide because I had a feeling he was just as tired as I was. Snuggled under the blanket, I thought it would be easy to fall asleep but I kept thinking about Shannon and Alexei.

Even though my sister had put me in extreme danger, I prayed that she had found somewhere safe to hide. I prayed that Ruben would finally do something smart and get her out of town. They needed to run fast and far and never look back. The list of men who wanted to hurt them was long and growing.

And Alexei? I prayed he would come back safe and unharmed. If he got hurt protecting me, I would never forgive myself for drawing him into this stupid, crazy mess.

"Stop worrying," Stas chided. "You're going to wear a hole in that blanket if you keep rubbing it between your fingers."

Not even realizing I was fidgeting, I looked down to find the blanket clamped between my thumb and forefinger. "I can't help it."

"Alexei is a legend in the underworld. He's survived shit I can't even fathom, okay? What he's facing tonight? It's nothing."

Stas' reply didn't comfort me. If anything, it awakened an insatiable curiosity. Earlier this evening, Alexei had given me a glimpse of his history by explaining some of his tattoos. I had got much more up-close-and-personal view of his history when he had rescued me. Now I wanted to know all the dark, dangerous and difficult things that had shaped Alexei into the man he was today.

"You picked a good man, Shay." Stas folded his arms behind his head. "He'll give you a good life if you can just figure out how to keep him happy."

If only it was that simple…

"IS THAT IT?" Boychenko asked as he stuffed the blood stained clothing and leather shoes into an industrial-sized furnace.

"Yes." Alexei rolled his shoulders and straightened the collar on the clean suit he now wore. He grimaced at the sight of his favorite Armani lace-ups surrounded by flames. He eyed the sputtering furnace with concern. "Where the hell did Kostya find this thing?"

The great big beast of an incinerator belched like an angry dragon as Boychenko tapped at the dials and locked the door. "He picked it up in Mexico. It belonged to some medical waste disposal company that went bankrupt."

Picked it up in Mexico? Alexei shuddered to think what sort of ghoul had sold this terrifying piece of machinery to the cleaner. He doubted very much that it had ever been used for legitimate purposes. More likely, it had come out of some cartel hell hole. If it had been in cartel hands, there was no telling what, *exactly*, had been incinerated inside the thing.

"Where are we headed next?" Boychenko asked as he strode to a sink in the eerily lit warehouse and scrubbed his hands clean.

"To Shay's home," he said, waiting for the younger man to dry his hands. He eyed the snarling furnace. "Are you just going to leave that thing on?"

"It runs on a cycle." Boychenko shrugged into his leather jacket. "Trust me. I've spent a lot of time with this horrible thing over the last few months. It's old and cranky, but it's dependable."

Alexei decided he didn't want to know what other terrible shit Boychenko had destroyed in that furiously hot furnace. Instead, he headed for his SUV and told the kid to follow him. The drive to Shay's place was uneventful. The silent night and easy traffic gave him too much time to think.

When they reached the mobile home park, the place was unnaturally quiet and dark. Alexei didn't like it. Teeth on edge and fingertips buzzing, he drove slowly through the narrow streets and diverted his hawk-like gaze left and right, scanning for any signs of trouble. He passed all of the larger double wides before reaching the streets packed with single wide trailers, most in serious states of disrepair, all crammed together with tiny strips of brown grass between them.

He didn't pull into Shay's driveway. Wanting to be able to leave quickly, he parked parallel to the broken sidewalk and killed the engine and lights. Boychenko crept along behind him and found a spot to park on the opposite side of the street. The young soldier didn't get out of his car. He kept his engine idling but cut his lights. He probably had a gun on his lap and another close at hand.

Alexei reached into the backseat for Shay's purse and dropped it onto the console. He felt uncomfortable going through her personal things and found her keys quickly. Holding the small set in his hand, he traced her stamped initials on the small leather rectangle and the beautifully stitched edge. When this bullshit with her sister was done, he planned to ask her to make him something, maybe a wallet or a belt.

He left the SUV. Brittle grass crunched under the soles of his shoes. He had mounted exactly one step on the small, rickety staircase leading to her front porch when he heard the unmistakable whir of a spinning revolver chamber. The click of the chamber locking into place made his heart skip a beat. Frozen stiff, he waited for the steel bite of a bullet tearing through his skull.

But it never came.

"You're awfully jumpy tonight, Alex." Spider's raspy voice drifted from the side of the small mobile home. A moment later, the snap of a lighter and the bright orange glow of cigarette helped Alexei locate the outlaw vice president. He leaned against the edge of the home, right behind a bush and crape myrtle.

"You fucking asshole," Alexei hissed. "What the hell is wrong with you? My friend might have shot you."

"Not before my two prospects shot him," Spider answered between puffs.

Alexei glanced toward Boychenko and found the kid leaning against the door of his car, arms crossed against his chest, while two young men wearing the Calaveras colors stood on either side of him. Not liking this situation at all, Alexei stepped off the stairs and back onto the grass. He walked toward Spider to face him like a man. "Is there a problem here?"

"Not at all," Spider replied in that slow, easy way of his. "I'm here to protect my property and make sure that you get out of here unscathed."

The irritation in Spider's voice was impossible to miss. "I don't blame you for being pissed off about all of this. I realize that you're in a bad situation here, but I'm grateful for the help you gave Shay earlier today. I fully intend to pay back that favor."

Spider stepped out of the shadows and flicked his cigarette ash toward the ground. "You better believe I'm going to take full advantage of that debt, but I would have helped Shay regardless of her connection to you." He took a long, final drag on his cigarette. "She's a good person. She doesn't deserve any of this shit."

"I know she doesn't."

Spider stubbed out the cigarette on the bottom of his boot. "You two kept your relationship quiet."

The suspicion in the biker's tone came through clearly. The last thing Alexei needed was Spider digging around in his personal business or making trouble for them. "Shay is a private person."

"She's a good girl." He tossed down the cigarette butt. "She deserves to be treated properly. Her old man is cold and dead in the ground so he isn't here to keep you in line, but I am. If I hear one fucking whisper about you hurting her, I'll start with your kneecaps and then I'll let the rest of the club have a turn."

Alexei took the threat in stride. He could see that Spider felt strongly about Shay's welfare. He was glad that she had a father figure looking out for her. "My intentions toward Shay are what you would want from any man who dated your daughter."

Spider issued a harsh laugh. "There isn't a man in Houston

with balls big enough to ask me to date my baby girl." He gestured toward the house. "Do you need keys?"

"I have Shay's set."

"You want some help?"

"Sure." Alexei climbed the stairs, crossed the porch and unlocked the front door. Shay had left on a lamp in the living room. A pleasant cinnamon and vanilla scent lingered in the air. Just like the last time he had visited her home, the place was neat and tidy. There was a new throw and pillows on the old, worn out sofa and more recent pictures of the two sisters on the wall.

"The girls are some of my best tenants," Spider said as he shut the storm door. "Shay always pays the rent a week early. She keeps the house and the yard clean. I never have to worry about late notices for the utilities." He rested his arm on the wall and shook his head. "I'll be sad to see the girls go."

Alexei hadn't considered that Spider might toss them out of their home. He had been planning to let Shay stay at his apartment until she felt safe to come home or able to make a decision about her future without the added pressure of homelessness hanging over her head.

"You understand why I can't keep them here." Spider reached into a vest pocket and retrieved a stick of gum. "I've spent most of the year cleaning up this neighborhood. I'm moving in families and oilfield guys. I can't have the trouble that followed Shay and Shannon home in my park."

"I'm a businessman. I understand when hard choices have to be made to protect your bottom line."

"I know you won't let Shay end up on the streets or sleep-ing in her car. Shannon?" He shrugged and jammed the stick of gum into his mouth. "If she survives the weekend, it will be a fucking miracle."

It was a cold, unfeeling statement but that didn't make it any less true.

Not wanting to waste any more time talking, Alexei crossed the cramped living room and kitchen. There was a short hallway just off the kitchen. He stopped at the first door he reached, opened it, switched on the light and peeked inside. Even before he spotted the worktable against far wall, he knew it was Shay's room.

If he had felt uncomfortable going through her purse to find her keys, he felt completely out of his depth standing in the middle of her bedroom. It was decorated simply and plainly. She seemed to have sacrificed her sleeping comfort to make room for a wall of industrial shelving that held finished handbags, wallets, belts and packaging and mailing supplies. He investigated the tiny space, running his hands over the tools she used to make such beautiful handmade items. The mismatched initials etched into the tool handles convinced him she had probably purchased these at pawn shops and garage sales.

The laptop on her bed captured his interest. He dragged his finger over the mouse pad and awakened the sleeping machine. A sticky note tacked onto the corner of the screen had her password printed in bright green ink along with a reminder for Shannon to recharge the battery. A faint smile played upon his mouth as he imagined Shay getting irritated with her sister for the millionth time over that.

He typed in the password and found himself staring at extremely detailed spreadsheets. With a couple of clicks, he was able to read through Shay's current profit and loss statement, her bank account balances and her projected expenses and profit for the coming year. A word document in another window showed a five-year business plan broken down into yearly, quarterly and monthly goals and tasks.

By the looks of it, Shay was well ahead of her goals. She was very cautious with her money, putting almost all of it back into the business or into a savings account marked for the store she wanted to open with a friend. He noticed the friend's current savings were much lower than Shay's and her expenses were higher too.

She wouldn't like it if he started nosing into her business, but he felt a duty to talk through the problems of partnerships with her. He had been so desperate to get out of the mafia life that he had taken on Nikolai as a silent partner without a second thought to how it would impact him years down the line. Now that he was so very successful, he wanted nothing more than to shed those old connections to organized crime, but it was impossible. He was chained to the mafia for the rest of his life.

But maybe he could save Shay from making that mistake. If she wanted to go into business with a friend, she needed to do it with those beautiful brown eyes of hers wide, wide open and with an airtight contract in place.

He opened another window and discovered the household budget and her shopping list. He wasn't surprised to see that Shannon had been running short on cash or that Shay had been covering the household expenses on her own. Judging by the extremely short shopping list and the stack of clipped coupons he had spotted on her worktable, Shay had been cutting every possible corner to stay afloat.

Closing her laptop, he set it aside and returned to her closet to grab the one suitcase hidden away there. He wouldn't be able to fit much inside of it so he chose carefully from her wardrobe. He was picking his way through her dresser and lamenting the lack of lacy, silky things when Spider appeared in the doorway.

"If you want, I can have the prospects box up the house room by room. We can store it over in the building behind the main office."

"Start with Shay's room," he instructed. "I want this all boxed up carefully."

"I'll see if Marley can come over and take care of Shay and Shannon's things," Spider offered.

"I would prefer that." As he packed up Shay's tools, he gave Spider instructions for the delivery of her things. He found a couple of empty boxes on the supply shelf and put everything she might need for her work into them. He recognized a handbag from her virtual storefront, a site that he often found himself checking out late at night when he was thinking about her. It was among her most popular designs but the work she put into each one made it difficult for her to produce at a fast rate.

Her leather goods were made by hand, but there was no rule that said they had to be made by *her* hand. The seed of an idea blossomed. He needed to investigate the feasibility but he might have discovered a way for Shay to grow her business while maintaining her high quality standards.

He left Shay's bedroom and stopped in the bathroom to gather up her toiletries. He wasn't sure which toothbrush was hers but it was easy to pick out her shampoo and conditioner with a simple sniff. He ducked back into her bedroom to grab a couple of things off the top of her dresser like her hairbrush and watch.

She didn't have much jewelry, just a pair of gold hoops, a set of tiny diamond studs that were less than a quarter carat and a fragile golden heart necklace. He carefully traced the thin heart shape. This was the type of jewelry a father gave a young daughter on her birthday or for Christmas. He imagined Shay wearing the necklace and thinking of the father she had lost so suddenly.

Very carefully, he wrapped the necklace and earrings in a monogrammed handkerchief. He tucked it away in the interior pocket of his suit for safekeeping. Finished packing, he gathered up her things and left the house. Spider waited for him to lock the door and trailed him down the front steps and over to his SUV. The raucous laughter coming from the prospects and Boychenko made them frown.

"Young, dumb and full of cum," Spider remarked dryly.

Alexei let loose a snort of laughter at the biker's rough way of describing the trio. What he could hear of the salacious, raunchy tale was enough to make him shake his head. The wild parties thrown by the motorcycle club were infamous around the city. Poor Boychenko would never experience debauchery like that in Nikolai's service.

Tuning out the filthy story, he loaded up his SUV and held out his hand. "I've got a bottle of Dalmore with your name on it."

Spider gripped it hard. "Should I be flattered that you remembered it's my favorite?"

Alexei grinned and let go. "You know where to find me when you're ready to claim that favor owed."

"Remember what I told you about Shay."

"I heard you."

"If there's anything you need from me—for her—you just have to ask."

"I will. Thank you."

Alexei whistled at Boychenko, signaling that it was time to leave. He slid behind the wheel and drove away from Shay's home. Boychenko shadowed him to the first drug store where he picked up a toothbrush, toothpaste and two pints of the ice cream that he had seen on her shopping list.

By the time he reached the apartment building and waved off Boychenko, it was nearly three in the morning. As he was gathering up Shay's things and trying to figure out how he would get everything upstairs in one trip, he heard a vibrating sound. Thinking it was his phone, he patted his jacket but then realized it was coming from under his seat. He reached down and smacked around on the floorboard until he patted a cell phone.

During his rush to throw her handbag and the bloody evidence into the SUV earlier in the night, Shay's cell phone must have fallen out of her purse and under his seat. He studied the screen and noticed four missed calls and five increasingly more worried text messages from someone named Kylee and exactly one text message from Shannon.

I'm sorry. I'm so sorry.

Alexei gritted his teeth and dropped the phone into her handbag. Sorry? Shannon was fucking sorry? She had almost gotten her sister raped and murdered tonight. Sorry didn't come close to fixing all that.

He wasn't going to take a hard line with Shay tonight about her sister. She had been through enough and needed to be treated gently. But tomorrow? Tomorrow, he would have to tell her that the relationship she once had with her sister no longer existed. It was the only way for Shay to survive.

Upstairs, he unlocked the door and was immediately greeted by the sight of Stas striding toward the opening door, his hand on the gun holstered at his hip. The street soldier relaxed and hurried to help him with the luggage and boxes.

"Is she asleep?" Alexei asked quietly as he carried the ice cream into the kitchen.

"No, she's not asleep," Shay piped up from the living room.

He glanced toward the television and sofa but couldn't see her. She must have been huddled down and curled up under a blanket. "You should be in bed."

"I'm not five," she replied lightly. "I can choose my own bedtime."

Stas looked terribly amused by the back-and-forth. He was wise enough not to say a word. Instead, he toted her things to the master suite.

After stowing the ice cream in the freezer, Alexei shrugged out of his jacket and draped it over a chair. He strode toward the sofa and looked down at Shay. Wrapped up in a different blanket, she had her head propped up on a round pillow and watched an infomercial. She was so deeply burrowed he could barely see the side of her face. "What happened to the other blanket?"

"Stas made me hot cocoa, and I spilled some of it." She tugged down the blanket and glanced up at him. "I'll tackle the stain tomorrow."

"Leave it," he said with a wave of his hand. "You aren't a housekeeper. You're a guest."

"For how long?" she asked rather bravely.

Alexei chose to ignore that question as Stas reappeared in the living room. "Were there any problems tonight?"

Stas glanced at Shay and seemed to be waiting for her to answer first.

She sat up slowly and shared what could only be described as a secret smile with Stas. "We had a nice time."

"We're both reality TV junkies." Stas jammed his feet back into his shoes. "I think we can make this work."

Alexei wasn't so sure he liked the budding friendship between the pair. "I'm glad to hear it went well."

"Do you want me to stay for the rest of the night?" Stas gathered up the plate and cups on the coffee table and carried them to the dishwasher. "I'm on your payroll now so you give the orders."

"Try to remember that," he muttered softly, already worrying that Stas might be trying to get too friendly with Shay. "Go home and get some sleep. I'll need you back here by nine."

"Night, Stas," Shay called out as he walked her new bodyguard to the door.

"Goodnight, Shay."

Alexei followed Stas into the hallway. "I spoke to Carlos, the night concierge, about our situation. You and only you will be allowed to come and go freely to this floor. Anyone that you bring with you has to be cleared through me. Any of Shay's visitors need to be cleared through me also."

"I understand."

"In the morning, I'll leave some cash in an envelope for your daily expenses." Touching Stas' shoulder, he said pointedly, "Whatever Shay wants, she gets. No questions asked."

"No questions asked," Stas repeated with a nod. "You can be sure of that."

He watched the young street soldier get into the elevator before closing and locking the door and returning to the living room. Still wrapped up in the blanket, Shay hugged her knees and watched him as if curious to see what would happen next. In truth, he had no idea, but she looked to him for guidance and reassurance so he endeavored to be strong for her.

Toeing off his shoes, he left them behind the sofa and walked around to join her. He dropped down on the spot Stas had occupied earlier and tugged at the knot of his tie, loosening it and tossing aside the long length of striped silk. Working on the top buttons of his shirt, he said, "I went by the house and got some clothes for you. I boxed up the tools and projects on your table. I grabbed your laptop. Your jewelry is in my jacket," he said, patting his chest as the memory suddenly hit him.

"Thank you," Shay whispered with a soft, warm smile. "I really appreciate everything you've done for me." Her mouth slanted with a frown, and she gestured to her forehead. "You're starting to bruise."

"Am I?" He touched the sore spot there and winced. "My head isn't as hard as it used to be."

"You probably should have gone to the emergency room for a CAT scan or something."

"I'm fine. This?" He pointed to the small bruise. "I've survived much worse."

"What will your employees think tomorrow?" She worried her lower lip with her teeth.

"Don't do that. You'll break the skin again." He touched her wrist and welcomed the spark of heat that traveled through his fingertips. "My employees will think whatever they want to think, but they'll keep their mouths shut and work."

She shot him a perturbed look. "You shouldn't be so harsh with them."

"Selling cars is a tough business. They don't need me to coddle them." Alexei held out his hand, silently beckoning her closer. She placed her palm against his and yielded when he gave her arm a gentle tug. He expected her to slide closer and sit next to him, maybe even let him put his arm around her shoulders, but she stunned him by resting her head on his lap.

The sweetly intimate act made his heart do a wild flip. He wasn't quite sure what he was supposed to do now. His need to make her feel safe and secure overwhelmed him. He grasped the blanket and pulled it up around her shoulders. For a moment, he held tight to the blanket before finally surrendering to the urge to brush his fingers through her silky hair.

"Alexei?"

"Yes?" He combed through her wavy locks from the crown of her head down to the very ends.

"What happens now?"

Wanting to banish that quaver of fear in her voice, he decided it was time to make his intentions clear. "What happens now is what I should have done months ago."

"And what is that?"

He stroked her cheek and marveled at the flutter of her eyelashes. "I like you, Shay. I'm attracted to you, and I want you." He trailed his thumb along her jaw. "I think you're attracted to me. I think you want me." He traced her full lower lip. "Do you, Shay?"

"Yes." Her answer came breathlessly but without hesitation. "I want you."

He resumed the steady combing motion, hoping it would lull her to sleep. Closing his eyes, he leaned his head back against the cushion and relaxed his tired, tight shoulders. In the morning, he would probably regret falling asleep like this, but right now, only a fire would force him to shift away from Shay. "Then, as long as you want me, I'm yours."

CHAPTER EIGHT

W HEN I WOKE up a few hours later, I blinked with confusion and glanced around in a disoriented fog. The dim light of a television illuminated a space that was definitely not my bedroom. More perplexing were the strong arms wrapped around my shoulders and holding me close to a warm, powerful and very male body.

Alexei.

I didn't dare move as I tried to figure out how the hell I had ended up on top of him. Sometime after I had dozed off, he had stretched out across the long, wide sofa cushions. He had either dragged me on top of him or—more mortifyingly— I had crawled on top of him like a koala bear seeking heat and comfort.

Though my dating experiences included some serious heavy petting and wild make-out sessions, I had never, ever found myself in this position. I grew intensely aware of the hard, masculine form beneath me. The scent of his cologne teased me, and I wanted nothing more than to burrow in against him and inhale that intoxicating scent that was so perfectly him.

But I couldn't do that. This wasn't right. We hadn't even shared a real kiss. I had no business sleeping on top of him with our legs entwined and our bodies lined up in a dangerous way. Embarrassed by the thought of him waking up to find us so dangerously entangled, I planted a hand on the back of the couch and started to push up as slowly and easily as possible.

"Don't even think about moving," Alexei warned in a gruff, sleep-roughened voice.

I was startled by how attuned he was to his surroundings, even in his sleep. "But I'm crushing you."

A deep rumble of laughter escaped his throat. "Impossible."

"This can't possibly be comfortable for you."

"I've never been more comfortable in my life." He let his hand drift from my upper back along the bow of my spine and right down to the fleshy curve of my bottom. He gave my backside a gentle pat and then a playful squeeze. I sucked in a shocked, excited breath and tried not to hyperventilate as he touched me so intimately. "I think this might be my new favorite sleeping position."

Alexei's sensual, commanding presence left me trembling inside. I was beginning to understand why other women had eagerly agreed to be his mistress and to abide by whatever stipulations he had for occupying that role. He made me want things that had always frightened me. He made me want to throw caution to the wind and let him discover all the secrets my body had yet to share. I clenched my thighs together to assuage the pulse of heat building between them as I imagined his masterful hands roaming my naked body and making me cry out in pleasure.

He swatted my bottom, and I gasped. "I'm trying to get some rest, but if you keep squirming like that, I'll have no choice but to take this new relationship of ours to the next level right here on this couch."

Instantly, I froze. The mention of our new relationship perplexed and excited me. What did he mean by relationship? Was he offering me what he had offered countless other women or was he offering me something different?

I wasn't sure I could accept the first possibility. When he had asked me if I wanted him, I had answered truthfully. I did want Alexei, but I wanted him *my* way and on *my* terms. I didn't want to play his mistress game.

You don't have a choice. Alexei is the only thing between you and bunch of racist thugs and one pissed off drug kingpin.

The advice Stas had given me went round and round in my head. If I could keep Alexei happy, he would take care of me. If I wanted something more than he was offering, I would have to either find a way to come to accept his terms or show him that I was worth more than some seedy arrangement.

"Shay," he whispered sleepily. "Stop thinking and relax. It's late, and we both need rest." His arms tightened around me and his hand gently pushed my head back to the comfortable spot it had occupied against his chest. "Go back to sleep."

I held my breath when his lips brushed the top of my head. Safe in his arms, I let my tired, overwrought mind shut down. The slow, even thud of his heartbeat under my ear lulled me to sleep again.

When I awoke the second time, I was alone on the couch. For a second, I panicked, thinking that Alexei had left without a word, but then I smelled coffee. Sitting up, I pushed aside the blanket covering me and combed my fingers through my unruly hair. The memory of Alexei doing the same thing last night made my stomach flutter.

I rose from the sofa and went in search of him. I had just walked into the master suite when the door to the bathroom was flung open suddenly. With only a fluffy white towel around his trim waist, Alexei strode out of the steaming hot bathroom. My brain misfired as I tried to take in all six plus feet of his deliciously sexy manliness. The well-defined muscles of his chest and abdomen were incredible. There were even more tattoos on his chest, arms and legs. Some were bleak prison pieces with a bluish tint while others were more elaborate and richly colored professional artwork.

As if he walked around half-naked in front of me every day, Alexei strode toward the garment bag resting flat on the bed. "You must have been really tired. You didn't even move when my clothing was delivered."

"Which minion brought that?" I asked with a teasing smile.

He grinned at me, and I swear my heart skipped four whole beats. "My housekeeper's son."

Taking a seat on the edge of the mattress, I watched him take out a charcoal black suit with a fine pinstripe and a sky blue shirt. When he produced a pair of boxer briefs, I glanced away. My eyes widened as I heard him drop his towel, but I kept my gaze fixed on the wall, refusing to indulge the over-whelming desire to peek at his nakedness.

It was as though Alexei had flipped some switch. Yester-day morning, we were friends, and our relationship had been strictly platonic. Now, the very air between us was sexually charged and sizzling. He wasn't hiding his attraction to me or shielding me from his very flirtatious ways.

Desperate to find something to talk about that didn't include his naked body that was only a foot or two from me, I said, "I'm surprised you don't keep more clothing here."

"I've never spent the night the here."

"What? Never?" I heard his legs swooshing against the fabric of his perfectly tailored pants and judged that it was safe to look at him again. "You have this ridiculously expensive apartment, and you've never slept in it?"

"I didn't buy it for sleep," he answered matter-of-factly while zipping his trousers.

"Oh. Right." My face burned hot as I imagined what types of erotic delights kept him awake all night here. A pang of something that was far worse than jealousy stabbed at my chest. Memories of earlier that morning, of Alexei caressing my body and the way he had alluded to the physical relationship he wanted with me reminded me that I was wholly out of my depth here.

Didn't he understand? Couldn't he see that I wasn't mistress material? I didn't have the first idea of how to seduce him or please him. I didn't fit the mold and I didn't belong in a place like this. He was a man who strutted around daily wearing thousands of dollars in clothing and shoes. I was a girl who shopped the clearance racks and thrift stores.

Feeling inadequate, I tugged the bottom of the hoodie I still wore down around my knees. Thinking of how the women who entertained him here must have looked, I could only imagine what a disappointment I was in the cold light of morning with my mussed hair and ill-fitting clothing. He was probably used to silk lingerie and elegant robes and artfully arranged hair, not this hot mess I presented.

As if confirming my suspicion, he suggested, "You should shower and get dressed before Stas arrives." Alexei slipped into his shirt. "We'll have breakfast before I leave."

"All right." I pushed off the bed and gave him a wide berth as I headed for the bathroom.

"Shay." He snatched my hand before I reached the bathroom door. With a little tug, he pulled me toward him. When he stepped into me, forcing our bodies into contact, I held my breath and wondered what would happen next. He cupped my face and trailed his fingertips over the bruise on my cheek and the healing split in my lip. "This looks better than I expected."

"It doesn't hurt as much as I thought it would." Gazing up into his handsome face, I let myself wonder what it would be like to wake up like this every morning, to sit in bed and watch him dress, to have breakfast together, to have his warm, possessive hands on me.

"I should apologize for the way I groped you this morning when I was half-asleep," Alexei said, "but I don't think I will. I think you understand the sort of man I am. I could pretend to be someone else but that's disingenuous. I won't have lies between us."

"It surprised me," I admitted, "to have you touch me like that when you've always been so careful to *not* touch me." Feeling brave, I placed my palm against his bare chest. "But I liked it."

"Good." He dipped down and teased me with ticklish kisses he pressed along the curve of my throat. "You need to understand that *you* are in control of this part of our relationship." His hand moved down my spine until it rested on my lower back. "Until you're ready, I'll wait."

I leaned into him, resting my cheek against his hard chest, and closed my eyes. I wanted to tell him that I was ready *now*, that I had waited long enough to experience everything he had to offer, but I knew that it wasn't the right time. We were both still reeling from last night's traumatic events. We needed some time to figure out what *this* was.

Very slowly, I stepped out of his embrace and walked over to my suitcase. I wasn't quite sure what I would find inside but I was pleasantly surprised to see what Alexei had packed. After choosing some comfortable yoga pants, a long-sleeve tee and underclothes, I grabbed the small selection of toiletries and locked myself in the bathroom.

My one indulgence every morning was a long shower, but this morning I wanted to have more time with Alexei before he left for work. Knowing the hours he kept, I probably wouldn't see him again until well after dark. As I showered and changed, I made a short list of questions I needed answered. Without a blow dryer at hand, I wound my damp hair into a loose coil, secured it with a hot pink elastic band and left the bathroom.

Alexei was plucking piping hot English muffins from the toaster when I found him. He flashed that sexy grin of his, the one that made my knees week, and gestured for me to take a seat at the island. "We can eat at the formal dining table, if you prefer."

I hopped onto a chair and picked up the glass of orange juice waiting for me. "No, I like this."

He dropped an English muffin onto my plate of scrambled eggs and fresh fruit and walked to the other end of the island to grab my purse. He brought it back to me. "Your phone ended up under my seat. I found it last night when I got back from the trip to your house. You had some missed calls."

Anxious to hear from my sister, I snatched my phone out of my purse and scrolled down the screen. There was only one message from Shannon.

I'm sorry. I'm so sorry.

She was sorry? Feeling uncharitable and angry with my older sister, I wasn't ready to accept her apology. She had nearly gotten me killed—and for what? Money? It was ridiculous and horrible.

But I still loved her. No matter what mistakes she had made, she was my sister, and I loved her.

Call me. I need to know you're okay.

There were more than a dozen messages and seven missed calls from Kylee. By the looks of them, she was freaking out. Not wanting her to get the cops involved and make things worse for me or Shannon, I hastily composed a text and hit send.

I'm okay. I snuck a glance at Alexei who was busy stirring creamer into his coffee and smiled at the thought of using Kylee's nickname for him. *The Russian fox saved me. I'll call later with details.*

As if she had been waiting for my answer, Kylee zipped back a message only a few seconds later.

OMG. I was so worried. You sure you're okay?
Yes. I'm fine. Really.
Call me. ASAP.

I will.

"Is everything okay?" Alexei stabbed at his eggs. "I don't want to pry into your personal business, but if the police become involved…"

"No, everything is fine. It's just Kylee. She's my best friend. We worked together last night. I guess she got back to Clean-Rite and saw my busted up car and really freaked out. She went by the house this morning, and I wasn't there so she assumed the worst."

"Invite her over. Let her see that you're safe." He sipped his coffee. "We'll put her on the visitor list downstairs, but she has to come alone."

I played with my fork as I considered the authoritarian tone he had just used. Maybe it was better to just get all of the uncomfortable questions out of the way. "Alexei, am I your mistress now?"

"Yes." He eyed me over the rim of his coffee cup. "Unless you've changed your answer from last night?"

"No."

He put down his cup and studied me. A vulnerable expression flashed across his face. "But?"

"But I don't know what you want from me or what you expect from me, Alexei." Clenching my fork, I admitted, "I don't know how to be a mistress."

He pried the fork from my hand and slowly unfurled my fingers. "What I want is you, Shay." He stroked my fingers. "I've wanted you, just as you are, since that night I took you home. If you only knew how hard it's been for me…" He clasped my hand and gave it a squeeze. "All I want is for you to be happy. That's it."

"Nothing is that simple, Alexei." I wanted to believe it could be, but I had seen enough heartache in my life to know better. "You've offered me sanctuary, and you've put your life on the line for me. I'm so eternally grateful for that, but I don't want you to think that I'm here with you now only because of that. I don't want you to think that I'm trading myself—my body—for safety."

"I don't think that, and if I did, I wouldn't be here. I don't want to take advantage of you. I don't want to hurt you or make you feel used. I offered my help freely. You can say no to this arrangement of ours at any time, and I'll still make sure you're protected."

He seemed to be intent on making that point very clear to me. He wasn't asking me to pay for safety with sex. He was giving his protection freely because we were friends and because he cared for me. I would never be able to adequately thank him for what he had done. Alexei had willingly put himself in extreme danger for me.

"As for what I expect from a mistress? The rules are simple." Alexei lifted my hand and kissed each of my fingertips as he ticked off his rules. "You will not have any male visitors in this apartment. Period. You will not have any overnight guests in this apartment without clearing it with me first. You will not smoke or take drugs. You will not work. You will be available to me whenever I call."

It took me a few seconds to take all of that in and process it. Indignation swelled within me. "I'm not giving up my work, Alexei."

He seemed surprised that I was pushing back so quickly. "I don't want you cleaning floors or waiting tables anymore.

Your handbag business is different. In fact, I want you to put your full focus on it."

"But how am I supposed to support myself? I have school loans. My car was probably totaled last night. I have health insurance costs and—"

"The car is easy enough for me to replace, and I'll take care of your monthly expenses."

The thought of Alexei paying for my living expenses made me so uncomfortable. "Alexei, I've been working and supporting myself since I was, like, sixteen."

"And it's high fucking time you got a break," he grumbled roughly. Reaching out to touch my cheek, he urged, "Don't fight me on this. Let me take care of you."

It was a tempting offer, one that I would be stupid to cast aside in my current predicament, but a lifetime of broken promises had taught me to be wary. I desperately wanted to pursue a relationship with Alexei, but I had to be careful. He was obviously a man used to getting his way in all things.

"Look at you," he said with a faint smile. "You're so grim. Is what I'm offering really so bad?"

He was trying to tease but I sensed he was hurt by my reaction. Taking his hand between both of mine, I held his gaze. "This isn't easy for me. My past…"

"I know," he murmured. "I know." He seemed to truly understand my wariness. "Just give me a chance to show you that I can be trusted to come through for you." He leaned in and brushed a tender kiss to my cheek. "Always."

My skin was still alight with the tingling pressure of his lips when he put my fork back in my hands and urged me to eat. While we had breakfast, he talked to me about the building's amenities and the nearby shops.

"But I don't want you going out by yourself," he warned before finishing his coffee. "Stas will be following you like a shadow. That's non-negotiable."

"Until?" I pushed grapes around my plate with the fork.

"Until I say it's safe," he replied matter-of-factly and polished off his orange segments. Pushing away his plate, he said, "We need to talk about your sister."

I really didn't want to talk about Shannon. I feared what Alexei would say, but there was no way around it. "All right."

"If your sister is smart, she's already crossed two or three state lines. If she's not, if she's still in Texas, she's in a lot of trouble. That means you're in trouble, and I can't have that." He tapped his fingers against the granite. "Your sister is not welcome in this building. Frankly, I would prefer you have zero contact with her, but I know that's impossible for you."

"I'm not cutting my sister out of my life, Alexei."

"I won't force you to rat your sister out to Nikolai or Mueller or Lalo, but I have to put my foot down when it comes to seeing her again."

"Alexei, she's my sister. She's all the family I have. You're asking to turn my back on my blood."

"I'm asking you to be smart and to help me keep you alive," he countered. "I know what I'm asking is difficult and it hurts—but you have to do it. Shannon made her decision when she chose to help Ruben with this scam. Don't let her put all that guilt on you when she's the reason this is happening. You're just reacting to a bad situation in the best way you can."

"She's my sister," I reiterated. "She's all I have left."

Alexei started to say something but then he clamped his mouth shut. A second later, he finally said, "Whatever happens with Shannon, you are not alone. I'm here for you."

"Until you get tired of me like you did your other mistresses," I replied in a quiet but firm voice. It was a petulant thing to say, and I instantly regretted it. Alexei's head snapped back as if I had smacked him. In a way, I had, only I had used words instead of my hand.

Before I could apologize, he was pushing out of his chair and gathering up our dishes. "Stas will be here any minute. I need to finish up some last minute arrangements for him."

"Alexei…"

"We're fine, Shay." He had his back to me as he dropped our plates and silverware in the dishwasher. "You should unpack and get settled."

Not at all used to being dismissed like a naughty child, I nevertheless slid off my chair and returned to the master suite. It didn't take me long to unpack my one suitcase or the two boxes of tools and materials. I was examining the handbag I had been working on yesterday when Alexei appeared in the doorway of the bedroom.

"Stas is here." He leaned against the frame. "I need to leave."

Not wanting him to leave with all this tension existing between us, I set aside the handbag and crossed the bedroom. "Alexei, I'm sorry about what I said."

"Why should you be sorry? You didn't say anything untrue. I did get tired of the other women before you. Six months? Seven months? The flame burned out, and I sent them on their way."

His description of his earlier relationships caused a painful clenching sensation in my stomach. Was he trying to tell me that I shouldn't get too comfortable with him? That we were already running the clock on the expiration date for our new relationship?

He shoved off the frame and closed the short distance between us. "Do you know the friendship I've had with you is the longest I've ever shared with any woman? We're closing in on twelve months, Shay." He eyed me curiously. "All this time, you've had me right in the palm of your hand, and I've never even kissed you properly."

That big, warm hand of his cradled my nape, and he slowly lowered his face, all the while searching my eyes as if looking for a sign that he needed to stop. Just before his lips touched mine, he whispered, "Is this all right?"

I clutched at the lapels of his suit jacket and lifted on tiptoes to meet his descending mouth. "Yes."

Our lips met cautiously, but Alexei quickly took command. Eyes closed, I clung to his powerful frame and reveled in the wicked, wicked way he kissed me. When his tongue flicked against the seam of my lips, I answered his silent plea for entrance by shyly touching my tongue to his. He groaned, the low, rumbling noise reverberating through me, and tugged me tighter to his body.

With a little pressure, he guided me toward the closest wall. Trapped against his hard chest, I surrendered to his sensual onslaught. I slid one hand to his shoulders and combed the fingers of the other through his short hair while he plundered my mouth, taking and taking until I was shaking and breathless. The ache between my thighs left me quivering with need.

I shuddered as Alexei kissed the fingertip bruises on my throat and then skimmed his lips along my jaw. He claimed my mouth one last time and traced my swollen pout with his thumb. "I'll see you this evening. Stay inside with Stas, and you'll be safe."

"I will." Still a bit dazed from his kisses, I sagged against the wall. He backed away slowly and left the bedroom. Trying to get my racing heartbeat under control, I shook my head and touched my tingling mouth.

What have I gotten myself into now?

CHAPTER NINE

"**B**OSS, YOU HAVE a visitor waiting in your office." Audrey, one of the weekend receptionists, greeted him with a cup of coffee and a stack of messages. "It's An Trinh."

An, the eldest daughter of Mr. Lu, the well-known importer and not so well-known underworld don, ran the legal side of her father's business empire. She was very highly respected around the city and ran in some of his social circles. In a few short weeks, they would begin serving on the board of directors for the Chamber of Commerce, and both had entertained the idea of putting together an organization to support small businesses owned by minorities and immigrants.

But why would An be in his office this early on a Saturday morning? "Did you offer her coffee or tea?"

"Yes, sir. I made sure she was comfortable."

Taking the coffee and messages, he gave Audrey a few quick orders for the morning. "Send one of our tow trucks to CleanRite to pick up a car from the lot. They'll know which one it is when they see it. Have them take it to Merkurie Motors. Give the crew at Merkurie a call so they'll know to expect it. Make sure they know I'm handling all the estimates and bills."

"Yes, sir."

He handed her his key fob. "Will you please grab the handbag and wallet on the front seat of my SUV? And bring me a new hire packet, too."

"For a salesman?"

"No, for one of the hourly positions." He needed to get Stas on the payroll by the end of the day. "After you've brought me the box and the packet, hold my calls until I'm finished with my meeting."

"Yes, sir."

Upstairs, he entered his office and found An sitting in one of the chairs across from his desk. Lithe and willowy, she eyed him with what could only be described as cool disdain. He didn't let her expression intimidate or concern him. In all the years he had known her, she had never once smiled.

"Good morning, An." He shut the door and shifted the items he held so he could shake her hand as she rose from her chair. "Did we have a meeting on the schedule?"

"No." Her bony, fragile hand was cold in his, but she had a strong grip. He had a feeling men underestimated her all the time—and suffered for it. "But I thought this needed to be dealt with face to face."

"All right." He moved behind his desk and took a seat. Before he could ask her what they needed to discuss, she retrieved an envelope from her purse and tossed it onto his desk. He opened it and found an invoice for a new security system. Confused, he asked, "What is this?"

"The next time you want to take a bat to a bunch of thugs I suggest you check for security cameras." An shook her head and played with the elegant gold band encircling her wrist. "You're damned lucky that young kid with you knew the dishwasher boys who were working last night. They disabled the system before the police could get their hands on it. Unfortunately, their method of disabling was permanent."

His stomach pitched at the mention of police. "I forgot the restaurant was under your family's control. I didn't mean to make trouble for you or your father, especially not now when he's so ill." Alexei hadn't heard any news about the old man's fight with cancer. "How is he?"

"He's stubborn." She clearly didn't want to talk about it. "Look, I despise John Mueller and his ilk so I'm going to turn a blind eye to the mess you made in our parking lot. What really concerns me is the way you put yourself at risk." She tut-tutted at him. "You're smarter than that."

"The circumstances were extreme."

An actually smirked at him, her primly set mouth quirking up just a bit. "They usually are when a woman is involved."

"I can't argue with that." Not wanting any bad blood with An or her father, he offered, "I am truly sorry for last night. I know how hard we all try to keep our illicit connections clear of our legitimate businesses. I should have contacted you, in person, to apologize."

"We're fine," An assured him. "For what it's worth, my father and I are willing to back you in whatever way that you might find useful in this matter. There is no love lost between my father and Mueller, not after that horrifying bit of business his people tangled us up in last year."

Though he didn't know all of the details, Alexei had heard the tale of Mr. Lu discovering too late that cargo shipments he had been hired to shepherd through customs contained cargo of a human variety. It had been a very public black eye for the old man, especially when he had been suspected of possible involvement in Vivian's kidnapping.

Audrey knocked at the door, and he gave her permission to enter. She carried the box holding Shay's handbags and the new hire packet to his desk. After whisking away An's empty coffee cup, she left the office.

Setting aside the box and the packet, Alexei said, "Listen, I know some of our contracts are up for renegotiation in early January. For the trucking services my company provides for your restaurants and for the food and supplies the company I own with Nikolai ships out to your locations," he clarified. "I'm sure we can take this favor," he waved the envelope, "into account when we settle on new terms."

"I'm counting on it." She gestured to the box on his desk. "Is that a handbag I see?"

"It is." Smiling, he rose from his seat and started unpacking the box. "I actually planned to visit your office so we could talk about these handbags and wallets."

"It's a few weeks too early for Christmas so I'm assuming these aren't gifts for me." The faint smile on her face hinted at a mischief streak he never would have guessed she possessed. "This is lovely." She picked up the larger handbag and ran her fingers along the blush pink Saffiano leather. "Who made these?"

"My girlfriend," he answered proudly. Only a moment later did he realize what word he had used, not mistress or lover but girlfriend. It was a word that had always struck him as so very juvenile, but it suddenly seemed clean and new and entirely more suitable for Shay. Because no matter how hard he tried to shove her into that role, she was never, ever, ever going to the perfect little mistress. After all, this morning, his *ptichka* had shown him her claws with that six month remark.

"She's very talented." An examined the wallet. "Oh, look at how slim this is! The design is wonderful. Is she self-taught or did she go to college for this?"

"Both," he said, running his fingers over the elaborate stitching on the clutch. "She currently sells her leather goods in an online boutique, but she's planning to open a proper store front soon. I'd like to help her find a way to increase her productivity."

"Well, she needs a team who understands leather goods and attention to detail," An murmured. "Let me work my contacts. I'm sure I can get you some names by the end of the week."

Alexei had suspected An would be able to help him. There were a number of small factories under her family's control and protection that employed seamstresses and cobblers. Surely, a few of them had experience with leather goods. "I would appreciate it."

"It's no problem." She glanced at her watch. "I need to go. My daughter has figure skating practice in half an hour, and I never miss it. I'll have my assistant call you with those names. I'm sure you won't have any trouble getting a production line set up."

"I hope not."

After An left, Alexei settled into his chair and went through the usual Saturday morning routine, holding a sales meeting and talking one-on-one with his salesmen and managers before returning calls and answering internal emails. When he had a chance, he dialed Fox, Kostya's hacker who had set up the computer systems across his dealerships.

"Henhouse Security Services," a sunny female voice answered. "Fox here. How can I help you?"

The name of her company brought a smile to his face. "Fox, this is Alexei Sarnov."

"Oh! Hey, how are you? I was going to call you later to talk about the attempted hacking."

An uproar of hooting voices and clapping erupted in the background. It didn't take him long to figure out that she was standing in a room of raucous gamers. "Is this a good time to talk?"

"Yes, it is. Just…um…hang on a sec. I need get back into my office." A door squealed loudly and slammed into place. "Sorry about that. We're testing a new version for Maisie. Like you cannot even believe how gore-tastic this new zombie shredding version is!"

Having seen enough violence and bloodshed firsthand, Alexei didn't need video games to give him a vicarious thrill. "I'll pass."

"Right. Um. Okay. So I spent the night clearing out all the malware and virues and all that awful shit that had attempted to infect your systems. It was all quarantined so no sensitive information was compromised. The system worked the way it was supposed to and saved your virtual backside."

"Well that's a relief." He rubbed his sore neck. His days of sleeping on couches were long behind him and he was paying for it this morning. "Do you have any recommendations for preventing something like this in the future?"

"Vet your cleaning staff better?" she hazarded a smart-ass guess. "No, but really, Alexei? Shit like this happens. It's just part of the business. Your best offense is a good defense. You just need to keep your systems up to date and well-protected. This why you pay me an outrageous amount of money every month."

He finished off the last of his lukewarm coffee. "So I assume by the cleaning staff remark you know who was behind this."

"I figured out the identity of the hacker who wrote this program before I heard the news that he had gone missing. His signature is one I recognize easily. Edgar has been a wannabe black hat for years. He's good, but he's not elite." She sighed sadly. "That's some bad, bad business there."

Wondering if she was just as plugged in to the underworld as Kostya, her benefactor, he asked, "Have you heard who might have been interested in buying this stolen information?"

"I haven't heard any specifics, but it's a good bet they come from your old stomping grounds. Identity theft is big business over there. Would you like me to poke around and see if I can find out the name of the buyer?"

"No," he said quickly. "I don't want you to put yourself at risk. Let's just leave this alone."

"All right. I'll probably swing by your dealerships on Monday just to take a peek at the systems again and run some diagnostics."

"Thank you, Fox."

"No problem."

After she hung up, he drummed his fingers on his desk. He didn't want to think that Nikolai might be more involved in this than he had initially let on, but it was entirely possible that Nikolai might know the identity of the buyer.

His cell phone rattled across his desk. Fearing it was Shay calling with a problem, he snatched it up and glanced at the screen. It was Nikolai's name that flashed at him. "Hello?"

"Lyosha, can you get over to Kazimir's? I'm headed that way to pick up something for Vivian. I need to speak with you."

He pulled back his cuff and looked at his watch. "Sure. It may take me half an hour or more to get over there."

"Take your time."

As Nikolai ended the call, Alexei remembered the jewelry he had tucked into his handkerchief last night. "Shit."

He quickly scrolled through his list of recent calls, found Shay's number and hit dial. While he waited for her to answer, he logged out of the computer system and locked away the files on his desk. When she didn't answer in time, the call went to her voicemail.

"Hi! You've reached Shay Sandoval. I can't come to the phone right now. Leave me a message, and I'll get back you!"

Although her bright voice made him smile, he didn't leave a message. Why wasn't she answering? Fearing the worst, he started to call Stas but Shay returned his call first. "Shay? Is everything okay?"

"Hello to you, too," she said with a laugh. "Yes, everything here is okay. Are you all right?"

"I'm fine. You didn't answer, and I started to worry."

"Alexei," she murmured his name. "You shouldn't worry so much. I'm safe here with Stas. We are working together in the kitchen. I left my phone in the bedroom so I had to run across the apartment. Now I'm all out of breath!"

He could think of a dozen ways he'd like to take her breath

away, but right now wasn't the time to indulge in fantasies. "Did the concierge send up someone for my suit?"

"No. Why?"

"I asked for laundry service. Will you find my suit in the closet please? I put your jewelry in a handkerchief and tucked it into my jacket pocket. I'd hate for it to get lost at the cleaner's."

"Oh. Okay. Hang on." A short time later, she announced, "Found it! Thank you so much for bringing this to me."

"I could tell it was important to you."

"I don't have much jewelry, but what I do have means something. The necklace and the hoops were a Christmas gift from my dad. He's the only person who has ever given me jewelry."

Instantly, Alexei knew exactly what he was going to do when he got to Kazimir's. Not wanting to tip her off, he changed the subject, "So you've put Stas to work?"

"He's really good at punching holes in leather. I might let him try grommets next. He's been teaching me to count in Russian which has been cool."

A zing of jealousy snapped through him. As childish as it was, he wanted to be the one who taught her how to speak his language. "Well I'm glad to hear that you're finding him useful."

"Shay, do you want to order something for lunch?" Stas bellowed in the background. "I'm starving."

"You just ate three oranges and a banana!"

"Like an hour ago," Stas called back. "Do you like Chinese? There's a place a few blocks from here that's pretty good. Or how about Thai?"

"Do you realize how loud you are?" Shay scolded Stas with a laugh. "I'm just in the next room, but you're shouting so loud they can probably hear you down in the lobby."

"I'm starving."

"You're a drama queen."

"I'm about to start chewing on this leather. That's how hungry I am."

"Oh my God!" Shay laughed. "We'll order Chinese, okay? Can I finish my call now?"

"Is that your friend? We can wait to order lunch until she gets here."

"No, it's Alexei. Now quiet down and get back to work."

"Yes, ma'am."

"So anyway," Shay said, returning to their call. "We're good here. Kylee is going to come over later and spend some time with me. I thought we might take Stas and go see my car later?"

He noticed the way she phrased it as a question. "That's not necessary. I had your car towed earlier this morning. I'm handling it."

"Oh. Well…what am I supposed to do about the insurance claim?"

"There won't be one. We'll see what the car is worth and sell it. You can use the cash for your business."

"I'll have to use the cash for a new car. Well—not a *new* car. A used car that's new to me," she said.

He already had his eye on a sporty Jaguar coupe for her, but he sensed this wasn't the type of conversation that would go well over the phone. "We'll figure it out, Shay."

"I'm sure we will. Look, I'm going to send Stas out for groceries later. Otherwise the takeout bill here is going to be sky high."

Knowing how stubborn she could be, he warned, "Don't even try to give him money for the groceries. I left him funds to cover your daily expenses."

Shay started to answer him, but a loud shout of pain interrupted her. Stas began cursing angrily in Russian. "Uh-oh. Sounds like Stas just had his first on-the-job injury. I hope your workman's comp coverage is good, Alexei."

"You mean you hope *your* coverage is good," he corrected with a teasing laugh. "He's currently working for you."

"What? That is so not fair!"

"Welcome to the cutthroat world of business, sweetheart." Listening to Stas swear nastily, he added, "Tell Stas that he is forbidden from teaching you that colorful language. If I hear any of those words come out of your mouth, I'll know who to blame."

"When he stops crying, I'll let tell him."

"See that you do." Even though he'd like nothing better than to stay on the phone with her, he had to get moving. "I'll call you later."

"Be careful out there, Alexei."

"I will."

When their call ended, he held his phone to his ear a moment longer than necessary. He was so tempted to leave the office for this meeting with Nikolai and not come back until Sunday afternoon or even Monday morning. Only the gut feeling that they were going to get slammed with customers later in the day kept him from doing it. He couldn't leave his employees in the lurch like that, especially not when so many of his them were doing their damnedest to earn their holiday bonuses. He needed to be here to work deals and push through financing.

Down on the main sales floor, he walked the perimeter to ensure customers were being treated the way he liked and that all of the salesmen were busy. The quickest way to earn a pink slip at any of his dealerships was to be discovered standing around, shooting the breeze or laughing with coworkers. The only thing he hated more were high-pressure salesmen. He liked ambition and drive, but he didn't want the salesmen skulking after customers, breathing down their necks and pushing financing and trades that weren't a good deal for both sides.

Satisfied that the sales floor was operating like a well-oiled machine, he pulled aside the general manager for a chat. With his temporary absence squared away, Alexei left the dealership and headed for the luxury jewelry store operated by Kazimir and his daughter, Zoya. He hadn't visited the jeweler in more than a year. Marissa, his last mistress, had preferred a different high-end jeweler so he had indulged her with gifts only from there.

Finding parking at Kamizir's was a nightmare as usual. Why the man hadn't moved to a better location Alexei would never understand. He spotted Nikolai's Land Rover and pulled into a space a few cars down. Ilya, one of the boss's handlers, leaned against the hood and smoked while keeping an eye out for trouble.

It wasn't so long ago that Ilya had been the young kid on Alexei's street crew. Now he had advanced to the inner circle and was poised for a promotion to street captain. He stopped to shake Ilya's hand and couldn't help but read the new ink on his hands and neck. Apparently, he had been busy.

When he stepped inside the store, he was instantly greeted by Kazimir who directed him to the cozy room where clients with expensive taste could inspect jewels and designs in privacy. He found Zoya and Nikolai there.

"Lyosha." Nikolai pointed to an empty seat. "We're almost done."

"How are you, Alexei?" Zoya drew sunbursts on her sketchpad. "It's been awhile since we've seen you."

"You should go ahead and unlock the diamond safe," Nikolai joked. "I have a feeling you're going to be seeing a lot more of him."

"Oh?" Zoya's bright blue eyes lit up excitedly.

"We'll talk after you've finished with the boss." Alexei waved toward their work.

Taking the hint, Nikolai said, "Zoya, this gift needs to be something beautiful but simple. The bracelet has to be something Vee can wear every day. I want her to see it on her wrist and think of our son and me and the life we're building together."

Zoya smiled warmly as she sketched out some ideas on her notepad. "That's so lovely and sweet."

"And the other gift? It needs to be regal." Nikolai emphasized the description with a flourish of his hands. "We need to stay away from anything too gaudy, but I want her to have something incredible to mark the birth of our first child."

"I've gotten to know Vivian's tastes very well this year. I have an idea of what she likes and what you like and how to make it work." Zoya jotted down her notes. "Do you have any preference for gemstones for the necklace and earrings?"

"Sapphires," he answered. "I want them to be as blue as her eyes."

"Platinum? Gold? White gold?" When Nikolai gave her a look, she let loose a twitter of laughter. "Right. Platinum. Always." She jotted down more notes. "I should have some preliminary designs in a week. Does that work for your timeline?"

"Yes, that's fine. Would you mind stepping out for a few minutes? I promise I'll let you have your room back as soon as we're done."

"Of course," she graciously replied.

When the door closed behind Zoya, Nikolai reached over and smacked him on the back of his head. It wasn't a hard hit, but it was enough to get his attention.

"Hey!" Alexei winced and smoothed down his hair. "What the fuck was that for?"

"Did you really think I wasn't going to find out you went behind my back and asked Besian for help? Huh? How the fuck do you think that makes me look?"

"*Shit.* That's not—I didn't go to Besian for backup. I went there for information. I didn't know what was happening with Shay's sister, but I knew that he would. I never asked him to publicly stand for me."

"Well he fucking did," Nikolai shot back. "I had John Mueller on my doorstep this morning complaining that Besian's Merkurie Motors boys towed his truck from the restaurant he was at last night. This morning, they picked up his wife's SUV while she was at the gym. Needless to say, he got the message."

"I didn't ask Besian to get involved. He promised he would have my back if things went sideways but he didn't tell me he was going to harass Mueller and his wife."

"Apparently, Mueller went by that marble monstrosity of yours this morning, but there was no answer so he decided to walk over another street to bother me. Do you know how I like to spend my Saturday mornings?"

Alexei had an idea of what Nikolai enjoyed doing on Saturday mornings, but it was too graphic and dirty to say to Nikolai's face, especially where Vivian was concerned. "Probably not having coffee with the Mr. White Is Right."

Nikolai leveled that cold no-nonsense stare of his so Alexei eased off the sarcasm.

"Look, obviously, this was not how I envisioned any of this happening, okay? So get off my fucking back, Kolya."

Nikolai's jaw tensed. He spun his wedding band around his finger, a gesture that seemed to have replaced his old habit of tossing that lucky lighter of his back and forth between his hands. "It seems An Trinh is mixed up in this mess now. She's threatening to blackball Mueller around town. She even told Mueller that all it would take is a few words from Vivian and Bianca and Holly to have his wife blacklisted around town." Nikolai shook his head. "That woman fucking scares me. I can't get a read on her at all. I used to dismiss that rumor about her poisoning her husband but now I'm not so sure."

Alexei had heard the rumor and had instantly believed it. The man had been in his late thirties when he had died while on vacation abroad. The official word had been a heart attack but the whispers were poison. That marriage had always had problems apparently.

"An is giving us a free pass for that bullshit that went down behind her family's restaurant, but she's blaming Mueller for his men trespassing on her turf and trying to beat an innocent young woman to death behind one of her businesses."

"She came to see me this morning. I've agreed to pay for the replacement of the security system that was disabled."

"Keep her happy," Nikolai ordered. "She can make trouble that we don't need."

"Understood."

"Besian is pushing for the council to sanction Mueller. This is the third time he's trespassed into someone else's territory. He's done it to Spider and the MC twice. First it was the kidnapping at Spider's trailer park when all that shit went down with Step's girlfriend and her little brother. Yesterday his men trespassed again to shakedown your girl. Then trying to beat her up in the Lu family's backyard? *Blyad*." Nikolai rubbed his face. "They're too fucking reckless."

Alexei held his tongue and waited to see what Nikolai would say.

"I told Mueller that he's going to have to eat the cost of his downed men and that whatever bad blood there is between his side and yours ends today." The boss slashed his hand through the air. "You and Shay are free and that score is settled. I made it clear that if his men even look at Shay, I'll let you gouge their eyes out. It's done. Over. *Finished*."

"And the sister?" Alexei didn't have high hopes for Shannon's case but he had to ask.

"She's not my problem." Nikolai cast a pointed look his direction. "Or yours. Don't be stupid like Vanya was with

Erin's junkie sister. You stay away from Shannon and Ruben. Let Lalo's men sort that shit out."

"Have you heard anything about Lalo?"

"He's looking for Shay." Nikolai reached into his jacket pocket and retrieved his phone. He swept his finger across the screen and read a message that made his mouth twitch with amusement. There was only one person in the entire world who could make him smile like that. "I sent Danny over to talk to him this morning and to let him know that Shay belongs to you and that I've taken an interest in her. Lalo assured Danny that he only wants to make sure that Shay is safe."

"Lying little prick," Alexei groused.

"Don't worry about him." Nikolai typed a reply. "I went over his head and cleared Shay's safety with Hector Salas. Lalo's boss will put him back in his kennel where he belongs. Just keep her away from him until his wounded pride heals." Nikolai pocketed his phone and grinned. "Danny said Lalo has two black eyes, a broken nose and a bandaged head. I guess he must have slammed face first into the ground. That'll teach the little bastard to try to assault some poor woman again."

The image of Lalo so badly wounded amused Alexei but it wasn't nearly enough pain for what he had tried to do to Shay.

"How is she?" Nikolai seemed genuinely curious. "Last night, she looked badly shaken."

"She's much better this morning. Having Stas there seems to be helping."

"Are they getting along well? I haven't spent much time with him, but so far I like him."

"Shay enjoyed his company last night, and they seemed to be getting along just fine earlier." Alexei didn't want to dwell on the uncomfortable feeling he had about Stas and Shay alone together and getting so chummy. "I wanted to let you know that Boychenko really came through for me last night. He made sure there was no evidence on the security tapes to implicate me. He went above and beyond, Kolya."

"He's a good kid," Nikolai agreed. "He reminds me of me. He's hungry and he's got something to prove. I'm torn between assigning him to guard duty for my son when he's born or putting him out on the streets with Ilya. He's not big enough to be an enforcer but he's got that instinct, you know?"

"I've been watching him train at the warehouse. The kid is getting better in the ring. He'll never be as good as Sergei or Vanya but he's developing some skill."

"He better develop fast. We need a new champion before the spring fights start. The family has a reputation to uphold after you, Ivan and Sergei."

"You could always throw Ten in there."

Nikolai laughed. "That P.O. of his is way too uptight to let that pass. Hey," he said, swiveling in his chair and tapping the tabletop, "can we talk about that strip of buildings you own uptown?"

"Sure." He had acquired two empty lots ripe for development and a strip of retail space in the fire sale that had followed real estate developer Jonah Krause's arrest for attempted murder. The sorry son of a bitch had hired thugs to kill Dimitri Stepanov and his then-girlfriend Benny Marquez but the couple had fought them off and survived.

"Those retail spaces are still wide open, right?"

"They are," he affirmed. "The area there is developing and growing, but it's taking time to fill the prime spots. I've been kicking around an idea about one of the corner retail spaces. Shay wants to take her online handbag boutique to a proper storefront. The area is high traffic, and it's right there next to the Galleria."

Of course, getting Shay to agree to take the space would be an uphill battle. He had seen her savings and the working capital she planned for her business. She didn't have anywhere close to the budget to afford prime real estate like that, but he wouldn't charge her, not at first. He would eat the cost to help her get that business off the ground. It would be a solid investment. He believed in her and her dreams. Someday, she would pay him back and make good on the debt.

"You'll need another business on the other corner to anchor that space," Nikolai remarked. "I think I have the perfect one."

"Oh?"

"When Vee had her art show in London, it occurred to me that she really needs her own gallery space. It needs to be in a high traffic area, and it needs to fit the profile of the neighborhood. That strip of retail space that you own is perfect, Alexei."

He could already see the way the retail strip would look with Shay's luxury handbag boutique on one end and Vivian's high-end gallery on the other. "But what would go in between? That space in the center would have to be something truly special."

Nikolai gestured around them. "Kazimir has been looking for a new space, one with better access and room to grow. Zoya's designs are becoming more and more popular. In five years? Ten? She'll be a household name. She needs a beautiful place that draws in flush customers. Just think of Vee and Shay sitting on either side of one of the most popular jewelry stores in this city."

He was thinking about it, and he liked it. Certain there was a catch, he asked, "What sort of deal are you looking for here?"

The boss shook his head. "This would be above board and clean from the start. It would all be in Vivian's name and using her money." He drummed his fingers on the table. "I would expect that she be given a break on the contract and lease." He flicked his tattooed fingers. "We can work out the exact details later. What do you think?"

"I like it." He leaned back in his chair and let his mind race with all the possibilities. "I've been thinking about my goals for next year. Maybe it's time to finally do something with all that property."

"I'd like it if you would consider Sergei and David's construction company for any of the work that needs to be done. Maybe bring in Mueller for a piece of it. Just a few crumbs from the table, you understand?"

"I do." Whatever his personal disagreements with John Mueller, the man had a lot of money behind him and the potential to cause problems down the line. "Viktor is coming to Houston next week. I'll talk business with him and see what he thinks about that property. He might have a better idea of how to structure this."

"How is he doing? The ruble falling like a rock must have him all twisted up," Nikolai remarked with feeling.

"He's like Yuri and Evgeni, you know? Five steps ahead of the market and always hedging his bets when it comes to Putin and the government policies back home," Alexei replied. "I'm sure he's taken a hit, but you watch. He'll come out richer than he was before this shit went down. He always does."

"I hope you're right." Nikolai glanced at his vibrating phone and smiled again. "I need to go. I promised Vee we would pick out nursery furniture today. If I make her wait much longer, she's going to take Ten with her and bankrupt me. You would not believe what a crib costs, Lyosha! Don't even get me started on rocking chairs, changing tables, dressers, linens, toys, clothes—it never ends."

"You can complain all you like but we both know you've never been happier." Alexei had witnessed the change in Nikolai since he had married Vivian. The announcement of the impending arrival of their first child had caused the boss to go into a fiercely protective mode but he was also smiling more and seemed lighter and happier.

Nikolai's expression turned serious for a moment. "You don't know what you stand to lose until you finally have it all. A wife? A son?" His eyes turned dark with ferocity. "I'll burn this fucking city to the ground before I let anyone harm them."

That wasn't hyperbole or an empty statement of bravado. He meant it. There wasn't a throat he wouldn't cut to keep Vivian and the baby safe.

Reaching out to tap the table in front of Alexei, Nikolai said, "You'll understand that soon enough, I wager."

"I don't know about that," Alexei nervously answered. "Marriage and children? That's not for me."

Nikolai seemed surprised. "Then you'd better cut Shay loose," he advised. "That's the type of woman who wants a husband and a family. She's not the type that will be happy with expensive trinkets and a posh apartment for very long."

It was a warning that Alexei couldn't shake even after Nikolai left and Zoya returned to help him pick out some jewelry for Shay. As he examined different watches, he conceded that Nikolai had only affirmed what he had always known. Shay deserved better than what he had offered her, but he wasn't sure he could give her anything more.

Marriage? Children? He didn't know the first damned thing about being a husband or a father. His own miserable childhood hadn't taught him anything useful. Then again, neither had Nikolai's or Ivan's and they both seemed incredibly happy. Things weren't always perfect, but they were making it work.

Could I do that? He honestly didn't know. The thought of failing Shay, of disappointing or hurting her, turned him inside out. Maybe it was better to have her for a little while and then set her free. Yet even as he tried to convince himself that was the right thing to do, he could hardly breathe. The idea of another man swooping in and taking Shay away from him hit him like a punch to the gut.

"So that's a watch, necklace and bracelet for everyday wear. Would you like to look at something special?" Zoya placed the items he had chosen on a velvet-lined tray. "I have some new designs that haven't been put out onto the showroom floor yet."

"Let me see what you have." The idea of gifting Shay with something truly spectacular appealed to him.

Zoya unlocked a safe and produced three different covered trays that she placed on the table. She carefully revealed the jewelry sets on each one and described them. "This is 18k rose gold with pink sapphires. I'm really pleased with this one. I think I might do more rose gold this year."

"It's very pretty." Alexei thought it was the sort of jewelry that would look beautiful on Ivan's wife, but it wasn't right for Shay. His gaze slid to the next set on offer, a spectacular display of white diamonds and platinum, but it was the final set that really caught his eye. "Are these yellow diamonds?"

"Aren't they gorgeous?" She gingerly picked up the cascade necklace and draped it around her neck to show it off under the lights. "This was hands-down my favorite piece to design this year. I chose to keep the earrings simple so the main focus is on the necklace."

"It's perfect." He didn't even bother looking at the sky high price tag. All he could think about was how incredible the white and yellow diamonds would look against her gorgeous skin. "I'll take it."

But as he left the jewelry store with his neatly wrapped packages, Alexei couldn't shake the feeling that diamonds simply weren't enough.

CHAPTER TEN

"**S**HAY, I'M GOING to the store." Stas poked his head into the master suite where I sat waiting for Kylee to model her next design. "That front door locks behind me and it doesn't open again until I get back. Understood?"

"Yep."

"If you need anything call me, okay? If I don't answer, call Alexei."

"Got it." I thought he was going way overboard. Here in Alexei's apartment, I was perfectly safe. No one could get onto this floor without one of the keycards and the two keys were currently in Stas and Alexei's wallets. "We'll be fine."

"I'll be back in less than an hour."

"All right. Bye."

"So what do you think about this one?" Kylee announced as she paraded out of the master bathroom and modeled one of her designs. She walked the length of the bedroom and circled back. The camisole style of the top and the feminine flounce suited her thin frame. "I was a little worried about the length but I think I'm sold on this mid-thigh hem."

"It looks really good," I agreed. "That fabric is amazing." I touched the shiny metallic dots printed on the black background. "It reminds me of fireworks."

"It's fun, right?" She gave a whirl and laughed. "Speaking of fireworks, I want the whole story about you and Alexei. Now that your bodyguard is gone, you can tell me all the juicy details."

I sat down on the bed and leaned back against the mountain of pillows. "There are no juicy details."

"Bullshit." She flopped down next to me and wiggled into place. "The guy came to your rescue, brought you to this million dollar apartment and *nothing* happened? Come on, Shay. I know you're, like, a Super Virgin, but you expect me to believe you weren't the teeniest, tiniest bit tempted by that hot Russian?"

"I was tempted, but after what Lalo tried to do to me?" I touched my neck and felt the bruises there. "I really wasn't in that kind of mood, you know? Alexei is always so respectful toward me and gentle. He was careful with me last night."

"If I ever see Lalo, I'm going to run over him with my truck." She made a sad face and cautiously traced one of the ugly bruises. "He's such a piece of shit. It's too bad I broke it off with Eli. He and the rest of his MC brothers would have put the hurt on Lalo for this."

"Are you kidding me? Lalo has a hundred heavily-armed drug dealers and gang members on his team. I don't want anyone to get hurt because of me. It's bad enough that I put Alexei in this position."

"Honey, that man would have come running if you had stubbed your toe. I know I've teased you about the way he watches you, but I'm being serious now. It's clear to anyone who has ever seen you two together that he's head over heels for you. After last night, what other proof do you need?"

I didn't dare believe Kylee. It would hurt too much if she was wrong. "I kissed him last night," I finally admitted. "And then he kissed me this morning. Like *really* kissed me."

"I knew it!" she exclaimed triumphantly. "And then?"

"And then nothing," I said with a shrug. "He went to work."

"Well, maybe that's for the best after this," she said, gesturing to my neck and cheek. "Slow and steady has always been your preferred mode. It's always steered you right in school and money so it's probably the best choice for a relationship." She hesitated before asking, "I mean, that is what this is, right? You two are dating now?"

"I don't know," I confessed with a rush of emotion. "I don't know what he wants or expects. He said this apartment was for his mistress, right? You know, like his kept woman or lover or whatever. But then he told me that it's been vacant since February so I thought he was trying to tell me that he's been waiting for me or maybe he wants something different this time."

"But?"

"But then last night, before we fell asleep, he made it pretty clear that he sees me as just his next mistress." I bit my lower lip and tried to ignore the ball of disappointment clogging my throat. "I told him I didn't know the first thing about being a mistress. He gave his list of ground rules, kissed me and left."

She winced with sympathy. "That's pretty cold."

"Right? It's like there's this wall," I said while drawing one in the air, "between him and everyone else. Last night, he asked me what I wanted. I swear it was as if he was afraid to ask for what *he* really wanted."

"What? Like it might make him too vulnerable? Because I could *totally* see that from him," Kylee commented knowingly. "That man is driven by some powerful need to be successful and wealthy. He's all battle-hardened from his years working on the streets. Can you imagine how hard it must be for a man like that to let his guard down? To let someone like you inside? To put his heart at risk?"

The disappointment and fear dissipated as I listened to Kylee. "If I hug you right now, I'm going to squeeze the air right out of your lungs." I laughed and let all that pent-up stress escape. "You are seriously the best friend who ever lived."

"I know," she said and jokingly polished her nails on her dress. "I am pretty fucking amazing."

"You really are."

"You know," she said, leaning back against the pillows, "this is probably why he's so drawn to you, Shay. You two are exactly alike. You've always been afraid to get involved with a man because you saw the way your mother got knocked around and the way she let her boyfriends hurt you and Shannon. You've always been driven to be something great, to be somebody, to break away from your humble beginnings, and I bet it's the same for Alexei. He's been in prison and ran the streets for a Russian mob boss. God only knows what he's seen. I'd be damned afraid of falling in love, too, if I had seen how truly terrible people can be to one another."

Everything Kylee said made sense. "But how do I get through to him? Because, Kylee, I really, really care for him, but I can't be just a mistress. I can't be this pretty little thing he dresses up in jewels and parades around town. I need to matter."

"You do matter, Shay. He's just fooling himself if he thinks he can keep you locked away up here like a fairytale princess. Deep down inside, he knows you aren't kept woman material." She sat up suddenly, as if a thought had struck her. "You need to be the best damned mistress he's ever had. You need to show him what he'll be missing when you walk away." She climbed off the bed and crossed the room to grab her cell phone. "Because you do have to walk away, Shay. At some point, if he doesn't give you what you deserve, you have to get up and walk out."

"I know," I murmured sadly. "I thought about that all morning. It's so tempting to get caught up in this fairytale he's offering, but that isn't real life."

"No, it's not." She tapped away at her phone. "Okay. Seriously, you would not believe how many articles there on how to be a kept woman! This is wild, Shay."

"No." I pushed off the bed and shook my head. "I'm not playing by those rules. If I'm going to do this, I'm doing it *my* way."

"Yeah, but these women are like professional about it, Shay. They have tips and tricks and—"

"No. He told me that he wants me, just as I am, so that's what he's going to get. Me. Simple, quiet, unadorned me."

"That's all well and good," she said, tossing aside her phone, "but what are you going to do about the sex? Because last time I checked you've only rounded second base and that was when you flipped out on Luke Garcia the night we graduated high school and he stuck his hand in your panties."

"That wasn't the only place he stuck his hand," I muttered

unhappily. "It *hurt*."

"He was a jerk. You shouldn't have let that one bad experience put you off sex forever. There were so many great guys you dated in college. They would have been good farm team sex partners, you know? Now you're in the big leagues, and you've never even hit a base run!"

"It's too late for what-ifs, Kylee. I'll just have to figure it out as I go."

"If I had to guess, Alexei is one of those one-in-a-million lovers. Let him take the lead."

I laughed nervously. "Like I have any other choice!"

"Maybe we should watch some—"

We were interrupted by my ringing cell phone. The sound of my sister's ringtone had me flying out of the bedroom and racing through the living area to reach my phone in time. I snatched it off the counter and answered in a breathless rush, "Hello? Shannon?"

"Shay!" She sobbed my name. "Oh my God! Are you okay? Please tell me you're okay!"

Sagging with relief upon hearing her voice, I leaned against the counter. "I'm okay."

"I heard about what happened to you last night, about what Lalo did to you." She wept. "I'm sorry, Shay. I never meant for any of this to happen. We just thought… We never… It wasn't supposed to go this way."

My earlier anger with her vanished. "It's all right. I know you didn't mean for me to get hurt."

"But you did," she sobbed. "You did, and this is all my fault."

"It's too late for that, Shannon. We don't have time for

this. Where are you?"

"I'm hiding out in a hotel in Pasadena."

"Pasadena?" I was already calculating how fast I could get there. "Where is Ruben?"

"I don't know." She started crying again. "He went out to get some money, but he didn't come back."

I had a bad, bad feeling about that. "Listen, Kylee and I are going to come get you. Okay?"

Appearing beside me, Kylee nodded vigorously as she tugged on her boots and slipped into her jacket. She raised her voice, "We'll drive all night if we have to, Shannon, but we'll get you out of Texas. We can hop on the interstate and get her to New Orleans."

"I'll need money, Shay. I'll need to go underground and stay off the radar."

"I'll get it. Just hold on and wait for us, okay?"

"Okay. I love you, Shay. Please be careful."

"I will be." After hanging up, I glanced at Kylee. "Where the hell am I going to get cash this late on a Saturday after-noon?"

"Do you have your checkbook in your purse?"

"Yes. Why?"

"We'll go see Abby at Kirkwood's Pawn. She'll give you a fat chunk of cash. She knows you're good for it." Kylee grabbed my arm when I started to run for the door. "Shay, are you sure you want to do this?"

"What are you talking about? Of course! She's my sister. She's scared. She's alone. She needs me."

"Yes, she does, but you promised Alexei you wouldn't leave the apartment."

My heartbeat pounded against my eardrums as I realized I had to choose between my sister, my flesh and blood, and the man who had risked his life to save mine, the man who had offered me protection and security, the man I had been secretly in love with for almost a year.

"If I don't help Shannon get out of Texas, they'll kill her. Nikolai Kalasnikov sat right here in this kitchen and told me that last night. Shannon is a dead woman if she stays here." My heart broke as I accepted that I was going to ruin everything with Alexei even before it had really begun. "There's no choice here, Kylee. I have to save my sister."

"Then we need to move," she urged and thrust my hoodie into my hands. "We need to get out of here before Stas gets back."

Like a couple of spies trying to escape a covert operation, we took the stairs down eleven floors rather than risk running into Stas. By the time we reached the parking level, we were breathless and promising each other that we would take up CrossFit because we were so weak. Somehow we managed to avoid seeing anyone in the garage but that didn't stop Kylee from racing out of there like a bat out of hell in her truck.

"This is one of those times where you really want to thank your lucky stars we've networked so much," Kylee said as we pulled into the parking lot across the street from Abby Kirkwood's pawn shop. "Bet you never thought all those business major mixers we went to would lead to this."

"No, I sure didn't." I hopped out of the front seat of her truck and waited for her to join me before dashing across the street and into the shop.

Thankfully, it wasn't very busy. There were a handful of

customers milling around the place, most of them in the electronics section. I had hoped to run into Marley, my neighbor and a longtime employee of the pawn shop, but I didn't see her anywhere.

"Shay! Kylee!" Abby Kirkwood stepped out from behind the jewelry counter to come over and give us big hugs. "It's good to see you! Are you here to pick through my vintage handbags again?"

"Oh, don't tempt me!" Abby had some really fantastic fashion items come into the shop. I had been lucky enough to grab a vintage Chanel 2.55 last Christmas for a steal. "But, actually, um, I was hoping you could cash a personal check for me." I didn't see any reason to beat around the bush. "I recognize it's asking for a big favor but—"

Abby smiled knowingly and slid her arm around my shoulders. "Come over to the window."

Kylee stayed behind to look through the showcases of jewelry while I walked with Abby to the bulletproof windows at the rear of the store. Leaning close, Abby whispered, "I heard about your sister. Whatever you need, it's yours."

"Thank you, Abby," I whispered right back and blinked away grateful tears. "I feel bad asking, but all the banks are closed so—"

"It's not a big deal. I know your check is good." She squeezed my shoulder. "I'll even give you a break on the interest," she teased with a playful wink.

While Abby unlocked a door and entered the reinforced and protected cashier area, I walked down to the open window and began filling out a check. I hesitated when I got to the amount. How much would Shannon need to survive in a new city? How long would she be unable to work? I made a hasty calculation and wrote out the five figure amount. I decided not to think about how long it would take me to earn all of that back. My sister's life was worth every penny in my bank accounts. I would give them all to her if it meant she would stay alive.

Abby glanced at the check after I pushed it through the small opening in the bulletproof window. She didn't even blink at the amount. "I'll have to do a mix of big and small bills. Is that okay?"

"Yes, it's fine. Whatever works for you, Abby."

"All right. Hang on. I'll be right back." She disappeared into a locked room where I assumed they kept their safe.

I glanced back to see Kylee inspecting gold chains. It wasn't the type of jewelry she liked to wear so I suspected she was looking for something to use in a clothing design. Feeling anxious and exposed, I looked around the shop, counting and recounting the customers. I didn't recognize any of them, but the paranoia gripping me made me sensitive to every glance.

"Okay," Abby said as she reappeared at the window with a stacks of bills still wrapped in their bank yellow, purple and brown bank bands. She counted it out for me twice before placing the money inside shopping bags. "Can I see your ID, please?"

"Yes." I slipped it through the small window. While I waited for her to record the necessary information, Kylee wandered over and joined me. "I guess you didn't see anything you wanted?"

"Nah," she said and then nervously looked over her shoulder. Moving closer, she whispered, "There's some guy watching us. Don't look back!" She hissed when I started to turn my head. "Brioni suit? Bruno Magli boots? This guy isn't part of Lalo's crew or those backwoods skinheads. I can't see any tattoos on his hands or neck. I don't think he's part of the Russian crew either, but he looks dangerous and familiar."

Mouth dry, I smiled at Abby who gestured toward the locked door after pushing my ID back at me. "Let me come around and meet you. I'll have one of my security guys walk you out to your vehicle."

"Shit," Kylee whispered frantically. "That guy is coming toward us. Keep walking. Keep walking."

Just as Abby stepped onto the main floor, she looked behind us and broke into a wide grin. "Besian! I didn't know you were stopping by today!"

"I thought I would come into the store and browse." His raspy voice carried an accent that was quite unlike Alexei's. When he stepped into view, I noticed that Kylee's dangerous description fit the man perfectly. He wasn't as tall as Alexei or as muscular, but there was a menacing, intimidating air about him. My internal alarms went crazy. I needed to get away from this man and quickly. "I never know what might catch my eye."

"Uh-huh," Abby dryly remarked. "Marley's not working this weekend so your eye will just have to keep on wandering." She pressed the bag of money into my hands. "Take care of this."

"I will." Surprised by the weight, I held it close to my chest.

"Shay, Kylee, do you two know Besian? He's, um, a very successful local businessman," Abby said with obvious amusement. "But we won't talk about what type of business he's in because this is a family friendly store."

Besian laughed. "You make it sound so scandalous, Abby. They're just clubs, and it's only dancing." He turned his full attention to me. "I haven't had the pleasure of meeting Shay, but I think we have a good friend in common."

"Oh?" I asked weakly, already knowing the answer.

"Alexei." He studied me closely. "I have to admit I'm rather surprised to see you." His gaze flicked around the store. "Is Stas waiting for you outside?"

"That's none of your business, Mr. Strip Club Owner," Kylee interjected forcefully, "and we've got somewhere to be." She put her hand between my shoulders and propelled me toward the exit. "See you around, Abby."

"Wait! Let me get a security guard—"

"No need," Kylee said quickly and pushed me forward. "We're fine."

"Thank you, Abby," I called over my shoulder as Kylee hustled me out of the store. When we hit the street, I glared at her. "That was rude!"

"Fuck that guy," Kylee grunted. "I remembered why he looked so familiar to me. He's a loan shark, Shay. He used to run a book for the Albanian mafia thugs over at the Black Eagle Club. He's one of the bastards who used to own my dad's debt. He took our boat and our car and my horse." She hurried across the street at my side. "He's one of the reasons Daddy put that rope around his neck in our barn."

"Shit, Kylee." I hated that such awful memories had been dredged up for her. She had been fifteen when her father had hanged himself in the barn where she had kept her beloved horse—the horse he had been forced to give to Besian only a few days earlier. "I'm so sorry."

"It's not your fault. Nobody made Daddy gamble or embezzle. He did that himself." She wrenched open her truck door and hopped inside. As she cranked the engine, I buckled my belt. "But assholes like that made it too easy. They took advantage of him when he was down. They kept feeding him credit because they knew they could collect on all his collateral, even after he died."

As she hit the gas, Besian stepped out of the pawn shop, a cell phone pressed to his ear, and watched us drive away. Never one to go quietly, Kylee actually rolled down her window and shot him the finger. "Vulture!"

"Oh my God! Are you crazy?" I twisted in my seat to see the gangster's shocked reaction as she punched the accelerator and tore down the busy road. "You just sat here and told me that guy is affiliated with the Albanian mafia. Are you seriously trying to pick a fight with someone like that?"

"I'm not afraid of people like that anymore." Kylee gripped the steering wheel tightly. "I'm over being pushed around by criminals."

Still aghast at the trouble she had probably made for herself, I pulled my phone out of my purse and called Shannon. She didn't answer so I texted her for the name of her hotel and the address.

Hey! We have the cash. We're headed your way. Be ready to leave as soon as we get there. What's the address?

"Why isn't she answering?" I asked, worry edging into my voice.

"Maybe she's almost out of battery. Maybe she's in the

shower. Maybe she went out to grab something from a vending machine." Kylee reached over and gave my hand a reassuring squeeze. "Don't panic. I'm sure everything is okay."

"I hope so."

A few seconds later, my cell phone chirped with a message alert.

"What's she say?" Kylee asked as she merged onto the loop.

"She's at the Spanger Motel." I opened a map app on my phone and punched in the name to get directions. "Take the loop to 225."

"We'll have to grab 146 to get up to Baytown and then hit the interstate to take us into Louisiana," Kylee said, already thinking five steps ahead. "It's nearly five, and it's getting dark. It's going to be a long drive."

"We'll trade off behind the wheel."

My phone started to ring. It was Stas. I ignored the call, but guilt gnawed at me. Staring out the window, I chewed on my thumb. "Alexei is going to be so angry with me."

"Yep." Kylee didn't even bother trying to convince me otherwise. "I would suggest you wait to call him until we cross the state line. By the time we get your sister situated in New Orleans or Baton Rouge and make it back to Houston, he'll cool down."

"No, he won't." My stomach churned violently as I accepted the truth of the situation. "I said I trusted him. I told him I would stay put and let him protect me."

"Yeah, you did. He swore to protect *you*. He didn't say shit about your sister. He can't expect you to sit in that apartment, living the high life, while your sister gets her throat slit by some cartel hitman."

I ran my thumb up and down the screen on my phone. "What if there's another way? What if he can help her?"

"You need to stop second guessing your decision, Shay." Kylee glanced away from the windshield and held my gaze. "You told me what happened last night with Nikolai. As far as Alexei's old family is concerned, Shannon is as good as dead. If you call Alexei, if you tell him where she is, do you really think he's going to choose between his old mob boss and you?"

"He won't betray me. He's not like that."

"No, he probably wouldn't, but at what cost?" Kylee bit her lip and shook her head. "You're his mistress, his girlfriend. *Sort of.* You're not his wife. The loyalty he owes you doesn't come close to what he owes Nikolai. You're a bright, shiny new thing in his life. That history he has with Nikolai? That shit goes way back, Shay. Can you imagine what Nikolai will do to him if he finds out that Alexei knew about your sister? That he helped you get her out of the city?"

A shudder rocked me right to the core. "I don't want Alexei to get hurt." Thinking of her safety, I added, "I don't want you to get hurt either."

"We'll be fine."

I couldn't tell who she was trying to convince more—me or her.

"He'll forgive you," she insisted. "He'll forgive you for this."

Feeling sick, I sadly murmured, "No, he won't."

"Don't say that."

"It's the truth. That wall he built around himself? The one I was telling you about earlier? The same things that made him build that wall are the same things that will make it impossible for him to forgive me for this."

Alexei was such a complicated man with a dark and complex history. The rules he had given me this morning weren't so much about control as they were about testing my commitment to him. Like me, he had spent a lifetime being disappointed and hurt by people. Unlike me, he had chosen to protect his heart by closing it off and only allowing himself to indulge in these romantic arrangements with mistresses, these easily controlled emotional transactions.

I was officially the worst mistress in the history of the world. I hadn't even lasted one full day. He would see my decision to go after Shannon as a betrayal of everything he had done for me. I was flinging it all back in his face, and he would punish me by turning his back on me and sending me away.

"Don't get all weepy on me." Kylee playfully punched my arm. "I'm all out of tissues, and I don't want you getting snot on my new dress."

"I'm not going to cry." I blinked rapidly to clear away the wetness threatening to spill onto my cheeks. An hour ago, we were excitedly discussing my blossoming relationship with Alexei but now? I was sitting here bereft and silently planning its funeral.

Angry with Shannon, I clenched my hands together on my lap. I would get her out of the state and give her a clean start, but then she was on her own. I couldn't keep doing this. I couldn't allow her to drag me down again. This had to be the final time.

Glancing down at the navigation screen on my phone, I motioned to the next exit. "Get off at Center Street."

Kylee followed my directions until we found the rundown motel. "Holy shit," she exclaimed as we turned onto the property. "I've seen motels in horror films that looked nicer than this."

I couldn't argue with that observation. Only one light worked in the parking lot. From what I could see, the moldy green paint was peeling and half of the windows didn't have drapes. My jaw dropped when I saw a hooker walk out of a room still fastening her shirt. Her skirt was hiked up around her thighs so high I could see that she wasn't wearing underwear. She combed her fingers through her stringy hair before sliding into the front seat of a car driven by a man I could only assume was her pimp.

"Jesus," Kylee breathed in horror. "This place is a cesspool!"

"Let's just grab Shannon and get out of here."

"Which room is she in?"

I looked at her message and then at the numbers on each door. "Fourteen. Over there."

"Hang on." Kylee swung the truck wide and backed into the closest spot. "We aren't sticking around here any longer than necessary."

"Stay here." I flicked off my belt and tossed my phone onto the dashboard. "I'll grab her, and we'll get the hell out of here."

Kylee looked around nervously. "Hurry. This place gives me the creeps!"

I practically jumped out of her truck and ran to the motel door. I knocked twice. "Shannon! Shannon, it's me. Come on! Let's go."

The rattle of a door chain met my ears. A moment later,

the door opened—and a pair of hands grabbed the front of my hoodie and hauled me inside the motel room. Before I could scream, a hand cruelly slapped over my mouth, muffling the sound as I kicked and flailed wildly. With a rough shove, I was thrown face down on a bed. The scent of mildew and much, much worse filled my nose. I pushed off the dirty, smelly blanket and lost my balance, rolling off the bed and onto the floor.

As I tried to make out the shapes in the darkened room, I heard a tussle near the door. Kylee was thrown through the door and fell onto the stained carpet. She scrambled toward me on hands and knees. Eyes wide, she latched onto my side and gripped my hand.

And then the very last face I ever wanted to see appeared in the open doorway.

With his broken nose and black eyes, Lalo looked like he had been in one hell of a fight. The hatred etched into his face warned me not to make a sound or any sudden moves. My heart stuttered when I noticed he held the same paperweight I had used to beat him unconscious. The door slammed closed behind him, and he smiled evilly at us.

I thought the fear I had experienced last night had been the worst of my life, but I was wrong. I experienced a whole new level of terror as I realized that Lalo and his two henchmen were going to kill us. There was no chance of escape tonight.

We were going to die in this dirty, filthy motel—and Alexei would never know how much I cared about him or how sorry I was for disappointing him.

CHAPTER ELEVEN

"**G**IVE HIM AN extra grand on the trade," Alexei said as he glanced at his watch, "and get this deal closed. He's had Jake tied up on this sale for six fucking hours." He hated these doctor pricks who swaggered onto the sales floor with big dreams and even bigger demands but maxed-out shit credit.

"Do you want to keep this one on our lot?" Peter asked as he handed off the signed deal sheet to the salesman working with the surgeon.

"No. Get it detailed and serviced. Send it over to James. We move a lot of BMWs at that dealership. It'll be a fast turnaround."

"Done."

Alexei's gaze moved to the windows. The sun was setting, and the clouds seemed heavy and ominous. With the threat of bad weather and the ongoing issues with Lalo's crew, he didn't think taking Shay out to a restaurant was a good idea. Still wanting to do something special for her, he decided he would pick up a nice dinner for them. He patted his pocket in a search for his cell phone so he could ask her what she would like, but his phone was missing.

I must have left it upstairs. On the way to his office, he was sidetracked twice to give approval for two more deals. His instincts had been right. The afternoon and early evening had been busy and productive.

When he walked into his private space, he could hear his phone vibrating and rattling on his desk. He hurried across the room and snatched it up. "Hello?"

"Where have you been?" Stas demanded. "I've been trying to reach you for almost an hour!"

Not liking Stas' tone, he asked, "What's wrong?"

"She's gone."

Alexei thought he must have misheard. "What? Who is gone?"

"Shay," the street soldier said with exasperation. "I came back from the store, and she was gone."

Alexei's stomach dropped, the swooping sensation threatening to drop him. Had she been kidnapped? Had she opened the door for a delivery and been grabbed? "Did someone break into the apartment? Did someone get by the concierge and the security?"

"No. I went down and asked to see the security tapes. I found Shay and that fucking troublemaking friend of hers running down eleven flights of stairs. They raced out of the parking garage." He exhaled with disgust. "I knew that blonde was bad news. I could smell it on her."

"Where are you now?" Alexei didn't want to panic. *Stay calm. Think this through.* "Did you go by her house?"

"I went there first. The neighbors haven't seen her since she left yesterday. The nosy lady who lives a few doors told me where Kylee lives. One of her kids is doing a fundraiser and Kylee's address was on the form."

"And?"

"The girls aren't here."

"Fuck." Fury surged within him, blackening his heart with smoldering soot. "I told her to stay put. What the hell is she doing?"

"I don't know, but I haven't got the first fucking clue where I should go now. I've called her six times. She isn't answering."

Was she dodging Stas' calls or was she unable to answer because something terrible had happened to her? Alexei's anger was quickly replaced by fear. If she had been caught by Lalo's men…

He scoured his memories of their conversations for a hint of any place she might go. She didn't have many places to hide. "I don't care who you have to call or what it costs. Get men out on the street looking for her."

As soon as the phone call ended, he immediately dialed Shay. When she didn't answer, he dialed again and gathered up his things. He flew down the stairs, pausing just long enough to tell Peter that he was in charge for the night, and raced out to his SUV. He let the Bluetooth connection pick up his third try as he left the lot and stayed on the line to leave a voice message.

"Shay, I don't know where the hell you are, but you need to call me right now. This isn't a fucking game. You're in danger. Call me."

Without any idea where to go, he hopped onto I-45 South. Dread pooled in his belly as he watched the setting sun. The thought of Shay wandering around the city at night with that fluorescent target painted on her back was enough to make him ill. *Where is she?*

His phone began to ring, and he punched the button on his steering wheel to answer it. "Yes?"

"Alexei, it's Besian."

"Look, Besian, I don't have time—"

"You'll make time for this," the Albanian boss interrupted. "You will never guess who I just saw at Kirkwood Pawn."

His gut clenched. "Who?"

"That luscious dark-eyed beauty of yours," he said with what could only be described as glee. "My men told me she was pretty, but they were wrong. That woman is stunning. I can see why you wanted to keep her a secret."

"Cut the bullshit, Besian. Is she still at the shop?"

"No. She was in a hurry to leave with that rude little friend of hers. She had a bag full of money. Probably ten or fifteen grand. Easy."

"What?" Alexei's mind raced. "Why the fuck would she need that much…?" His voice trailed off to nothing. Swearing, he slapped the wheel. "She's gone after her sister."

"I figured as much," Besian agreed. "Luckily, I had Jet with me as a driver. I sent him after them. He thinks they're headed to Pasadena. The last time he checked in, they were in Deer Park."

"*Blyad.*" In his mind, he quickly recalled a map of the city. All those years on the streets had given him a sixth sense for navigating the Greater Houston area. Spencer Highway was up ahead. If he got off the freeway and onto that smaller highway, he could get out to the Pasadena area quickly. "I'm heading that way. As soon as Jet gives you a location, call me."

"I will. I'm waiting for Devil to pick me up and then I'll

join the hunt."

Clenching the wheel, Alexei tried to keep his temper in check. He was furious with Shay for leaving the safety of the apartment, for ditching Stas, and running out on her own. *Why didn't she call me when she heard from her sister?*

"Because she doesn't trust you," he muttered angrily. Trying to ignore the pain in his chest, he didn't want to admit to the feelings that had him all twisted up inside. *Weak*, he silently berated himself. *She's made you weak.*

He tamped down his wildly vacillating emotions and walled them away in that cold pit he had mentally constructed years ago. He had no idea what to expect when he found her and needed to be able to think clearly. Later, when he had her safely back in the apartment and he was back at his own home, he would allow himself to sort through his feelings.

When his phone started to ring again, he answered it quickly. "Yes?"

"Jet says they just turned into a motel on Spencer. It's a shit hole. He spotted a couple of Hermanos parked at the tire shop half a block down. There's an SUV parked at the car wash that he recognizes. It's one that Ben modified for Lalo."

Jesus Christ. Whatever anger Alexei felt toward Shay evaporated in that moment. Did she have any idea that she was walking into a trap? Would she even know what to look for? After what had gone down with Lalo last night, that little bastard would be bloodthirsty for revenge. How much damage could he inflict in five minutes? In ten?

Desperation took hold. "Which motel?"

"Spanish Trail. Be careful, Alexei. We're stuck behind a fucking accident. The rain is heavy this way. We'll get there as fast as we can."

Alexei smashed the accelerator and dialed Stas. He didn't even utter a syllable before Stas talked over him.

"Yeah, I know. She's at Spanish Trail. Jet called me. I'm almost there. Less than ten minutes."

"I'm closer."

"Don't do anything stupid before I get there. Nikolai will kill me if anything happens to you."

The line went dead, and Alexei zoomed around a truck. A light drizzle was falling now, slicking the road and forcing him to be more cautious. Wrecking a few blocks from the hotel wouldn't help Shay.

When he raced onto the parking lot, he hastily sized up the situation. There seemed to be twenty rooms. Maybe half of them were rented and probably to drug addicts or whores. Whatever was seen or heard tonight would be easy enough to cover up with a liberal application of money—or so he hoped.

He spotted the SUV that probably belonged to Lalo. Those shiny rims practically blinked at him. The idling truck was a different story. Did it belong to Shay's friend?

The sight of a heavy-set guy in a black T-shirt rolling into the middle of the lot caught his attention. A moment later, Jet appeared from behind a parked car. He wiped at his bleeding mouth before giving the downed man a good kick. Two more men ran at Jet, but the gangster just laughed and leaped back into the fray. Alexei threw his SUV into park and bailed out of the driver's seat. He rushed toward Jet but the Albanian enforcer shook his head. "I've got this."

A woman's scream erupted from behind a closed door. A heartbeat later, he heard Shay shouting, "Don't touch her!"

Tunnel vision overwhelmed him. Not fearing what he might find on the other side of that door, he ran toward it and planted his foot right above the handle. With a crack, the door slammed open and right into the back of one of Lalo's thugs. Using the momentum of the kick, Alexei rushed forward, grabbed two handfuls of leather jacket and swung the thug right out into the now pouring rain. He rammed the bastard head first into the tailgate of the idling pickup and dropped him to the pavement.

Spinning around, he stormed into the hotel room and faced off with another one of Lalo's henchmen. He blocked the punch that flew at his head and buried his fist in the other man's paunchy belly. The guy he fought was younger but stupid and unskilled. He was no match for Alexei who had years of fighting experience on his side. A couple of punches to the ribs and a knee to the face finished off his opponent. He threw him right out the open door.

Amid the squeal of tires that signaled Stas' arrival and backup for Jet who was still fighting those three men, Alexei whirled back to face his next opponent—and found himself staring right into the barrel of Lalo's gleaming Five-seveN. The irony of the moment was laughable. Years ago, he had helped move shipments of the Belgian-made handguns from Russian to Mexico. South of the border, they called the armor piercing ammunition used in the guns *matas policias*—cop killers.

"No!" From the space between the dingy beds, Shay jumped in front of him, putting her small, fragile body between his and Lalo's.

"Shay!" He tried to grab her and throw her out of the way, but Lalo pointed the gun right at her head. Alexei froze, suddenly fearful that any move would provoke the wild-eyed kingpin. *What the hell is she thinking? He'll kill her.*

"You are not going to hurt anyone else that I care about," she stubbornly stated. "I'm the one you hate. You punish me."

Hush, ptichka. He desperately wanted her to be quiet. Lalo was clearly a man on edge. He had a crazy gleam in his eye, and Alexei feared there was more going on here than just a man hell-bent on revenge against the young woman who had humiliated him.

"Oh, I'm going to punish you," Lalo promised. "Maybe I'll start right here." He swung the gun toward Kylee who was crouched on the floor next to him, her nose bloodied and her eyes wet with tears. She flinched, as if expecting to be shot, and then he swung the gun back toward Alexei's head. "Or maybe I'll spray your boyfriend's brains all over the wall."

"No!" Shay stepped forward, right toward Lalo, and drew his aim. "You are not going to hurt them."

"I'm going to hurt you," Lalo promised, his evil gaze raking Shay from head to toe. "All night long," he added nastily. "Fuck it. Maybe I'll record it so Alexei can see how a real man makes a woman scream."

Infuriated that Lalo would even think to threaten such a thing about Shay, he growled, "The only motherfu—"

"If you let Alexei and Kylee walk out of here right now," Shay talked over him, "I'll go with you. I'll walk out of here without a fight, and I'll do whatever you want."

"No!" He couldn't allow her to prostitute herself, to bargain with her body and her life, for him. "You aren't going anywhere unless it's with me."

"Be quiet, Alexei!" Shay glanced back at him, her dark eyes

pleading with him. "It's my turn to save you."

"This *pinche* Russian was dead the moment he decided to take you from me," Lalo snarled. "You're mine. You've always been mine."

"I was never yours," she retorted with disgust.

"You. Are. Mine." Lalo annunciated each word. "You were bought and paid for when Shannon took my money to fund this little scam of hers."

Alexei watched as Shay's shoulders slumped with shock. He couldn't quite believe it either. Suddenly this whole fucking mess was more twisted and tangled than he had ever imagined.

"Fine," Shay said with resignation. "You're right." She seemed desperate to please Lalo now. "I'm yours. I'm all yours." She said the words the wannabe kingpin had wanted to hear for months and months. "Just let Alexei and Kylee leave, and I'll be yours as long as you want."

"No!" Alexei couldn't allow it. He would take a bullet to the brain before he let Shay leave with Lalo.

But he wouldn't have to make that choice. He had been so intent on watching Lalo and that damn gun that he hadn't noticed Kylee inching along the edge of the bed until she was directly behind the drug dealer.

In a flash of blonde hair and with a banshee's scream, she hefted up a blood-stained crystal paperweight and slammed it right into the back of his head. When Lalo lurched forward, Shay rushed him and grabbed his wrist, shoving the gun's muzzle toward the ceiling.

"Shay!" Alexei cursed loudly and raced to intervene. "*Fuck!* No!"

Kylee swung the paperweight high and cracked Lalo on

the side of the head this time. Just then, a bright bolt of lightning hit nearby and lit up the room with a shocking blast of light. A heartbeat later, a crack of thunder shook the paper-thin walls of the motel. In that same instant, Shay threw her knee into Lalo's stomach—and the gun fired.

The eardrum piercing crack of the bullet momentarily deafened him. Amid the muzzle fire, he spotted a burst of blood. His heart stuttered painfully in his chest. He grabbed Shay by the shoulders, picking her up and swinging her out of the way and onto the closest bed. Unable to breathe, he frantically looked her over. There was blood all over her skin. His fingers slipped in the messy stuff, but he couldn't find the source. "Where did the bullet hit you?"

"I'm okay!" she shouted hysterically. "I'm okay. It's not me."

There was blood on her face, neck and chest but it wasn't hers. Before he could fully process how the blood had gotten on her, Kylee screamed again. Like a woman possessed, she hit Lalo with the paperweight, this time between the shoulder blades. The drug dealer slumped forward and flopped onto the ground.

Blood poured out of his mouth and pooled on the carpet. In the struggle, Shay or Lalo had caused the weapon to fire and a bullet had ripped through his face, entering just under his chin and taking off most of his lower mouth and jaw. Lalo's limbs shuddered wildly, as if he were having a seizure, and then he expelled a ragged, noisy breath. Had the bullet lodged in his brain? Had the multiple blows from the heavy crystal paperweight finally killed him?

With a sob, Kylee dropped forward onto her knees. The

crystal teardrop hit the carpeted floor with a loud *thunk*. Shay scrambled off the bed and half-crawled, half-stumbled her way to her best friend. She wrapped her arms around Kylee and rocked her like a mother would a small child.

"Holy shit."

Alexei whirled around at the sound of Besian's voice. The boss stood in the doorway of the motel room, his hair wet from the rain and the hem of his neatly pressed trousers soaked. Devil, his face a ruined mess of scars, stood behind his boss and looked on with little emotion. Like Sergei, Devil had been hired for his size and strength and his ability to intimidate with nothing more than a glare.

Without taking his eyes off the mess in front of him, Besian ordered, "You need to get her out of here, Alexei. Right now. I'll deal with the mouthy blonde."

"Oh, no you won't!" Shay growled like a mama bear, her voice so filled with hatred that it stunned Alexei. "You aren't touching Kylee. You already killed her father. I won't let you hurt her."

Completely confounded by Shay's accusation, Alexei shot his attention to Besian who seemed totally thrown by the charge. He tilted his head, studying Kylee's face, and then recognition dawned. "You're Monty Benson's little girl. The one with the horse."

"I'm not so little anymore." Kylee stood with Shay's help and roughly wiped at her wet nose and cheeks, smearing Lalo's blood on her skin. "And you took my horse, you asshole."

Besian didn't take kindly to anyone calling him names. "Your father was the asshole who got into debt he couldn't service. No one made him bet on those games or races. No one made him come into the club to play cards. He put that rope around his neck because he was a failure as a provider, a husband and a father. Don't even think about putting that shit on me."

"Boy, you're real tough, aren't you? Stealing a little girl's horse? Having your thugs beat up my daddy? Taking the life insurance money and the house and driving a sick woman and her kid into a homeless shelter. You're just some big fucking gangster hero, aren't you?" Kylee stepped over Lalo's bent legs and raised a fist as if to strike Besian. "I've already taken out one gangster tonight. Maybe I'll go ahead and make my score an even two."

Shit. Alexei moved in front of Kylee, shielding her from Besian's wrath, and Shay grabbed her friends arm, desperately pleading for her to hush. "She's had a shock," Alexei insisted. "She doesn't know what she's saying."

"She better learn to keep that mouth of hers shut unless she wants Hector Salas to send one of his hit squads after her—and Shay," Besian added with a threatening edge.

Because there were years of friendship and history between them, Alexei understood Besian wasn't actually threatening to hurt Shay. The boss was trying to put the fear of God into Kylee, to make her shut up and get in line.

"She'll be quiet." Alexei cast a warning glare at Kylee who eventually nodded stiffly.

Devil edged his way into the room and unfurled the tarp. "Lorik and Jet have the Hermanos boys tied up and tossed in the back of Bek's Tahoe. I sent Lorik with Bek to stow them away at the safe house until you decide what to do with them."

Alexei wondered if those five men understood their lives

were held in Besian's hands now. What the Albanian boss would do was anyone's guess.

"Do you have any cash on you?" Besian patted his pockets. "Because I'm clean out."

"I have a little," Alexei said, already reaching for his wallet. "But not enough to buy the silence of an entire motel."

"I have money." Shay rubbed at the drying blood spattered on her cheek. "It's on the front seat of Kylee's truck. It should be more than enough."

Besian glanced at Jet who lingered in the doorway waiting for orders. "Get the money and bring it to me. Then take the loudmouth home and sit on her until I've secured her safety."

Wordlessly, Jet left the doorway and returned a few moments later with the sack of cash. He handed it to Besian and then motioned for Kylee to join him. She walked toward him on shaking legs. Jet tugged the black hood on her jacket over her blonde hair. It was a surprisingly gentle action from a man with a ruthless, cold-hearted reputation. "Can you drive?"

"Yes."

"I'll follow you, but we're taking the back roads. Got it?"

"Yes." She glanced back as if seeking Shay's approval.

Shay nodded encouragingly. "I'll be okay. Go."

When Stas' familiar face appeared in the doorway, Alexei grasped Shay's upper arm and guided her toward the street soldier. "Get her out of here. Take her back to the apartment. Get her cleaned up, but don't let her out of your sight."

Seemingly stunned by his callous regard, Shay blinked at him. "Alexei—"

He ignored her entreaty and kept his gaze focused on Stas. "Take away her phone. I don't want her contacting anyone."

"Come on." Stas clasped her hand and tugged her out of the dingy motel room. "Move."

The hurt etched into her beautiful face bothered him, but he wasn't going to show her an ounce of kindness or softness right now. She had deliberately broken his rules. She had put not only her life but her friend's in danger. Lalo Contreras was dead, and there would be hell to pay for this, from Hector Salas and the cartel, from Diego and the Hermanos street gang loyal to Lalo, from Nikolai for upsetting the fragile balance of power in the city and from the police who would no doubt start sniffing around when Lalo's disappearance became public knowledge.

"I'll deal with this. You contact Nikolai." Besian thumbed through the cash in the bag. Alexei hated to even think about how long Shay had worked to earn that money. "You should get out of here before anyone recognizes you."

He cast one final glance at Lalo's now lifeless body before heading for the door. When he reached it, he paused and looked back at the room. "Where is Shannon? Shay must have come here looking for her so where is she? Was she ever here?"

Realizing they might be one girl short, Besian looked under both beds and then in the bathroom. When he came back, he said, "It looks like she went out the back window. The glass is broken, and there's blood." He waved a cell phone. "She left this behind. Do you want to give it to Shay?"

He took the phone from Besian and tucked it away in his pocket. Looking around the room, she said, "If you find anything else that belonged to Shannon in this room, trash it."

His instructions given, Alexei put his head down and ventured into the stormy night. The rain was cold and miserable and so heavy, but the lightning and thunder were useful. With all the noise of the storm, the fight and gunfire seemed to have gone unnoticed by the other occupants of the rat hole motel.

Sitting behind the wheel of his SUV, he inhaled a long, steadying breath. He needed to find a pay phone as far away from here as possible. Nikolai's fury would know no bounds tonight. All of the pain and punishment for this would land squarely on his shoulders. He had claimed Shay as his—and now he had to pay the price.

CHAPTER TWELVE

S HAKING FROM THE cold rain and an adrenaline rush, I pulled my arms out of the sleeves of my hoodie and crossed them against my chest. I burrowed down into the warmth of the slightly damp fabric and wondered if I would ever stop trembling. Stas' wild driving wasn't helping any. Every time my teeth stopped chattering, he would veer around another vehicle or stomp the gas even harder. "Can you please slow down? You're going to wreck and kill us!"

"Oh, now you're worried about people getting killed, huh?" Stas glared at me. "Jesus Christ, Shay! Do you have any idea what you've done? God, if you were my girlfriend, I would toss you across my lap and beat your ass for this stunt!"

"If you were my boyfriend, I'd throw myself out of this moving car before I let you hit me!" I slid closer to the door, almost as if threatening to do it.

"I didn't mean it like that." Stas reached over and smacked the lock button on the doors, just in case. "Don't be childish."

"Don't be such a jerk! Do you think I wanted this to happen?"

"I don't know what to think about you anymore. I thought you were a smart girl. I thought you understood what Alexei was risking for you. I was wrong. You just shit all over everything he did for you. Do you have any idea what Nikolai is going to do to him? What Hector Salas is going to take from him?" Stas shook his head. "You've ruined Alexei."

The guilt I felt for helping take a life, even if it was the life of a miserable, cruel man, was nothing compared to the new guilt I experienced upon fully accepting my responsibility for hurting Alexei. What would Nikolai do to him? Would he have him beaten up or worse? And what would Hector Salas want? Money? His businesses? His home?

Fresh tears burned my eyes. Flashes of the fighting and the gunshot and the horrible gurgling noise Lalo made as he died tormented me. I still couldn't make sense of any of it. How had everything gone so bad so fast?

Shannon was still missing. My best friend had helped me kill someone. Alexei was going to lose everything he had worked so hard to build. It was all my fault.

You've ruined everything. Suddenly, I was ten-years-old and cowering in a corner as my drunken mother screeched at me for running off her latest boyfriend. It didn't matter that I had caught him trying to hurt Shannon or that he had tried to put his hands in my shorts. She had been so furious with me. The awful things she had said still cut deeply, the wounds unhealed and forever sore and bleeding.

I rolled my shoulders as the phantom strikes of the extension cord she had whipped me with made my skin crawl and sting. *Stop thinking about that. It's over. It's done. She's gone. She can't hurt you anymore.*

Too soon, we arrived at the parking garage. Stas pulled into the second assigned spot and shut off the engine. He looked me over and then shrugged out of his leather jacket.

"Put this on and cover up that blood. Pull up your hood again and keep your face down. You've got Lalo's blood all over your face."

"I know." The stickiness and the coppery stink of it turned my stomach. Desperate for a shower and a good scrub, I did what Stas told me and followed him up to the apartment.

After grabbing a trash bag, he marched me right into the master bathroom and started a hot shower. "You know the drill. Strip. Put everything in here. Toss it out the door when you're done."

"Even your jacket?" I asked, eying the expensive leather with guilt.

"You got his blood all over it. It's going to the incinerator."

"Stas, I'm sorry for—"

"Spare me," he meanly retorted. "Just get clean." He tossed the garbage bag onto the vanity and walked toward the door. Pausing there, he turned back to me. "Didn't I tell you that you needed to keep him happy? Didn't I warn you?" He exhaled roughly. "I would strongly suggest you spend the time you have thinking about all the ways you can make this up to him. Or at least figure out a way to keep him happy tonight," he added. "Because if he puts you out on the street? You won't make it to sunrise, Shay."

His warning given, Stas stalked out of the bathroom. The door slammed behind him, and I jumped. Heart racing and stomach churning with anxiety, I stared at my reflection in the mirror. The bruise on my cheek was now decorated by dried specks of blood. Every time I breathed, I smelled the acrid stink of the gunfire. My eardrums still ached from the close proximity of the shot.

Again and again, I replayed the moments before the gun fired. Lalo's finger had been curved against the trigger. My hands had been wrapped around his wrists. He had either jerked the trigger when I kneed him in the stomach or when Kylee whacked him with that paperweight he had been using to threaten us. Technically, he had shot himself but I feared that was a thin, weak defense.

What happened if someone decided to talk to the police? Alexei, Stas, Besian and his crew—they were all highly recognizable men in the underworld. I feared a taste of hush money would be just enough to whet the appetites of the motel occupants. They might resort to blackmail or worse to get more money.

Would the police believe me if they picked me up? Would I even survive a night in lockup while the facts were sorted out? There were probably a dozen cops on the cartel payroll and twice as many inmates in the county jail ready to stab me in the neck for what I had done.

You're panicking. Calm down. You can't change anything now. It's done.

I shrugged out of Stas' jacket, peeled off my hoodie and jammed both into the garbage bag. The rest of my clothes followed. Naked and shivering, I stepped into the shower and let the hot water blast my skin. I couldn't get to the soap fast enough. I scrubbed and scrubbed until my skin was raw and sensitive and then shampooed and rinsed my hair three times just to make sure every single strand had been stripped of Lalo's blood.

While I let conditioner soak in, I touched my forehead to the milky white marble and closed my eyes. *Where are you,*

Shannon? Are you still alive? I figured Ruben had ratted her out and Lalo had gone after her. She had either escaped before he could grab her or she had been kidnapped and hauled away before I had arrived.

Remembering what Lalo had said before he died, I wondered how deep the identity theft scam really went. I suddenly understood why he hadn't fought to protect Ruben after the scam had been uncovered by Mr. Mueller. He must have known that it was only a matter of time until his connection was made public, either by a panicking Shannon or a scheming Ruben. Letting Mueller's men hunt them down and kill them meant they would be silenced quickly.

But it hadn't worked that way. Ruben and Shannon had escaped. I suspected Lalo had planned to use me as bait to draw Shannon in and silence her. That hadn't worked either. It had all blown up in his face—literally.

Done with my shower, I dried off and wrapped up in the towel. I poked my head out of the bathroom door and discovered Stas leaning against the door frame, texting someone. He glanced up at me and then back down at the screen. "Where is your phone?"

"Kylee's truck," I answered, still hiding behind the door.

"If you're lying to me—"

"I'm not!" Shocked by the way he was treating me, I snapped. "Oh my God, Stas! Yes, I made a huge mistake, but I'm still the same girl who watched reality TV with you last night. I'm the same girl you pinched with chopsticks at lunch when I stole one of your dumplings. I'm the same girl you taught to count to twenty in Russian this morning."

"And I'm still a street soldier who takes orders and does

what he's told," he retorted simply. "You made your choice. These are the consequences."

"So what? I'm a prisoner now?"

He shoved his phone in his pocket and leveled a no-nonsense look my way. "I'd be very careful using that argument with Alexei. This so-called prison of yours is a hell of a lot nicer than the ones he knew."

Neatly put in my place, I swallowed nervously. "Will you please step outside so I can get dressed?"

"You have five minutes. Bring that bag of clothing to the living room."

After Stas left, I tried not to break down into tears again. He was right. If this was my punishment, it was so much better and easier than what I probably deserved. I was safe here, and no matter how angry Alexei was with me when he came back, he would never hurt me. He was probably going to yell but he wouldn't put his hands on me.

I quickly slipped into the only nightgown that Alexei had packed for me. Feeling underdressed, I picked up the Markovic MMA hooded sweatshirt I had been wearing last night and put it on, leaving it unzipped and wearing it like a short-hemmed robe. I grabbed the bag of soiled clothing and left the bedroom.

Stas actually glanced at his watch as if to reinforce that the rules were different now. He took the bag of clothing from my hand and gestured to the kitchen. "You should eat something. Toast, juice, an orange—you need to put some food in your stomach. After that, we're going to talk about your alibi. Then you're going to sit quietly on the couch and wait for Alexei. Understand?"

"Yes." I understood perfectly. The bright promise of a future with Alexei and the glimmer of friendship I had hoped to share with Stas had been shot to hell with one stupendously bad decision.

PARKED IN THE rear section of a junkyard owned by one of Besian's people, he waited for Nikolai. He wanted to be anywhere except the Pasadena area, but he had been given his orders so he here sat. Glancing at the clock, he made a face. How much longer was this going to take?

Alexei drummed his fingertips on the dashboard and scanned his dark surroundings. The heavy rainfall obscured most of his vision. Already on edge, he stared hard at the shadowy shapes of stacked and crushed cars and tried to decide if he was really seeing movement or not. It would be so fucking easy to ambush him.

He wasn't a man prone to nervousness but tonight? Shit, his stomach was in knots! This was two nights in a row Nikolai had been dragged away from Vivian to deal with problems caused by Shay or her sister. If the boss wasn't in a very charitable mood, it could be disastrous for her.

The longer he sat here, the more Alexei worried. What if he had been sent here by the boss so Stas could take Shay to some remote location? What if the boss double-crossed him and handed her over to Hector Salas as a peace offering?

He wouldn't do that to you. Stop fucking panicking.

But if Alexei was wrong, if his trust in Nikolai had been misplaced, he would never forgive himself for the cold, callous was he had sent her away.

Just when he started to despair, a pair of headlights bounced off the dented grille of a car. He leaned forward and spotted first one SUV then another and another and another. When it was all done, there were two SUVs parked on either side of his and four surrounding them. He recognized the guard vehicles driven by Danila and Ilya as well as the Escalade that had brought Besian and the silver Land Rover that Nikolai preferred but the ice white G-Class was unknown to him.

Street soldiers poured out of their vehicles, some of them taking up positions facing out toward the junkyard to keep watch and others hustling to open doors for their bosses. Boychenko hopped out of driver's seat of the Land Rover and quickly popped open an umbrella. He hurried to Alexei's door and rapped his knuckles on the glass.

Answering his summons, Alexei stepped out into the rain and grimaced as cold, dirty water rushed around his ankles. Boychenko shot him a *you are so fucked* look before gesturing with a jerk of his head. Shielded by the umbrella, Alexei crossed the short distance to Nikolai's vehicle and slipped into the passenger seat open next to the boss.

A moment later, the driver's door opened and Besian slipped behind the wheel. As Besian combed his fingers through his wet hair, the front passenger door opened and none other than Hector Salas slid onto the empty seat there. Surrounded by some of the most dangerous men in the city, Alexei wondered if he was going to end up shot and tossed into the trunk of a car.

"You really know how to celebrate a man's birthday, Nikolai," Hector Salas remarked with a dry laugh. Not yet thirty, the former cartel enforcer had carried out a coup against

Lorenzo Guzman with ruthless efficiency. Reputed for his Machiavellian intelligence, he had the good looks of a model and the well-honed body of a fighter. It was no surprise men had been willing to betray their leader for him. He was the sort of man other men emulated and followed. "I didn't even have to blow out my birthday candles to get my wish."

Thrown by Hector's comments, Alexei glanced at Nikolai. The harsh expression on the boss' face warned him to keep quiet.

"This wasn't the way I wanted this go down," Nikolai finally said. "We needed more time to groom your man and get the pieces in place before Lalo was neutralized."

As if sharing Alexei's confusion, Besian twisted in the driver's seat for a better look at Nikolai. "When did we greenlight a hit on Lalo?"

"We didn't," Nikolai replied. "Not yet."

"Is there something I'm missing?" Besian asked, clearly exasperated.

"That raid on his house for that dog fighting ring put him on my shortlist, but finding out he tried to rape some girl backstage at a concert?" Hector picked at something on the lapel of his jacket. "That was the last straw for me. Brutalizing women isn't part of my rulebook. I won't allow it."

Alexei's estimation of the young drug lord rose a few notches.

"Look, my business is moving product to the right salesmen and keeping my customers happy and satisfied. That's it," Hector said. "Lalo was always a greedy little fucker, skimming and taking and running his side deals. I turned a blind eye to it when I needed him to take on Lorenzo, but when that was done, I warned him to cut that shit out and walk the line. He thought he was smart enough to run his games behind my back, but I see everything. This bullshit with Ruben and the identity theft? It's too much heat. This is the kind of shit that will send the FBI and INTERPOL right up my ass. Fuck. That." Hector slashed his fingers in front of his throat. "That *puto*? He needed to go."

"We didn't bring this to the council because the hit was never supposed to happen here." Nikolai's irritated glare made the fine hairs on the back of Alexei's neck stand right on edge. He had seen men on the receiving end of that look before and it never ended well. "We were going to wait until Lalo was in Hector's territory, down south of the border. Romero was going to take care of it."

"It's easier to spin my version of the tale down there." Hector turned in his seat and smirked back at them. "But I guess your girlfriend wanted to become part of the underworld legend."

"Shay didn't kill him," Alexei insisted. "Neither did her friend. They were trying to defend themselves. Lalo shot himself while he was fighting Shay for control of the gun."

When Nikolai glanced at Besian for confirmation, the Albanian boss nodded. "It looked that way to me and Devil. The gun was still in Lalo's hand when he fell. His finger was wrapped around the trigger. So, technically, Lalo iced himself."

"Technically isn't going to sell very well on the streets," Nikolai warned. "Those five men you picked up at the hotel? The ones you have tied up in your warehouse? They have big mouths and loud voices. All we need is one street thug with a soft spot for Lalo. He can make this very messy, very fast."

"They'll see things my way—or they won't see at all." Hector jabbed two fingers toward his eyes. "When they find out how much money Lalo was hoarding while they were starving on the streets? Their loyalty will vanish." He snapped his fingers. "So you let me deal with them."

"What do we do about the power vacuum?" Besian unwrapped a jawbreaker and tossed it in his mouth. "The last thing we need is violence on the streets."

"There won't be a vacuum," Nikolai promised. "Hector is going to talk to Diego as soon as we're done here. He's the obvious choice and the best man for the job. He's worked his way up from the streets to the top of the Hermanos hierarchy. He understands the men who work for him, and he's earned their loyalty and their trust."

"He's quiet," Hector said. "He's not flashy. He believes in discipline. He'll keep things quiet and calm."

Seemingly reassured, Besian visibly relaxed. "What do you need from me?"

"Show your support to Diego," Nikolai ordered. "Keep your men in your territory. The last thing we need is an incident while things are unsettled."

"I'll look up Nickel when I leave and get him on board," Besian offered. "Do you want me to hit up Mueller?"

Nikolai shook his head. "I'll handle him."

"What about the motel?" Hector turned his attention to Besian. "Do you need my help with the cover up?"

"It's done—and it cost me nothing," Besian remarked with a bit of amusement. "Alexei's girlfriend took care of that."

"What?" Nikolai shifted in his seat. "What does that mean?"

"It seems that Shay was headed to the motel to help her sister escape the city." Alexei hadn't asked her for the details but he had assumed that to be the most likely scenario. "She was able to get her hands on ten grand at Abby Kirkwood's pawn shop. By the time she arrived at the motel, her sister was gone and Lalo was waiting for her. She offered her cash as hush money."

"Where is the sister?" Nikolai asked the question on everyone's minds.

"We don't know," Alexei admitted. "There was blood in the bathroom. She left her phone. We think she ran."

"Or Lalo kidnapped her and his men dragged her away somewhere before Shay and her friend got there," Besian proposed an alternative theory. "We just don't know."

Nikolai blew out a frustrated breath. "That's a loose end that needs to be clipped—and fast."

Before Alexei could even try to plead for Shannon's life, Besian said, "I'll take care of her. Leave it to me."

Something about the way Besian so quickly leapt at the chance to have that job bothered Alexei. Was there something else going on with Shannon that he didn't know?

"What's the punishment for Shay and her friend?" Nikolai put the issue that concerned Alexei the most right on the table. He held his breath as he waited to see what the boss would suggest. "My vote is that they get a pass. These were extraordinary circumstances."

"I want this to end here," Hector interjected firmly. "These two girls? I want them to walk. Untouched," he clarified. "They have my guarantee of safety and protection. This shit ends tonight. There's been enough bloodshed in this city. Let's end the year on a better note than we started. Yeah?"

"Yeah." Besian rolled the jawbreaker around his mouth, knocking it into his teeth. "Let's put this to bed."

"Then it's settled," Nikolai declared.

Sagging with relief, Alexei leaned back against his seat while the three bosses talked out a few minor details. Hector exited the vehicle first. Besian left a short time later. Alone with Nikolai, Alexei blew out a pent-up breath. "I know that sorry doesn't even come close to apologizing for all of this."

"It's done, Alyosha. Leave it." He rapped his knuckles on the window, signaling Boychenko. "Put on your seatbelt. We're going for a ride."

Not liking the sound of that one bit, Alexei did as told. He glanced back at his still running SUV and wondered if the damn thing would even be there when they got back. Waiting for Nikolai to say something, he stared out the window and tried to figure out where they were going. Very quickly, he realized they were headed back to the motel.

As if reading his mind, Nikolai said, "Since Kostya is still out on vacation, we had to call in some professional help for this one."

The Professionals. Four anonymous brothers who proffered their services to Houston's underworld and the city's elite. The Collector. The Fence. The Cleaner. The Liquidator. They were men who were whispered about but never seen. Even the evidence of their crimes was nearly impossible to spot.

Up ahead, the blink of red, white and blue lights from emergency vehicles caught his attention. A police cruiser blew by them, the siren squawking so loud he winced. Wondering where it was headed, Alexei leaned forward for a better look. A violent wave of orange streaked the dark night sky and took his breath away.

The Spanish Trail motel was totally engulfed in flames.

Jerking back, he glanced at Nikolai in shock. "Why?"

"What else could we do? There were too many unknowns and too much risk. Was Shay's blood on the carpet? Was the friend's? What about the sister? What the hell were we going to do with Lalo's body? That isn't a death we can sweep under the rug, Alyosha. This isn't a man that can just disappear."

Nikolai had his lucky lighter in hand now. He flicked it opened and closed as he gazed out the window at the destruction he had wrought. "This was the best choice. Tomorrow, when the sun is up and the flames are out, they'll find Lalo's body and the right gun and that's it."

"The *right* gun?"

"We have a weapon in our possession that was used during Hector's coup earlier this year. The bullet that killed Lalo tonight was removed and his gun was destroyed. The other gun was used to fire some bullets into the body and the wall. The cops will trace these rounds and the gun left at the scene to the deaths earlier this year." He brushed his pant leg as if to sweep away lint. "It will keep them busy chasing their tails while we deal with the transition."

It was all discussed so calmly. Alexei had been out of the life long enough that he had forgotten how blithely Nikolai decided these things. Who lived. Who died. Who to frame. It was a simple act of arithmetic for him.

"But the fire, Kolya," Alexei protested. "It's dangerous. The motel guests—"

"No one died in this fire. The brothers took care of it. It was all very clean."

"God, I hope you're right." Alexei cringed as Boychenko slowly glided through an intersection and away from the frantic scene. Another fire truck raced toward the blaze. He prayed no firemen were hurt tonight. That was a guilt he didn't want on his conscience or Shay's. "Fire is nasty business, Kolya."

"It's never my preference," the boss admitted, "but these were extenuating circumstances. Once Besian took a step back and truly considered the situation, he knew there were too many risks if he tried to haul that body out of there. We're just lucky this all happened in the dark, in a shitty part of town, and in a rainstorm where it's easier to manage the spread of the fire."

"What happens to the people who were living in that motel? Where do they go now?"

"John Mueller is about to get some new tenants in his apartment complexes." He snapped his lighter closed and dropped it into his pocket. "You can expect that bill soon."

Alexei swore under his breath but accepted the out of pocket costs for housing those people were a small price to pay. Considering how badly this might have gone for Shay, he didn't dare complain. It seemed uncouth to call tonight's events a stroke of luck, especially when one man was dead and someone's business had just been burned to the ground, but he silently called it that.

"I swear our lives were never this complicated before we started welcoming all these women into our inner circle," Nikolai grumbled. "Who would have thought falling in love would be so fucking complicated?"

Out of habit, he started to correct Nikolai, to laugh at the very notion that he was head over heels in love with Shay, but the reality of what had happened in the last forty-eight hours slapped sense into him. There was no point in lying to himself or trying to convince anyone else that what he felt for Shay was anything less than love. It had crept up on him so slowly over the last year that he hadn't even recognized the subtle shift from infatuation to friendship to love.

"Vanya, Dima, Yuri, Sergei, Kostya, you, me... Who's next? Danny?" Nikolai laughed as if he had just heard the funniest joke ever. "Hell, maybe it will be Ten!"

Up front, Boychenko snorted with amusement. Alexei shook his head at the outlandish idea. "I don't think there's a woman alive who can tame Ten."

"Stranger things have happened," Nikolai replied. "So—is it true? Did she really step in front of a gun for you?"

Alexei's heart stuttered as the memory of Shay jumping in front of him flashed before his eyes. "Yes, she did."

"She must love you very much."

"I don't know about that." Alexei didn't dare hope that Shay's action was proof of her love for him. "She's a good person. She would protect anyone from a bully like Lalo."

"Yes, but she protected *you*. She saw you fight for her last night. She knows what you're capable of doing, but she still stepped in front of a possible bullet for *you*. That was an action spurred by the heart," Nikolai touched his chest, "not the head."

"She should listen to her head more," he said, suddenly uncomfortable talking about all of this with Nikolai. "I'm not the type of man who knows what to do with a woman's heart."

"You'll learn." Nikolai stretched out his legs. "I know what you're thinking. You think no one could possibly love you because of the terrible things you've done, but you're wrong. We're all worthy of love. Even the worst of us," he murmured. Their gazes clashed in the shadows of the rear seats. "A woman like Shay is an extraordinary find, Alyosha. It takes a big heart to love men like us, and those big hearts are easily damaged. She fucked up tonight. That's not up for debate— but we've all made big mistakes in our lives. We've all done things we wish we could take back."

They drove in silence, all three occupants of the Land Rover thinking of their misdeeds and blunders. When they pulled into the junkyard, Nikolai inhaled a deep breath. "Go home to her. Scold her if you must but show her love tonight. She needs to feels safe again. Her entire life has fallen apart in the last two days. She needs you to be her rock. Give her something to cling to," he urged. "A woman who will throw herself between you and a gun? That's a woman you should deny nothing and give everything. Even if you lose everything tomorrow, Shay will walk beside you."

The boss's powerful counsel made Alexei's head spin. As he drove away from the junkyard he couldn't stop thinking about everything Nikolai had said. Though he was still angry with Shay for taking such a risk and for defying him, he understood why she had made the decision to go after her sister. Hadn't he done far, far worse and stupider things to save Ivan or Nikolai in the past?

When he entered the apartment a short time later, he discovered Shay seated at the island in the kitchen and staring at a bowl of melted ice cream. Stas sat on the opposite end of the polished slab, his expression hard and his arms crossed. Frosty was the first adjective that came to mind. The cheerful, easy friendship that he had witnessed between the pair last night had vanished.

"What's going on here?" Alexei dropped his gym bag on the floor and glanced back and forth between them. Shay lifted her head, and her swollen, red eyes helped him fill in the blanks. Thinking of the cruelty she had known as a child, he cast a sharp glance at Stas. "What did you do to upset her like this?"

"Nothing," she answered quickly. As if terrified to make either of the men in the room angry, she smiled brightly but it didn't reach those beautiful eyes of hers. "We're fine. How…how are you?"

"No, Shay. We aren't doing this." Alexei slashed his hand through the air. "You and I have always been honest with each other. You don't ever have to pretend with me."

Shay swallowed and bit her lower lip. She gripped the edge of the counter so tightly he feared her thin, delicate fingers would snap. "I'm sorry, Alexei. I'm so sorry."

The words were whispered so softly he barely heard them. Certain they were on the verge of some new development in their relationship, he glanced at Stas and hooked his thumb back toward the door. "Go home."

Stas gathered up his things and the garbage bag of ruined clothing. "She left her phone in the friend's truck. I can pick it up tomorrow."

"That's fine." He followed Stas to the door and locked it behind him. When he returned to the kitchen, he took a deep breath and finally met her anxious gaze. Hating to see her looking so wounded and afraid, he insisted, "I'm not the men who abused you when you were little. I'm not going to hurt you. There is nothing for you to fear from me. *Ever.*"

"I'm not afraid of that," she assured him, her voice steady but soft. "I know you won't hurt me…even though I nearly got you shot and dragged you into that nightmare at the hotel."

"I dragged myself into this mess, Shay." He combed his fingers through his hair and expelled a loud breath. "Look, I *am* angry with you for risking your own life. You had no business in that motel! You had no business going after your sister! You know what these people are like. You're a very smart woman. Why the hell would you go after Shannon like that?"

Blinking rapidly, she said in a tremulous voice, "I thought I could get there quickly and get Shannon out of Texas. We were going to take her to Baton Rouge or New Orleans."

"You were going to drive to Louisiana? With your sister? The girl who has a price on her head?" His blood pressure shot through the fucking roof. "And then what, Shay? What was the plan?"

She shrugged nervously. "I don't know. Leave her there with some money and burner phones, I guess. She would have to figure out the rest herself."

"And what did you think I was going to do when I came home and you were gone?" Had she considered the rampage that would have followed that discovery? The damage he would have done to this city to find her?

"I was going to call you and explain everything."

"That call would have come too late. Stas had already

called to tell me you were missing. I was gunning for Lalo. Because that's what I assumed, Shay. I assumed he'd gotten his dirty fucking hands on you—and I was ready to kill him."

Her eyes widened at the strident tone of his voice. Had she truly doubted his reaction? Didn't she understand how far he would go for her?

"You can't do that, Alexei." She was deadly serious now. "Promise me you will never cross that line for me."

"I can't. I won't. You're mine, and there is nothing I won't do to keep you safe."

She exhaled a shocked breath. Then, shaking her head, she said, "If I'm yours, why did you send me away with Stas? Why didn't you come with me?"

Remembering Nikolai's advice, he said, "I shouldn't have dismissed you like that, Shay. I shouldn't have sent you away from the motel without making sure you were okay. It won't happen again." He cleared his throat. "I know that you're sensitive about these things. I should have been more careful with you."

"No, Alexei." She shook her head. "*I* should have been more careful. After everything you've done for me, this was the way I repaid your kindness. I—"

"You don't owe me anything." He needed her to understand that. "This isn't a relationship built on debts and payments."

Her grip on the counter eased as she seemed to accept what he was telling her. "I should have called you, Alexei."

"Yes, you should have."

"I should have trusted you to help me again."

"That's what hurts the most." His admission seemed to

surprise her. "After everything we went through last night, you went off on your own instead of coming to me. You said you trusted me—"

"I do trust you!"

"Do you?" He wasn't so sure. "If you had trusted me, you would have called me the moment you heard from your sister."

"I trust you to be good to *me*, but I didn't know what you would do if I told you about Shannon," she tearfully confessed. "I'm sorry. I know how awful that sounds. I really do! But it's the truth. You promised you would protect me but Nikolai sat here last night and he made it clear that Shannon is dead to him. I couldn't take the chance, Alexei. I didn't want to force you to choose between helping me and being loyal to one of your oldest friends."

As she sobbed out her explanation, he finally grasped her position and her reasoning. He couldn't blame her or punish her or scold her for any of that. She was right. What would he have done if she had called him? He would have run to her side in an instant but Shannon? He would have tried to help her, but he wouldn't have crossed Nikolai to do it. It was an ugly, painful truth to acknowledge but there it was.

"But you still came for me," Shay murmured, almost in awe. "You came for me *again*, and you saved me."

"You don't need to keep testing me, Shay. I gave you my word. I will never break it."

Certain her reluctance to trust him completely would be the biggest stumbling block for their continuing relationship, Alexei decided to leave it for tonight. He might have discovered that he loved her, but she was clearly in a different place.

There was no point in rushing or pressuring her. He had waited nearly a year just to kiss her. He could wait as long as she needed for all the rest.

"I need to shower." He wanted to hold her, to feel her skin beneath his hands, but he was filthy from the mud and rain. "We'll talk more when I'm finished."

"May I come with you?"

It seemed to take a great deal of bravery for her to ask that. Sometimes she struck him as so incredibly naïve. He was beginning to question how much experience she actually had with men.

"I don't want to be alone. I know how silly that sounds but…"

"You're not silly." He held out his hand. "Come here, *ptichka*."

Shay glided toward him, her footsteps silent and light, and grasped his hand. Her fingers were cold, and her hand trembled in his. He was taken aback by the realization that she had been so afraid that she was shaking.

Had she been sitting here waiting and worrying that he would put her out on the streets? That he would leave her to fend for herself? That he would turn his back on her because she had made a bad choice and a stupid mistake?

Stas.

The answer came to him instantly. *Of course.*

The street soldier had probably been filling her head with all kinds of bullshit. Alexei decided he would set Stas straight in the morning.

Her fingers tightened around his hand, and she stepped into his personal space. She pressed her cheek to his chest and slid her other arm around his waist. His breath caught in his throat as she burrowed into him, seeking his warmth and protection. He encircled her and drew her in even closer.

"I don't know what I'd do without you, Alexei."

A choked laugh escaped his throat, the sound muffled by her thick hair. "After the last two days, I don't even want to think about what you would do."

She released him slowly and tipped her head back. Gazing up at him, she had the most vulnerable look on her face. The surge of affection he felt toward her left him reeling. But this wasn't simple affection anymore. Nor was it infatuation. No, it was something else. It was exactly what Nikolai had guessed.

He kissed her forehead and then backed away from her. "I need to get clean."

"Stas took my clothes from earlier. What are you going to do with yours?"

He glanced down at his messy pants and ruined shoes. "I'll have to get rid of them tomorrow."

"I'll go grab a bag for you."

He entered the bathroom and stepped into the private toilet area, locking the door behind him. When he was finished, he stepped out of the room and found Shay sitting on the counter. His appreciative gaze lingered on her crossed legs. The hoodie she was wearing had ridden up to mid-thigh and revealed an incredible swath of silky brown skin that he wanted to touch. Holding out the trash bag she had fetched from the kitchen, she seemed wholly unaware of the effect she had on him.

Standing in front of her, he toed off his shoes and peeled off his socks. He tossed them into the bag and then slipped out of his jacket. He hated to lose another of his favorite suits, but it had to go. They couldn't risk any evidence tying them to that motel. His belt and shirt followed. When he started lowering the zipper on his pants, he noticed the way her gaze flicked from his waist right back up to his chest. She seemed determined not to look.

Wanting to tease her a bit, he asked, "Aren't you the least bit curious?"

"About?" Her eyes were fixed on his face now.

"Whether it's boxers or briefs?"

She shot him a saucy look. "Knowing you? You're probably commando under those pants."

He laughed as he stepped out of his pants and dropped them in the bag. He gestured to his boxers as if to say, "See?"

She rolled her eyes and gave the trash bag a little shake. This time she let her gaze wander down his chest until it settled on his waist. There was no mistaking the way she was breathing a bit faster now. If he put a hand to her neck, he expected to feel her pulse pounding under his fingers.

He stripped slowly, drawing his boxers off in an effortless sweeping motion. He wasn't hard—yet—but he'd always been proud of what he considered his rather impressive offering to the women in his life. It struck him suddenly how very strange this was. Usually, he was the one sitting fully clothed while his mistress disrobed for the first time. He was always the one enjoying the strip show.

But, then, Shay wasn't a typical mistress, was she? It was no surprise she'd gotten the best seat in the house and her own private show tonight.

Naked as the day he'd been born, Alexei strode to the

shower and adjusted the knobs until he had the right tempera-
ture. He stepped inside the shower and felt the chill of the tile
under his feet. The hot water spewing from three showerheads
quickly steamed up the oversized space. He grabbed the bar of
soap he kept here and lathered it between his hands.

"Alexei?"

"Yes?" He spread soapy foam along his chest.

"Do you think Shannon is still alive?"

His hand stopped halfway down his stomach. He couldn't
lie to her. Not after everything they had survived in the last
two days. "I don't know, Shay. There was blood in the bathroom. She left her phone behind."

"A lot of blood?" She seemed afraid of the answer.

"No. If I had to guess? She probably cut herself trying to
get out that small window. I think she's still alive, and I hope
she's smart enough to lay low for a while. She has everyone
looking for her now."

"Even that Besian guy?"

"Everyone," he repeated.

"You two go way back?"

"Me? And Besian?" He took special care to clean his hands
and feet, not wanting any lingering blood or mud under his
nails. "We've known each other for years. Even before we
came to Houston," he added. "We ran in the same circles back
home."

"Oh." She didn't sound particularly impressed by that but
didn't press for more information. "Alexei, where is Tirana?"

"Albania." He glanced out the foggy shower door. Still
seated on the counter, she had her head down and seemed to
be drawing shapes on the marble. "Why?"

She lifted her head and met his gaze through the steamed up glass. "Stas said something yesterday about Tirana and Shannon. I wasn't sure what he meant."

Tirana? Shannon? Alexei had a bad feeling Stas meant that Shannon's secret buyer for the information she had stolen was none other than Zec. Which explained why Besian had been so helpful about finding Shay's sister!

"Tell me about Kylee and her history with Besian." He stepped under the nearest showerhead. "What the hell was all that back at the motel?"

She didn't answer him immediately. He suspected she was trying to sort out her loyalty to Kylee and her desire to be honest with him. Eventually, she said, "Kylee's dad was an investment guy. I'm not really sure what his job title was exactly, but he managed a lot of money for really wealthy people. She used to live in Carlton Woods in one of those stupid crazy huge mansions on the golf course there."

He grinned at her description of the area. That particular development was the ritziest in The Woodlands—and that was saying something. He had briefly considered settling there when he'd been in the market for a home, but his ties to Nikolai and the rest of his "family" had proven too strong to break. Now he lived a few blocks from the boss in one of the newer homes in Houston's most expensive zip code.

"Anyway," she continued, "her dad got into some trouble gambling and betting on horses and sports, I guess. He started stealing from clients, and the whole thing blew up in his face. Besian was the guy who came and took her horse, their vehicles, the boat and all of her mother's jewelry and paintings. Her dad was indicted a few days later and hanged himself that night." She got quiet. "Kylee found him swinging a rafter."

Alexei went still under the water. It was a horrible tale. "That must have been very difficult for her." Now he understood why Shay's friend had reacted so badly at the motel. "But she can't go around threatening him like that, Shay. He isn't like Nikolai. He doesn't make exceptions for women. He's hard—and dangerous."

"I think, deep down inside, she's still that scared but really angry little girl," Shay said. "She didn't just lose her dad and their home and the life she'd always known. Her mom was really sick when all that money trouble started. She had Huntington's disease."

He reached for the bottle of shampoo. "That's genetic, right?"

"Yeah, but Kylee doesn't have to worry about it. Her mom and dad used a donor egg to have her. They wanted a baby, but not the risk of the child inheriting her mother's disease."

Alexei wouldn't admit it aloud, but he was getting to an age where thoughts of children were occurring to him more and more often. Watching Ivan become a husband and Nikolai become a family man had awakened something in Alexei that he didn't quite understand. He had gone to visit Dimitri and Benny after the birth of their daughter, and holding that baby had sparked something unexpected in him. Not a desire to start a family, exactly, but a curiosity.

"Her mom was so sick when they got kicked out of their house. I met Kylee when she transferred into my school. They couldn't afford the tuition to the private school she went to, and they were living in a women's shelter here in Houston that was zoned for my school. We met in home economics. I had smuggled in a copy of *Vogue*, and she wanted to look at the dresses while I looked at the handbags and shoes. Within a couple of days, we were sketching outfits together and dreaming about owning a business someday." Her voice drifted off for a moment. "Her mom died a few weeks later, and my own mom split a few months after that. I think those experiences pretty much sealed our bond as friends forever."

Hearing that made him worry. If she considered Kylee a sister, what would she do to keep her friend safe? Would she get in between Kylee and Besian if those two went after it again? The thought of all the trouble their friendship could cause down the line had him vowing to schedule a sit down with Besian in the next few days. The Albanian boss needed to understand how far Alexei would take things.

Finished with his shower, he switched off the water and stepped out onto the mat. He grabbed a towel from the nearby shelf and wiped his face and hair before dragging it along the back of his neck and then securing it around his waist. He caught her staring at him. Recognizing that gleam in her dark eyes was easy enough.

She wants me.

Even though he ached to be with her, to connect in the most intimate way possible after everything they had survived tonight, he refused to be the one to make the first move. He didn't want any regrets, not after they had both waited so long to be together.

As if reading his mind, she held out her hand. "Alexei?"

It was an invitation he couldn't refuse. In three long strides, he was in front of her. She took his hand in hers and dragged him closer. Her other hand touched his chest, gliding over his skin until it stopped along the side of his neck. She pulled down gently, and her lips finally touched his in a gentle, seeking kiss.

But when her tongue shyly flicked at his, all thoughts of going slow, of taking this one step at a time, of doing this differently were incinerated. Not wanting to overwhelm her, he tore his mouth away, but she wouldn't have it. She peppered ticklish kisses along his neck and jaw and slid her hands to his shoulders. Every kiss, every touch, caused a wild flare of need.

"If you keep that up, I'm taking you to bed," he warned. He wasn't sure if she understood what that meant. He doubted she had ever been with a man who shared his tastes. Tonight, it might be too much for her.

She answered him by winding one slim leg around his waist and hooking her heel against his thigh. Leaning back and meeting his heated gaze, she said, "I'm ready."

With two softly spoken words, she shattered his control. Tangling his hand in her hair, he crashed their mouths together in a burst of pent-up desire. She mewled, that kittenish sound traveling through him and settling right in the bottom of his stomach.

Tonight? Tonight, he was going to give her exactly what she wanted and everything he needed.

CHAPTER THIRTEEN

I COULDN'T BREATHE. My heart was beating like a panicked hummingbird's. With shaky fingers, I clung to Alexei's broad, powerful shoulders as he kissed me like a man starving for affection. Maybe he was. Or maybe he was feeling that earlier rush of adrenaline fade after our harrowing experience at the motel. Did he crave the heat and touch of another person as I did?

Something had changed in him. Something I had said or done had flipped an invisible switch. I was finally seeing the passionate, dominant man that had always been hinted at but never revealed. I had given him the permission he needed, and now he was totally in control. I didn't think I wanted it any other way. Not tonight. Not my first time.

My first time.

Surrendering to the stab of Alexei's tongue, I whimpered softly and clawed at his bare back. A deep growling sound rumbled from his throat, and he picked me up off the counter. While our tongues danced, he guided my legs around his waist before settling his big, strong hands on my bottom. Holding me close, he walked toward the bedroom.

This is really happening.

I panted against his mouth and nipped at his lip. He repaid me for that little bite with a swat that left my ass stinging. I clenched my thighs, squeezing his waist and drawing another groan from him. He murmured something in Russian before unceremoniously dumping me on the bed.

"Alexei!" I squealed with surprise and excitement as I bounced on the mattress.

He threw back his head and laughed as I pushed up on my palms and waited to see what would happen next. He walked around the bed and turned on the nearest lamp, illuminating the room in a warm glow of light. Able to see me fully, he raked his gaze along my form and then dropped the towel wrapped around his waist.

I swallowed hard when I saw his cock. It was every bit as thick and long as I had expected, maybe even more. As if tired of watching me study him, Alexei crooked a tattooed finger and gestured for me to crawl toward the edge of the bed. I knew what he wanted even before he asked, but I wasn't sure I could satisfy him. The mechanics of giving head were easy enough, but I hadn't every actually done it.

When I reached the edge of the bed, I waited to see what would happen next. Should I tell him? Would he want to know that we were sailing into actual virgin waters here? Worried that he might stomp on the brakes, I decided to keep the status of my V Card a secret for now. I didn't want this night to stop. I wanted this. I wanted it with him.

Fake it. I could hear Kylee's voice in my head as I considered my next move. *Just fake it.*

Emboldened by desire and curiosity, I shamelessly grasped his shaft. Alexei growled and pressed into my hand, wordlessly urging me to stroke him. So I did. I slid my hand from the blunt tip all the way down to the base of him before gliding it back down again. Hot. Hard. Soft. Steel. I explored him with my fingertips.

Touching him like this, I had a better feel for his length and girth. A quiver of panic stabbed my stomach. There was no way around it. This was going to hurt. Even if I was one of those lucky girls who had a relatively easy first time, putting something this big inside me was going to an experience I would never forget.

But right now I was more interested in seeing how he would react when I licked him…

Leaning forward, I grasped the base of his shaft and swiped my wet tongue along his penis. Staring up at him, I sucked the tip between my lips. Alexei gazed down at me, his dark eyes smoldering, and his breath coming in sharp pants. I might not have the skills of his former mistresses, but he clearly enjoyed what I was doing. My confidence growing, I used my tongue to paint his shaft and then tried to suck him a little deeper this time.

Alexei let loose a loud groan of approval. "Open your mouth a little wider, baby." I relaxed my jaw, and he sighed. "*Da*. Yes. Like that."

He gathered my hair in one of his hands, drawing it to the back of my head, and gently thrust into my open and willing mouth. I tensed up, suddenly afraid he would take things too fast or too hard, but he was careful as always, reminding me yet again why he owned my trust. He wasn't going to hurt me. He wasn't trying to debase or degrade me or force me to do anything I didn't want or like.

Alexei took his time enjoying my mouth. His cock glided

across my tongue with slow, measured thrusts. He caressed my face with his free hand and continued to hold my hair with the other. Every now and then, he slid a little deeper, almost as if to test me, and each time I swallowed every inch he offered. Something about pleasing him, about making him groan and pant, invigorated and excited me. I liked knowing that I could make him feel like this.

"Look at me," he ordered in a strained voice. I glanced up at him. Lips stretched wide around his cock, I locked into his lascivious gaze. He pushed deeper into my mouth, so far back that I felt my throat start to tighten. A momentary quiver of panic rattled my core, but I shoved it down. *He won't hurt you. Relax. Feel. Enjoy.*

"Shay." His nostrils flared, and his breaths were heavy and fast now. "You look so fucking beautiful like this." He retreated ever so slowly, dragging his cock out of my mouth until just the tip remained. I tightened my lips around him, refusing to let him go just yet. He groaned and then said on a harsh breath, "Suck. *Da.* Harder. More."

I gave him what he wanted until it was too much. He drew back with a sharp intake, pulling free from my mouth and panting for air. Tangling his fingers in my hair, he hauled me upright until I was kneeling. He claimed my mouth in a fierce kiss. I spread my hands along his smooth, tattooed skin and finally gripped his shoulders, hanging on for dear life.

"Shay," he murmured in between kisses. He grasped the oversized hoodie and my nightgown and dragged them up and over my head. He tossed them over his shoulder, leaving me clad in only a plain pair of cotton undies. Whatever embarrassment I might have felt at being so sorely underdressed for the occasion, I quickly lost when I noticed the way he looked at me. That hungry, needy gaze left me trembling inside.

"Look at you." His muscular chest heaved with each breath as he gazed at my nearly naked body. He smiled, his mouth curving slowly as one of his hands reached for me. He traced a line from the dip of my lower neck to the valley between my breasts. His finger traveled to my left nipple, and I inhaled a shuddery breath as he circled my flesh, causing it to pucker and throb.

Alexei put a knee on the bed and cupped the back of my neck. Holding me at the nape, he titled my head back and skimmed his lips along the curve of my throat. I clutched at him, gripping his incredible biceps as he kissed and nibbled his way down my neck to my breasts. When he latched onto my nipple, I experienced a piercing jolt of delight that left my clitoris throbbing almost painfully.

He must have known what he was doing to me because his other hand slid down until he gripped the back of my thigh. He forced my thighs apart and pushed his leg between them. The sudden friction of his muscular thigh against the most sensitive part of me was too much. I tried to pull away, but he held me right there, silently daring me to move.

But I couldn't. I was too embarrassed to rub against him in the way I wanted most. This was happening so fast, and I was quickly realizing that I was way out of my depth here.

Alexei's mouth moved to my other breast. He suckled and grazed his teeth over me while kneading my bottom in his big hands. When Alexei pushed me back on the bed, I pressed my knees together to assuage the pulsing ache between my thighs. He grinned knowingly, his sexy smile making my stomach do wild flips.

Crawling toward me, he gripped the waistband of my panties and tugged them down my hips. I lifted my bottom to help him, and with one good jerk, he swished them down my legs. Completely naked now, I leaned back on my elbows and waited to see what he would do next. He sat back on his heels and idly stroked his shaft. Seeing his hand moving over his cock was a shock to me. He was so comfortable in his skin and seemed wholly unfazed by touching himself like that in front of me.

"Open your legs, Shay."

I gulped and did as instructed, slowly widening my thighs so he could see me.

He swore under his breath. "Use your fingers. Show me everything, Shay."

Fingers trembling, I reached between my legs and parted the lips of my sex. Slick with arousal, I glistened down there. My clitoris throbbed, and I couldn't help myself. I circled the aching bud with the tip of my finger, but it wasn't enough. It wasn't nearly enough.

Growling in Russian, he abandoned his cock and moved toward me. Dipping his head, he kissed the top of my left foot before skimming his lips up my calf toward my knee. He repeated the same kissing maneuver on my right leg and then peppered light kisses along my thigh up to my hip. His mouth danced across my lower belly, hesitating at my navel where he placed a noisy kiss that made me laugh, and then continued its trek down the curve of my hip and thigh to my left knee.

His mouth shifted course when he reached my knee. He dragged his tongue along my inner thigh. Lightheaded, I inhaled quick, shuddery breaths as his tongue moved closer and closer to that spot where I was throbbing and aching. I gasped when he swiped the length of my slit. He did it twice more before dotting a kiss right on top of my clitoris.

The heady sensation he evoked left me clutching at the covers and desperate for air. I wanted him to use his mouth on me even more, but I wasn't brave enough to ask. This was all too new, and I wasn't sure what to do or how to do it.

Alexei continued kissing his way up my body, across my stomach and along my ribcage and didn't stop until he reached my neck. I could feel his cock rubbing against my belly. Arching into him, I lifted my hips and rocked into him. Alexei groaned and grabbed my wrists in one big hand. He dragged them above my head, pinning them to a pillow, and shoved my legs apart with his knee.

Suddenly his captive, I experienced the most delightful thrill. Alexei buried his face in my neck and nipped at my sensitive throat. His other hand rode the outline of my body, sliding down my ribcage to my hip before gliding between my thighs. He cupped my pussy and pressed his lips to my ear. "Do you know how long I've wanted to touch you like this?"

I licked my lips and shook my head.

"Do you know many nights I fucked my own hand while thinking about you?" His fingers traced and then parted my labia. I whimpered when he found my swollen nub and started to strum it ever so slowly. His hand touching me so intimately felt nothing like my own hand, and I didn't want him to stop.

"Feel how wet you are?" His fingers slid down even lower and dipped into me. There was no resistance as he carefully probed. One finger slid inside me, curling just a little. His thumb rubbed side to side over my clitoris. It felt so good. My toes curled against the duvet, and I lifted my hips, desperate for more. I was getting close. So close…

"You're ready for my cock, aren't you?"

Overwhelmed by sensation and unable to speak, I nodded. He grinned that sexy grin of his that made my stomach wobble. Burning up for him, I widened my thighs in a silent plea for him to keep going. I wanted this. I wanted him. Right now. Inside me.

He reached down and wrapped a hand around his shaft. Dragging the fat head of his cock through my folds, he teased me with the promise of what was to come. Pulsing with desire, I moaned and surged against him, wanting to feel his shaft on my clitoris again. "Please! Alexei!"

Without a moment's warning, Alexei thrust forward, slamming into me and sheathing himself right to the hilt. Hissing, I recoiled with the shock of the sharp pain that gripped me.

Too hard.

Too fast.

Too deep.

Too much.

"Shay?" Frozen above me, Alexei stared down at me with a panicked expression.

No, no, no, I thought. *Don't stop now!*

"Please," I panted. "Don't." I tried to catch my breath. "Stop."

THE MOMENT HE surged forward, Alexei had recognized

something was different. The unexpected resistance had registered a second too late, but the hiss of pain was impossible to ignore.

A virgin!

A fucking virgin?

Of course.

It all made sense now. The mixed signals? Her shyness? He should have seen it. He should have been paying more attention.

Like right now, he thought, glancing at her pained expression.

I'm hurting her. The taut muscles in her face and neck told him everything. She was in agony right now. He'd been so desperate to finally have her that he had rammed into her without warning.

Feeling like the worst asshole in the world, he replayed her pained words. "Please! Don't! Stop!"

I swore I would never hurt her, but I did.

Desperate to make this right, Alexei started to withdraw from the unbelievably tight sheath now gripping him, but Shay frowned up at him. Wrapping her legs around his waist, she shook her head. "Please don't stop," she practically begged. "I want this with you."

The tension in his chest eased. He had misunderstood that part at least, but there was no mistaking the signs of pain on her beautiful face. Letting go of her wrists, he caressed her cheek. "I'm hurting you, *ptichka*."

She shook her head. "I don't care." She slid her hands along his arms until they rested on his shoulders. "I've wanted this just as long as you have."

He believed her. She spoke with sincerity. There was no denying their mutual attraction or desire, but it shouldn't have happened like this.

Ashamed of how selfish he had been, he leaned down and captured her mouth with loving, tender kisses. She deserved better than this, to be rushed and used so roughly. If he'd known—if she had told him that she had no experience with men—he would have taken his time with her.

Watching her face, he slid forward only an inch or so and then retreated. She winced, and he froze again. Was this the right thing to do? Should he stop altogether? Should he keep going? He didn't know much about virgins. In fact, he had always gone out of his way to avoid them. There was too much responsibility involved. If he fucked this up tonight, Shay would be cheated of a wonderful experience.

So don't fuck it up. Go easy. Trust her to tell you what she needs.

"Should I keep going? Do you want to stop and try again later?"

"It's not that bad." She placed her hand against his cheek in a reassuring gesture. "I promise, Alexei. It doesn't hurt. It's just…different." Her eyes closed for a moment and a smile flitted across her face. "A very *good* different."

He skimmed his lips along her jaw. He couldn't get enough of her soft skin. His hand moved along her neck and across her collarbone before slipping down to her breast. He marveled at her silky skin and the dark puckered flesh of her nipple. Unable to help himself, he suckled her gently. Almost instantly, he felt her pussy clamping down on his cock. His breath escaped his lungs on a rushed exhalation as he reveled in that wild sensation. He did it again, suckling harder this time and even biting down just a bit.

"Alexei!" Shay rocked against him. Her pussy fluttered around his dick, and he thought he might die in that moment. Heart racing, mouth dry, he kissed her again, tasting her sweet mouth and wishing they could stay like this forever.

More relaxed, Shay lifted her legs and hooked them at the small of his back, crossing her ankles and anchoring herself to him. The shift in angle felt amazing for him. By the look of wonder reflected in her eyes, it felt pretty damn good for her too. He couldn't believe how wet she was now. He was able to thrust without even the slightest bit of drag.

Shifting his weight to one knee, he trailed his fingertips from her hairline to her lips. He outlined her mouth and then pressed his fingers to her pout. "Lick."

Always a good girl, she followed his order and flicked her tongue over his skin. He kissed the tip of her nose and then lowered his now slick fingers to the place where their bodies met. He framed her clit between them and rubbed slowly while thrusting into her. He didn't go very deep or very hard. He took his time, moving with leisurely strokes and kissing her over and over again.

He wasn't sure if she would be able to come like his. He had always heard that it wasn't very good for women the first few times. Not wanting her to associate pain or disappointment with him, Alexei was determined to try to help her find pleasure with him.

But, fuck, it was hard to hold back. Everything about this coupling was different. He'd never been this excited in his life, not even *his* first time. Beneath him, Shay started to move. Her body was tense now but for a different reason. She gripped his shoulder and hip, her short nails digging into his skin. She was so damn tight and wet and hot and—*blyad*!

Fuck.

Fuck.

He suddenly realized why this felt better than it ever had. In their rush to bed, he had broken his only sex rule. He never fucked without a condom. *Until now.* He had always been careful, fearing an unwanted pregnancy or disease.

Pull out. A small and very responsible voice in the back of his head urged caution, but then Shay gripped the back of his neck and dragged him down for a kiss that made his damn toes curl. His self-control imploded in that moment.

He felt that familiar buzzing sensation building at the base of his spine. *Too fast. Too soon.* But he couldn't stop it. Not when Shay started rocking her hips to meet his measured thrusts. Pressing her forehead to his, she whispered his name again and again. "Alexei. Alexei. *Alexei.*"

Hearing her breathing his name like that broke him. Thrusting deep, he came so damn hard his vision started to dim. His entire body trembled with the aftershocks as wave after wave of incredible pleasure gripped him. Shay's thighs tightened around his waist, almost as if she were determined to hold him prisoner. Desperate to eke out the last few moments of incredible sensation, he rolled his hips, thrusting shallow and fast until ever last drop of cum had been milked out of him.

Falling forward, he tried to catch his breath as he drowned in a wave of guilt. Silently berating himself for ruining her first experience with a man, he stayed fully sheathed in her slick heat. She combed her fingers through his hair and kissed his cheek and jaw. He didn't deserve her sweet gestures, not after failing her in this.

"I'm sorry," he said, his voice muffled by her throat. Embarrassment gripped him. For a man renowned for his sexual prowess, he had just made a complete fool of himself by coming so fast. "I'm so sorry."

"For what?" Shay sounded confused as she stroked his back.

Lifting his head, he gazed down into her beautiful face. Didn't she understand that he'd just cheated her of something special? "I should have had more control. I hurt you—and then I finished first."

Shay pressed her lips to his in a lingering kiss. "You didn't hurt me, and I don't care that you finished first." Smiling tenderly, she brushed her fingertips along his jawline. "We'll figure out the timing eventually."

In awe of her, Alexei nuzzled into her and noisily kissed his cheek. Very carefully, he withdrew from her body and rolled onto his side. He slipped one arm under her body and embraced her from behind, dragging her back against him. He grasped her knee and pulled her leg up and over his, opening her thighs and giving him the right amount of access. Cupping her hot mound, he nibbled her earlobe and said, "Tell me what feels good."

"Everything you do to me feels good," she said breathlessly. "Like that," she whispered when he rubbed his finger around her clit in a lazy circle. "Especially that."

Listening to her moans and hitched breaths for guidance, he played with that pink pearl hidden away between her legs until she started to tremble. Holding her like this, he was able to tease her with kisses and fondle her incredible breasts. He focused his attention on her clitoris, rubbing and stroking, but didn't let his fingers drift any lower. After the way he had just battered her poor body, she was probably aching and sore.

She gripped his thigh and pushed back against him. Her perky little ass brushed against his stiffening cock. He'd always been quick to recover but even this was fast for him. With his fingers sliding in her wetness, he grew more excited, his blood heating in his veins and coursing through him with renewed vigor. He wanted nothing more than to bury his dick in her again—but it was too soon.

With a shocked groan, Alexei surged against Shay when she reached down between her spread legs to stroke his shaft. Her nimble fingers moved over his solid length, gliding down from the tip to the base. She was growing bolder with him and more curious. He fucking loved it.

But when she cupped his balls, Alexei's fingers faltered. He nipped at her earlobe. "What are you doing, Shay?"

"Can we try again?" she asked, her voice tinted with excitement and uncertainty.

He gulped. "Are you sure? I don't want to hurt you again."

"You won't," she assured him. "I know what I want, and I want you. Again."

His dick throbbed, and heat rolled through his belly. "I'll be gentle."

Shay looked back at him and smiled. "You always are with me."

The absolute trust reflected in her dark eyes drove him crazy. Someday, he wanted to deserve it. He wasn't a good man. He'd done some terrible shit in his life, but he had tried to make amends. He'd tried to live clean and right. Gazing down at Shay, he wondered if she was his reward for good behavior.

Instead of pushing her onto her back, he kept her glued to his chest like this. Spooning would keep him from losing control again. Clutching his cock, she guided him into place, and he carefully, *slowly*, pressed into her. She licked her full lower lip and wiggled her hips until she found just the right angle. "Oh," she breathed out on a long sigh. "Alexei."

"Does this feel good?"

"Yes. So good."

Fully sheathed in her wet heat, he didn't move. Instead, he traced a tight circle around her clit with two fingers. She shuddered when his fingertips flicked a certain way so he kept doing that—again and again and again until she panted and squirmed. Their coupling was unhurried and slow. Pushing, thrusting, rocking—he carried her closer and closer to the edge. She squeezed him with rhythmic spasms until finally— *finally*—she came apart in his arms.

"Alexei!" Shay cried out with ecstasy, her entire body undulating with sheer pleasure.

Exquisite. He watched her closely, enjoying the wonder and astonishment brightening her gorgeous face. His own orgasm was close behind, thrumming and building and pulsing with greater intensity. But he clamped down on it, refusing to let go until Shay was satisfied.

She had just come down from her first climax when she shifted away from him and onto her back. Clutching at his arms, she tugged on him in a silent plea for him to climb on top of her again. He wasn't about to deny her anything she desired, especially not tonight.

Sliding into her, he was careful not to take her too fast or too hard. He crashed their mouths together while snapping his hips, burying him cock in her. She clawed at his back, leaving burning trails along his skin. Feeling her staccato breaths on his cheek and neck excited him more than anything. He grasped her hand and dragged it down to the place where their bodies were joined.

"Make yourself come again," he all but ordered. Nipping at her bottom lip, he caused her to hiss. "Show me the way you touch yourself when you're alone."

Throwing her head back, Shay cried out as he thrust into her with a little more force. She played with her clit, rubbing fast circles around it while rising up to meet his every move. He could tell she was close again by those quick breaths she inhaled and the deep flush racing along her skin. Enthralled by her breasts, he bent his head and latched on to her dark nipple.

She came suddenly, her entire body wracked with the explosion of pure bliss. He didn't stand a chance. He dove off the edge with her and plunged into the same wave of pleasure.

They came down together, kissing, touching, whispering. She had the sweetest, softest smile on her beautiful face. She kissed him so tenderly, her eyes shimmering with unshed tears as she started to giggle. "That was amazing," she murmured against his lips. She embraced him in a hug he never wanted to end. "I'm so glad it was you."

In that moment, he knew everything had changed. All his plans for her? They crumbled in a spectacular crash. She could never be *just* his mistress. Not after this.

No, she was meant for something far greater.

Mine, he thought and gathered her close. *Always*.

CHAPTER FOURTEEN

LONG AFTER SHAY fell asleep in his arms, Alexei stroked her bare back and arm. His mind raced in ten different directions. What would happen once the underworld woke to the news that Lalo Contreras was dead? Would Shay and Kylee's involvement in his death stay secret? Would the police come sniffing around for answers?

And what the fuck was he going to do about Shannon? She was out there somewhere, probably hurt and scared, and would need to be rescued. If she was smart, she would get as far away from Texas as possible. She would go north to any place not connected to the cartel and start a new life. But was she that smart? The choices she had made so far in life didn't inspire much confidence.

Shay hummed in her sleep and turned on her side. Even before he slid closer, she was snuggling back against him. His mouth lifted in a smile as pulled her in tight and kissed the side of her neck. His smile faded when he noticed the scars crisscrossing her back. Earlier, he had felt the raised bumps under his fingertips, but he had been so fascinated by her lithe body that he hadn't paid them much attention.

But now? Now he couldn't stop looking at them.

He knew what they were.

Someone had struck Shay, repeatedly, with a cord of some kind. The scars curved around her back the way something flexible would when it hit skin. He didn't have to think very hard to find a culprit for the abuse she had suffered. It was either her horrible mother or one of the scumbag assholes she had brought into their home.

Rage burned hot and heavy in his chest as he traced the thin scars. They spurred a memory he had long since buried. While imprisoned in that juvenile camp, he and Ivan had watched another boy, a weaker boy, who had been singled out by the three of their guards. For every little infraction, that poor kid had been hauled away and taken to the secret block where terrible things had been done to him.

Once, the kid had been thrown back into their dormitory cell completely unconscious and with his back ragged and torn from a whipping. The next day, Ivan had coaxed the truth from the younger boy, learning about the extension cord that had been used on him and the other terrible things that had been done. That was the day Ivan had decided he had finally seen enough of that kid limping and bleeding around their cell block.

Three nights after that, he and Ivan and a few of the older boys had led a small revolt on their sadistic guards. By sunrise, those guards had been on their way to a hospital and an unspoken agreement between the warden and the inmates had been struck. Not another kid had been touched while Ivan was there.

Staring at his hands, he could almost feel the hot blood spilling onto them. If he closed his eyes, he could smell the sharp bite of fear in the air. He could hear that extension cord

Ivan had stolen smacking into bare skin. He could see the panicked stares of those guards when they had realized their days of beating and raping young boys were over and that they were going to leave the prison on stretchers.

Disgust soured his stomach. The things he had done to survive in that place…

Alexei lifted his hand from Shay's back and held it away from her as if he feared infecting her with the darkness and shame still clinging to him. She was the most pure and good thing he had ever had in his life. If she ever found out about the horrible things he had done?

She'll leave me.

Panic overwhelmed him. He couldn't stand the thought of losing her. He would do anything to keep her. Anything.

Thinking of the unseemly way he had brought her into his life left his stomach in knots. He had been so stupid to ever think that asking her to be his mistress would work. What must she have been thinking when he'd said that last night? Had she been afraid of what would happen when he discovered she didn't have the skills a mistress usually possessed? Had she felt pressured to let him have her tonight?

No. He didn't believe that last one. She had been the one who came onto him tonight. She had been the one to urge him to continue every time he had hesitated. She had made the decision to enjoy this with him. He only hoped that she was happy with that decision.

I'll never be good enough for her.

It was a troubling thought, and one that threatened to turn him inside out. He wasn't sure how to navigate these uncharted relationship waters. He couldn't just give her pretty, expensive things and expect her to be happy. She would need him to be open and honest with her, to talk about his feelings and to share his thoughts with her. He'd never done that with a woman before and didn't have the first notion of how to make it work.

But I have to try.

She had given him a precious gift tonight. She had trusted him with something she could give no other man. Forever and always, this experience was theirs and theirs alone. As he drifted off with Shay in his arms, he vowed then and there to never give her a reason to doubt that decision.

Sometime later, Alexei bolted awake to the sensation of movement. Confused, he lifted his head from his pillow and saw Shay sliding out of bed. He touched her hip, stopping her. "What's wrong?"

"Nothing." She glanced back at him and smiled sleepily. "I'm fine." Leaning back toward him, she kissed his cheek. "Go back to sleep."

When she got out of bed, she turned off the bedside lamp, plunging the bedroom into darkness before he could fully appreciate every sexy inch of her body. The bathroom door clicked when it closed and a faint sliver of light illuminated the strip of space beneath it. On the verge of dozing off again, he heard the shower start. She wasn't in there very long, maybe two or three minutes, before it switched off.

A short time later, she left the bathroom and climbed back into bed with him. He reached for her in the darkness, and she cuddled into him. He smoothed his hand down the long strands of her hair. The ends were wet so he swept her hair away from her back and onto the pillow behind her. He had his suspicions about her shower, but he didn't want to pry or make her uncomfortable. Still—he worried she might be in pain after the way he had taken her not once but twice in such a short time.

"Shay?"

"Yes?"

"Is everything all right?"

She didn't answer immediately. "I woke up, and I was all sticky."

There was no mistaking the embarrassment in her voice. "Oh." Smiling, he kissed her temple and gave her bottom a little pat. "Sorry."

She drew shapes on his shoulder. "It's all right. I'll...I'll be better prepared next time."

Next time? Shit, he started to get hard just thinking about fucking her again. *No, not fucking*, he silently admonished. It wasn't fucking. Not with Shay. It was something more. Something better.

Feeling her shiver from the chill in the room, he reached down and grabbed the covers. She burrowed into him when he dragged the sheet and duvet over their naked bodies. Almost shyly, she tucked her leg over his in a search for the most comfortable position. He placed his hand on her thigh in a reassuring gesture, wordlessly letting her know that this was all right.

It didn't take him long to fall asleep again. Like Shay, he was exhausted from the last two nights. Unfortunately, he was programmed to wake early. He lingered in bed with Shay for half an hour before carefully extricating himself. Wanting her to get some much-needed rest, he tucked the covers around her and gently kissed her cheek before backing away from the bed.

He took a shower in the guest bathroom and changed into the clean set of workout clothes in his gym bag. While he waited for his coffee to brew, he couldn't shake the feeling that he had forgotten something important. Halfway through his first cup, it suddenly hit him.

No condom.

Twice.

What were the odds that a woman who wasn't sexually active would be on birth control? Not very high. Thinking about everything he had packed for Shay, he didn't remember seeing any pills in her bathroom or bedroom. She didn't have any in her purse either.

It would figure that innocent, virginal Shay would conceive a child on her first night of lovemaking. That was the way these things usually worked. Worried that she would wake up and regret what they had done, Alexei decided he would do the one thing he could to make this right. He found his phone and texted Stas who answered back mere seconds later that he was already in the parking garage downstairs.

A few minutes later, Stas was at the front door, a fast food bag in one hand and a cup of coffee in the other. He headed straight for the kitchen, dropped his bag on the counter and retrieved Shay's phone from his pocket. "I was up early so I went by the friend's house to get Shay's phone. There weren't any missed calls."

"Did you hear anything last night?" Alexei finished his coffee and put the cup in the sink. He pocketed Shay's phone for now.

Stas shook his head. "I went straight home."

"And this morning?"

Stas shrugged out of his jacket. "People have noticed Lalo is missing. I've heard a few different theories. Some people think Shannon and Ruben killed him and ran. Others think Lalo killed Shannon and Ruben and is laying low. The one that I heard more than the others is that Hector Salas came to town to clean up Lalo's mess and whacked Lalo, Shannon and Ruben. Everyone knew that Lalo was skating on thin fucking ice with Hector. After that bust for the dog fighting? The books were opened on how long Lalo would last."

"And Shay? Her friend? The motel?"

"Shay and Kylee were never there. You were never there. I was never there. Besian and his crew weren't either. Last night didn't happen."

"Let's hope it stays that way," Alexei grumbled. "I'm going out for a little while. I won't be long."

"We'll be fine." Stas dumped the contents of the bag onto the counter, sending Egg McMuffins and hash browns rolling across the granite.

"Don't let her eat any of that horrible, greasy shit if she wakes up before I'm back," Alexei warned. "I'll make her a proper breakfast."

"Whatever." Stas stuffed a greasy hashbrown in his mouth.

Annoyed by the sound of the guard's chewing, he pointed toward the closed bedroom door. "Don't bother her. She needs to get some rest. The last few days have been difficult for her."

Stas swallowed his mouthful of food and reached for his coffee. After a quick sip, he said, "I'll be quiet."

"See that you are," Alexei replied, his mouth settling into a frustrated line. "And no more of your bullshit, Stas. I don't know what you said to her yesterday—and I don't want to know—but if I come home again and you've upset her, I'm bouncing you back to Nikolai."

Stas wiped his mouth with a paper napkin and balled it up in his big fist. "I didn't say anything to hurt her purposely. I just—I wanted her to understand what she'd done."

"That's not your job. She's mine. If she needs a lesson in the way the world works, I'll be the one who gives it to her. You keep your mouth shut and stop filling her head with stories that scare her. Shay and I? We have our own way of doing things."

Stas eventually nodded. "You're the boss."

Fucking right I am, Alexei thought crossly. "Don't let anyone inside the penthouse while I'm gone."

"I'll keep her locked up tight for you."

Alexei shot Stas a warning glance before gathering up his phone, wallet and keys and leaving the apartment. He waited in the hallway until he heard the deadbolt engage. On his way out of the building, he questioned whether Stas was the right fit long-term. He seemed to be a man who was used to getting his hands dirty, not following a nice woman around town and keeping her safe.

Maybe it was time to look for a permanent solution to the issue of Shay's security. This thing with Lalo and Shannon would blow over soon enough. Of that, he was sure. Nikolai and the other bosses wanted last night's secret to stay buried. Only a complete idiot with a death wish would say anything. He just had to get Shay through the tension of the next week, and everything would be all right.

But he did have enemies. He would never fully escape the underworld or the awful shit he'd done in that past life. Some grudges never faded. Now that he finally had someone that he loved in his life, she would be a target. He needed to know that she was safe.

As he drove home, he considered calling Dimitri. His security company had survived its bumpy start and was now among the most highly regarded in Texas, but hiring a team from Dimitri might be overkill. He could just imagine the look on Shay's face if he hired a pair like the two that Yuri had following his beloved Lena everywhere.

Shay seemed willing to let him coddle her to an extent, but he had no doubt she would push back if tried to attach retired SAS or SEALs to her. She didn't need hardcore security guards with special ops backgrounds. She needed one or two men he trusted to keep her safe, to drive and escort her around town.

Alone in his house, he changed into a pair of jeans and a shirt and slipped into a comfortable pair of boots. Standing in his master bathroom, he eyed the empty second closet that was part of the suite. He walked over to it and opened the door. It had been designed for a woman with plenty of rack space, built-in shelving for shoes and even a marble topped island for storing lingerie.

He had no trouble imaging Shay in here every morning, picking through her clothing and slipping into all the sexy, tiny, lacy things he intended to buy her. She would need more handbag space though. That was one habit he would support without complaint.

Feeling strangely excited by the prospect of Shay moving into his home, Alexei backed out of the bathroom. He cast a glance at his bed and decided that he would have her in it tonight. This business with keeping her in the penthouse was done. Nikolai was right. She didn't belong there. It was seedy and beneath her. She belonged here. In his home. Sharing his life.

After locking up, he left the house and drove to the nearest twenty-four hour drug store. He headed straight inside and right to the contraceptives aisle. He wasn't quite sure how these morning after pills worked. He'd never needed them until now. He studied the options on the rack and finally chose the one that seemed easiest for her to take. He also grabbed the biggest box of condoms he could find.

At the pharmacy counter, he stared right back at the pharmacist who leveled a judgmental look his way. It wasn't that old prick's business why he needed the medication. Seeing the pharmacist's reaction convinced him that coming here was the right thing to do. The last thing Shay needed was someone treating her like a whore after their night together.

Bag in hand, he left the drug store and stopped at the closest bakery. He had been planning to buy some nice pastries or muffins until he saw the stack of freshly made challah. The accompanying recipe cards for French toast seemed simple enough to handle. He chose a bottle of organic maple syrup from the nearby display before heading to the cashier.

Breakfast and medication purchased, Alexei returned to the penthouse. He sat in his SUV for a few minutes after parking and held the plastic bag and the pill it contained. His desire to protect Shay from the unintended consequence of their night together was strong, but he would be a fucking liar if he said that he was happy about buying this for her.

Some primal instinct within him decried the idea of Shay taking this and preventing a pregnancy that might be hours away from taking hold. Knowing he was the only man she had ever been with was powerful stuff. He didn't like admitting that. He had always been a man who didn't care about those kinds of things. The number of notches on a woman's bedpost meant nothing to him.

But he couldn't stomach the thought of another man knowing the sounds Shay made when she climaxed or the feel of her naked body rocking against his. He wasn't proud of that. He wasn't proud of these unexpected and very old school feelings creeping over him.

It's because she's the first woman who has ever been only mine.

It's because she trusted me.

It's because she chose me.

Alexei exhaled roughly. He wouldn't break her trust by putting her in a situation she wasn't ready for or wanted. Shay was just getting started in life. She was on the cusp of success in her career, and she was also facing the very real prospect she might never see her sister again. The last thing he needed was an unexpected pregnancy complicating her life.

Even so, he couldn't shake the image of Shay holding a baby and smiling at him. It was a powerful image, one that made his chest ache with desire and need. *Someday,* he promised himself as he stepped into the elevator. *Someday, when she's ready...*

CHAPTER FIFTEEN

WAKING UP ALONE was a jarring sensation, especially after being wrapped up in Alexei's arms all night. I sat up slowly and glanced around the bedroom. It was late, probably nine or ten in the morning. I ran my hand over the spot where Alexei had slept, but the sheets were cool to the touch. He had been awake awhile.

A sadness I didn't understand engulfed me. It was silly to feel so slighted about something like this, but I had envisioned something different. I had expected to wake up curled next to him, breathing in his scent, feeling his heat, maybe even sneaking a kiss or two.

Stop being ridiculous. You're a grown ass woman, and it was just sex.

Except it wasn't just sex. As I showered and pulled on some leggings and an oversized sweater, I tried to sort out my jumbled feelings. Not much about my first time had gone as I'd envisioned. No mood lighting. No wine. No music. Last night hadn't gone according to any plan. It had just…happened.

But I was glad it had happened. I had loved every moment of making love to Alexei, even the sort of painful parts. Maybe the first time hadn't been romance novel worthy, but the second time had been amazing. Frankly, I couldn't wait to try it again.

While I blasted my hair with a blow dryer, I debated how much to tell Kylee. She had always been incredibly open with me about her experiences. It was only fair that I shared my news and all the juicy details with her. I could just imagine the smug look on her face when she heard the story I had to tell. She had called this months ago and was going to make sure I remembered it.

Winding up the cord on the blow dryer, I stopped suddenly. Thinking of all the details I would share with her, I remembered one very important thing.

Oh no. Oh no no no no no.

We hadn't used protection. At all. Either time.

Kylee was going to flip when I told her that detail. We had always promised each other that we would be safe. I had gotten so wrapped up in the lust and excitement that I hadn't even stopped to think about the risks.

Calm down.

Think.

Count.

For once in my life, I rejoiced at my clockwork period. For years now, I had run on a perfect schedule of thirty-three days. I quickly did the math and breathed a sigh of relief. Aunt Flo was due in less than a week. Unless my body was up to some seriously weird things, I had already ovulated and was in the clear.

Combing my fingers through my hair, I stared at my reflection and shook my head. *What were you thinking? You need to slow down and act responsibly. You are not ready to be a mother!*

My fingers drifted over the bruises on my throat and cheek. They were starting to turn a deep shade of plum. It would be another week or two before they faded completely. I rarely wore more than a little BB cream, but I would definitely have to find a way to work some concealer into my usual routine until they were gone.

Today, though, I didn't see the need to spackle on the heavy duty stuff. I dabbed on some lip balm before leaving the safety of the bedroom. The scent of vanilla wafted through the penthouse, and I discovered Alexei making French toast for me. In all the time I had known him, this was the first time I had ever seen him in jeans. He looked so sexy in them. Those rolled up sleeves of his shirt highlighted his corded forearms and the swath of tattoos swirling from his fingers along his wrists and right up to his elbows.

Sensing my presence, Alexei turned toward me and grinned. He turned back to the range just long enough to switch off the gas. With powerful, confident strides, he closed the distance between us and slid an arm around my waist. Cupping my face, he tipped back my head and teased his mouth across mine. It was a tender, seeking kiss that stoked the lingering flames from last night.

When he pulled back, he brushed his knuckles along my cheek. "Good morning."

I smiled shyly up at him. "Hi."

He pressed his lips to my forehead and then dotted kisses along my temple and right up to the crown of my head. He inhaled deeply. "You always smell so fucking good."

I rubbed my hand over his chest. "You were up early."

"Old habits." He brushed his fingers through my hair. "I hope you're hungry. I managed to time breakfast just right."

"Oh?"

"I heard the shower and started following the recipe." He gestured to a recipe card propped up against the backsplash. "I hope you like French toast."

"I love it."

"Come eat while it's still hot." He guided me to the nearest barstool and helped me settle onto it. I sipped the orange juice he'd already placed at my spot while he dished up our breakfast. I liked watching him at these domestic chores. Even with something as simple as French toast, he was so careful in plating the dish. He added blueberries and strawberries to each serving along with a healthy dollop of butter and swirl of expensive maple syrup.

"Thank you." I smiled at him when he slid my plate in front of me.

"You're welcome." Alexei leaned down and kissed me. His newfound ease of displaying affection seemed so natural this morning.

Glancing back toward the living room, I asked, "What about Stas?"

"I sent him on some errands. He'll meet up with us later." He gestured with his fork toward my plate. "Eat."

Side by side, we devoured our fluffy stacks of French toast and berries. We talked quietly, mostly about the best breakfasts we had ever eaten. I noticed the way he seemed to be going out of his way not to mention the motel or Lalo or Shannon. Eventually, we would have to talk about it, but it was such a lovely Sunday morning. I didn't want to spoil it with something so ugly either.

When we were finished eating, he pushed my plate out of the way and leaned closer. He brushed a few strands of my hair behind my ear and traced the shell of it with his fingertip. "We need to talk about last night."

Something in my chest clenched painfully. Was this it? Was he going to tell me it was a mistake? That I was a nice girl but I wasn't exactly mistress material? Or that he'd finally decided that all my baggage was too much to handle? Stomach churning, I said softly, "Okay...?"

As if reading my mind, he shook his head and ran his thumb along my lower lip. "That's *not* what I meant, Shay." He claimed my mouth in a lingering, lovingly sweet kiss. "I have no regrets about last night." He kissed me again. "None." And again. "Not one." Leaning back, he searched my eyes for something. "Do you?"

"No." My answer was swift and sure.

He tilted his head. "Not even the way I was too rough with you the first time?"

I sensed his guilt and hated that he felt as if he had hurt me or done something wrong. Touching his cheek, I said, "Alexei, I should have told you that I hadn't ever gone that far. You shouldn't feel guilty about anything that happened last night."

"Why didn't you tell me?"

I glanced down, suddenly embarrassed. "I guess...maybe...I was worried you wouldn't want me."

"What?" he asked, seemingly incredulous at the very thought. Tilting my head up with fingers beneath my chin, he stared at me in utter confusion. "How could you ever think that I wouldn't want you?"

Didn't he understand? Didn't he realize how high his dating stock was compared to mine?

"Alexei, you're this ridiculously hot guy with a long history of lovers and mistresses who have rocked your freaking world. I can't compare with that. I don't know what I'm doing. I'm just…stumbling along behind you, trying to catch up."

"If you feel like you're stumbling behind, say something, Shay. I want you to walk beside me. Don't ever let me pressure you into doing something you don't like just because it's something I enjoy."

"But how will I know if I enjoy it if I don't try it with you?"

He didn't have a quick answer for that. "We'll have to take it slow. You have to promise me that you will always tell me to stop if you don't like something we try. I can't stand the thought of hurting you, Shay." He touched his forehead to mine. "It would fucking destroy me if I found out you felt used or abused or forced into something."

"You would never let it get that far."

"I'd like to think I wouldn't, but I can't read your mind. You have to speak up, Shay."

"I will."

"Promise me, Shay."

"I promise, Alexei."

As if remembering the other thing I had said, he added, "And you don't ever have to compare yourself to the other women in my past." His gaze bore into me. "Do you understand that?"

"Yes."

"All I want is you, Shay. Just you. Exactly as you are."

"That's a good thing." I slid my hand down to the side of

his neck and ran my thumb back and forth along the under-side of his jaw. "That's all I can offer."

"It's more than enough, Shay." Turning his head, he kissed my palm before turning his worried gaze to me. "But," he said with a sigh, "we made two mistakes last night."

Instantly, I knew what he meant. "I'm so sorry, Alexei. I swear I didn't do it on purpose. I've never been so irresponsible. I never thought—"

"Hush." He pressed his lips to mine, silencing my rambling. "There's more than enough blame to share. The bulk of the blame is on me, Shay. I'm older than you. I'm more experienced. I seduced you, and I should have been prepared."

"It's my body. I should have been more careful with it."

"I would never put you at risk of any sort of disease, Shay." He rubbed the back of his neck and glanced away briefly. He seemed reluctant as he said, "I served time in prison and tuberculosis is rampant there. The worst kind. The one that doesn't respond to drugs. Even though I know I'm clear, I still go in every year and demand a test from my doctor. It's crazy to do that. I haven't been exposed in decades but I can't shake that worry."

His eyes closed for a brief moment, and I witnessed the dark shadow of his complicated history cross his face. "When I used to fight underground, there was a lot of blood." He cringed as if remembering the mess in those cages at the end of fight night. "A lot of blood," he repeated. "Back then, they didn't test anyone. They just threw us in the ring and had us beat the shit out of each other until one man was left standing. Now? Now Nikolai and Besian make sure everyone has papers proving they're clean."

He cupped the back of my neck and stared into my eyes. He was being totally open with me and seemed to be trying to reassure me that he was telling the truth. "I've been tested for all the horrible blood borne diseases. I've also been tested for everything to do with sex. The tests are always negative. It's been years since I fought in a cage, and I've always been careful when I fuck around so it's definitely overkill to be tested so much. I know it is. But I would hate myself if I hurt a woman who shared my bed."

Seeing this side of Alexei surprised me. He was letting me see the real him beneath that ultra-confident shell. Deep down, he was vulnerable and unsure. At the purest part of him, he wanted to be a good man, to care and provide and protect the woman in his life. It was an old-school sentiment—and one I was starting to find intensely attractive.

Not wanting him to beat himself up over our mistake, I said, "Alexei, I'm sure we're fine. You obviously monitor your health closely. I'll have my doctor run some tests the next time I see her if that will put your mind at ease."

"I can show you my latest results, if you'd like. I have them in my electronic medical chart that the hospital uses."

"That's fine." We had flirted with danger last night, and we couldn't do it again. But I wasn't going to berate him when it was clear he had been diligent about protecting himself.

Clearing his throat, he said, "Last night was the first time I've forgotten a condom. I'm not sure if you're taking something…?"

I shook my head. "I'm not."

"Well, we'll have to do something about that," he said. "Until then, I'll wear a condom. If you want to keep having sex with me," he added.

"Of course, I want to keep having sex with you!" I couldn't even believe he would ask something that crazy.

He laughed. "Good. Because I want to keep having sex with you." He reached into the back pocket of his jeans and shifted on his seat. "About last night? Just in case, I got this for you when I went out this morning."

I didn't know what to say when Alexei placed the familiar box in front of me. I had seen the morning after pill in a few stores and had even bought it for Shannon once when she was too embarrassed to go in and buy it herself. Uncertain about how to take it or whether I even wanted to take it, I picked it up and turned the box over to read the back.

Alexei gently grasped my wrist and lowered my hand holding the box so he could meet my gaze. "If you want to take it—"

"If?" I seized on that surprising start to his sentence.

"I won't force you take it. I won't even ask you to take it. This is your decision, and I will support whatever choice you make."

For a man so inclined toward rather alpha, dominant behavior, I was pleasantly surprised by his stance on this issue. My heart beat a little faster when I considered the possibilities of what could happen if my dates were wrong. I hadn't ever given much thought to babies or motherhood, but it suddenly seemed like an interesting idea and one I very much wanted to pursue.

With Alexei.

But just not right now.

"I'm sure I've already ovulated. I, um, I have a cycle that

runs like a clock." Struck by the awkwardness of discussing my cycle with Alexei, I ducked my head. "But, um, I can take this anyway. If you want me to, I mean." I glanced at the box again. "It's not foolproof. If I've already ovulated—and I'm sure I did—then this pill won't do anything because there is no egg to delay. If I ovulated yesterday, biology is going to win because this pill won't work. There's still a risk that we might be shopping for diapers in nine months."

I started to open the box but Alexei snatched it out of my hand. He seemed as shocked by his action as I was. Very slowly, he placed it on the counter and pushed it back toward me. "I'm sorry. I shouldn't have—"

"Alexei." I pinned him in place with an imploring gaze. "Tell me what you want me to do."

He raked his fingers through his short hair and rubbed the back of his neck. "I don't have any right to ask you to not take it but I don't want you to feel pressured to do something just because I want it."

"Is that what you want?" I searched his handsome face for the answer. His expression was one I couldn't quite place. Was it yearning? Did he want a family? *With me?*

Gently covering his hand with mine, I said, "Alexei, I know my body, and I doubt we even need to be having this discussion. I don't want you to get your hopes up about the tiniest, slimmest of possibilities." Interlacing our fingers, I gave his hand a squeeze. "But if I was at a place in my life where starting a family seemed like a good idea, you would be at the top of my list for a partner in that adventure."

His surprised gaze shifted to meet mine. "Why?"

Bemused by his confusion, I touched his face with my oth-

276 | ROXIE RIVERA

er hand. "Alexei, look at what you've done for me in the last two days! You protected me. You defended me. You took care of me." I leaned in and kissed him tenderly. "Someday, you're going to be a very good father."

His hand tightened around mine. "I would take care of you, Shay."

"You already do."

Alexei trailed his fingers down my arm until they rested on my hand. "I want you to pack your things. You're leaving this penthouse today."

Taken aback, I asked, "Are you throwing me out?"

"No!" Alexei hurriedly stood and gathered me close to his chest. Crushed in his arms, I relaxed. "I'm not throwing you out, Shay. I'm taking you home with me."

Pushing back on his chest, I gazed questioningly up at him. "But I thought—"

He touched my lips, gently interrupting me. "You don't belong in this place." He glanced around the luxury penthouse he had used as his private playground for many years. "Maybe I don't belong here anymore either." His gaze returned to me. "Maybe you've changed me."

"Is that a good thing?" Considering all the trouble I had caused him, I wasn't so sure.

"The very best thing." He brushed his thumb along my jaw. "After we get you settled in at the house, I'm going to the gym. It's my normal Sunday afternoon routine. We need to try to behave as normally as possible this week, just in case the police come sniffing around about your sister or Lalo. What do you typically do on a weekend?"

"Work."

He exhaled a rough burst of laughter. "Why am I not surprised?"

Feeling a bit defensive, I thumped his arm. "Some of us have bills to pay and wayward older sisters to support."

"Not anymore," he said, capturing my hand and bringing it close for a kiss. "From now on, you work on your handbags and that's it. I'll handle the rest."

I didn't want to argue with him so I decided to let it go for now. Later, we would have to sit down and have a realistic discussion about my finances and his expectations in a relationship.

He let go of my hand and retrieved his buzzing cell phone. After answering a text, he set it aside. "Stas is going to meet us at my house."

"So I have to keep the bodyguard even if I'm living with you?"

"Bodyguards are non-negotiable from this day forward."

"Even after we fix this mess with Shannon?"

He nodded. "You know my history, Shay. I have enemies—and now I have a weakness."

I cocked my head to the side. "Is that supposed to be a compliment?"

"I've never worried about anyone coming after a woman of mine until you. Take that as you will." His thumb glided along the outline of my mouth before sliding toward the bruise darkening my cheek. "I can't let this happen to you again."

I nuzzled into his strong hand. "This wasn't your fault."

"Maybe not, but it's a reminder of how close I came to losing you." He softly kissed the bruise. "Twice."

"I nearly lost you when Lalo turned his gun on you," I

murmured, thinking of how horribly it all could have gone wrong. "I nearly lost my best friend, too."

"Shay, you have to promise me you will never again jump in front of a gun like that," Alexei ordered. There was a panicked look on his face that I never wanted to see again. He seemed haunted by the memory of last night.

"I won't." I placed my hands on either side of his neck and leaned in to kiss him. It was a gentle kiss, the kind that sealed a vow. Ending it, I leaned back just enough to look into his eyes. "I won't ever do anything that puts us in danger again."

Alexei's worried expression faded. A slow smile spread across his handsome face. "Us?" He wound a tendril of my hair around his finger. "I like the sound of that."

"So do I," I whispered, my heart racing and my stomach fluttering excitedly.

He playfully tugged my hair. "Get packed. I'll clean the kitchen and then we'll leave."

"It won't take me long to pack. I only have a few things here." I stood and started to back away from him but stopped. A nagging question wouldn't leave me. If I was moving in with Alexei, what did *us* mean?

"What is it?" He read me so easily.

"What about our arrangement? What about your rules?"

"You blew that arrangement straight to hell last night." He walked toward me and cupped my face. "We're playing by new rules today."

I had a sneaking suspicion I was really going to like this new game. Walking my fingers up his chest, I rose on tiptoes and brushed my lips to his. "I can't wait to play."

CHAPTER SIXTEEN

D RIPPING WITH SWEAT and breathing hard, Alexei continued pushing through the burn of another set of bench
dips. He eyed the whiteboard mounted on the closest wall
where Ivan had scrawled the workout plan for today in that
terrible handwriting of his.

One-Arm Kettlebell Push Press
Dumbbell Bench Press
Side Lateral Raise
Push-Ups
Lying Dumbbell Tricep Extension
Bench Dips
Chest Dips
Handstand Push-Ups
Push-Ups
Bench Dips
Chest Dips.

Ivan seemed intent on exercising him to death today. If he
didn't know any better, Alexei might think Ivan was pissed off
at him, but this was pure Ivan. He ran his gym with an iron fist

and demanded the members meet the workout goals—or fuck off across town to Connolly Fitness.

"Watch your form," Ivan barked as he left another workout station and strode closer. He spun a towel like a windmill as he drew near. "Your arms are fatigued." As if to prove his point, Ivan kicked him right in the ass as he dipped down too low. It wasn't a hard blow, barely more than a tap, but it drove home the point. "You've gone beyond set failure. Stop. Recover."

The burn in Alexei's arms had spread to his chest by now. Knowing Ivan was right, he eased off the bench and into a standing position. Shaking out his hands, he walked to the whiteboard and slashed his finger through the set he had just finished, smearing the dry erase marker. Only one set of exercises remained to be completed but he needed more time to recover.

Hotter than hell, Alexei ripped off his t-shirt and wiped his sweaty face and neck with it. He caught the water bottle Ivan tossed at him and took a long drink.

"I see the rumors are true."

"Huh?" When Ivan gestured to the mirror, he contorted his upper body to get a better look. The angry red scratches on his shoulders and lower back were impossible to ignore. A quicksilver flash of something dark and possessive ignited within him as he remembered Shay grasping and scratching at him while he thrust into her.

Without warning, Ivan popped him across the back with the towel he had been carrying. "Don't start bragging. I'll make you cover up."

Hissing with the sharp bite of pain, Alexei jerked the towel away from Ivan and whacked him right back with it. "Like you haven't walked around here with love bites from Erin all over your neck?"

Ivan yanked the towel back and landed a vicious snap right across Alexei's ass. "That's my wife you're talking about."

He grinned at Ivan's reaction. "I didn't see Erin today."

Ivan's happy demeanor switched to one of frustration. "She's visiting her sister."

Alexei had to tread carefully here. Ivan's feelings about his incarcerated sister-in-law were well-known to him. "Is Ruby getting out soon?"

Ivan nodded. "They're letting her out in January."

"To a halfway house?"

"No, to *our* house."

Alexei knew enough about the history between Erin and her sister to tread carefully. "You don't sound happy about that."

"I'm not." Ivan pointed to the parallel bars, silently ordering him to finish the final exercise on the list. "But I can't say no to Erin, not after I moved Ten into the house without asking her." Even all these months later, Ivan winced with the memory of his mistake. "I really stepped deep in the shit on that one."

Alexei agreed with a grunt as he raised and lowered his body using only his arms. *Up. Down. Up. Down.* He focused on the wall, keeping his rhythm steady and his pace measured. Keeping his voice low, he asked, "How is Erin doing after..?"

Ivan didn't need him to finish that sentence. He had been away in Vegas with Sergei when their women had been attacked by cartel henchmen hell bent on avenging their overthrown boss. Artyom had taken a nasty gut shot and two to the shoulder to protect Erin. Other street soldiers had taken beatings and worse, especially the younger ones who hadn't ever been in a street war. Roman and Danny wouldn't be so easily overpowered the next time blood spilled in the streets.

"She's fine." Ivan's clipped answer spoke volumes to Alexei. It was a response that told him to drop the issue. Arms crossed, Ivan watched him carefully, his keen eyes taking in Alexei's form. "Looks good. Keep going."

When he neared the point of failure, Alexei pushed through for two more dips before carefully lowering his feet and stretching out his arms.

"That was good." Ivan tossed him the towel and his water bottle. "Walk with me."

Alexei mopped at his face and rehydrated while they walked the length of the warehouse toward the sparring cages. Ivan's fighters were all working toward upcoming matches so the gym was a busy place even on a Sunday afternoon. Sergei and Kir, both matched in size and strength, sparred lightly in one cage. They lingered there for a few minutes before moving to the next cage where Zel, a Croatian fighter who had been the first to join Ivan's professional stable, sparred with a fighter Alexei didn't recognize.

Closer to Alexei's age than Sergei's, Zel was nearing that point in his life where it was time to hang up the gloves. Alexei sipped his water and relaxed his stance while watched Zel fight. "I thought he was done."

Ivan held up a single finger as if to say he had one match left in him. "This next tournament is his last."

"Vegas?" Alexei had been planning to fly out for the fights

at the Mandalay Bay, but he hadn't realized Zel was fighting. "I didn't realize he was on the card."

"He wasn't, but there was an opening and the promoter and the league wanted him in that slot." Ivan ran his tongue along the inside of his lower lip. "I shouldn't have let him take this one, but the money was too good for him to pass up."

Alexei cast a worried glance at Ivan. "Is Zel in trouble?"

"He still owes money on his debt to Luka Beciraj."

"What? After seven years? Eight years?" Stunned, Alexei did the math. "He's still paying on that shit?"

"Interest and penalties," Ivan replied. "You know what those fucking loan sharks are like."

Alexei turned his attention to Zel and watched him work his floor games. Zel had one hell of a standup game, but he had always been weak on the floor. Even now, he was struggling to break free from a hold.

Growling with frustration, Ivan moved closer to the cage and gripped onto the chain link. Snarling in Russian, he barked orders at Zel. "Watch that elbow! When it hits the ground, push up into him and fucking throw him off! Use your hips! Come on!" Ivan banged his hand against the cage. "Buck! Harder!"

Alexei watched as Zel finally got a good grip on his opponents' sweat-slicked arm and did exactly as Ivan instructed. He arched off the mat and used the momentum of his move to push the other fighter up and off of him. It was a swift maneuver that sent his partner rolling onto his back. Zel quickly pinned the other man to the mat and moved into a dominant position, earning Ivan's clap of approval.

After a few more pointers and discussing Zel's grappling

game with a trainer, Ivan returned to Alexei's side. He seemed troubled as he watched his fighter continue his Sunday session. "He's losing his fire."

The words were spoken softly, but Alexei heard them clearly. Watching Zel, he acknowledged that the Croatian seemed to have lost his passion for fighting. Of course, after the hellish year he had survived, it was no wonder. "He's had a rough year."

"Losing his boy broke him. That kid was the reason he fought. Now?" Ivan's lips sank into a flattened line. "Now he just fights to clear his debt to Luka and move on with his life."

"Fighting for money is dangerous. That's how men get hurt." He cast a look Ivan's way that communicated exactly what he was thinking. *That's how* we *got hurt.*

"Yes, it is." Ivan crossed his arms again. "I offered him the money. I even offered to speak to Luka directly to see if they would write off the balance. The boy is dead now. All that money Zel spent getting them here and then paying for his son's medical bills was wasted. Making him pay it all off now is rubbing salt in a fresh, deep wound."

"He's a proud man." Alexei stated the obvious. "Would you take the money if you owed the debt?"

Ivan didn't answer immediately. After a while, he shook his head. "No."

"We'll have to help him," Alexei decided. "I'll talk to Besian. I'll find out the balance and then place some strategic bets when I get to Vegas. Maybe we can make Zel enough money to clear his debts and a little bit to start over."

"Be careful with that," Ivan warned. "The last thing you need is to get caught up in some underground gambling shit."

Alexei grunted in agreement.

"Are you bringing her?"

"Shay? To Vegas?" Alexei shook his head. "No."

Ivan gawked at him. "You're going to Vegas without your new girl?"

"Our Vegas trips are always men only."

"Not anymore," Ivan shot back. "I'm taking Erin with me."

Alexei wasn't surprised, not after what happened the last time Ivan went to Vegas. "She's your wife. It's different."

Ivan made a grumbling noise. "You better be careful saying shit like that around Shay."

Alexei shifted uncomfortably under his friend's stare. "I don't think Shay would enjoy the Vegas scene."

"Have you asked her?"

"It hasn't come up yet."

"It better come up before you step on that plane and leave her here in Houston," Ivan warned. "You might come back to an empty penthouse."

"It's already empty. She moved into my house this morning."

Ivan seemed taken aback. "You're really moving fast with her."

You have no idea. Alexei wondered just how much Ivan knew about Shay and what was going on with her sister. Even though he was out of the life, he lived right on the edge and always had his ear to the ground. There weren't many dirty deeds he didn't hear about eventually.

As if reading his mind, Ivan said, "You should be careful with your cleaning lady." He held up a hand to halt Alexei's retort. "Listen to me, okay?"

286 | ROXIE RIVERA

Alexei relented unhappily and nodded stiffly.

"Sisters are trouble." Ivan grasped his shoulder and gave it a squeeze. "Take it from me. I know. They come as a package deal," he warned. "I fell in love with Erin and married her—but that means her sister became *my* sister. Because she's now my family, I owe her a fresh start when she finally gets out of lockup. It's a burden, but I went into this with eyes wide open. For Erin? I'll do anything—even if it means paying for protection for her sister while she's doing her stretch or pushing around money and favors to get Ruby a job once she's out. It's never-ending, Alyosha."

"I get it," Alexei assured him. "Shay's sister is—"

"A fuck up?" Ivan supplied.

"Difficult," Alexei replied. "She's difficult, but the girls had a hard life." He had been thinking about Shannon and Shay during his workout. "I think Shannon did the best she could. Sometimes it wasn't enough, but she tried. Shay loves her for that. She respects her big sister for sticking around and trying."

Ivan shook his head. "You better be careful thinking like that. You need to snip those strings." He made a scissoring gesture with his thick fingers. "If what I've heard is true, Shannon nearly got her sister killed *twice*. Don't let her have a third chance, Alyosha. She might finally succeed."

The chilling thought wouldn't leave him as he gathered up his gym bag and left the warehouse. Driving across town, he couldn't stop thinking about Ivan's warning. He didn't want to push Shay to cut her sister out of her life, but what other choice did he have?

When he arrived at the house, he slipped his SUV into its

slot in his five-car garage and dropped his gym bag on the built-in bench in the mudroom. He found Stas eating an apple in the kitchen. "Do you ever stop eating?" he asked the enforcer-turned-bodyguard.

"No." Stas crunched a huge bite of apple between his teeth. He gestured toward the ceiling with the fruit clamped in his hand. "She's upstairs."

"You can head out," Alexei said. "We'll be fine for the rest of the day."

"Same time tomorrow?"

Alexei nodded. "You can work for me until you find a different position or Nikolai decided he needs you somewhere else. I know this isn't how a man with your skillset wants to spend his days."

"It's the best job I've had since I joined the family. Even with all the shit that went down last night," he added.

"If you hear anything about Shay tonight—"

"I'll make sure you know," Stas interjected. "But I wouldn't worry about it. Those secrets died with Lalo."

"Let's hope they stay buried," he muttered.

After walking Stas out and locking the door behind him, Alexei went upstairs in search of Shay. He found her curled up on an armless upholstered chair in the master bedroom texting with someone. He didn't want to accuse her of talking to her sister so he held his tongue and waited for her to say something.

"It's Kylee," she explained and flashed him her phone as if to prove it. "We haven't said anything about last night. We're just talking about normal things. I wouldn't say anything that might get us all in trouble."

"I trust you to be safe." He spotted her suitcase still sitting where he'd left it. "Why didn't you unpack?"

She seemed to shrink back into the chair. "Well…"

"Shay." He pinned her in place with a no nonsense look. "What's wrong?"

"There weren't any hangers," she said, her excuse sounding feeble to both of them.

"I'll pick up some more tomorrow. Until then, you can borrow some from my side." He could tell that wasn't the real reason she hadn't unpacked. "What's really going on here?"

When she didn't answer immediately, he crouched down in front of her and gently took her phone from her hands. He tossed it onto the bed and held her hands instead. Capturing her gaze, he said, "Talk to me."

Hesitantly, she admitted, "It made me too nervous."

"Nervous? Why?"

She swallowed anxiously and dropped her gaze, staring straight down at her lap as if embarrassed. "I've been interested in you for so long, and I used to fantasize about something like this happening. About you asking me to live with you," she explained. "And now I'm *here* in *your* home and we're together. and I wanted to be excited and optimistic about us— but then I remembered why I'm here—"

"You're here because I want you to be here," he cut in quickly and drew her gaze. "You're here because I care about you and because I want to share my home with you."

"My sister—"

"Isn't part of the equation, Shay," he insisted. "If this was just about keeping you safe, I would have left you in the penthouse. You were perfectly safe there." Leaning forward, he kissed her tenderly. "You're here because I wanted you in my life." He kissed her again and relished the way she responded so sweetly. "You're here because you're special to me."

Her dark eyes lit up as he described her as being special to him. "You're special to me, too."

This time, she was the one who kissed him. Her small hands slid along his arms, over his shoulders and up the sides of his neck until she clasped his face. He let her have control, surrendering to her searching tongue and her soft, soft lips. After his workout, his legs were killing him in this cramped, crouched position, but he didn't dare move or complain. He would let his toes go numb before he ended this kiss.

When Shay shifted her hold on him, he answered her silent urging and put a knee onto the chair. He shivered when her hands slid under his loose T-shirt and stroked his bare stomach. The memories of her hands on his body last night were so new and fresh. Making more of them sounded like a very good idea right now, but he desperately needed a shower.

Shay eased off their increasingly more erotic kisses and smiled up at him, her expression relaxed and happy. Running her finger along his chin, she murmured, "This chair is too small."

"I'll buy us a new one tomorrow." He nibbled at her amused grin. "The biggest, widest chair in the store."

"Or we could just move to your big, comfy bed," she suggested seductively and tapped his chin.

"Or," he nipped at her finger, "I can show you why this chair is the perfect size and height." Her dark eyes sparked with interest and excitement. Taking that as permission, he gently pushed on her shoulders. "Lean back, baby."

She allowed him to maneuver her into the position he wanted. When he slid his hands under her oversized sweater and gripped the waistbands of her leggings and panties, she bit her lip in an anxious and uncertain way. He wasn't surprised by her nervousness. This was another first for her.

As he dragged the leggings and panties down her legs and whisked them off her bare feet, he considered how fucking selfish he had been last night. He should have spent half the night with his face buried between her thighs, but he had been so focused on his needs that he hadn't even considered that she might want more than a few teasing licks. He intended to rectify that oversight right now.

Running his palms over her slim legs, he marveled at the smooth, brown skin under his scarred and tattooed hands. Starting at her ankles, he dotted light kisses toward her thighs. He could feel the tension beneath his lips as he moved higher and higher. He assumed it was a mixture of excitement and nervousness that gripped her now.

Holding her curious gaze, he grasped her knees and pushed her thighs wide apart. He gently kneaded her inner thighs, massaging the stiffness and tension from her legs until they fell open in a relaxed way. Dragging his knuckles down her slit, he smiled devilishly at the way she shuddered. Her shaky breaths and the flush to her skin told him all he needed to know.

Using his thumbs, he explored her pussy. Soft. Pink. Wet. He dipped his thumb into her and gathered the slick heat there. Sliding easily now, he moved to her clit and traced the little pearl with the pad of his thumb. Her sharp intake of breath encouraged his movements. Drawing slow circles around that tiny bud, he teased Shay until she dropped her head back against the chair and closed her eyes.

Alexei leaned down and swiped her slit. Her taste reminded him of the sea and he couldn't get enough. Hands on her inner thighs, he held her wide open and flicked at her clit. He took his time, nibbling and licking until she whimpered and clutched at his forearm. When he tugged the little bud between his lips, she arched off the chair, lifting her hips off the cushion and crying out as he tormented her.

Loving her reaction, he gripped her bottom in both hands and held her tight to his mouth as he feasted on her slick, soft heat. She made the wildest sounds, and he couldn't get enough. She was always so quiet, so reserved and sweet. He wanted Shay to lose control. He wanted to unleash that wanton wildcat that he knew was hidden just beneath her surface.

Forcing her thighs farther apart with his broad shoulders, he traced her clit with steady strokes. He didn't care if he was on his knees for the next hour. He was going to make her come and make her come *hard*.

Shay sucked in sharp, shaking breaths. He could feel the tension building in her legs. It wouldn't be long now. Fluttering his tongue faster and more firmly, he zeroed in on a rhythm that made her scratch at his forearm. He would have a few more marks for Ivan to tease him about at the gym tomorrow.

"Alexei," she whispered. "Alexei, please don't stop."

Always so polite, he thought with some amusement. But she didn't need to bother asking. He wasn't going to stop.

With a thrust of her hips, she pressed against his mouth

and came with a ragged groan. He licked her right through that orgasm, cupping her perky ass and ravishing her with his tongue until she sagged against the chair. Wanting to give her a chance to recover before he pushed things to an even more intense level, he abandoned her clit and gripped the backs of her thighs. He pushed her knees toward her chest and grinned wolfishly at the way she was so beautifully displayed for him.

"What are you doing to me?" Shay's fingers were in his hair now, her short nails scratching at his scalp.

"What I should have done last night if I wasn't such a selfish asshole." He dipped his tongue into her and smiled at her little squeal of delight. Licking a finger, he got it nice and wet before sliding it into her tight channel. Worried she might still be sore after the way he had taken her last night, he eased his way inside and pumped slowly.

He returned to that pink pearl begging for his attention and fluttered his tongue over it. She gasped and swiveled her hips, silently urging him to continue. He understood her body now and it didn't take him very long to find the right rhythm this time. Her thighs fell open as he pushed her closer and closer to the edge. She draped one leg over his shoulder as he added a second finger and thrust deeper.

When he curled his fingers inside her pussy and stroked just so, her shoulders shot off the chair. She surged against him, and he had to hold her down with a hand firmly planted on her lower belly. Massaging a slow circle there, he worked her with his tongue and fingers until he drove her right into a powerful orgasm. Rocked by the pleasurable waves, she cried out his name until she fell back against the chair in a blissed out state.

Satisfied that he had made up for his shortcomings last night, he placed a lingering kiss right on top of her clit and then dotted a line of them right up to her navel. He slid one of his hands across her belly and under her sweater. She wore no bra under the oversized top, and he appreciated the easy access to her lush breasts. He circled one nipple and then the other while taking in her relaxed, happy smile.

Brushing her fingers along his jaw, she said, "I've changed my mind. This chair is the *perfect* size. I think we should keep it."

He laughed and kissed her stomach. "Whatever you want, *ptichka*."

CHAPTER SEVENTEEN

STILL THRUMMING WITH aftershocks, I leaned back in the chair and watched Alexei strip in the bathroom. His lean body rippled as he tossed his gym clothes into hampers tucked away in a cabinet. In the full light of day, I could see all the tattoos on his back and legs. Someday I wanted to ask him about each and every one of them. Even if the stories weren't particularly nice, he wouldn't hide anything from me.

Because he trusts me.

The weight of that realization struck me suddenly. Alexei seemed to prefer a language of *doing* rather than *saying*. Today, by inviting me into his home, he had shown me exactly what I meant to him and how much he trusted me.

For the first time in forever, I truly felt special. I felt as if I mattered. Knowing what it had taken for me to place my trust in Alexei, I imagined it had been similarly as difficult for him. I had to respect that and treat his trust as a gift. I expected him to do the same for me.

I won't screw this up.

He came out of the bathroom wearing only a pair of swim trunks. They were black and fit his body like a glove. His erection was outlined in the thin fabric, and I wondered why he hadn't asked me to help him with that. He must have noticed my gaze lingering there because he said, "This can wait until tonight."

"You're sure?" I was more than willing to climb into bed with him.

"I'm sure." He crossed the room and leaned down to kiss me. "It's not quid pro quo with us, Shay. Sometimes I'm just going to throw you down, push your legs open and eat your pussy because I feel like it. I don't expect anything in return."

Reeling from his description, I flushed with heat. "You say the dirtiest things."

"And you fucking love it," he remarked with a devilishly sexy grin. After he kissed me one more time, he stepped back. "I'm going down for a swim."

"It's raining," I reminded him and gestured to the window overlooking the lush backyard with the incredible pool, pergola and outdoor kitchen.

"There's a smaller indoor pool downstairs." He combed his fingers through my hair. "When you're done unpacking, come find me. We'll talk about dinner."

"All right."

"The security alarm is on so you're safe inside the house."

"And if I need to go out or answer the door?"

"I would prefer that you didn't do either one of those without me, but the code is 1113." He glanced away briefly, and I realized there was a significance to that number. It didn't take me long to work it out. It was a date. A very significant date.

"The first time they sent me to your dealership was last November."

Alexei nodded stiffly. "It was the thirteenth."

There was a flutter of something sweet and warm in my chest. "I see."

"Do you?" He pinned me in place with a searching look. "I had that security system installed two months after you started working at the dealership. Two months of seeing you once a week and I was already infatuated with you."

"I think maybe I had the same feelings for you after my first night there," I confessed, not wanting him to feel exposed.

"But we wasted all those months avoiding the obvious," he said with a shake of his head.

I grasped his hand and gave it a reassuring squeeze. "You know what they say about the best place to hide things…"

"Right under your nose," he said, a tender expression crossing his handsome face. He leaned down and kissed the tip of my nose. After stroking my jaw, he backed away and pivoted toward the door.

When he disappeared from the room, I found the strength to push out of the chair and onto my feet. My legs were wobbly as I pulled on my panties and leggings. I tugged my suitcase through the master bathroom to the insane closet where Alexei wanted me to store my things.

Standing there, I was reminded of the stark difference between his lifestyle and mine. My entire mobile home would have fit in his master suite. The closet alone was bigger than my bedroom and Shay's combined. I ran my fingers along his designer clothing, noticing the way he had everything organized so neatly. His collection of leather belts held my interest. Some of them were beautifully made and I admired the stitching.

Spotting the stack of hangers he had placed on the marble-topped island, I took the hint and started unpacking my things. There wasn't much in my luggage so it didn't take long. I found the hamper for my dirty clothes and decided to investigate the rest of the house so I could locate the laundry room.

When I was finished unpacking, I left the master suite and walked around the upper floor of Alexei's mansion. I opened doors and poked my head inside the many rooms. I was a bit taken aback when I realized only two of the rooms were furnished. I clearly wasn't lack of money that kept him from finishing the guest rooms on the second floor. There had to be another reason for it—and I had a good feeling I knew what it was.

As I walked downstairs, I began to suspect that Alexei had purchased this grand mansion in River Oaks as a way to prove to everyone else that he had arrived. He was a man who liked to nice things and liked to use luxury items like his watches, his suits and his fleet of vehicles to prove that he was successful and wealthy. That wasn't my style, but I understood it. I had seen what it was like when the people I grew up with got a taste of money. They immediately went for new cars or shiny rims or expensive clothes.

I suspected Alexei had done the same thing. He wanted to prove he belonged. He wanted to prove that he had left behind his criminal past and was a man of worth and success.

But it had to be lonely in this beautiful house of his. All the marble and hardwood and expensive, luxury furniture in the world couldn't make up for the coldness of an empty mansion. Without anyone to share this incredible space with, he must have grown disinterested in decorating and furnishing after tackling the first three bedrooms upstairs. The other four had been left to languish, unused and empty.

Downstairs, I finally found the laundry room. There were two washers and two dryers plus a wall of built-in cabinets and an obscene amount of marble countertops. I tried to imagine what size family would need that many machines and that much folding space. Considering the dry cleaning tags I had seen upstairs in Alexei's closet, I doubted he got much use out of this room at all.

The ringing doorbell startled me. Alexei hadn't said anything about visitors. Wondering if Stas had come back for some reason, I left the laundry room and made my way to the front of the house. The custom double doors made of wood and iron filigree had glass panels on the upper portion of the doors. I could see the outline of a single man through them and hesitated in the entryway.

I hadn't located Alexei's indoor pool yet so I had no idea where he was or if he could even hear the doorbell. I backed away from the door, hoping the man out there hadn't seen me yet, and winced when the doorbell rang again. After the hell I'd been through in the last three days, I was naturally suspicious and easily spooked.

And then I caught sight of the security system console mounted on the wall around the corner. The small screen showed a live feed from a camera mounted somewhere above the front doors. I recognized the man standing there almost instantly—and my stomach knotted with distress.

What is he *doing here?*

Inhaling a steadying breath, I punched in the code Alexei had given me and walked to the front door. I turned the deadbolt and door knob locks and opened the door a few inches. Trying to hide my anxiety, I faked a warm smile and hoped to hell Detective Eric Santos couldn't tell my hands were shaking.

"Hello," I greeted softly. "Can I help you?"

"Shay?" Eric Santos's face registered shock. He took a step back and gazed up at the façade of Alexei's house as if to reassure himself he was in the right place. "What are you doing here?"

"I sort of live here," I said, still not quite believing it myself. I didn't add that it was a temporary situation. I didn't need Eric digging around in my personal life. "Are you here to speak with Alexei?"

Eric nodded. "I came here to speak with him about you actually."

"Me?" Oh, this wasn't good.

"Well you're missing—"

"I'm not missing, Detective. I'm right here."

He shot me a perturbed look. "I think we need to talk."

I didn't want to talk to him. I really, really didn't. But I knew that if I acted odd or gave him any reason to suspect something wasn't right, he was going to make trouble for Alexei.

I stepped aside and waved him into the house. "Come in, please."

Eric entered, and I shut and locked the door behind him. I walked him into the living area and gestured toward one of the couches there. I took a seat in a chair across from him and tried to look calm and relaxed. I thought about asking him if he wanted something to drink, but I wasn't familiar enough with the house. If he saw me peeking through cabinets or going down the wrong hall, he would automatically know something was up.

After taking his seat, Eric whipped out a notebook and pen and flipped to the page he wanted. "Your neighbors said they saw a truck at your house on Friday evening. They said three or four men got out of the truck and hassled you. Your landlord and his crew intervened." He lifted his gaze from his notes. "Does that fit your recollection of the evening?"

"Yes." I leaned back in the chair, drawing up my legs and crossing them. I tugged my oversized sweatshirt over my knees and reminded myself to be very, very careful with my answers.

"And do you want to tell me who those men were?"

"They were just some guys looking for Ruben." The lie came so easily. I sort of hated myself for not telling Eric the truth. He had been trying to help Shannon get straight for years. He was a good guy, and he was someone I had trusted— until my loyalty shifted to Alexei.

"And?"

"And they left when I told them he wasn't there."

Eric's expression remained impassive. I couldn't tell if he believed me or if he was using those super detective powers on me. "We've been trying to find your sister and Ruben."

"Why?"

"Because we think they may have had something to do with the disappearance of this man," he said and flashed me the screen of his iPhone. "Do you know this guy?"

Expecting to see Lalo's face, I reluctantly glanced at Eric's phone. The license photograph wasn't his. It was some blond guy I had never seen. "No."

"His name is Edgar Vasquez. He went to school with Ruben. They seem to have kept in touch and the rumor is that they're working together."

"Detective Santos, you know that I don't have anything to do with Ruben or the life he lives. I barely tolerate Shannon's involvement."

"Is that why you've moved in here?"

"I live here because Alexei asked me to live with him. It has nothing to do with Shannon." Lies. Lies. Lies.

"How long have you been dating?"

"I don't think my personal life has anything to do with that man." I motioned toward his phone. "I'm not going to answer questions about my relationship with Alexei."

Eric seemed surprised by my reply. Had he expected to push me around that easily? As if trying to push my buttons, he asked, "And those rumors about you and Lalo Contreras?"

My face wrinkled with disgust. It was a reaction I couldn't hide. "There has never been anything between me and Lalo. Those rumors are all lies."

"Even the one about you and Lalo going into a back room together at the Arena on Friday night?" His arched eyebrows dared me to lie, and I knew I was caught.

Carefully, I explained, "I went to the Arena on Friday night looking for Shannon. She was supposed to be there with Ruben." Not wanting to talk about what had happened in that back room, I came up with another lie on the fly. "I ran into Lalo there. I couldn't hear him over the music and the crowd so he took me to a quiet room in the back. We talked for a few minutes about Shannon and the show and then I left."

"You just talked?" He didn't believe me. "You're sure

about that?"

"Yes." I didn't know what else to say.

"Because those bruises on your throat and on your face tell me another story, Shay."

Shit. I had completely forgotten about my busted up face. Alone with Alexei and Stas, there had been no reason to smear on concealer and foundation.

"Those bruises tell me a story I've heard from other girls who were unfortunate enough to run into Lalo on a bad night," Eric said. "They tell me that he tried to get rough with you." He tilted his head and studied me. "But I think you fought back. I think the story I heard about Lalo getting the shit beat out of him by a pretty little dark-haired doll is true."

I swallowed nervously. "It was self-defense."

"I don't doubt that it was," Eric assured me. "Lalo is a pig. He got what he deserved." Sliding his pen into the metallic coils atop his notepad, he admitted, "I saw the footage of you going into the Arena. I also saw you going into the back of the building with him. I didn't see you come out the front or back exits, but I did see him stumbling out the back with a bloody towel on his head."

"I went out a window," I said quietly. "It was the only way out of that room."

He didn't have to ask why I hadn't called the police. "You realize he's not going to take that embarrassment lightly."

"I'm not worried about what Lalo or anyone else thinks. Alexei won't let anything happen to me."

Eric narrowed his eyes. "I know what Alexei used to be. I know what he still is."

"And what is that?"

"Take off those designer suits and those expensive watches and he's nothing but a gangster with money. He's a criminal who lives in a fancy house. He's got blood on those tattooed hands, and it doesn't wash off, Shay."

"Are you trying to scare me away from him? Because it won't work."

"Obviously," he said with a dark laugh. "You and your sister seem to have a type. I always thought you were the smarter sister. The one with goals. The one who was going places." He glanced around the beautiful room with its lavish décor and vaulted ceilings. "Looks like I was right about you going places and having goals. I was just wrong about the type of goals you had and what you were willing to do to attain them."

His barb hit its mark. Like a bullet to the chest, it burned through me, spreading humiliation and embarrassment as I realized what he was insinuating. *He thinks I whored myself out for a big house and money.*

"When was the last time you saw your sister?"

Still hurting from his cruel remark, I said, "Friday afternoon."

"And you haven't talked to her since then?"

"She texted me a few times. She heard about my run-in with Lalo." It was close enough to the truth. "We haven't talked since yesterday."

"You should know that I'm going to pull Shannon's phone records. If you're lying—"

"Yesterday was the last time we spoke."

"May I see your phone?"

"Do you have a warrant?"

Eric shot me a warning look. "I can get one."

"When you have one, come back and ask me again."

"You should be careful playing these kinds of games, Shay. You don't have nearly as much experience as Alexei. You're bound to get burned."

I didn't have a smart reply to that.

"Was Ruben with Shannon the last time you spoke to her?"

"I didn't hear him, but they never spend much time apart so who knows."

"And Lalo? The last time you saw him?"

"Friday night," I lied.

"You haven't had any contact with him since then?"

"No." The lie came quickly and without a hint of emotion. I would take that secret to the grave rather than put Alexei and Kylee in danger.

"Tell me about your car."

His question threw me off but I quickly recovered. "It's in the shop." Not exactly a lie.

"The body shop, you mean," he interjected. "Because your boss told me someone beat your car to hell in the parking lot. He said that some guys in a truck that looked exactly like the one in front of your house took bats and crowbars to the car."

It seemed Eric had done quite a bit of snooping before coming here to talk to Alexei. "That's what he told me, too."

"And?"

"And nothing," I said with a careless shrug. "I called Alexei, and he had one of his friends tow it to a shop."

"And that's it? No insurance claim? No police report."

"Alexei took care of it," I reiterated.

Narrowing his eyes, Eric asked, "Is Alexei going to *take care* of Lalo?"

And that's when I realized that Eric didn't know Lalo was dead.

Treading carefully, I said, "No."

"I find it hard to believe a man like Alexei is going to let someone like Lalo put his hands on his woman and not doing anything about it."

You have no idea, I thought grimly. "Believe whatever you want, but I'm telling you the truth."

"Maybe I'll ask Alexei about Lalo," Eric said in a threatening tone.

"Fine." If Eric thought he could outsmart Alexei when it came to something like this, he was a fool. Eric had said it best. Alexei was a gangster through and through. He was never going to let the police get a step ahead of him. "That's why you're here isn't it?"

"I'm here because I heard a rumor on the streets that Alexei was playing sugar daddy to a cleaning lady. I figured he might know where you and your sister were hiding."

"I'm not hiding. I'm right here."

Eric grunted in annoyance. "Where is Alexei?"

"He's swimming."

Eric shot me a disbelieving look. "It's raining."

"In his other pool," I corrected. "It's indoors."

"Of course it is," he grumbled and rose to his feet. Stuffing his notepad into his pocket, he said, "Tell your boyfriend I'm going to come see him at the dealership tomorrow."

Eric should have known that type of intimidation tactic wasn't going to work on Alexei. "I'll make sure to let him know to expect you."

"You do that."

I stood up, and Eric thrust one of his business cards at me. "If you hear from your sister, you need to call me." He stared down at me, and I tried not to look away, desperate not to reveal my guilt. "That friend of Ruben's? Edgar? His neighbor called in a disturbance, but when the police went inside his apartment, you know what they found?"

I shook my head slowly, not wanting to hear Eric's answer.

"Six fingers and a cracked computer monitor with his blood and hair on it," Eric said in an ominous tone. "That's it."

I didn't even want to think about what had happened to the rest of Edgar. "Why are you telling me this?"

"I'm telling you this because your sister is in deep shit, Shay. This is so much bigger than the dog fighting a few weeks ago. This is bigger than even the drug dealing Ruben does."

"I don't know anything about Shannon or Ruben or this Edgar guy. That's not my life, Detective."

"You better hope to hell it isn't," he warned. "If I'm knocking on this door looking for you, who else do you think is coming next? Lalo? Those men who hassled you at your house and totaled your car?"

Eric was so far behind on this case. I almost felt bad for him. He had no idea that Lalo was dead or that Ruben and Shannon had double-crossed him. He probably assumed Ruben was dead and maybe even thought the same thing about Shannon.

Stay out of it, Shay. Don't say a word. You have to protect Alexei and Kylee.

"I'm a big girl, Detective. I can take care of myself."

"No, you can't." Eric's mouth flattened into a grim line. "But that mobbed-up boyfriend of yours can."

For a long moment, we simply stared at one another. Eric must have sensed that I wasn't going to say anything else. He turned on his heel and marched toward the front door. I let him out, and he left without another word.

Thinking of what he said about other people coming to look for me, I locked the door and switched on the security system. Feeling ill at ease and worried about this new complication, I went in search of Alexei. I finally found him in a room connected to his home gym.

It was like walking into a high-end spa with the honey-colored travertine and glass walls and doors. There were potted plants and miniature trees in the corners of the room and plenty of comfortable seating. The French doors along the back wall overlooked another part of his property that I wanted to explore when the weather wasn't quite so bleak.

I stepped into the pool room and watched Alexei gliding through the water. The rectangular pool was narrow and long and perfect for swimming laps. It seemed a bit wasteful to me to have two pools, and I didn't even want to think about the upkeep costs of an arrangement like that. More and more, I suspected Alexei's money wasn't just from his dealerships and that trucking company he owned. There was no way he was clearing enough money from those businesses to live like this.

But I wasn't sure I really wanted to know where the money came from. I remembered what Stas had said. I shouldn't ask questions, right? Maybe Stas had the right idea. He had obviously figured out a way to survive in the shadowy world Alexei had once lived in and I would do well to heed his advice before I found myself in even more trouble.

Not wanting to disturb Alexei while he swam, I sat on one of the lounge chairs near the pool and waited. It was no hardship watching him. His powerful body cut through the water at a steady speed. I envied his ease in the water. Swimming had never been a skill I had tackled. Even now, water deeper than a bathroom tub made me nervous.

I hadn't been sitting there long before Alexei noticed me. He paused at the far end of the pool and wiped the water from his face and eyes. His happy expression turned to one of concern, his forehead furrowing with worry when he had a good look at me. After Eric's mini interrogation, I didn't have the energy to smile and look pretty.

Alexei swam to my side of the pool and rested his forearms on the tile deck. "*Malysh*? What's wrong? You look upset."

I held up the business card. "Eric Santos was just here."

Alexei's expression turned stormy. "The detective? He was here? In my house?"

Even though he hadn't raised his voice, I could tell he was upset. "Yes."

Alexei swore under his breath. "You shouldn't have let him inside, Shay. It's not safe to have the police poking around in our business."

Hearing him call this mess *our* business made it seem somehow less daunting. "I'm sorry. I didn't know what else to do. He was standing on the front porch, and I didn't think it was a good idea to let him walk away without answering."

"It's all right. I know this is new territory for you. The next time you see Eric, you tell him that you're not talking to him without a lawyer."

"I don't have a lawyer, Alexei."

"You will. Tomorrow morning, I'm getting you one."

"That seems a bit extreme."

"Do I need to remind you of all the shit that's happened since Friday? You *need* a lawyer." Running his fingers through his wet hair, Alexei asked, "What did Eric want?"

"He was looking for me. Apparently, I'm missing."

Alexei cursed again. "And he came here because...?"

"I guess there's a rumor about you and me going around," I said with a sad smile. "People like to talk."

"Yes, they do." Clearly unhappy to be the subject of the underworld rumor mill, he asked, "What else did Eric want?"

"He knows that Lalo and I got into an altercation at the Arena. He has video evidence."

"Fuck."

"Yeah. But he doesn't seem to know about anything else." I didn't want to say the words, and I didn't need to because Alexei understood.

"None of it?" Alexei seemed surprised.

"He warned me to be careful about Lalo. He also told me to call him if I see or hear from Shannon or Ruben."

"He doesn't have the faintest fucking clue, does he?" Alexei shook his head in disbelief. "Well that's good news for us."

"I guess."

"It is," Alexei assured me.

"Eric told me to tell you that he's going to visit you at the dealership tomorrow."

Alexei snorted with amusement. He wasn't the least bit

intimidated. "As if he can rattle me with a threat like that!"

"Alexei," I said pleadingly. "Please be careful. I've known Eric a long time, and he is not the sort of man to let things go. He's like a dog with a bone, and if he thinks there's a chance you're involved with this whole mess, he will make your life a living hell."

"I'd like to see him try," Alexei replied, totally unfazed. "He doesn't scare me. My relationship with Eric goes back years. Back to the days when he was a patrol cop." Clearly interested in my history with Eric, he asked, "How do you know him?"

"Eric was the first cop to bust Shannon. That was way back when Mom was still around," I said, my brain bombarded with memories I didn't want. "He also responded to some of the 9-1-1 calls when things got out of hand between Mom and her boyfriends."

"I'm sorry that you had to go through that, Shay." The tenderness in his gaze was enough to make me forget all about Eric's visit. "You deserved a better childhood than that."

"I survived it, and I'm better for it." In so many ways, I believed that. "You had a rough start in life, too. You didn't deserve that either."

"Most of the rough things in my background were my own fault." Not wanting to talk about his past, he held out his hand. "Come into the pool with me."

I gulped and shrank back. "No, thank you."

"Come swim with me, Shay."

"I don't have a bathing suit." I stated the obvious and gestured to my leggings and sweater.

"We're alone in the house. Take it off, and get in the water with me." He ran his hand through water. "It's warm."

Feeling embarrassed, I realized I couldn't come up with enough excuses and finally admitted, "I don't know how to swim. I never learned."

Alexei's eyebrows arched with surprise. "As hot as it is here in the summers and you never learned to swim?"

"There weren't many pools in the neighborhoods I grew up in," I said somewhat bitterly.

"Take off your clothes," Alexei all but ordered.

"What?"

"Strip."

Biting my lip, I thought about telling him no but he had that gleam in his eye. Slowly, I rose to my feet and started peeling out of my clothes. Naked and feeling vulnerable, I stood in front of him.

"Come sit on the edge of the pool." He patted the space right in front of him. When I hesitated, he promised, "I won't pull you in or try to do anything stupid like that. Just come sit here and put your feet in the water."

Trusting him, I did as he asked and sat on the cold tile. I slipped my feet into the pool. The warm water lapped at my calves. It felt nice, but I was terrified of going in any deeper.

As if sensing my fear, Alexei put his hands on my waist. "You're perfectly safe with me, Shay."

"I know." I rested my hands on his shoulders. "I'm just afraid."

"It's okay to be afraid." He touched his lips to mine in a sweet kiss. "This water isn't that deep. I'm standing flat footed right now."

The water hit him mid-chest, but with our height difference, I was pretty sure it would cover my head.

He must have been reading my mind. "If you wrap your legs around my waist, I'll hold you up."

I narrowed my eyes at him. "Wrap my legs around your waist, huh?"

He laughed. "Humor me."

Swallowing anxiously, I nodded. "Okay."

Alexei enveloped me in his strong arms and lifted me off the edge of the pool. I wrapped my legs around his waist as he gently lowered me into the water. "I've got you, *ptichka*."

Even though I knew he never would, I begged, "Please don't let go."

"Never," he promised and kissed me again. Floating in the warm water and safe in his arms, his sensual kiss ignited my passion like a spark to dry tinder. His incredible body, hard and honed, supported me so easily. He flicked his tongue against mine, and my thighs tightened around him in response. There was a flutter in my lower belly, and I moaned against his mouth.

Pulling back, I gazed down at him and whispered, "I have a feeling I'm not going to get that swimming lesson."

"Probably not," he agreed, a relaxed smile playing upon his lips. "But there's always tomorrow."

As Alexei kissed me again and slid one of his big hands down to cup my bottom, I had a pretty good feeling we wouldn't get to the swimming lesson tomorrow either…

CHAPTER EIGHTEEN

W HEN ALEXEI'S ALARM sounded early the next morning, he did the unthinkable. He slapped the top of the annoying machine until he found the button to switch it off and then curled around Shay's lithe body. She made a soft, kittenish sound as he kissed a lazy line from her shoulder to her neck and up to her ear. He didn't want to wake her so he left it there and simply held her until her breaths deepened and she relaxed completely.

Long conditioned to be out of bed before the sun, he wanted to linger in bed with her this morning. The thought of being separated from her during the coming day was almost too much to bear. A small voice in the back of his mind reminded him that he was the boss and he could take the entire day off if he wanted. Those were the perks of running his own businesses.

But that was a slippery slope. He'd seen what happened to businesses run by absentee owners. If he gave in to the urge to call off and stay in bed with Shay today, Tuesday would be even harder and Wednesday damn near impossible.

Deciding to skip his usual morning run, he closed his eyes and breathed in her feminine scent. Flashes of their evening together taunted him. Once he had her in the pool with him, it hadn't taken him long to show her all the different ways they could enjoy the water. They had ordered delivery and kicked back in his media room to watch the Food Network which was, apparently, her favorite channel. She started to nod off during one of the cooking competitions so they had cut their night short.

It wasn't a particularly remarkable night, but he had enjoyed it more than any other night he could remember. Sitting there next to Shay in his media room, he had realized just how lonely he was and how empty his life had become. In his drive to amass more wealth and more expensive things and his desperate need to keep himself walled off from other people, he had starved himself of the most necessary things for a man.

When Shay had placed her head in his lap and dragged his arm over her waist so she could hold his hand while watching television, he had experienced the strangest yearning sensation. Like a lump he couldn't swallow, his emotions had balled up in his throat. She would never understand how something so innocent could affect him in such a way.

"You're going to be late," Shay murmured sleepily.

"I have plenty of time to get to work." He nuzzled the back of her neck and stroked her stomach through the thin cotton nightshirt she wore. "Hear that rain hitting the windows? I have no desire to lace up my running shoes and splash through that when I can stay right here with you for another hour."

Shay interlaced her fingers with his and dragged his hand under her shirt. "I have an idea how you can still burn some calories here in bed with me."

Laughing softly, he nipped at her earlobe. "Show me."

Shay guided his hand to her bare breast. He could feel her heart beating as fast as a hummingbird's underneath his fingertips. With her hand resting atop his, he caressed her silky skin. He cupped her breasts and brushed his thumb over her nipples, feeling them pucker and harden as she breathed a little faster and shallower.

Reaching back, Shay slid her smaller hand into the loose shorts he liked to sleep in and discovered his hardening cock. She stroked the length of him, coaxing him to grow harder and longer. As he kissed her neck and shoulder, she pushed back against him, rubbing her tight little ass against his dick in a daring way.

Never one to turn away an invite like that, Alexei grasped the bottom of her shirt and dragged it up her body. Shay shifted so he could remove it and helped him when he tugged on her panties. It didn't take him long to kick off his shorts.

Skin to skin, they kissed passionately. He couldn't get enough of this woman—*my woman*—and wondered if she had any idea of the powerful sway she held over him. Like a witch, she had enchanted him and held him right in the palm of her hand.

When Shay arched onto her back and tried to wrap her legs around his waist, to draw him inside her and get the satisfaction she craved, he made a low warning sound and lifted off her nubile body. He manhandled Shay, drawing an excited laugh from her, and flipped her right onto her belly.

Shoving aside her hair, he nibbled her nape and kissed across her shoulders. She wiggled her bottom, and he gave her a good smack, causing her to yelp and hiss. But she wasn't daunted by that brief bite of pain. She pushed back even

316 | ROXIE RIVERA

harder, almost as if to test his resolve. He answered her teasing wiggle with another swat and another.

"Alexei!" Desperation filled her voice. "*Please*."

"Please what?" He skimmed his lips down her spine. Those scars crisscrossing her back still hadn't been discussed, but they would have to be soon. For now, he put them out of his mind and concentrated on the beautiful, sexy woman begging him to fuck her.

"I can't take anymore," she said, nearly breathless. "Don't make me wait."

"*Kotyonok*." Smiling, he brushed his mouth over her back. "Patience."

He nudged her thighs apart and cupped between them. Shay inhaled a ragged breath of excitement, the sound urging him to continue. She was already wet for him when he probed her with one finger and then two. Dropping her head to the mattress, Shay moaned as he worked her with both hands, thrusting into her pussy with two fingers on hand and strumming her clit with the other. She swiveled her hips, and he moved his hands at a faster pace until she came with a strangled groan. Her back bowed as she rode his fingers until the last burst of bliss left her.

Gripping her hips, he hauled Shay onto her knees and pushed them apart. He sheathed himself with one swift thrust. She clawed at sheets and rocked back against him. He took her easily at first, enjoying the leisurely pace and sweeping his hands up and down her back. The grey light creeping through the windows washed over her body, but it wasn't enough to highlight the sensual curves he'd grown to love so much.

Cloaked in shadow, he ran his palms over her perfect ass.

Wondering if she might be interested in one of his favorite bedroom activities, he dragged his thumb between her plump cheeks and then circled the tight pucker hidden away there. She gasped when he touched her so intimately, but she didn't pull away or tell him to stop.

Permission granted, he drew lazy circles around it, applying a subtle pressure, but he didn't try to penetrate her. She wasn't ready for that yet, and he'd only hurt her if he tried to slide in dry. But he could tell by her excited breaths and movements that she liked the way it felt. She was definitely curious, and he intended to help her explore that curiosity soon.

Alexei slid his hand along her waist and down the slope of her lower belly until he touched her clitoris. She bucked against his hand, and he grinned devilishly. She responded so beautifully and easily. The combination of his deep, measured thrusts and his rubbing fingers was enough to push her over the edge again.

Her orgasm felt incredible for him. The sensation of her snug pussy gripping him as she cried out his name made his balls ache. Dropping his hand, he gripped her hips and took her faster. She jerked on the sheets, her fingers fisting around the fabric as she met each powerful thrust. Deeper. Harder. Faster. He chased that burning, throbbing pull building at the base of his spine.

Taking her hair in one hand, he pulled her head back, gently but with some force, and bit the side of her neck. He wanted to leave a love bite right there, a little mark to remind her that she belonged to him and that she drove him fucking crazy when they were together. Shay's shocked gasp was the trigger for his orgasm. Buried deep inside her, he closed his eyes as a pleasurable bolt rocked him.

They collapsed together onto the bed. Tangled in the sheets that had popped free, they panted and trembled. When Shay turned toward him, he gathered her hot body in his arms and drew her in close. She pressed sweet, soft kisses on his jaw, each one causing his heart to swell with his unspoken love for her.

The urge to confess it all was so strong, but he knew she wasn't ready. Instead, he declared, "Fuck running! I'm going to set my alarm for this every morning."

Shay giggled and pressed up on one hand. Looking down at him, she caressed his face. Her hair fell around them like a curtain. He almost couldn't believe how beautiful she was. Running her finger around his lips, she whispered, "You amaze me."

"If you think this amazing, wait until you see what I have planned for tonight."

Shay laughed again and bent down to kiss him. Drawing back, she said, "I'm going to take a shower and then I'm going to cook you breakfast."

"You don't have to do that."

She rolled her eyes at him. "Let me guess. Mistresses don't cook breakfast, right?"

"No, they don't." *But wives do*, he thought wistfully.

Touching her forehead to his, she whispered playfully, "Then I guess it's a good thing I've never played by the rules."

He patted her bottom. "A very good thing."

Shay kissed him one last time before crawling over him and sliding out of bed. He gave her a few minutes of privacy in the bathroom and waited until he heard the shower running to join her. Glad for the multiple shower heads, he went through his usual morning routine, but he kept sneaking glances at Shay as she washed and conditioned her hair, shaved her legs and soaped up her body.

He had always dreaded this kind of closeness with another person. With earlier relationships, he had feared sharing his home with a woman with a nearly claustrophobic desperation. Today he couldn't bear the thought of Shay straying beyond arm's reach.

When she stepped out of the shower, he switched off the water and followed her. Watching her dab the water from her skin and rub lotion into her legs and arms was better than a striptease. Wrapping a towel around his waist, he decided he liked how comfortable she had grown with him. They'd come a long way since that first night at the penthouse when she had covered up like a nun and run for cover behind a door to avoid being seen.

Standing at the counter, he leaned down at the sink and splashed hot water on his face before reaching for his shaving brush and the canister of shaving soap he preferred. He had just started to work up a lather with the brush when he noticed Shay standing in front of her meager selection of clothing. Wearing only her panties, she held a pair of those black yoga pants she liked and reached for the last remaining clean shirt.

As he lathered up his face, he said, "We'll have to get your things from the house."

"If we don't, I'll have to raid your side of the closet."

The thought of Shay in his button-downs brought a smile to his face. When she was dressed, she wrapped her damp hair in a towel and brushed her fingers across his back. He paused his shaving to quickly sneak in a kiss before she moved out of reach.

"Alexei!" She laughed and wiped at the shaving foam on her chin and nose.

Chuckling, he handed her the nearest towel. "Sorry."

"I doubt it." She cleaned her face and put the towel back on the counter. She leaned toward the mirror and eyed the love bite on her neck. "And this?"

"Not sorry," he said, scraping his razor down his cheek.

"Just remember that two can play that game," she warned as she backed out of the bathroom. "Maybe tomorrow I'll send you to work looking like the quarterback after the homecoming dance…"

He wasn't so sure that was a bad thing, but he didn't dare tell her that. He finished his morning routine and put on a crisp black suit and shoes. He picked out a watch and cufflinks, slung his jacket over his shoulder and left the master suite. Downstairs in his office, he crouched down to open the safe hidden in the credenza behind his desk.

As was his habit, he counted the neatly stacked envelopes of cash, ensuring not a single one was missing. Each envelope contained a mix of cash, the notes bound tightly in their brightly colored currency straps, and the dollar amounts contained within written on the upper right corner of each one. He had a good idea of the monthly salary Shay brought home so he added it to the allowance figure he had in mind for her so she could cover her expenses and have plenty extra to spend on herself.

After he gathered up the envelopes he needed for Stas and

made a mental count of the amount of replacement cash he needed from the bank, he eyed the extra set of house keys and the key to the garage lockbox. When he'd called in a locksmith to change all the locks the day that he closed on the property, the locksmith had assumed he would need a set for his wife. Alexei had dropped them in the new safe a few days later, and the set had been waiting here ever since.

Waiting for her...

His phone started to ring as he was locking up the safe. Tossing the envelopes of money and the keys onto the credenza, he answered it. "Hello?"

"Alexei?"

"Yes." He closed the cabinet door guarding the safe and rose to his full height. He pocketed the extra set of keys.

"It's Spider. I wanted to let you know that my girl is boxing up Shay's place. I'll have some of my guys drive the truck over to your penthouse this afternoon."

"No, have them bring it to my house." He rattled off the address while gathering up the envelopes. "Stas can help your men unload the truck."

"Whatever you want," Spider replied.

"Is there a balance on the lease?"

"They just renewed in May."

"Have someone run a bill to my office. I'll cut a check to cover the rest of their lease."

"If that's the way you want it," Spider said. "But you should know that the police were crawling all over that house yesterday."

"So I've heard," Alexei confirmed with irritation.

"I trust you know how to handle your business." Spider

322 | ROXIE RIVERA

didn't need to say anything else. "If you need my help, you know where to find me."

The call ended and Alexei pocketed his phone. Envelopes in hand, he made his way to the kitchen, his stomach growling as he inhaled the delicious scents wafting from there. When he arrived, he was stopped in his tracks by the sight of Shay cooking.

Lingering in the doorway, he watched the way she moved around the kitchen with ease, tending a pan on the gas stove and keeping an eye on something in the built-in ovens at the same time. She was totally at home in this environment.

Sensing his presence, Shay glanced back at him. "I'm almost finished."

"I'm in no rush." And he really wasn't. He would find any excuse to enjoy every single moment of his first morning with Shay in his home.

He entered the kitchen and placed the envelopes on the counter, out of the way. He noticed the damp towel draped over the back of one of the tall chairs at the counter. Shay had quickly and loosely braided her damp hair to get it out of the way. He gave the end of her braid a playful tug as he passed behind her to reach the coffee pot. "Do you want some coffee?"

"No."

"I think I have some orange juice in the refrigerator." He wasn't ever sure what he had in there, to be honest. Denise kept the place stocked with the things he liked, and he magically never seemed to run out.

"That's fine." She returned her attention to the breakfast she was cooking. He glanced at the stove as his coffee sputtered into its cup and watched her spread some of the creamy white béchamel she'd made onto the golden brown ham and cheese sandwiches she had been toasting in the oven. She carefully slipped the pan back into the oven before flipping the eggs she was frying.

Alexei put away the ingredients she had finished using and poured a glass of juice for her. He set the table in the breakfast nook and had just taken his seat when she brought over two plates with piping hot croque-madame. There was a sprinkling of chives on top of each egg. She had decorated each plate with thinly sliced oranges twisted to form figure eights and sliced, fanned strawberries.

"You didn't have to go to all this trouble. I'm glad that you did because it looks delicious, and I'm starving, but I would have been happy with a bowl of oatmeal."

"Remember that tomorrow when I slide a bowl of gruel in front of you," she warned and took her seat.

"It wouldn't be the first time I've eaten watery thin *kasha* for breakfast." He stabbed his fork into the soft yolk and watched the yellow cream mix with the béchamel. "That's standard prison fare."

He was just cutting through his sandwich when he noticed Shay wasn't moving. He glanced up and frowned at her stricken face. "What is it?"

"I'm so sorry, Alexei. I shouldn't have made a joke like that."

"Shay," he said with a quiet laugh, "it doesn't bother me to talk about that part of my life." He paused to reflect. "What I should say is that it doesn't bother me to talk about that part of my life with you."

"Why doesn't it bother you to talk about prison with me?" She seemed genuinely curious.

"I don't know," he admitted uncomfortably.

Shay popped her egg yolk with the tines of her fork. "Maybe you don't mind talking to me because you know I won't judge you. I'm basically the poster child for a dysfunctional family."

"Maybe," he agreed quietly. Her mention of dysfunctional families made him think of those scars on her back. Asking her about them in the bedroom or shower had seemed like a bad idea. He didn't want her to feel attacked or self-conscious about her body. Here in the kitchen, he felt relatively safe asking her about them. "Shay?"

"Mmm-hmm?"

"Can we talk about the scars on your back?"

Shay froze. Like a deer caught in the headlights, she panicked right in front of him. She opened her mouth and then shut it quickly. Focusing all of her attention on her breakfast, she stabbed at it with her fork. "No, we can't."

"Shay," he pushed gently, "I've told you about my tattoos. The stories behind these," he gestured to the markings on his left hand, "are surely a thousand times worse than the story about your back."

"You're probably right, but it's *my* story to tell when I'm ready to tell it."

"And when will that be?"

She dropped her fork. It bounced off her plate with a noisy clatter. Exasperated, she asked, "Seriously, Alexei, what is the big deal? They're scars. End of story."

"If it's not a big deal, you should have no problem telling

me how they happened." Unable to comprehend why she was being so cagey about this, he began to fear something truly horrific had happened to her. Worried he might unknowingly do something to trigger pain or fear, he insisted, "I think I have the right to know about your body."

"Why would you think that? Because we had sex? You think have ownership over me?" Obviously angered by his remark, she said, "I'm not a car, Alexei. You don't get a rundown of all my dings and scratches before you buy me."

Realizing he had pushed too far, he hurried to fix things between them. "I didn't mean it like that, Shay. I only meant that I think I have the right to know who hurt you."

"Why? Look, it happened a long time ago. It's done. It's over. I don't want to think about any of that ever again, okay?" Her appetite gone, she stood up and grabbed her plate. Before retreating to the sink, she snapped, "If the scars bother you that much, I'm sure you can find someone else to sleep with, Alexei."

"Stop right there, Shay!" He was on his feet in an instant and intercepted her before she reached the island. Taking the plate from her hand, he set it aside and then gripped both of her small hands in his larger ones. Knowing that he had caused the pain and embarrassment that was etched into her face made him feel like the biggest dick in the world.

"Shay," he whispered, trying to figure out how to make it right. "*Malysh.*" He pulled her in tight and touched his forehead to hers. "I didn't mean to upset you like this. It was stupid of me to push and push like that."

He lifted his head and gazed down at her, trying to gauge her emotional state. Her lower lib wobbled precariously, and he knew that apology wasn't enough. She needed to know why.

Stroking her cheek, he explained, "Our first night together, I didn't have all the facts, and I hurt you." She opened her mouth to argue with him, but he silenced her gently with a finger against her soft lips. "I did hurt you, Shay. I don't ever want to hurt you again. If something happened to you, if someone hurt you so badly they left scars, I need to know how it happened so that I never do anything that might make you think of person or that time when we're alone together."

Not sure she understood exactly what he meant, he continued, "I've popped your backside three or four times since we've been together, Shay. I grabbed your wrists that first night and held you down while I made love to you and—"

"I liked it," she admitted quietly. "I *really* like it when you do those things." With a blush in her cheeks, she said, "I hope you don't stop just because of some scars on my back."

"I told you before, Shay. You're in control of that part of our life together. Whatever you want, I'll give you."

She nodded once. Then, with a tired sigh, she said, "Unless your bedroom kink includes beating me with an extension cord and then locking me in a dark closet for two days, I don't think you need to worry about setting me off on some spiral into my horrible childhood memories."

Alexei sucked in a sharp breath at her description of the events that had led to the scars on her back. The shock he felt was quickly subsumed by raging fury. "How old were you?"

"Ten," she said.

He remembered seeing the photos of Shay and her sister when they were younger on the walls of her house. Just imagining that sweet, innocent pigtailed little girl treated so brutally sickened him. He wanted to hurt someone for her. It might be thirteen years too late, but he wanted to give her justice. "What was his name?"

"What?" She seemed confused by his question.

"The man who hit you," he clarified. "Tell me his name."

She put a soothing hand on his chest. "It wasn't a man." She hesitated before admitting, "It was my mother."

"Why?" He couldn't think of any reason a mother would beat a child so terribly.

Shay dropped her gaze to the floor, and instantly, he knew he wasn't going to like what she had to say. "I came home one afternoon, and Mom's boyfriend was trying to hurt Shannon. He had her boxed into a corner and had his hand up her skirt. I didn't know what else to do so I hit him with my backpack and kicked him."

He wanted to ask what happened next, but he didn't want to interrupt or pressure her. She needed to tell this story in her own time.

"Shannon ran out the back door, and she left me there with him. I think she was so traumatized that she wasn't thinking straight."

Bullshit, he thought angrily. Even back then, Shannon was only concerned with herself.

"He got up and…" Shay's voice faded. After a few tense seconds, she said, "He sort of leered at me and then he told me that if I was jealous of his attention toward Shannon he had plenty to give me."

Oh no. God, no, Alexei silently begged.

"I backed up into the kitchen, and he kept coming toward

me. He was excited, but I didn't really understand it then. It wasn't until I was a little older that I understood it all the things he said to me and the way he was touching himself."

Shay gripped her left wrist with her right hand and rhythmically squeezed it in a way that could only be described as a nervous tic. Not wanting her to feel alone right now, he took her hand and interlaced their fingers, giving her something to squeeze and hold onto for support.

"But he made a mistake backing me into that kitchen," Shay said, her voice stronger now. "I had done the dishes the night before so they were laid out neatly in the dish rack. I grabbed a knife, and I cut him." She touched her arm and chest and neck. "I just slashed at him. It wasn't very deep, but he was bleeding everywhere when Mom walked into the house. She had just gotten off a double shift, and she lost it when she saw the blood and the knife."

Knowing what a kind, gentle soul Shay was, he could hardly fathom how terrified she must have been to lash out in violence to protect herself. "What do you mean? Lost it how?"

"He started telling her all this bullshit about me and Shannon, telling her that we were lying little whores and that we wanted to break them up because we wanted him all to ourselves. He told her that we flirted with him all the time when she was at work and that we liked to walk around half-naked after our showers in the evening. She just ate it right up. He said he was leaving, and they started fighting. It was awful, and I just—I wanted to get out of there, but I didn't know where to go. It was almost Christmas, and it was so cold…"

"And your mother took her anger out on you," Alexei guessed, doing everything he could to hide the disgust he felt.

"Pretty much," Shay sadly agreed.

Alexei had never hit a woman in his life, but an exception would have to be made if he ever crossed paths with Shay's mother.

"Shannon came home two nights later, and I was still locked in the closet. She got me out of there and took me to Ruben's apartment. He was living on his own by then, and he and Shannon had already been making plans to run off and get married as soon as she was old enough. But then Mom split and Shannon's dreams of getting married went with her."

"Is that why you let Shannon get away with so much?" He was finally starting to understand the depth of Shay's guilt when it came to her older sister. If she imagined herself to be the reason her sister wasn't able to get married and start a new life, there was nothing she wouldn't do to help Shannon now.

"The Shannon you know isn't the Shannon I grew up with," Shay insisted.

"If you say so," he replied.

"I do say so—and I know what you're going to ask next," Shay said with a frown. "You're going to ask about that boyfriend of Mom's."

"I was," he admitted. "He deserves what he's got coming to him."

"He deserved a lot of things, but he's dead."

"When? How?"

Shay shrugged uncertainly. "New Year's Eve of that year. He was stabbed to death in the bathroom at a club."

"Ruben?" For a young man with aspirations toward the inner circle of a street game, the dishonor that was done to Shannon would never have been allowed to stand. Ruben would have been expected to spill blood to avenge Shannon.

Shay nodded. "For all his faults, he loves Shannon. He would do anything for her."

Alexei didn't correct her verb tense. It was better that she referred to Ruben as alive rather than dead, especially if Eric Santos was going to be snooping around her.

Cupping the back of her neck, he tilted her head back and held her gaze. "Are we all right?"

"We're good."

"I'm sorry I upset you." He kissed her lovingly. "I didn't mean to ruin our morning."

"You didn't ruin it." She kissed him right back. "We're probably going to argue like this more often than either of us would like. Especially right now," she added, "when our relationship is so new."

"I wouldn't know," he replied carefully. "The women I dated before you didn't argue with me."

She actually snorted with laughter. Arching one of those winged brows at him, she warned, "Don't expect a free pass from me."

"I wouldn't dream of it." He didn't tell her that he sometimes enjoyed the way she pushed back. He needed a woman who wouldn't let him get away with bullshit. He needed a woman brave enough to call him out when it was required.

Holding her hand, he picked up her plate and led her back to the table. He made himself a second cup of coffee before joining her.

"Is it okay if Kylee comes over today?" she asked in between bites.

He was struck by the uncomfortable way her query made

him think of a child's relationship with a parent. Their relationship already had problems of inequality when it came it money, age and experience. He didn't want to add another layer to that. "Shay, you don't need to ask permission to have guests."

"But, at the penthouse, you said—"

"That was different." He cringed at the memory of the things he had said to her there. *Fuck.* She must have thought he was a controlling asshole with all his rules and stipulations! Now, knowing what he did of her experience with men and relationships, he realized that it had obviously never occurred to her to negotiate with him. That was part of the give-and-take between mistresses and their benefactors.

Wanting a fresh start, he stated, "The arrangement between us has changed. I would prefer to be told before you have guests in the house only because I'm concerned about your safety. This home is your home."

She pushed food around her plate. "For how long?"

Forever. But he didn't say that. It would scare her if she found out he was thinking long-term after only a few days. She needed time to get comfortable with their living arrangement and to decide that she wanted to stay with him. "For as long as you would like," he said instead.

She seemed satisfied with that response. "Do you mind if I work in here? I have some orders that need to be finished this week."

"You can set up your workshop wherever you'd like. The kitchen probably has the most available space." He glanced around the room and sized up the work surfaces. "But you might like the privacy of my office more. Denise rarely goes in

332 | ROXIE RIVERA

there so she won't bother you much."

"When does she get here?"

"Around ten." He glanced at his watch to make sure he had enough time to get to the dealership in time to prepare for the morning sales floor meeting. "I let her come in late because she takes her grandchildren to school. Her daughter works an overnight shift at one of the hospitals downtown. She's usually out of here by two or three so you'll have the house to yourself most of the day."

"Except for Stas."

"Yes, and that reminds me…" He lifted his hips so he could get his hand into the pocket of his trousers to retrieve the keys. Taking her hand, he turned it over and placed the keys on her palm. "These are yours. This key opens the front door. This one opens the door between the mud room and the garage. This one opens the lockbox in the garage where I store the keys to my vehicles. You may drive any of them."

Alexei closed her fingers around the keys. "You're the only with these keys. Denise has a garage door opener that allows her into her parking space, and I leave the side door open for her. Stas will need you to open doors for him. You'll have to pick the car you'd like him to drive each day."

"Do you have, like, a minivan with two different colored doors and maybe rusted out rims? Because I'd really like to see Stas driving that around town today," she said with some irritation.

"Shay," he said carefully, "Stas isn't used to dealing with women. He's a street soldier. You have to make some allowances for his behavior. Not all of it, but some of it. I spoke with Stas yesterday and made it very clear that he isn't to upset you again."

Shay sat back in her chair and played with the keys he had given her. "I don't think he meant to be a jerk. I think he really was trying to be helpful. In his own way, he was trying to protect me."

"That's what I pay him to do."

"For how long?" Shay twirled the key ring around her finger. "I don't think he actually enjoys this line of work."

"It doesn't matter what he enjoys or doesn't enjoy," Alexei said matter-of-factly. "Nikolai owns him. He'll do what the boss says or he'll find himself on a plane back to New York."

"Did Nikolai own you?" Shay bravely asked.

"Maksim, his boss, did," Alexei explained. "When Nikolai got the green light to come here, I jumped ship and came with him." Motioning around them, he said, "It worked out for the best. I've made more money here than I ever dreamed possible."

"Is it all legit?" she asked carefully.

He wasn't sure he was ready to divulge all the dirty details of his rise to this level of wealth. "Every penny in my bank accounts today is legit. It's all clean."

"But it was dirty once?"

"Some of it," he said. "It's complicated, but if you really want to know all the secrets I have, I can tell you about it some other time. It's not something I can do in ten minutes." Certain she was concerned about his well-being and safety and the security he could provide, he assured her, "I don't owe outrageous debts, Shay. This house will be mine in two years. I have a comfortable amount of money tucked away in various safe places."

"And what about all the favors you've called in to protect me? What kind of debts are you going to owe because of me?"

"You don't need to worry about any of that." Rising out of his chair, he came around to her side of the table and leaned down to kiss her. Gliding his hand over her braid, he said, "You're worth every fucking penny, Shay."

The doorbell rang, interrupting their moment, and he left her in the kitchen to answer it. He found Stas on the porch and welcomed him into the house. "Shay is finishing her breakfast. She's expecting company today. She'll let you know what else she wants or needs to do. There will also be a delivery later this afternoon."

"What kind of delivery?" Stas removed his damp jacket and placed it in the coat closet Alexei pointed out to him.

"Spider is having Shay's house boxed up this morning. They're bringing the truck when they're done. Take the boxes upstairs to one of the extra bedrooms. Shay will let you know which boxes need to come into the master suite."

Stas nodded. "Consider it done."

"She has the keys and access to my garage. I would prefer that you drive her around town in one of my vehicles."

"All right."

Alexei flicked his fingers and Stas followed him into the kitchen. He found Shay standing at the sink washing dishes by hand. It didn't surprise him that she was cleaning up after herself even though a housekeeper was on her way.

Picking up an envelope, he checked it to be sure it contained the proper amount and handed it to Stas. "To cover her expenses and yours," he said in Russian. "Whatever is left at the end of the week, you can keep."

Stas nodded and slipped the envelope into the back pocket of his jeans. Rightly guessing that Alexei wanted to be alone with Shay for a few minutes, Stas left the kitchen.

Envelopes in hand, Alexei came up behind Shay and embraced her. He kissed her temple. "I have to go."

Shay leaned into his kiss and reached for a dish towel to dry her hands. "What time will you be home?"

For the first time in his life, Alexei had a reason to come straight home. The house wouldn't be empty. Shay would be right here waiting for him. "Seven or eight."

Turning in his arms, she put her hand on his chest. "I'll make something for dinner."

"You don't have to cook. We can go out for dinner."

"Not like this," she gestured to her healing face. "I need a few more days and some strategic makeup buys before I can go out in public. I don't want people getting the wrong idea."

He didn't fancy the idea of people assuming he had been the one to hit her either.

"Do you need any errands run today? Anything specific you want done around the house?"

He realized what she was doing. "You don't have to earn your keep, Shay."

"I'd feel better about taking money from you if I was actively doing something around here to help. Otherwise, I'm basically earning my salary on my back."

He didn't care for that comparison but he understood she felt strongly about the money issue. "Listen," he said, an idea forming, "why don't you sell me a piece of your company."

"What?" She seemed baffled by the offer. "Are you serious?"

"Yes. I've seen your business plan."

"You saw my business plan?"

"At your house," he explained. "When I went to pack up some of your things. It's a solid plan. I've seen your work. You produce quality pieces. You have strong sales. What you need is a capital injection." He handed her the envelopes. "Consider this your first disbursement. Use it to cover your living and operating expenses."

Shay hesitantly took the envelopes from him. "We need a contract or something legal between us, Alexei. Someday you're going to want to be repaid for your investment."

"We'll talk about it tonight." He captured her mouth in a lingering kiss. "Thank you for breakfast." He kissed her again. "Try not to get Stas in trouble today."

"Alexei!" She smacked his chest with the envelopes, but he kissed away her annoyed retort.

He allowed himself a moment to simply appreciate how lovely she looked. "Call me if you need anything."

"I will."

Not wanting to leave her, he pivoted on his heel, picked up his jacket from the back of the chair where he had draped it and left the kitchen. Out in the garage, he slid behind the wheel of his SUV and cranked the engine. Rolling down the private driveway, he experienced the strangest sensation of dread and fear. It took him another block of driving before he figured out why.

I'm happy.

He was finally, truly happy—and it terrified him. After the intense stress of the last few days, after Shay had nearly been killed twice, Alexei was painfully aware of how easily and quickly she could be taken away from him.

His first instinct was to clamp down and keep Shay isolated, but she would wither away and die like a flower starved of sunlight if he did that. She needed her freedom, and he wanted her to have it.

And if that meant he had to make deals with some of the city's worst devils? So be it.

CHAPTER NINETEEN

"HOLY. FUCK." KYLEE exclaimed for probably the twentieth time as she followed me on a tour through Alexei's house. "I mean, the house I grew up in was big but this place is crazy, stupid huge. What the hell does he do here all by himself?"

"I don't think he spends that much time here." I led her into Alexei's office and shut the door after sharing a look with Stas. It was going to take some time for our fledgling relationship to recover. Right now, I wanted privacy and I didn't want to have to worry about getting in Denise's way as she worked.

"Really?" Kylee walked around the perimeter of the room before plonking down in an overstuffed leather club chair. "Why do you think that?"

I shrugged and dropped into the chair across from her. "Think about the hours he puts in at work. Then add in the time he spends at the gym, restaurants, bars…"

"You'd think he'd just keep that penthouse," Kylee remarked. "Less upkeep, lower monthly expenses and all that."

"I'm sure he had his reasons."

"Listen to you being all protective of your Russian sugar daddy!"

I rolled my eyes at her teasing. "He's not my sugar daddy."

"Did he or did he not give you stacks of cash in envelopes this morning?"

"Well…"

"Exactly," she announced triumphantly.

"It's not like that and you know it," I insisted, feeling a bit hurt.

She must have realized that I wasn't keen on her teasing because she immediately stopped. "You know I don't mean it in a bad way, Shay. He's a good guy, and he obviously adores you. Hell, after seeing him in the motel the other night? I'm pretty sure Alexei is like legit in love with you."

"Don't say that," I pleaded quietly.

"Why not?" Perplexed, she blinked at me. "Shay, the guy kicked in a door for you. He beat up all those men. He let Lalo put a gun in his face for you. I thought he was going to cry when he thought you had been shot. He was panicked because he thought you were hurt." She sat forward in the chair. "He loves you."

"I want to believe that. Alexei loving me is the one thing in the world I want, but if I'm wrong, it will gut me, Ky. His track record with relationships is terrible. Right now, I'm new and interesting, but in six months? Seven months? I don't know." I rubbed my face between my hands and tried not to cry as I imagined him walking away from me forever. "I need to be realistic. I don't want to be my mother, always chasing after men who will never love me."

"You are *not* your mother. You will *never* be your mother." Kylee leaned forward and squeezed my hand. "Alexei is showing you how much he loves you. You just need to trust what he's shown you and be brave enough to love him back.

God, Shay," she said with a laugh, "what else does he have to do to prove what you mean to him? Actually get shot?"

"No!" My stomach lurched and twisted painfully at the very idea of such a terrible thing.

"You worry too much. You're always waiting for that other shoe to drop. You need to live in the moment. We aren't guaranteed a tomorrow, Shay."

I placed my hand on top of hers. "I don't know what I'd do without you. You always know what I need to hear."

"That's what best friends do." Leaning back in her chair, she mirrored my cross-legged position. "Speaking of other shoes that are about to drop…"

I made a face. "What now?"

"A detective came to see me yesterday."

"And?" I held my breath as I waited to hear what she had to say.

"He was looking for you. I told him you were spending the weekend with your boyfriend. He seemed to be really curious about your relationship with Alexei."

"Was it Eric Santos? The detective, I mean."

"Yeah. I sensed that you two had some history. I was careful in what I said. I told him you two had been an item for a while and left it at that. Anything I should know?"

"Eric was one of the cops who used to come to our house when the neighbors would call 9-1-1 on Mom. He works in some gang unit now. He's been in it for a few years. Remember when Shannon got busted in high school?" Kylee nodded. "He was the cop who cut her a break and helped her get community service instead of juvie."

"It didn't help her much."

"I don't think Shannon was ever interested in being helped or saved. I think she is a true ride-or-die girlfriend. She'll do anything for Ruben."

"Even die for him?" Kylee said what we were both thinking. "Because I've got to tell you, Shay, I have a feeling that Ruben is wearing cement shoes and sitting on the bottom of the Gulf. We haven't seen or heard from Shannon since Saturday. That isn't good."

"I think Ruben is dead too," I agreed somberly. "But I don't think Shannon is." I touched my chest and tried to explain how I knew. "I think I would feel it if something had happened to her. Shannon must have escaped the motel and went underground. She's hiding out somewhere. I know it."

"If she's smart, she'll stay hidden. People are going to start asking questions about Lalo, and they're going to draw the obvious conclusions about her and Ruben. If she pops up alive? It won't be good for any of us if people realize we're the ones who killed Lalo."

"We didn't kill him!" I glanced at the closed door, suddenly paranoid that Denise might be lurking nearby and hear our conversation. "He shot himself."

"Yeah, after you shoved the gun to his face and kicked him in the stomach and I hit him in the head with the same paperweight that you bashed him with a day earlier," Kylee said.

"Well he shouldn't have tried to rape me or kill us," I argued. "It's not like we're psychopaths who go around beating people with crystal paperweights. And he shot himself in the face," I said forcefully. "I didn't pull that trigger. You didn't pull it. Alexei didn't pull it. He killed himself." Shaking my head, I said, "I'm not putting that on us. He was a *terrible* person. I'm not going to sit around and cry and feel guilty about defending you and Alexei or saving my own life."

"I'm not saying that we should feel guilty." Kylee bit her lip. "I just keep playing it over and over in my head trying to figure out where it went wrong."

"It went wrong the second we decided to go after Shannon without help. We shouldn't have done that. It was dumb and dangerous—and now we have to pay for that mistake by keeping this secret for the rest of our lives."

"Do you think it will stay a secret?" She was obviously worried. "That motel fire was in the news, Shay. It was just a short piece in the *Chronicle*, but it mentioned an unidentified body. What happens when the cops figure out it's Lalo?"

"I don't know," I admitted. "I really don't."

"We're so fucked," she said with dramatic resignation. "Like seriously screwed."

"Maybe not, Kylee. I mean, we're talking about drug dealers and mobsters, you know? I'm pretty sure they have ways of making things like this go away. When was the last time you saw one of these guys hauled in on anything bigger than a gun charge or slinging dope?"

"I hope you're right because I was not made for prison."

I didn't point out that we probably wouldn't survive the first night in county lockup. Either one of the *cholas* down with the Hermanos would take us out with a plastic shiv or one of the guards owned by the gang would turn a blind eye to us being beaten to death before we made it to our arraignment. But Kylee didn't need to hear that, and I didn't want to think about it.

"So, um, changing the subject," she said while reaching into the leather tote I had made her for Christmas last year, "I kind of did some research on Alexei."

"What?" Her admission startled me. "What do you mean?"

"Look, you know I love you like a sister. I needed to be sure there wasn't anything super sketchy in his background."

Not wanting her digging around in Alexei's criminal past, I said, "I already know about the sketchy things he did. I know he was in prison. I know he used to be part of the mob."

"Obviously," she said. "It's kind of hard to hide his tattoos."

"So why go looking into his history?"

"His recent history," she clarified. "You know I keep up with the gossip and society pages. I like to keep an eye on familiar faces."

What she really meant was that she had some serious hang-ups about the wealthy folks who had turned their backs on her and her mother and shunned them after her father's crimes came to light. Not a single one of her mother's country club set had lifted a finger to help them out. Sometimes I wondered if Kylee secretly had some crazy revenge plan in the works...

"So I remembered Alexei's face in some of the big galas and charity events around town," she said, "and I decided to have a look at his usual arm candy. It got me thinking that we really need to improve your game."

"What's that supposed to mean?"

Kylee retrieved her laptop and motioned toward Alexei's desk. "I'll show you."

Reluctantly, I joined her at his desk. I sat in his chair, and she stood beside me, plunking down her laptop in front of me and typing in her password. She brought up a browser window with twenty different tabs.

One by one, she clicked on them and introduced me to my competition. My heart sank as I got a good look at the incredible women Alexei had paraded around town at society events. Judging by the number of photos from the society pages and local gossip blogs, he had a very full social calendar. The same woman would be on his arm for three or four events and then a new woman would appear. My stomach ached as I imagined myself as just another in a long line of pretty faces.

And they were such pretty faces. Alexei seemed to have a type, and it worried me that I didn't resemble any of them. They were all taller than me with knockout bodies and lush blonde or red hair. Their cocktail dresses and evening gowns put my shabby collection of thrift store finds to shame. I zeroed in on their evening clutches and shoes and jewelry. They were so beautifully put together.

Elegant.

Sophisticated.

Confident.

Sexy.

"Oh my God." I sighed as the worst feeling in the world swamped me. Glancing down at my old, oversized tee and faded black leggings, I wanted to cry. "How the hell do I compete with that?"

Next to me, Kylee clicked her teeth and rolled her eyes. "Do you really think they look that good when they roll out of bed? Hell no! These women work their assets. We've just got to teach you to do the same thing."

"How?"

"I've already booked appointments for both of us at Al-lure," she said with a mischievous gleam in her eyes. "We're going tomorrow morning. The full package. Hair, nails, makeup, waxing—"

I squeezed my thighs together. "I am *not* going on a trip to Brazil."

"You are such a baby!"

"Look, I keep the landing strip tidy. My landscaping is neat." Feeling a bit smug, I added, "I didn't hear Alexei complaining."

"Wait. What?" Kylee slammed her laptop closed and whirled the desk chair so that we were eye to eye. "Did you—? Have you—? Oh. My. God. You *did*!" She hugged me so hard I nearly came out of the chair. "Why didn't you tell me when I walked in the door? That's the kind of news you lead with, Shay."

"I wasn't going to talk about my sex life in front of Stas and Denise!"

"Well they're not in here now and I want all the juicy de-tails. Like *all* of them." She hopped up onto Alexei's desk. "What's he like in bed? He's pretty good, right? Like a Russian tiger?" She pawed at me. "*Rawr!*"

I tipped my head back and laughed. Blushing as I tried find the right words to explain my experiences with him, I finally said, "He's very…generous."

Now she looked really interested. "Tell me more!"

So I did. We sat there and whispered and laughed for the next hour. Kylee offered a handful of tips that I filed away for later. For the first time in days, I felt totally relaxed and safe. It was like nothing horrible had ever happened to us.

"I'm going to miss seeing you at work." Kylee pouted. "It won't be the same."

I had to roll my eyes at her dramatic pout. "We text and Snapchat all day long. I'm sure we're going to see each other every day."

"I'll have to ask your sugar daddy for gas money," she teased. "The drive to your new palace is going to burn through my gas budget."

I thumped her leg. "He is *not* my sugar daddy!"

"Shay?" Stas knocked on the door to the office. "You have a delivery."

"I bet it's something totally ostentatious," Kylee guessed as she hopped off the desk. "Probably twenty dozen roses or a car."

I wouldn't put it passed Alexei to do something like that. Kylee followed me out of the office and down the hall toward the noise coming from the front door. When we rounded the corner, I nearly tripped over my feet as the boxes came into view. Moving boxes labeled in large red block letters were being carted into the house by men wearing the colors of Spider's M.C.

"Holy shit," Kylee hissed. "Is that everything from inside your house?"

Dumbfounded, I nodded. "I think so."

"Why are these strangers packing up your house?" Kylee seemed just as confused as me. "I figured we would do that when you were ready."

"So did I," I murmured in disbelief.

Alexei had officially gone too far.

I didn't know what to say as I stood there and watched my entire life come into Alexei's home in hastily tossed together boxes. The thought of strangers going through my personal things made me feel queasy. Worry gripped me. What about my supplies? My tools? My unfinished client orders?

Stas approached me with cautious steps. "This wasn't my idea."

"I'm not upset with you," I assured him. "Did Alexei tell you this was going to happen?"

Stas nodded. "But I guess he forgot to tell you."

"Obviously," I muttered.

"Where do you want all these boxes to go?" Stas gestured to the men waiting for instructions.

I want them to go back to my house.

But it was too late for that. The boxes were here, and judging by the crew that had delivered them, Spider didn't want me back in one of his properties. I cringed inwardly as I imagined the amount of trouble I had caused him. He tried to run a safe, clean park, and my sister and I had brought not only those skinheads onto his property but the police, too. He was probably in a rush to get rid of us.

With a resigned sigh, I glanced over the boxes and formed a plan. "Put the ones with my name on them in the hall outside the master suite. The ones labeled with leather or handbags or tools can go in Alexei's office. All the others can go into the empty room at the end of the hall."

Stas picked up a box and led a line of men upstairs. Kylee stepped closer and gave me a supportive smile. "Well, this got awkward real fast."

"Sorry about that," a familiar female voice remarked.

I glanced back at the open front doors and noticed Marley coming into the house with a smaller box. She set it on the nearest stack. With an apologetic expression, she explained, "Dad called me this morning and asked me go over and box up your things. I didn't realize that you hadn't asked for help until we got here. I am so sorry, Shay."

"It's okay, Marley." As long as I had known her, she had never struck me as the nosy or intrusive type. She was uncommonly generous and kind and would have dropped everything to come to the house to help pack up my things if she thought I needed help. "We're fine."

"Are you sure?"

"I'm sure."

"I was *really* careful with your stuff," Marley promised. "I made sure I personally boxed up your private things and Shannon's. I also wrapped all of your handbags in tissue paper and put your tools in bubble wrap." She opened up the box she had been carrying to show me. "See?"

"Thank you," I said as I poked through the box containing my collection of secondhand leather punches and stamps. She had done exactly as described, and I was thankful for her care with my things.

"I wasn't sure what to do with all the furniture, the food in your refrigerator or the potted plants around the house."

"I'll take care of them."

Marley hesitated. "Dad wanted me to tell you that he has new renters moving in next week so he needs the place cleared out as soon as possible."

I could tell she didn't want to be the messenger so I let her off the hook. "I understand. It's just business."

"It sure as shit shouldn't be just business," she argued. "Not with you, Shay. You've lived down the street from me for nearly four years. You were a wonderful neighbor, and I don't want you to think that you did anything wrong. It is so hypocritical of Dad to want you and Shannon out of the park when he's...well...*you know.*"

"I know." I had often wondered how Marley had turned out so normal when her family was even more dysfunctional than mine.

"Um, well," Marley glanced at the men coming back downstairs, "I'll run the unpacking of the truck and make sure we're out of your hair as quickly as possible."

"There's no rush."

After Marley stepped outside to direct the men, Kylee stepped up beside me. She glanced at her watch. "I'm sorry, Shay, but I've got to run. I have a marketing lecture and then I've got work."

It felt strange not to be thinking about work and the long night of cleaning, bending, lifting and sweating ahead of me.

"Listen, I'll text you later, and we'll figure out our plans for tomorrow, okay?" Kylee air-kissed my cheeks. Lowering her voice, she added, "You better lay down the law with that Russian of yours. He's hot as hell and the sweetest sugar daddy you'll ever find—but he can't do shit like this," she gestured toward the boxes, "without telling you."

She was right. It was a conversation I didn't look forward to having with him, but it had to be done.

When Stas and I were finally alone in the house an hour later, he shut and locked the door. Leaning back against it, he crossed his arms in front of his broad chest and asked, "What now?"

"Now?" I exhaled roughly. "Now we're going for a drive."

Stas groaned but didn't try to stop me. Shoving off the door, he said, "Yes, ma'am."

CHAPTER TWENTY

S TRETCHING HIS TIGHT neck, Alexei waited for the red light to turn green. In the passenger seats surrounding him, his marketing manager argued with his general manager about Alexei's expansion plans. They had spent the last two hours visiting a dealership in Sugar Land that he wanted to buy. The owner was ready to retire and had no children interested in the family business. To Alexei, it seemed like the ideal situation.

He didn't want to get pulled into the back-and-forth so he kept his focus on the wet streets. The rain was starting to pick up again. Spending the night at home with Shay was the perfect plan for weather like this. He planned to build a fire and open a bottle of wine to set the mood. He hadn't had a chance to properly seduce her yet. Tonight was that night.

When they reached his main dealership, Alexei parked in his spot and asked his team members to pull together their thoughts in emails. He already had his mind set on buying the Sugar Land dealership, but he wanted to give himself a day or two to consider any differing points of view. He usually had good instincts, but he valued their opinions, even if he didn't care for the back-and-forth bickering.

Two steps into the dealership, he was pulled aside by his

stand-in F&I manager who wanted him to sort out a salesman who had fucked up a deal by promising a rate and down payment that was way outside the customer's credit worthiness. Getting in between the supervisor and salesman reminded him exactly why he had a finance and insurance manager who usually handled these issues. But Donna was on maternity leave until after the New Year and somehow it fell on Alexei to mediate the disagreement.

"Enough, Dale!" Alexei said with some exasperation, cutting off the salesman who wanted to argue every single point that his supervisor brought up. "You fucked up with this customer. Own it like a man."

The salesman nodded and curtly answered, "Yes, Mr. Sarnov."

Exhaling roughly, Alexei glanced at James. "Give the customer the promised rate and down payment. We'll eat the difference."

Alexei pinned the salesman in place. "I'm giving you a pass today. Pull this shit again? You'll be joining the unemployment line."

"Yes, sir."

Alexei motioned toward the door of the supervisor's office. "Go."

Alone with James, Alexei asked, "Other than this, how is he? He came in with the new group we hired in August?"

James confirmed it with a nod. "Dale's a pretty good salesman. He's not top of the pack, but he's up there. I think maybe he's not suited for this lot. He would be better at one of our pre-owned lots."

"Call Tommy. Ask him if he can take Dale for a week or

two. Make sure Dale knows we aren't punishing him." Alexei could already hear the complaints. "Let him know that we're trying to find the most successful fit for him."

"I'll take care of it."

Alexei left James's office and crossed the main sales floor. He felt his pocket vibrate with a text message notification but didn't answer it. His attention had been pulled toward the all too familiar face walking through the double doors. *Blin.*

Never one to back down from confrontation, Alexei strode toward Detective Santos and held out his hand. "Eric."

"Alexei." Eric gripped his hand with a strong shake. "Do you have time to talk?"

"Of course." Wanting to control the situation, he gestured toward the second floor. "Come up to my office."

"Sure."

Alexei led Eric into his office and offered the detective a beverage that he declined. After closing the door, Alexei took his seat and pushed aside a stack of paperwork that needed his signature. "I suppose you're here to talk about Shay."

Eric got comfortable in his chair. "You don't want to hear what I have to say when it comes to you and Shay."

"Then keep it to yourself," Alexei suggested.

Eric cracked a smile. "There's the Alexei I've known for ten years."

"Almost twelve," Alexei corrected and settled back into his seat. "As I remember it, we never had problems, Eric."

"We never had problems because you respected the rules."

"I still respect them." He steepled his fingers and stared at Eric. "Do you?"

Eric's eyes narrowed. "I'm not a dirty cop."

"I didn't say you were." But Alexei knew that Eric had gone rogue with Nikolai when Vivian had been kidnapped. He might not have put on Kostya's black apron, but he had watched the former FSB operative do the dirty work.

"I'm not here to play mind games with you, Alexei." Eric sat forward. "I know what your crew is like when it comes to protecting your women. You'll keep Shay safe—but what about her sister?"

"What about her?"

"We know she checked into that motel that burned down on Saturday night. She used one of her well-known aliases to get the key. There was a body in the room."

Playing along and pretending he didn't know, Alexei asked in a voice laced with concern, "Was it Shannon?"

Eric shook his head. "It's a man. We don't have DNA back yet. The body was stripped and unrecognizable."

"Ruben?"

"I doubt it. Ruben was a big dude. This body was smaller and thinner." He paused. "I'm concerned it might be Lalo Contreras."

"Fuck." Alexei let the expletive loose for two reasons. One: to make Eric think that he was just as shocked. Two: because if Eric thought the body was Lalo's so did everyone else on the street.

"If Shannon killed Lalo…" Eric didn't finish his thought. "I need to find her before they do."

"I don't know where she is and that is the truth. I'm not bullshitting you, Eric." Alexei made sure Eric could read him. "Every second that Shannon is missing is a second that Shay is in danger."

"Do you know who Shannon was working for? With her little identity theft scam? She and Ruben didn't have the money to do it on their own."

Alexei shrugged. "It wasn't my family."

"I figured that out already. It wasn't the Asian syndicate or Nicky Jackson's boys either."

Wanting to give Mueller a taste of some police harassment after that shit he pulled with Shay, Alexei gave Eric a little nudge in the wrong direction. "The newest face in town has been having some problems gaining territory and creating a market for his wares. He might be interested in growing a new side business."

"Mueller." Eric grumbled the name with distaste and rose from his chair. "I've said all I need to say. You know how to find me if Shannon makes contact with Shay."

"I do."

Eric walked to the door but didn't open it. Looking back, he asked, "This thing you're doing with Shay? Is it real?"

"I'm not going to discuss my relationship with Shay."

"That's your prerogative, but I've known Shay a long time."

"And?"

"And I've known you a long time," Eric shot back.

Alexei understood what Eric meant. He didn't like the guilty feeling that clawed at him. Eric had every right to be concerned. He'd earned his reputation as a man who burned through mistresses for a reason.

"It's not like that with Shay," Alexei said finally. "It's different with her."

"It better be," Eric warned.

Alexei bristled at Eric's tone but let it slide. The last thing he needed was to get into a pissing match with a detective who could make his life a living hell. Even more than that, he couldn't stand the thought that Shay would be disappointed in him if he got into a fight with Eric. Instead, he stayed in his chair and watched Eric leave.

Thinking of Shay, he decided to call her and see what she wanted to do about dinner. He pulled his phone from his pocket and noticed the text message he had ignored earlier. He swiped the screen of his phone and opened the message from Stas.

Your little bird has flown back to the nest.

"Shit."

Alexei quickly cleaned off his desk and left his office, locking the door behind him. It didn't take him long to figure out what had sent Shay running back home. Feeling like the worst asshole in the world for forgetting to tell her about the move he had arranged, Alexei made sure the dealership was in good hands and hurried out to his SUV, texting Stas as he walked.

Is my little bird still in her nest?

He was backing out of his parking place when the reply came.

She's visiting a neighbor.

With his foot on the brake, he hastily tapped in his reply.

I'll be there soon. Keep her there.

The sun began to set as he drove across the city. The rush

of workers trying to get home slowed his progress and gave him plenty of time to think about his misstep. His first instinct was to do something special and give her an expensive gift to show how sorry he was, but as he pulled into the park and drove down her street, it occurred to him that Shay didn't want things from him. She would want him to apologize for being an asshole—and to *mean* it.

He parked in front of her mobile home and climbed out of the SUV, making sure to lock the doors behind him. He spotted his Maserati parked in her driveway. On habit, he checked the driver's door and found it unlocked. He had a feeling she had done that on purpose.

He climbed the rickety stairs to her small porch and knocked on the door. When there was no answer, he tried the door, found it unlocked and stepped into the house. "Shay?"

There was no reply. She was probably still visiting that neighbor.

He glanced around the living room and noticed how much larger it seemed without the furniture. He walked the length of the house and discovered every room was empty. The refrigerator had been cleaned out, and he could smell the lemon and pine scents of disinfectants and cleansers. Knowing Shay as he did, he was certain she had spent the afternoon scrubbing every inch of this place.

Without a place to sit, he left the house to wait for her outside. When he reached the bottom step, he heard the squeaky whine of bicycle tires that badly needed a shot of WD-40. He watched a young boy with a too-big backpack ride down the street, dodging potholes and puddles until he reached the SUV. The little boy clambered off the bike and popped the kickstand. Hitching his backpack up higher, the chubby kid asked, "Are you Shay's friend?"

"Yes. Are you?" He leaned against the hood of his SUV.

"Yep." The kid wandered over to the Maserati. Eyes wide, he carefully touched the gleaming silver paint, running his hand over side panel. "Is this yours?"

"Yes." He reconsidered his reply and corrected himself. "It's actually Shay's now."

"Really?" The kid seemed skeptical.

"Really," Alexei confirmed. Remembering how much he had loved cars at that age, he asked, "Would you like to sit behind the wheel?"

"Are you serious? Like for real?"

Alexei gestured to the door. "It's unlocked."

The kid laughed and raced around to the driver's side. He jerked open the door, yanked off his backpack and climbed inside. Ignoring the urge to tell the kid to be careful with those muddy shoes, Alexei walked around to the other side and sat on the passenger seat after moving the kid's backpack out of the way.

"I'm Hector," the boy said as he poked buttons and pretended to move the shifter.

"Alexei."

"You're Shay's boyfriend, right? She was telling my mom about you." Hector narrowed his eyes as if trying to decide if Alexei was worthy of Shay. "Mom thinks you're sketchy and controlling. She says Shay can have any man she wants and that Shay needs to remind you of that."

Alexei snorted at that. "You're mother sounds like a very smart lady."

"She is." Hector pretended to drive the car while he chattered away. "She was glad that Shay wasn't dead."

"Why did she think Shay was dead?"

"Pelon said that Lalo, Shannon and Shay were missing. Everyone thinks Lalo killed Shay and Shannon and ran off to Mexico."

"Who is Pelon?"

"My sister's boyfriend," Hector said. "He used to be in a gang, but he got out when they shot his brother. He's a roughneck offshore now, but he's still down. He hears all the good stuff." Hector twisted in his seat "Hey, do you want to buy some wrapping paper?"

The swift change in subject amused Alexei. He started to tell the kid no but changed his mind. "Maybe."

Hector reached for his backpack and dug around inside it until he found an ordering form and small catalog. "We're raising money for school. If I sell enough paper, I get to take a limo to a pizza party with my friends."

Alexei disliked the way the area schools pushed the kids to raise money like this. Every time he walked into the employee lounge at the dealership, someone was selling cookie dough or wrapping paper or some other bullshit. He hated the pressure to buy.

He flipped through the catalog and glanced at the order sheet. Shay's name was the last one on the form. She had purchased three rolls of wrapping paper and a box of Christmas cards. The little smiley faces she had drawn inside each zero made him grin. She really was the sweetest thing. Maybe Hector's mother was right. Maybe he did need a swift kick in the ass as a reminder that Shay could have any man she wanted.

Alexei did the math between what the kid had sold and what he needed to reach the grand prize level on the flyer. "I'm not interested in wrapping paper, but I'll make a donation instead."

"Really?"

"Yes." He wrote down the amount he was pledging in the correct spot on the form and then reached into his jacket for his checkbook. The last check he had written had been earlier that morning when one of the employees from the trailer park had come to the dealership with the invoice for Shay's lease. As he scrawled on the check, he said, "If you don't win that limo ride, you call Shay and she'll tell me. I'll make sure you and your friends get your party."

There was a knock at the driver's side window. A moment later, Shay's face appeared. Alexei tore free the check and handed it to Hector along with the form and catalogue.

"Thanks." Hector stuffed everything into his backpack. "For all of this."

"When you get ready to buy a car, come by the lot for a test drive."

The kid's eyes lit up. "Really?"

"Sure."

Hector practically bounced as he got out of the car. A few seconds later, Shay slid into the seat he had just vacated. She closed the door and put her hands on the wheel. Alexei waited for her to speak but it became clear that she wanted him to go first.

"I'm sorry, Shay." It occurred to him that this was the second time he had said it to her today. *You've got to be more careful with her.* He was painfully aware that Shay could have any man she wanted. Right now, she wanted him, and he needed to work to make sure that never changed.

"What are you sorry for *exactly*?" Shay turned in her seat so she could look at him. "Because I need to know if you actually get it, Alexei, or if you're just saying you're sorry because you think that's what I want to hear."

"I should have told you about Spider having his daughter pack up your place. I should have told you—and not Stas—that those boxes were coming today."

"You should have *asked* me if I wanted to move out of this house," Shay corrected. "I thought you asked me to move in with you as a temporary thing. This is a *huge* step, Alexei. You should have made sure I was ready for it. You should have let me decide what to do with my home and my things."

"I thought I was being helpful." Alexei tried to explain his reasoning. "I'm used to the women in my life enjoying the way I take charge. I thought you would be relieved to not have to deal with it after everything else that's happened in your life."

"You would think that," Shay said with a sad little smile playing on her lips. "And I get it, Alexei. I get that you show people you care by doing things like this."

"I do care, Shay." He reached for her hand. "I care more about you than I have any other woman."

Just fucking tell her that you love her! But he couldn't do it. He wasn't ready. *Coward.*

"I believe you," she said softly. "I do like the way you want to take care of me and help me—but you have to talk to me, Alexei. I don't like the feeling of losing control when it comes to big decisions like this."

"I will," he promised. "I'm not perfect, and I'm going to fuck this up again—but I'll try."

Still holding his hand, Shay glanced out the window into the darkening evening. "I needed to make the decision to move out of this place on my own, Alexei. You sort of blind-sided me with the penthouse and the mistress thing. I was still trying to wrap my head around that when you blindsided me with the move to your house. Then you shoved envelopes of money in my hand this morning. I'm just not sure where I stand anymore."

Leaning over, he touched her face and drew her gaze. "You stand next to me, Shay. That's where you belong."

"Is it? Because I'm not sure you want an equal partner who walks beside you. I think you want a woman who is happy to walk a few steps behind you. I think you want someone you can lead and someone who won't question your decisions."

Alexei shifted uncomfortably. Her questions needled him. "I'll be honest, Shay. I've always been the kind of man who likes to be in charge and in control of everything."

"I don't want to be controlled."

"I don't want to control you," he assured her. "But I'd be a liar if I sat here and said that I don't want to be the man of our house. I am who I am, Shay. I can change, but essentially, this is me."

"I like the man you are." Shay squeezed his hand. With a lopsided smile, she said, "You just piss me off sometimes."

"I wish I could say I won't piss you off again, but I'm a flawed man."

"Your flaws aren't that bad." She touched his jaw. "You're a good man. You've been nothing but kind and generous toward me."

"But you wanted to leave this house and this neighborhood on your own terms," Alexei guessed. "And with your own money?"

She nodded. "It feels like I didn't earn it."

"Fuck that," he swore roughly. "You're the hardest working woman I've ever met." Brushing his knuckles along her cheek, he said, "You don't have to be a martyr, Shay. It's okay to let someone—to let *me*—help you. It took me decades to get where I am. I want to spare you that."

Alexei captured her mouth in a tender kiss. He swept his finger down her jaw. "If I walked away right now, you would still make a success of your life. You've already proven that you can stand on your own two feet. You don't need me. You don't need any man to get where you want to go." He leaned in and kissed her again. "But I hope you *want* me there with you. I hope you'll let me help you reach your goals faster."

Shay cupped his face in her small hands. "I do want you with me."

"I just want to take care of you, Shay." He ran his thumb along her lower lip. "It makes me feel—"

"Proud? Like a good provider? Like a man?" she guessed.

He nodded. "It means something to me to be *your* man."

She leaned into him and pressed her warm lips to his. "It means something to me to be *your* girl."

Relieved she had accepted his apology, Alexei kissed her until her lips were swollen and red. He flicked his tongue against hers one last time before reluctantly easing off their kiss. He swept the long strands of hair that had escaped her loose braid behind her ear. "Let's go home. I'll build a fire and open a bottle of wine and then I'll spend the rest of the night making this up to you. How does that sound?"

"Like the best apology ever."

"Let me give my keys to Stas. He can drive my SUV back to the house. You can be my chauffeur for the ride home."

Outside in the chilly night, Alexei found Stas leaning against the door of the SUV waiting for them to finish. Sitting on the hood of the vehicle, a plate wrapped in aluminum foil rested on top of a thick blanket still sealed in its plastic packaging.

"Shay's friend decided I needed to be fed," Stas explained. "The blanket is Shay's. That surrogate mother of hers said she won it at bingo. It has a tiger on it."

"*Cobija*," Alexei said. "That's what they call these blankets. I used to have one," he admitted, eying the garish blanket with some envy. "One of the vendors at the flea market where I used to unload counterfeit shipments thanked me with a *cobija* when I got his mother some cheap diabetes medicine." He touched the blanket and laughed. "That was the warmest fucking thing. I lost it in a move and was so pissed off."

Stas pushed the blanket toward him. "Well now you have a replacement."

Alexei grabbed the blanket and tossed his keys to Stas who caught them in his meaty fist. "Follow us home. You can leave as soon as we reach the house."

Stas nodded and trudged around to the driver's side of the SUV. Alexei returned to the Maserati and slid into the passenger seat. Shay had turned on the radio and had the heater on low to warm the interior of the car. She waited for him to fasten his seatbelt before putting the car into drive. She was easy on the gas as they left her old neighborhood.

"*Malysh*," he scolded with a laugh. "Do you always drive like a little old lady on her way to church?"

"As a matter of fact, I do." She sent a warning glance his way. "And if you intend to backseat drive, I'll pull over and you can hop in with Stas."

Alexei smiled. "Fair enough." He waited a moment before adding, "I just came down the Beltway and 290. It's a mess. Take Sam Houston to 45." When she shot him a look, he held up both hands. "That isn't backseat driving. It's navigating."

"Make yourself useful and navigate us to a restaurant with takeout," Shay suggested.

"I know a place you'll like." Taking her hand, he lifted it and kissed the back of it. Holding it, he relaxed in his seat. Although he didn't want her to worry, he said, "Eric came to see me today."

"And?"

"He thinks the body in the motel belongs to Lalo. It's only a matter of time before it's confirmed." He hesitated. "He also told me that they know your sister was at the motel. She used one of her aliases for the room."

"So once they confirm it's his body, everyone is going to think she killed him."

"Yes. That's why Eric came to see me. He wants to find Shannon first."

"Good luck," Shay replied hotly. "Nobody knows where she is. She hasn't tried to contact me since that night."

"If she does contact you, I'll do what I can to get her out of the state. I can't promise anything more than that, but I'll try."

"You don't need to put yourself in any more risk, Alexei."

"She's your family. I wouldn't be much of a man if I let your sister get hurt when it's possible for me to protect her." He had been giving the issue with Shannon some thought. If something happened to Shannon and he could have prevented it, Shay would never forgive him. He didn't want that wedge driven between them.

Shay remained quiet as she drove, and he didn't push her by asking what she was thinking. When she was ready for his help or needed his opinion, she would ask. Until then, he was perfectly content to hold her hand…and wait.

CHAPTER TWENTY-ONE

S TANDING AT THE sink shaving the next morning, Alexei kept hearing the click of a cell phone snapping photos. Wondering what the hell Shay was up to, he finished shaving, wiped his face with a warm towel, stepped away from the sink and peered into the bedroom. In the soft morning light, she reclined against a mound of pillows and seemed to be making silly faces at her phone. Amused, he asked, "Baby, what are you doing?"

"Snapchatting with Kylee."

"I have no idea what that means." He didn't like admitting that. For the first time since the start of their relationship, he felt uncomfortably aware of their age gap.

"It's an app," she said before tossing her phone aside to give him her full attention. It was a small gesture, but he loved that she didn't constantly have her phone in her face. "It lets you message, send videos and snaps—photos—to friends. You can make stories, like a replay of your day, for your friends to view. The snaps disappear after they're viewed."

"What is the point of that? If you send me a picture, I want to keep it."

She smiled at him. "That's sweet."

"It's the truth."

"Well, maybe, some pictures shouldn't be kept," she said coyly, her gaze dropping to the comforter.

A flash of heat burned low in his stomach and arced through his chest. With a smoldering stare, he ordered, "Put that app on my phone right now."

With a giggle, Shay rolled onto her side and then crawled across the bed to the table where he kept his phone charger. As she moved, the shirt she had borrowed from his side of the closet rode up higher and revealed an enticing peek at her perfect little ass. Getting dressed no longer interested him. He tossed the towel back onto the counter and crossed the bedroom with long strides.

Grasping Shay's ankles, he tugged her across the mattress. She squealed with laughter at his sneak attack. "Alexei! What are you doing?"

He smacked her bare bottom and drew a shocked gasp from her throat. "Teaching you what happens when you tease me with this incredible ass of yours."

When he bent down and nibbled the curve of her bottom, Shay cried out in shock. He dotted kisses atop each plump cheek and then licked a long, slow trail up her spine that ended in a noisy kiss on the side of her neck. She shivered and gasped, but it wasn't enough for him. He wanted Shay to go wild.

Grasping her hips, he canted her bottom up higher and cupped her pussy from behind. He pushed between her shoulders to coax her into the right position. Face down. Ass up. "Perfect," he said, nipping at her backside. "Stay just like that."

Shay's toes curled, but she didn't move. Her ragged

breaths and the slick heat seeping from her betrayed her excitement. He traced her labia with soft strokes before gliding a finger down the seam of her pussy. He dipped a finger into her, gathering the moisture there, and then circled that wet finger around her sensitive clit.

Shay shuddered as he worked her with both hands. Thrusting. Rubbing. Pumping. Flicking. She pushed back against him, rocking on her knees, and moaned. He nipped at her fleshy bottom again, just a little tease of pain, and Shay cried out with ecstasy. She clenched around his fingers in a rhythm matching the waves of pleasure coursing through her incredible body.

She was still trembling and trying to catch her breath when she pushed up on both hands and spun around to attack him. Laughing, he fell back against a wall of pillows and wrapped his arms around her waist. As he hauled her on top of him, Shay smothered him with kisses. His stiff cock rubbed against her inner thigh and then nudged against her wet heat.

Hands on her hips, he guided her down onto the length of him. It felt so fucking good to slide deep inside her. "I did all the hard work last night." He palmed her ass in both hands. "This morning, it's your turn."

With a hand on his chest for support, Shay shyly said, "I don't know what to do."

"Move." Thrusting up into her, he dragged a low moan from her throat. He gripped her waist and pushed her back before pulling her forward. "Like this."

Her first movements were uncertain and embarrassed. Wanting her to relax, he kissed her breasts and the side of her throat while caressing her back. He tangled his fingers in her hair and dragged her closer for a kiss. "You're so fucking beautiful, Shay."

Seemingly reassured, she smiled back at him. Her uncertain movements grew more languid and relaxed. Eyes closed, she rocked back and forth on top of him. Content to watch and feel, he didn't try to rush or coach her.

It didn't take Shay long to find the rhythm and movements she liked best. Moving like a belly dancer, she sat up straighter. He was taken aback by how unbelievably sexy she looked in the pale morning light. Her long dark hair curled around her shoulders and back. Her breasts bounced, the nipples taut and begging for his touch. Her lips were curved with a heady smile.

He noticed the moment she found the right pace and friction. Her thighs squeezed his waist and her fingernails bit into his chest. Awed by her sensual beauty, he watched her come alive on top of him. Desperate need surged through him. Holding her waist, he held on tight as she rode him hard and fast.

Shay covered his hands with her own. She pinned him in place with her smoky gaze. In a husky voice, she begged, "Come with me, Alexei. I want to feel you come inside me."

"*Fuck*." Hearing her talk like that set him off like a firecracker. The first pulse of her tight pussy around his shaft was all it took. Helpless beneath her, he came hard while she rode him for all he was worth, taking her pleasure and giving him a taste of his own. Even after the last drop of cum had been milked from him, she rocked slowly back and forth until he shuddered and melted in a boneless heap of sated flesh.

Draping herself atop him, Shay exhaled a long, deep and

very satisfied breath. With a smile in her voice, she whispered, "I think I like that position best."

Swearing in Russian, he wiped a hand down his face. "I think it's my new favorite too."

She giggled softly and traced one of the tattoos on his chest. Quietly, she said, "We forgot again."

His stomach clenched with guilt. "I'm sorry."

"It's as much my fault as it is yours." Lifting her head, she said, "I'll call my clinic when they open and see if they can squeeze me in today or tomorrow."

He nodded. "That's probably the best idea since it appears I can't be trusted to remember to wear protection with you."

He had his suspicions about that, but he wasn't about to voice them aloud. In the deep, dark recesses of his mind, he wondered if he wasn't deliberately forgetting to wear a condom. That vulnerable, weak part of him that feared she would one day wake up and want a better man understood that a baby would tie them together forever.

"Do you have a preference?"

He shot her a look. "Shay, I don't know the first thing about birth control."

"Well, I mean, some couples want bulletproof contraception like an IUD."

"No," he said too quickly. "Not that one."

"Why not? Kylee has one, and she loves it."

"I had an experience I'd rather not repeat with one." He still winced all these years later as he remembered the unexpected and painful pricking sensation of those fucking strings jabbing the head of his cock. "I was afraid to have sex with Amanda for weeks after her IUD attacked me that night."

As if he'd just tossed a bucket of cold water on her, Shay withdrew from him. He lifted his head to get a better look at her. "What?"

Perturbed, she asked, "Really, Alexei?"

"Yes, really, Shay. What?"

"Maybe you could *not* talk about the other women you've fucked when you're still inside me?"

Shit. He squeezed his eyes shut and gritted his teeth. Was he ever going to stop making mistakes like these? *Stupid. Stupid. Stupid.*

Obviously upset and angry with him, Shay climbed off him and tried to escape the bed. He snatched her hand and prevented her from storming off. "Shay. Please."

She tugged hard. "Let go."

He did. "Running away isn't going to make this better."

"And staying here so you can regale me with stories of all the women you've slept with will?"

Sitting up, he insisted, "That's not fair, Shay. Telling a story about one of them isn't the same as listing all of them. You're the one who mentioned IUDs."

"Not so you could tell me about other women you've had sex with while we're still naked in bed together," she snapped back angrily.

"Why does it matter if I talk about those other women? You're the one I'm with right now." He cupped her face in both hands and ducked his head until he found her gaze. "Shay, I'll apologize for being crass and rude just now, but I won't apologize for my past. You knew my history when you got involved with me."

She took a moment before saying, "It's different now."

"How?"

"Because now I know what it means to be with you," she explained, her gaze downcast and her cheeks warm with what he realized was embarrassment. "What we just did felt so special to me and then you started talking about this other woman…"

"And then you didn't feel very special anymore," he finished for her. "Shay," he said, his voice filled with regret. "*Ptichka*." He brushed his knuckles down her soft cheek. "You might not be the first woman I've shared all these kinds of experiences with—but you'll be the last."

Her sad expression shifted right before his eyes. Her hopeful smile warmed his heart. Placing her hand atop his, she apologized quietly. "I'm sorry I flipped out just now."

"Don't." He kissed her. "You were right to call me out for hurting your feelings."

"Yes, but I shouldn't have reacted like a crazy, jealous girlfriend." Shay rubbed her face between her hands. "This is all so new to me. Maybe I'm not as emotionally prepared as I thought."

"Shay, we're having the most honest conversation I've ever had about a relationship." Brushing strands of hair behind her ear, he said, "I think you're more emotionally prepared than I am." Trying to put her at ease, he teased, "I'm glad I finally got to see you acting jealous. I was beginning to think you might not like me very much."

"Alexei!"

He captured her hand and tugged her close for a deep, lingering kiss. She melted into him, and he sensed that all was forgiven. *But not forgotten*, he thought as he stroked her hair and enjoyed her sweet mouth. He had to remember to be more careful with her soft heart. She had such a kind, innocent soul, and she was so easily injured, especially after the way her mother had treated her as a little girl.

Holding her gaze, he murmured, "You're special to me, Shay." He dotted a line of kisses along her jaw. "Don't ever forget that."

"You're really special to me, too, Alexei." Her eyes shimmered with unshed tears, proving to him that her feelings were just as deep and real as his.

Not wanting to end the honest intimacy they shared, Alexei remained in bed with her as long as possible. He would have to grab breakfast at the dealership, but he didn't mind. Shay's tender feelings were more important than anything else this morning.

"Put that app on my phone while I'm getting dressed." Alexei touched the fingerprint scanner before handing it over to her. "I expect at least three dirty snapshots of you today."

"Only if I get three from you," she replied with a saucy smile.

"Challenge accepted."

Laughing, Shay leaned back against her pillow and tapped away at his phone. He returned to the bathroom and put on his usual suit. While he picked out a tie, he decided it was time to get rid of the penthouse. He needed to show Shay he was cutting ties with his past and starting a new life with her.

He stood in the doorway of the bathroom and slipped into his jacket. "Are you still planning to meet up with Kylee today?"

"We're going to the salon."

"Pick up the tab for her. My treat," he added. "If you need extra cash—"

"Alexei, you gave me plenty yesterday. I'm fine."

He could tell the money issue was still a touchy subject with her. It was probably going to take a few months before she was comfortable with their new arrangement. He decided not to push it today.

She slipped back into the T-shirt she had slept in and beckoned him to sit next to her. "Let me show you how this works."

Sliding his arm around her waist, he watched her demonstrate the app. "It seems easy enough."

"It only gets dangerous if you have too many contacts and accidentally send a snap to the wrong people."

"Then I guess it's a good thing you're my only contact."

"Probably," she agreed. Lifting her phone high in the air, she cuddled up against him and snapped a quick photo of them. She checked her screen and smiled. "Oh! This is a good one."

"Let me guess? That's going to Kylee?"

Shay shook her head. "Nope. This one is just for me."

He combed his fingers through her long hair. He wanted to ask her not to cut it because he loved it long like this, but he didn't. "Please relax and enjoy yourself today, Shay. You need this."

"I will."

"Stay close to Stas."

"I'll stick to him like white on rice," she promised.

He kissed her temple and pocketed his phone. "I'll see you tonight."

Halfway downstairs, the doorbell rang. He switched of the alarm and let Stas inside. "Shay will be down later."

Stas followed him into the kitchen. "The boss wanted me to give you this."

Alexei stared at the folded slip of paper Stas held and doubted he was going to like whatever this message was. He opened it and scanned the message inside.

B&B Steakhouse. 7 p.m. Make it right.

Scowling, Alexei suspected that Nikolai's instruction to make it right was going to come at some expense. Walking over to the stove, he lit the message on fire and dropped it into the sink to burn. "Who am I meeting?"

"The boss didn't think I needed to know that detail, but—"

"But?" He glanced back at Stas.

"But the boss says if you do this favor for him, he'll do a favor for you. He'll make sure that Shay is safe while you go out of town for your birthday."

With everything else happening, Alexei had been on the verge of canceling his plane ticket and hotel reservations. Now that he knew Shay would be under Nikolai's personal protection he felt better about taking his annual Vegas getaway to gamble and watch the fights.

Plucking a K-Cup from the cabinet, Alexei asked, "Will you be part of the crew shadowing Shay while I'm out of town?"

"Yes. Also Danny and Boychenko."

All three men were capable. She would be perfectly safe with three of Nikolai's most trusted men watching her.

Alexei tossed a couple of ice cubes into his travel mug. "I'll talk to Shay about it tonight. My flight leaves at noon tomorrow." After pushing the lid on tight, he said, "The salon she's visiting is under Nikolai's protection. Vivian, Erin and all the other wives use it regularly and one of Nicky Jackson's nieces works there so it's neutral territory and on the safe list. You can give Shay some room today."

"Not a problem," Stas assured him.

Coffee in hand, Alexei left the house. He made it to the first stop sign before his cell phone chirped with an alert. Foot on the brake, he checked his phone. It was a message from Shay. Already grinning with anticipation, he opened it. A streak of heat burned white-hot through his stomach when he saw the snap she had sent him. The few seconds he was allowed to see the photo weren't nearly enough.

Dropping his phone back in the cup holder, he continued on his morning drive. By the time he reached the dealership, he had made up his mind. It was time to say goodbye to the penthouse.

Scrolling through his list of contacts, he found Marissa's new number and dialed it. They had parted on good terms, and he was happy to send some new realty business her way.

"Alexei!" She answered in that trademark husky voice. "I was just thinking about you!"

He doubted that very much, but he wasn't about to be rude. "Oh?"

"Well I was just about to put my suitcases in the car for my Vegas getaway," she explained. "Vegas. November. You. My mind tied it all together." There was no mistaking the smile in her voice as she asked, "Dare I hope you're calling about your birthday plans this weekend?"

He'd never taken a woman on his birthday trip, and he sure as hell wasn't going to start with a former mistress. He tried to let her down gently. "I'm calling about a business proposition, not pleasure."

Never one to back down easily, she replied, "Well, maybe if I'm a very lucky girl, we can make it a little bit of both."

Alexei didn't want to hurt her feelings so he changed the subject. "Do you have time for a meeting this afternoon? I'd like to discuss the penthouse."

"Oh," she said, her voice filled with interest. "I think I can make that happen. How about four?"

"That works for me."

"I'll see you then. Buh-bye."

Alexei pocketed his phone and stepped out of his SUV. With any luck, he'd have the penthouse on the market in a few days and a sale before Thanksgiving. As he walked into the dealership, an idea for what he would do with the profit from the sale began to form. It would be a grand romantic gesture, maybe even a bit too over the top, but if any woman deserved a gift like that it was Shay. He was going to make damn sure she got it.

CHAPTER TWENTY-TWO

"THIS PLACE IS crazy nice," I whispered to Kylee while clutching my mimosa. We were seated in the super luxurious waiting area of Allure and had already been treated to insanely delicious gourmet chocolate along with the champagne cocktail.

"It should be for the prices they charge," Kylee whispered back. "Good thing your sugar daddy is footing this bill," she added with a wicked smile and a bit too loudly.

Feeling the stares of the other women waiting with us, I pinched her arm. "Ky!"

"Sorry," she apologized quickly. She looked embarrassed as she insisted, "You know I was just teasing."

"I do." I glanced at the elegantly dressed blonde sitting across from us. Her perfectly painted lips were pulled into a taut thin line. Her jewelry glinted under the artfully placed lights. I couldn't help but stare at her handbag. Black Clemence leather. Gold hardware. The iconic shape and structure of the Birkin bag called to me, but it was a dream I would never attain. Even on the second-hand market, a pre-owned Birkin in good shape demanded a twenty-thousand-dollar price tag.

The elegant blonde caught me staring at her handbag and

shot me a cold look. After Kylee's teasing outburst, I could only imagine what she thought of me. Money-grubber came to mind. Even worse words circled around in my head. Sugar baby was the nicest of them—and I didn't like it. Not one bit.

Another woman in the lobby sized me up in the same way. There was something familiar about her, but I couldn't quite place her. She had beautiful red hair and striking blue eyes and classic fashion sense. She'd chosen a Chanel handbag and Jimmy Choos to complement her dove gray dress.

Suddenly self-conscious, I touched my neck and prayed the fading bruises I had painstakingly covered with fine layers of concealer and foundation were still hidden. I had chosen one of my nicer outfits from my meager closet, but it hardly compared. I glanced at Kylee who thumbed through a fashion magazine and sipped her mimosa. She fit so easily in this world, even after spending the last seven years watching it from the outside.

But me? Oh, I didn't belong here. Not at all.

"Shay?" A stylist with knockout curves approached me with an inviting smile. The bold coral jewelry she wore accented the black dress that hugged her thick hourglass figure. Even without her heels, she towered over me.

"Hi." I stood up and shook her hand.

"I'm Nisha. I'll be your stylist today." She waved at Kylee. "Hey, hon! Julie will be out in a few minutes. She's just tidying up her station."

"I'm in no rush." Kylee sat back with a smile. "Take good care of my friend. She doesn't indulge in beauty days very often."

"Well we'll have to change that, won't we?" Nisha linked

her arm through mine. "Come on over to the consult area, sugar. Would you like another mimosa or maybe a bottle of water or some tea?"

"I'm fine, but thank you."

"All right." She led me to a chair and sat down across from me. "So what would you like to today?"

"I think a trim," I said, touching the ends of my hair. "Maybe some color?"

"Do you color your hair often?"

I shook my head. "I haven't done it in almost two years."

"May I?" She asked for permission to touch my hair.

"Sure."

She stood behind me and examined my strands. "You have such gorgeous hair. It's very healthy. When you say you want some color, do you mean something very different or some subtle changes?"

"Subtle."

"Are you familiar with balayage?"

"Yes."

"So let me grab some color books and we'll talk shades, okay?"

We settled on soft caramel and toffee to complement my natural dark color. She combed her fingers through my hair as we discussed the upkeep and the haircut I wanted. It was clear from her consultation that she cared about my needs and satisfaction and wasn't going to push a style or color on me that wasn't right for my lifestyle. Feeling like I was in good hands, I finally relaxed.

After slipping into a smock, I took a seat at the color bar. The redhead from the lobby sat in the chair at the other end of the curved bar, and Kylee popped into the chair next to me. Grinning, she said, "By the time we leave here today, I want my hair so ice white I look like a Targaryen."

I snickered at her Game of Thrones reference. She had been a lover of the books for years and had dragged me into the show practically kicking and screaming. Two episodes into the first season, I had been hooked. Ever since then, we had been sharing the cost of an HBO subscription and stalking fan sites for the latest updates and spoilers. "We'll have to find you a Khal Drogo if you do that."

"Or maybe my Khal Drogo has already found me," she muttered.

"Wait. What?" I turned in my chair and leaned toward her. "What does that mean?"

"It just means that it's complicated." She shot me a meaningful look. "Really complicated and really Albanian."

Sitting back in my chair, I had a flash of that night in the motel and the guy from Besian's crew who had been so gentle with her. What was his name? James? Jim? Jet!

I wanted to ask her if I was right, but this very public place was not appropriate for that conversation. I didn't know how a relationship like that could work. Jet worked for the man who had basically ruined Kylee's life. Dealing with Alexei's history and his ties to a criminal enterprise were hard enough, but at least he was *out* of that life. Jet was still knee-deep in the Albanian mafia. His loyalties to his boss—to Besian—would always trump his loyalty to a girlfriend.

A platinum blonde built like a pixie stopped by the color bar to offer refreshments. Kylee insisted that I have another mimosa. With a designated driver waiting outside, I didn't put up too much of a protest. Soon, I happily sipped away at another glass while Nisha sectioned my hair and began applying color.

Conversations swirled around me. For the first time in days, I felt the tension and stress that had been knotting up my neck and shoulders start to release. The champagne had a lot to do with it. Escaping from reality in this bubble of luxury and beauty helped.

But I couldn't shake the guilt that pricked at my conscience as I enjoyed an afternoon of pampering. My sister was out there somewhere, alone and afraid, while I sat here drinking champagne and gossiping. It wasn't right. While I understood that helping Shannon was next to impossible now, a part of me wondered why the hell I wasn't crawling the streets of the city looking for her.

A shameful, horrible part of me knew why I hadn't fought against Alexei's decision to keep me safely tucked away at his house. Honestly? I was punishing my sister.

It was an ugly thing to admit—but there it was. For so many months, the resentment and anger inside me had been building to levels that had threatened to choke me some days. I had grown tired of supporting us both financially, of cleaning up after her and of worrying night after night that she was going to be hurt or arrested when she was out with Ruben.

Her bad decisions had nearly gotten me raped and killed. They'd put my best friend and the man I had fallen hopelessly and irrevocably in love with in danger. I was just so sick and tired of it all.

"You okay?" Kylee touched my foot with hers. "You look like you're in La-La Land."

"Just thinking," I said with a little smile.

"About?"

"Things," I said, deliberately evasive.

She let it go and returned her attention to her magazine. I leaned forward and reached into my purse to retrieve a small notebook I kept there and a pencil. While my color processed, I sketched out an idea I had for a gift I wanted to make Alexei. That wallet of his needed replacing.

As I drew lines on the paper, I overheard the redhead talking to her stylist about her weekend plans. They sure sounded more interesting than mine. She was headed to Vegas this evening and apparently had plans to meet up with an old flame. I couldn't imagine what man would have let a knockout like that walk out of his life. She seemed nice and funny and obviously had her act together considering the way she talked about her back-to-back appointments with her realty clients.

Kylee tapped my foot when the redhead left the color bar. "What do you think?"

"About?"

"You. Me. Vegas."

It was an interesting thought. "I'm listening."

"I'd be willing to work some overtime for a girls-only getaway." She smiled slyly. "You'd have to ask that Russian honey of yours for an advance on your allowance."

"Keep that up and I'll go to Vegas alone with my Russian honey."

Kylee pouted dramatically as Nisha returned. She checked my foils and said, "Looks good. Let's get you to the sink for a rinse and some toner."

I trailed Nisha to the wall of sinks along the far right side of the salon. The chair she directed me to was surprisingly comfortable. Eyes closed, I enjoyed the sensation of a warm shampoo and strong fingers massaging my scalp. After a good rinse, she applied the toner and left me to process for a few more minutes. I listened to the conversations around me and picked up on the redhead's voice again.

"He called me this morning—out of the blue—and told me he wanted to get together to talk about a piece of property in his portfolio. We're meeting at his place in a few hours."

"Uh-huh," her stylist said with a laugh. "Sounds to me like he's looking for a reason to get you alone again."

"Maybe."

"Are you interested in rekindling things with him?"

"I don't know," the redhead replied quietly. "We had a good thing when we were together, but he's not a long-term commitment type. He knows how to make a woman feel good. I mean, that man did things to my body that still make me blush and ache!"

The stylist laughed. "Oh, I remember those stories quite well."

"I'm ready to settle down, but I'm perfectly happy enjoying his company and no-strings attached sex until a better offer comes my way."

"All right, hon," Nisha said as she approached me from the side. "Let's get you rinsed."

A few minutes later, I sat in front of a mirror while Nisha combed out my freshly colored hair. We chatted while she snipped and texturized. It turned out that we had both lived in the same neighborhoods at different times. I had a feeling we had more in common than just crappy apartments and ramshackle houses.

As she gave me the best blowout of my life, I noticed Nisha staring at the barely visible marks on my neck. The bruise on my cheek had been easier to hide and camouflage than the ones of my neck. It didn't help that Alexei had made a habit of marking me with love bites. It was obvious by the taut line of her mouth what she thought. I hoped she wouldn't say anything, but I wasn't getting off that easy today.

"Listen," Nisha said as she walked me to the spa area of the salon for my remaining appointments, "I'm going to get in your business for a second. Please understand that I'm only doing it because I've been there."

We stopped in a quiet, private alcove, and I quickly said, "It's not what you think."

"Oh, honey," she said with a sad smile, "it's exactly what I think. Believe me. I know the signs all too well. I spent most of my teenage years and my early twenties hiding bruises from my boyfriend-turned-husband. You do not have to stay with a man who hits you. I can help you. I know people who specialize in this kind of thing."

"They're not from my partner," I said calmly. "But thank you for offering to help me. That's very kind of you."

She narrowed her eyes. "Those bruises came from a man. I know the span of a man's fingertips when I see them."

"You're right. They are." Carefully, I explained, "My sister got into some trouble with some very dangerous people. I became collateral damage."

Her tense expression relaxed. "I know about that, too," she said sadly. "My ex-husband used to run drugs and guns with Lalo Contreras. He screwed up a deal and I'm the one who paid for it."

"I'm sorry you had to go through that." After my run-ins with Lalo, I could only imagine what horrible things he had done to Nisha. "I know what he can be like."

A look of understanding passed between us.

"If you need some help, I know some people who can take care of that for you."

"It's been handled," I assured her.

"If you need protection, it can be bought. My uncle is Nicky Jackson. I can tell by the look on your face that you know what that means."

"I don't need to buy it. Alexei already has."

"Alexei?" Her eyebrows arched with surprise. "Wait. Do you mean Alexei Sarnov? The Russian with all the dealerships and trucking companies?"

"Yes."

Nisha glanced back at the salon. "Your relationship is kind of new?"

"Yes. Why?" Nisha bit her lower lip. I sensed she wanted to say something but wasn't sure if it was her place. Wondering what she knew, I asked, "What is it that you think I need to know?"

"I think—"—she looped her arm through mine and patted my hand in a motherly gesture—"—that you need to be very careful with your heart, sugar. You need a plan. You need to know how to get in and how to get out of a relationship with a man like that. Take advantage of whatever perks he offers you—jewelry, cars, money. You hoard it. Put it away some place safe. Someday, you'll need it to start the next chapter of your life. Enjoy him while you have him, but keep one foot out the door. You'll be glad you were prepared when the Cinderella story comes to an end, sweetheart."

Dazed by her advice, I didn't know what to say as she handed me off to the aesthetician. I managed a smile for her but inside I was a mess. Nisha didn't strike me as the type of woman to give advice like that just to be cruel. So what did she know about Alexei that I didn't?

As I endured the uncomfortable sting of having my eyebrows tidied up, I felt the worst churning in my stomach. How many of Alexei's girlfriends had come to this salon? Was I going to be the newest bit of gossip among the stylists? Would I become known as Alexei's hot new thing?

Stop, I thought insistently. *Just stop.*

There was no doubt in my mind that Alexei cared deeply for me. Our relationship was different than all the others. Wasn't it?

"Why don't you take a look in the mirror?" Emily suggested after she finished plucking a few strays. "You have a very nice natural brow shape so I just cleaned them up for you."

Shaken from my troubled thoughts, I hopped off the table and walked over to the full-length mirror attached to the adjacent wall. I checked out her work and smiled. "They look great."

"I'm glad you like them. Would like to add on any other waxing services?"

"Not today." The last thing I wanted was some stranger I hardly knew getting up close and personal with my lady parts.

"Would you like me to make a note about a return appointment? I usually see my eyebrow clients on a three to four week schedule."

I considered my normal plucking routine. "We should probably aim for three weeks."

"Okay. I'll make a note, and Billie or one of the other front desk girls will get you scheduled." She gestured to the door. "If you'll follow me, I'll take you to your manicure and pedicure appointment."

The quiet, relaxing hallway lined with rooms used by aestheticians and massage therapists led to a bright and open space where clients were pampered used by the nail technicians. Large potted palms filled the corners of the room and gauzy drapes gave the wall of pedicure chairs a luxury cabana feel.

Unlike the usual black pedicure chairs I was used to at the nail salons I had always visited, the chairs here were a creamy leather and had adjustable tabletops and shelves along each side for holding purses and shoes. Instead of black plastic foot baths, these chairs were attached to mosaic-tiled basins with gleaming faucets.

Emily led me to the kaleidoscope shelves lined with nail polish bottles and then wished me a good day before grabbing her next client from the spa waiting area. There were so many colors I wasn't sure where to start.

"Try a plum shade," a woman suggested from behind me. "It's a hot color for the fall."

Turning toward the sound of her voice, I discovered a dark-haired woman close to my age seated in a pedicure chair soaking her feet. She had one hand resting on a very prominent baby bump while the other held a home décor magazine. Diamonds glinted on her hands and ears as she added, "You should try the shellac." She flashed her paint-stained fingertips at me. "It's good for girls like us who work with our hands."

Bewildered, I asked, "How do you know I work with my hands?"

Her mouth slanted with amusement. "We haven't met, but we actually run in some of the same circles and have some of the same friends in common."

"Oh?"

"Hadley, Kylee, Alexei," she ticked off three names. "And, of course, my husband, Nikolai…" She held my gaze, and it was clear in that moment that she knew everything. "He speaks very highly of you."

Of course. I recognized her finally. Black hair. Blue eyes. Pigment-stained fingers. Vivian Valero.

Well. Kalasnikov now.

She was right. We did have friends in common. Kylee and Hadley had known each other when they were younger. Hadley had become one of her loyal customers, buying four or five of Kylee's designs every year. She also carried one of my tote bags and a hobo-style handbag. A few times, she had asked me to visit her art center to teach leather working classes.

With a gentle smile, Vivian touched the seat next to her. "Pick out your color and come sit next to me."

Like her husband, Vivian was not the kind of person I could refuse. "All right."

Taking her advice, I chose a deep plum shade with a hint of sparkle. Mandy, the nail technician assigned to me, seemed to approve the choice. She guided me to the chair next to Vivian. She offered me another mimosa but I turned it down in favor of a cup of tea.

"That's a beautiful bag. Is that one of your designs?" Vivian gestured to my handbag sitting on the shelf of the chair.

"Yes."

"I've actually been looking for something similar to that for a diaper bag. I want a leather tote but with more structure, you know? And with pockets and compartments."

"I made a bag similar to that a few months ago." I reached into my purse for my phone and started scrolling through the photos in my Dropbox app. When I found the right one, I showed it to her. "Something like this?"

"Yes!" She scrolled between the photos. "Exactly like this! But maybe in a brown leather? I'm not really a fan of black."

"All of my handbags are made-to-order. I can do any color you like."

"Do you have a shop?"

"I work out of my house right now. Well," I corrected myself, "I'm working out of Alexei's house at the moment."

"Oh! Well that works nicely. We live a few blocks away. I can pop over sometime if that's okay."

"It's definitely okay."

Vivian sipped from a water bottle and shifted in her chair. She swirled her feet through the hot water. "I work from home now. It's nice. I like being able to just walk downstairs and go to work, especially lately when I'm up all night with heartburn and insomnia."

As she rubbed her pregnant stomach, I was struck by the realization that we weren't that far apart in age. Seeing her so obviously happy about starting a family left me feeling conflicted and maybe even a bit envious. Alexei and I had been playing a dangerous game together, forgetting to use protection more often than not. Even though my usual cravings for salt and the discomfort of sore breasts seemed to confirm Aunt Flo's impending visit, there was always the slimmest possibility that I was wrong. It didn't scare me nearly as much as it should have.

"Where is your shadow?"

"My shadow?"

Vivian smiled as if we shared a secret. "Stas."

"Oh. Right. He's at the coffee shop next door. I assume your shadow is nearby, too?"

"Shadows," she corrected. "Two for me." She touched her stomach. "Two for him."

"I guess I should stop complaining about Stas. At least there's only one of him following me everywhere."

"Oh, it's not so bad. *Krisha* is just part of this life."

"*Krisha*?"

"Roof," she explained. "It's what they call the protection arrangements we have. Like a roof protects the house, you see?"

"Oh."

"You'll get used to it. My four shadows are like family now. Ten is really just a big teddy bear once you get to know him. Boychenko is a sweetheart. Ilya always has the best gossip and stories. Danny sneaks me *pan dulce* from Benny's bakery once or twice a week. Honestly? It's like having four seriously overprotective brothers. I was an only child and I always wanted brothers. It's like wish fulfillment twenty years later," she laughed.

Closing my eyes, I leaned back against the cushioned seat and enjoyed the hot water bubbling around my feet. "One older sister has been enough trouble for me."

"It will be all right," Vivian said softly. "Alexei won't let anything happen to you, and I can promise you that Nikolai won't either."

I glanced at her and saw the sincerity in her eyes. "I hope so."

She reached over and touched my hand. "I know so."

My cell phone buzzed, and I fished it out of my purse. The snap from Kylee made me giggle. She had taken a selfie with an exaggerated expression of pain as she waited in one of the aesthetician rooms for her waxing appointment. I snapped a quick photo of myself relaxing with a content smile and sent it her way.

"Are you Snapchatting with Alexei?" Vivian had her phone in her hand and seemed to be texting someone. "I've been trying to convince Nikolai to let me add the app to his phone for us to use, but he's all security this and NSA that so…" She rolled her eyes. "I tried telling him that the NSA doesn't care about our selfies but…"

"This one is from Kylee. She's in the back about to get up close and personal with some hot wax."

"Ouch!"

"I showed Alexei how to use Snapchat this morning." Amused, I admitted, "He sent me a snap of his blueberry muffin and a cup of coffee. I think it's going to take him a while to figure it out."

Vivian laughed. "Start sending racy snaps. He'll figure it out quick enough." Holding out her phone, she said, "Give me your number. We're neighbors now. We should get together for lunch or something."

"I'd like that." We exchanged phones and typed in our contact information. As I handed back her phone and took mine, Kylee strolled out of the spa, grabbed a funky sea blue shade of polish and hopped into the seat next to me. She leaned forward to wave at Vivian and soon they were chatting back and forth.

My pedicure and manicure finished before Kylee's so I settled our bills and tips and waited for her in the lobby. I snapped a selfie of my new haircut and color and sent it to Alexei. He responded seconds later with a phone call.

"Hello?" I answered quietly so as not to disturb any of the other patrons.

"You look beautiful."

"Thank you." Feeling giddy at the sound of his deep, dark voice, I couldn't help but smile.

"I'd like to take you out and show you off, but I have a meeting soon and then promised to do a favor for a friend tonight."

He didn't have to tell me who that friend was or why he had to do him a favor. I had a gnawing feeling in the pit of my stomach that Nikolai would expect many such favors from Alexei for the protection he had extended toward me.

"But I'll make it up to you when I get home," he promised. "I have to go. I'll call you when I'm headed home tonight. Stay close to Stas. All right?"

"I will." We ended our call with softly spoken goodbyes just as Kylee appeared in the lobby. We left the salon together and came face to face with two men in black leather jackets. They both had tattoos like Alexei's. The younger of the two men looked very familiar to me. He nodded toward me in acknowledgment. "Ma'am."

I suddenly remembered where I had seen him. He had come to my rescue with Alexei. "Mr. Boychenko."

His companion laughed and said something to him in Russian that made Boychenko's ears turn red. I sensed it was good-natured ribbing between two men who seemed close as brothers and left it at that. Kylee and I continued toward the coffee shop.

"What was that about?" she asked.

"Those are Vivian's guards. One of them—Boychenko—came to help me the other night."

We exchanged a look, and I could tell that I didn't need to tell her the rest of it. We entered the coffee shop and found Stas sitting at a table with two men that I assumed were Vivian's other guards. The bearded one shocked me with his size. Standing at full height, he was probably seven feet tall and all tattooed muscle. With a bear like that at Vivian's side, she was the safest woman in all of Houston.

Kylee and I ordered drinks and then left with Stas. She had an extra shift to get to so we dropped her off at her apartment. Before she got out of the car, she poked my shoulder. "We're still on for my birthday tomorrow, right?"

"Of course." My life might in the worst state of flux right now, but I wasn't going to abandon my best friend on her birthday. If we didn't go out as we normally did, it might arouse suspicions. We needed to keep to our normal routines.

"Whatever you two are planning, it needs to be cleared with Alexei," Stas warned. "And I'll have to go with you."

Kylee rolled her eyes. "Comrade, if you want to get dressed up, eat cupcakes and go dancing with us, you just have to ask."

396 | ROXIE RIVERA

Stas scowled at Kylee who laughed and clambered out of the car. "I'll call you later, okay?"

"Okay. Bye!"

"Comrade? She does realize that I'm not a fucking communist?"

"She was teasing," I said and put a hand on his arm. "She only said it because she knew it would bother you."

He grumbled under his breath and put the car in drive. "I need to make a stop on the way home."

"That's fine. I'm not in any rush. Where are we going?"

"I have to settle a debt."

"A debt?"

"That afternoon you and your friend ran away I promised the security guard a payment if he would let me access the tapes. It took me a few days to scrape it all together."

"Stas!" Guilt clawed at me. "Let me pay it. You shouldn't have to spend your own money on my mistakes."

"It wasn't money he wanted."

"What did he want?" Stas refused to meet my gaze or answer so I asked again, "Stas? What did he want?"

"It's not important, Shay. The less you know? The better."

More and more, those six words seemed to rule my life. As Stas navigated busy streets, I thought of Vivian. Was this how it was in her marriage? Did she blindly accept whatever Nikolai told her and not ask any questions?

No. She seemed to know a *lot* more about what was happening in Houston. I didn't imagine Nikolai told her everything, especially not the seedy, nasty, violent things, but I doubted he kept much from her. She didn't strike me as the type of woman who would take that shit.

So why are you?

It wasn't the first time I had wondered that. Alexei wanted to protect me by shielding me. I respected and understood that. Sitting here next to Stas, I accepted that there were actually some things I really didn't want to know. My life was complicated enough right now. I didn't want to know about the ugly, distasteful things that made the underworld work.

Stas and I no longer had the garage parking permit for the penthouse's private garage, but he was able to sweet talk the attendant into letting us through because she recognized him. He pulled into a visitor spot that was a tight fit and boxed in by pylons. "Are you coming in with me or staying here?"

"I'll stay here."

"I'm leaving the keys with you." He dropped the key fob into the cup holder between us. "Lock the doors. Don't open them for anyone but me."

"Yes, Warden."

Stas got out of the car and waited until he heard the doors lock to walk away from it. I leaned back in the seat and checked the notifications on my phone. I glanced up whenever I heard a vehicle approaching or noticed movement in the mirrors. Nothing seemed out of place or odd—until I recognized the black SUV rolling into the parking garage.

What in the world was Alexei doing here? I twisted in my seat to make sure it was actually him and it was.

Amused that we were in the same place at the same time, I called him. When he didn't answer, I decided to walk up the next level to his parking space. Stas would probably flip his lid if he came back to find me gone so I texted him my plan as I killed the engine and got out of the car.

I followed the incline up to the next level and came around the corner just in time to see Alexei step out of his SUV. I started to call out to him but stopped when I realized he was smiling at someone else.

What the hell?

Frozen in place, I watched as Alexei embraced a slender and very elegantly dressed woman.

It was *her*. It was the redhead from the salon. It was the woman who had plans to meet up with her ex.

Her ex?

My current boyfriend.

Alexei.

Shocked, I watched her slide her arm through his. They laughed and smiled at each other as they walked toward the elevator. Not wanting to be caught, I backed up quickly, hiding my body behind a concrete pillar. Putting a shaking hand to my throat, I tried to swallow the quivering ball choking me.

"What the hell are you doing?" Stas startled me as he came up behind me without warning. "I told you to stay in the car."

"I saw Alexei," I numbly replied.

"Alexei? Here?" Stas stepped around the pillar and spotted the SUV. "Why are you hiding here? If you saw Alexei, why didn't—"

"He wasn't alone." The words came out so quietly that I wasn't sure he heard me. "He was meeting a woman."

"*Blin.*" Stas grabbed my hand and tugged me back toward the car. "We need to get out of here right now."

The stupor that had momentarily taken hold was replaced by anger. What the hell was Alexei doing here with that woman? Why hadn't he told me he was meeting someone here at the penthouse?

I already knew that answer, of course. I knew that he wouldn't have lied to me about a business meeting and a favor for a friend if there was an innocent explanation for this. There was only one reason to take that woman to the penthouse in the middle of the afternoon.

Furious, I dug in my heels. "No!"

Stas whirled back to me. "Yes!"

"No!"

"Shay, we are leaving right now. If you don't walk, I will pick you up and carry you to that car. Do you understand me?"

"Screw you! I'm going up to that apartment and I'm going to confront him."

"No, you're not." Stas put both hands on my shoulders. His touch was surprisingly gentle as he lowered his face until we were eye to eye. "I'm not going to stand here and let you make a scene and embarrass yourself. You're going home. You're going to cool off and calm down and then you're going to make peace with this and keep your mouth shut."

"Why the hell would I do that?"

"You'll do that because you're going to go home and realize that without Alexei you have nothing. You have no home. You have no money. You have no job. Your sister is still missing. Mueller and the Mexicans have both painted a target on your back. That man is the only thing that stands between you and death. If you want to stay alive, you need him and you need to keep him happy."

Torn up inside, I blinked rapidly and tried to fight the tears burning my eyes. I didn't want to accept anything Stas

400 | ROXIE RIVERA

had to say, but deep down inside, I knew he was right. With-out Alexei, I was as good as dead. Sooner or later, Lalo's body would be found and I would be marked for death.

But I didn't want Alexei like this. I wanted him the right way. I wanted him to love me as much I loved him. I wanted him to be mine and only mine forever. I didn't want to share him with anyone else.

"This is so fucked up, Stas."

"Life is fucked up." Gently wiping away the tears on my face, Stas said, "It's time to grow up, Shay. You're sweet and kind and good. Alexei loves that about you. He's offering you the full package. He's offering you a home, money, access to powerful people and trendsetters. He's offering you a future."

"So what? You're saying I have to accept that?" I gestured toward his SUV. "That I have to just swallow his infidelity?"

"These whores get the penthouse. They get an hour of his time and then they're done. But you? You'll get the ring. You'll get the house. You'll get his name. You'll have his babies. He'll take care of you, and you'll be happy if you can learn to cast a blind eye to this bullshit. It's a small price to pay."

"That's not good enough for me, Stas."

His mouth flattened into a sad line. "Then you're a fool, Shay."

"I guess I am," I agreed miserably.

Stas awkwardly hugged me, wrapping his brawny arms around my shoulders and squeezing me tight. His embrace surprised me at first. He wasn't the most touchy-feely of guys, but deep down inside, he was a good man. He didn't always say the nicest things, but he was gentle when it counted. He understood that I was in pain and needed some support right now.

With his arm around my shoulder, he led me back to the car and helped me into the passenger seat. We didn't speak as he drove me back to Alexei's house. I stared out the window and tried to process everything that had just happened. I didn't know what to think or feel anymore. Everything I had accepted to be true about Alexei and about our relationship had been decimated. It was all lies. All of it.

I have to get out. I have to get out now.

But where would I go? Kylee? She was already on the hook for Lalo's death. If I ran to her, we would be two perfectly placed targets alone in that apartment of hers.

Shannon.

I could try to find Shannon and then we could disappear together. I had the money Alexei had given me, not a lot, but it would be enough to get us on a bus. We'd have to start over, but we weren't afraid of hard work. We could sleep in roach motels and eat ramen until we had enough scraped together to get an apartment.

"Don't even think about it," Stas warned as we walked into the house a short time later.

"Think about what?" I played dumb.

"You're thinking about running. It's not going to happen, Shay. Not on my watch. I'll handcuff you to me if that's what it takes to keep you safe."

He was dead serious. "Stas—"

"No, Shay. You are safe here. It might not be ideal, but you'll have to learn to accept it. For both our sakes," he added. Taking my hand, he dragged me through the house to the office I had taken over with my supplies. Flipping on the light, he pointed toward my tools. "The best thing you can do right now is take all that anger and pain inside you and turn it into fuel for work."

"Work? Right now? When I feel like I'm dying inside?"

"Yes. Right now." He gave me a little push toward the desk. "Alexei believes in you and in this business. He's not wrong about either of those things. He believes you'll be a success. Use him to get what you want."

"That's so cold, Stas."

"And fucking that other woman while you're here playing house isn't?"

I recoiled at the ugly way he framed it. "Stas!"

"It's the truth, Shay, and that's why you have to listen to me," he insisted. "You have a big, soft heart, Shay. Make your money. Get back on your feet. Then get the hell out before he ruins you."

He's already ruined me, I thought dejectedly. I had fallen for Alexei's charm like so many other women before me. I was a fool. I was just as stupid and pathetic as my mother had been, always chasing after the wrong men.

I had believed I was different, that Alexei could love me more than any of the others because I was special, but I had been dead wrong. I wasn't special. I wasn't different. Naïve. Childish. Hopelessly romantic. I was all those things.

Stas was right. It was time for me to grow up and see the world as it truly was. My life had taught me many painful lessons. This failed relationship with Alexei was just another one of them. I had been an idiot to place my safety and my future in the hands of a man. I had given up my home and my job for empty promises.

With renewed determination, I sorted out my projects and chose three of them. Two needed finishing touches. Punching holes in leather proved to be rather therapeutic. Setting grommets and eyelets felt even better. A few times, Stas came to the open door to watch me as I slammed a mallet down again and again. The thick board I used as a working platform absorbed most of the energy but the loud thud echoed in the office.

When I was finished with those two handbags, I wrapped them in pillowcases, tagged a note to each one and then then picked up the third order form. The client had chosen a fawn shade of leather for her handbag and wanted some feathery designs burned into it. I selected the pyrography tips I would need and attached them to the pens before plugging them in to heat.

Carefully, I unfolded the sheet of vegetable tanned leather and inspected it again for any blemishes. Satisfied with its condition, I measured out the leather I needed and cut it with my super sharp shears. I found the design we had settled on and used the copy of it as a template. I traced the template with a ballpoint stylus.

When I was finished, I set aside the paper and picked up the stylus pen I needed for the tracing. The heat radiating from the tip warmed my fingers and reminded me to use excess caution. In my early days of leather burning, I had scorched my fingertips so many times. It had taken two years of working with these tools regularly to feel comfortable with them. Even now, I worried about safety all the time, always looking for things that would melt or catch fire and keeping my fingers safe from the blazing hot tips.

While I methodically traced the imprint the stylus had created, I couldn't stop thinking about Alexei and the redhead. Embarrassed, I remembered the way she had looked at me when Kylee had made her ill-timed joke about my sugar daddy. Even worse, I remembered the way Nisha had glanced back at the salon's cutting floor when she was talking to me in private. She must have known that Alexei was stepping out on me with the glam redhead.

Feeling sick to my stomach, I realized what a fool I had been the last few days. The worst part? I had let Alexei put me at risk of not only pregnancy but an STD. I couldn't be sure he was telling the truth about always using protection with his other partners. Ashamed, I decided that tomorrow morning I would go straight to the clinic. My days of being cavalier with my health and future were over.

Distracted by thoughts of pregnancy and sickness, I wasn't paying attention when I reached out for the copy of the design to check my work so far. The cord of the pen I held tugged on the other pen plugged in next to it. I heard the other pen falling and reacted on instinct, reaching out to grab it before it fell on the floor.

Idiot!

"OW!" I screamed in pain as the sharp skew tip burned my fingers. The unbelievable pain as it simultaneously burned and sliced was so bad I shrieked again and ripped it away from my blistering skin.

Stas barreled into the room. "What happened?"

Gripping my injured hand, I sobbed in pain. "I burned myself."

He was at my side in a second. "Let me see." When I

pulled my hand back, he took it firmly and repeated himself. "Let me see it, Shay."

When I showed him, he winced. Reaching down, he unplugged the pyrography pens so we wouldn't start a fire. In a flash of speed, he scooped me up and rushed me to the kitchen. He put my hand under the faucet and started running cold water onto my wounded fingers. The heat in my fingers was almost too much to bear, and the cold sting felt even worse.

"I know it hurts but you have to cool it down." He found a plastic sandwich bag in a drawer and took it to the refrigerator where he filled it up with ice. He wet a towel under the faucet and wrung it out before wrapping the ice pack with it. "Put this on your hand. We need to get you to the emergency room right now."

It was the last place I wanted to go, but he was right. This wasn't a small burn I could fix with some antibiotic ointment and a bandage. Holding my hand to my chest, I followed Stas out of the house and into the car. He helped me fasten my seatbelt before jogging around and getting behind the wheel.

Backing out of the garage, he shook his head. "You have the worst fucking luck of any woman I've ever met."

Hand throbbing and heartbroken, I could only nod in quiet acceptance of that fact. The worst luck ever…

CHAPTER TWENTY-THREE

P ULLING INTO THE penthouse parking garage, Alexei wrapped up his phone call with Ivan and parked in his usual spot. It felt strange coming back here. This was usually a place that filled him with excitement and lust. Today he felt none of that. The woman he wanted wasn't waiting for him upstairs. She was on her way home.

Sitting here waiting for Marissa, he had never been more sure he was making the right decision to sell this property. Everything he wanted was waiting for him in the house that always seemed so empty and cold. With Shay's help, he would turn that place into a home. He wanted pictures of their smiling faces on the walls. He wanted her books on his shelves. He wanted her socks mixed in with his. Someday he wanted their noisy, messy children running through the halls.

He sighted Marissa's flashy Mercedes and exited his SUV. He buttoned his suit jacket and welcomed her with a smile. The elegantly dressed woman who embraced him in a cloud of floral and musk was nothing like the woman who had seduced and propositioned him over a year ago.

Back then, Marissa had been one of Besian's most popular girls, but she'd known her days were numbered on the stage. She'd been putting herself through school, but she'd needed connections and money to create a new life for herself. In that first negotiation, she had proven to him that she had a mind for business. He'd been impressed with her drive and ambition and had never doubted that she would find success.

"Alexei!" She embraced him and kissed his cheek.

"Hello, Marissa." Not so long ago, her shape and warmth had been so familiar to him. Today, he was surprised by how wrong it felt to hug her. Too tall. Too thin. Too much perfume. He mentally catalogued all the ways she was different from Shay.

Stepping to his side, she linked her arm with his. "So how was your day?"

"Busy but good." He escorted her to the private elevator. "You?"

"I had a business breakfast with John Mueller."

"Really? What did he want?"

"He asked me to join his firm." She preened like a peacock. "He wants to give me a department and everything."

Whatever his disagreements with Mueller over Shay and her sister, he grudgingly acknowledged that the man ran a successful business. If Mueller was being serious about asking Marissa to come onboard, it could be a huge career shift for her. "Get a lawyer and negotiate the fuck out of whatever contract he offers."

She laughed and stepped inside the elevator. "I heard your voice in my head while I was at breakfast with him. His terms were favorable, but I have some points I want to negotiate."

"Push hard, Marissa. He knows what an asset you'll be to him in this new market. Make him pay."

"You don't need to worry about that." They exited the elevator and walked to the door of the apartment. While she waited for him to unlock the door, she leaned back against the wall and smiled coyly. "I've missed that elevator ride and the walk to this door."

When she reached out and trailed her fingers down his arm, Alexei realized he had to say something. Though he had hoped to avoid any awkwardness, he could tell that was no longer a possibility. "Marissa," he said her name in the gentlest way possible, "I'm involved with someone."

Her smile slowly collapsed and her hand fell. "Involved?"

"It's serious." Not wanting there to be any doubt, he added, "I'm going to marry her."

Marissa seemed flabbergasted by that admission. "Is she pregnant?"

"No!" But he wasn't sure of that, was he? "It doesn't matter if she is or isn't. She's the woman I want to spend the rest of my life with," he answered simply.

Gawking at him as if she had never seen him before, she asked, "What makes her so special that you want to marry her? After all of us that have come through those doors?" She gestured to the penthouse entrance. "What does she have that we didn't?"

"It's not easy to explain. She just—she's the one." He touched his chest. "I felt it right here the first time I met her."

Narrowing her eyes, Marissa asked, "And when, exactly, did you meet her?"

He wasn't going to lie. "When we were together."

"I see." Her mouth thinned to a perturbed line. Knowing that Marissa could make trouble for Shay, he wanted to set the record straight.

"You don't. Shay had no idea about me and you or any of the others before you. Shay and I never dated or even kissed until months after we had ended things. I don't think she even realized I was interested in her until very recently."

"How is that possible? You are living, breathing, walking sex!"

Alexei shrugged. "She's not like us. She doesn't understand the games we played or the arrangements we enjoyed."

Marissa wrinkled her nose. "She sounds like a naïve little romantic."

"She probably is," Alexei agreed. "But that's what I love about her. She's a good person with a big heart."

"She makes you happy?"

"Very." Happy didn't even come close to describing how he felt with Shay.

"Then I'm glad you found her," Marissa said with a warm smile. "What we had together was fun, Alexei, but it never would have lasted. I'll confess that I was hoping this was an invite for another round of fun with you, but I won't pout now that you've told me you're getting married."

"Thank you. I appreciate that we can be adults about this."

"You never promised me forever. I never promised you forever. I'd like to think we can be friends." She paused. "Well—we can be friends if your soon-to-be wife allows it."

"She will." Despite that bit of jealousy this morning, Shay wasn't the controlling type. More than that, she would trust him to behave like a gentleman.

"All right." Marissa inhaled a deep breath. "Well, if you're done breaking my heart, let's get inside this penthouse and start talking numbers."

Relieved their conversation had gone well, he followed her into the penthouse and let her give him the rundown of the property's value. She had done her homework, presenting him with recent comps as well as a look at the current inventory of similar properties. She presented him with a plan for selling this penthouse and the other slightly smaller apartment he owned on this floor and admitted that she had four prospective buyers in mind.

"Give me a week to get it staged, photographed and listed. I can't guarantee a closed transaction by Christmas, but I'll work hard to make it happen."

"I know you will." Alexei extended his hand, and they shook on their deal. "Do I need to come by the office to sign paperwork?"

"I'll email you. We try to do as much electronically as possible in our office. It's easier for our very busy clients."

Their plan in place, they left the penthouse. Alexei made sure Marissa got into her car safely before getting behind the wheel of his SUV. He checked his watched and decided he had enough time to swing by his attorney's office to pick sign some paperwork and pick up a sample contract and business structure forms that he had requested.

By the time he was finished, he had just enough time to drive to B&B for the reservation Nikolai had arranged. When he arrived at the restaurant, he was quickly seated in a private corner and ordered a beer. He wasn't left to wonder about the identity of his dinner date for long. The moment he spotted Mueller coming through the door, he knew.

As Mueller drew near, his gaze shifted from their table to the various entrances and exits into the main room that put him at risk. Alexei had already taken the chair that put his back to the wall. If Mueller wanted to feel safe, he should have arrived earlier.

"Alexei."

"John."

Mueller took his seat and ordered a whiskey, neat, to start off his night. Picking up the menu, he glanced over it. "The boss decided it was better for the two of us to meet in public on neutral territory. At least he chose a restaurant where we can settle things over steak and whiskey." He glanced up and grinned. "Like real men."

Alexei let loose a rough laugh and sipped his beer. "Real men don't send hoodlums after innocent women."

The waiter stopped at the table and left Mueller's whiskey. They weren't ready to order yet so he offered to return in a few minutes.

Once they were alone, Mueller leveled a dark look his way. "I will admit that my men went beyond what was expected or authorized. Your girl was never part of my beef with the sister. They were only ever supposed to scare her."

"They succeeded." Alexei's jaw tightened as he remembered Shay's terrified face when he found her in that parking lot.

"And you succeeded in putting them all in the hospital," Mueller retorted. "You could have killed them."

"Touch Shay again and I'll do exactly that," Alexei warned.

"I suppose that would be fair," Mueller allowed. "If someone put hands on my wife, I wouldn't let them walk away either."

Wives. Children. Parents. The underworld code demanded that they all be protected from retaliation or harm. The men who broke those rules were considered untrustworthy and ostracized. If a man couldn't do business, he couldn't earn and that meant he couldn't eat.

"I know the score when it comes to Shay," Mueller assured him. "She's completely safe from me."

"Good."

"But you must realize that I can't be seen to just let you walk away without any consequence, Alexei." Mueller kicked back his Macallan. "You've been out of this world for a while, but you know the way it works. If I'm seen giving you a pass, it makes me look weak. I can't grow and build my business here if people think they can walk all over me."

"You should have thought of that before you went against Shay."

"She's not your wife. Hell," Mueller sat forward, "she's not even your fiancée. I had it checked out. She doesn't wear your ring."

"She will soon."

"But she wasn't when the attack happened," Mueller insisted. "How the fuck was I supposed to know she was protected by Nikolai? I can't read minds." He spread his hands out in front of him. "That's one rule I never break. Black, white, Mexican, Vietnamese—I don't give a shit what color your woman is. I don't touch them."

He didn't want to see things from Mueller's point of view, but he had to admit that the man had a point. Shay hadn't technically been his when the trouble had started. Mueller might have—probably would have—reacted differently if Shay had been openly claimed.

Alexei shifted in his chair and exhaled loudly. "What do you want?"

Mueller leaned forward. "We're starving on these streets. I'm boxed in tight. I need to grow."

"You know I can't help you with that. Your territory problems have to be sorted out by the council. That's a vote I can't sway."

"No? Because I hear you're very good friends with Besian…"

"That friendship goes back many years," Alexei agreed, "but he's a man with his own mind. He's looking out for his family first. It's about blood with them. I have absolutely no influence over his decisions."

The waiter approached their table again, and both men placed their orders. When the waiter was gone, Alexei drummed his fingers on the table. "There might be something else I can offer you."

"And what is that?"

"A piece of something legitimate."

"I'm listening."

Alexei laid out his plans for the pieces of commercial real estate he had been quietly and cheaply collecting for the last six years. He explained that he needed a partner to develop those sites, handle the leases and support the businesses that would occupy them.

Sketching out one of the buildings on the back of a business card as they ate, he explained, "This one is a special case. It's in a prime location. We're going to install a jewelry store in this center spot, an art gallery here on this side and a high-end luxury women's boutique here."

"We?"

"Nikolai and I," Alexei clarified.

"And the work?"

"Nikolai will expect that his construction firms get first pick. You would get second. We'll have to offer pieces of the action to the other families in town. If we don't, we'll run into problems with deliveries and supply thefts."

Mueller grumbled with irritation, but he nodded in acceptance of that fact. It wouldn't be easy parceling out the jobs to develop these properties, but it would have to be done.

Mueller would always be an outsider in the city. After his predecessors had so brazenly attacked Sergei's woman and caused all those problems for Nikolai, Besian and Mr. Lu, Mueller would never be able to reach the inner circle of the top bosses. He would be blocked at every turn. Furthermore, the AB syndicate's philosophies made it impossible for the crews under Nicky Jackson or the Hermanos and the cartels to trust them or work with them unless it was absolutely necessary.

But if Mueller played his cards right, he might be able to gain their trust and find ways to work with them that didn't violate either party's honor codes.

"And can I interest either of you in dessert?" the waiter asked as he cleared away their plates.

"None for me," Alexei said with a wave of his hand.

"I'll have another Macallan." Mueller touched his empty glass. "And then I'm done." When the waiter left, Mueller asked, "What have you heard about Lalo?"

Alexei turned it around on him. "What have *you* heard?"

"That he's missing." Mueller eyed him with thinly veiled suspicion. "That there's a burned up body on ice down at the morgue that is closed to his size."

Alexei shrugged. "He's not my problem. We ended things on good terms. We had no bad blood between us."

Mueller obviously didn't believe that lie, but the waiter returned with his Macallan before he could say anything else.

Alexei took the check and tucked a credit card into the black leather folio. When the waiter left their table, Alexei met Mueller's interested stare. "Wherever Lalo is and whatever happened to him, I trust that Nikolai and the other bosses have it under control." He made a quick slashing gesture across the front of his throat. "You know what they say about tall poppies…"

"I'll have to remember not to grow too tall."

"That's probably a good idea." Alexei grasped the folio the waiter handed him, added a sizeable tip to the check and signed his name across the bottom. "I enjoyed our dinner." He tucked his card back into his wallet. "We'll have to do a working lunch soon."

"I'll have my office set something up."

Their meeting finished, Alexei excused himself and left the restaurant. Despite the company, the meal had been delicious. He would have to bring Shay here.

Thinking of her, he wondered why he hadn't heard from her since their short afternoon chat. It finally occurred to him that he had switched his phone to Do Not Disturb during the morning sales meeting. He hadn't added Shay's number to the proper list yet so her calls and texts wouldn't have sent an alert.

As he walked to his SUV, he pulled his phone from his pocket and checked the screen. There were nine calls from

Stas, two from Nikolai and one from Shay. Stomach churning, he dialed Shay's number but there was no answer. He tried Stas next.

The enforcer answered on the first ring. "Where the fuck are you?"

Taken aback, Alexei said, "I just finished a business meeting. Why?"

"Shay is in the hospital."

"What?" Alexei's heart slammed into his sternum. It beat wildly as he tried to focus. Shay. Hospital. Feeling real fear, he demanded, "What happened? Which hospital?"

"We're at Methodist. The emergency room. She burned her hand. It's not good."

A burn? His heart slowed some. He had been envisioning the worst—a car accident or a gunshot wound. A burn could be healed. A burned hand wouldn't kill her.

But she would be in tremendous pain. His chest tightened as he realized he wouldn't be able to shield her from that. Knowing that she was alone and scared and suffering gutted him.

"I'll be there in fifteen minutes." He considered the time of night and the traffic. "It might be closer to thirty with parking."

Stas ended the call before he could ask to speak with Shay. Worried by the bodyguard's gruff tone, Alexei jogged to his vehicle. He had just gotten behind the wheel when his phone rang again. The Bluetooth connection picked it up so he could drive hands-free. "Yes?"

"Where are you?" Nikolai's exasperation came through clearly. "I just called the restaurant and they said you had left."

"I'm on my way to the hospital."

"So you heard from Stas," Nikolai deduced.

"Yes."

"You should know that there was a shooting tonight. One of Nicky's boys popped one of Diego's over a girl. Diego's soldier was taken to Ben Taub. I sent Boychenko to Methodist when Stas called looking for you. You shouldn't have any problems, but I'd rather be safe than sorry."

The last thing Alexei needed or wanted was to get caught in the crossfire of another's gang's retaliation. Everything was so tightly packed together downtown in the Medical Center. It would be hard to keep the two gangs separated if the Hermanos decided to seek retaliation.

"Call me see me tomorrow before you leave town so we can talk about your meeting. If you or Shay need anything, Vivian and I are only a few minutes away."

"Thank you."

Alexei made the drive in record time. He used the valet, handing off his keys and snatching the ticket before rushing inside the hospital. He scanned the packed emergency room and spotted Boychenko standing in a far corner.

"Where is Shay?" he asked as he drew near.

"They took her back about ten minutes ago."

"Only ten minutes?" The first missed call from Stas had occurred nearly two hours ago.

Boychenko nodded. "She's been waiting here forever. They're slammed tonight."

Alexei's chest ached at the thought of her sitting here in pain for so long. "I need to see her."

"Let me text Stas. He can switch out with you. They're only allowing one person in with each patient."

Boychenko sent his text. A short time later, Stas appeared at the double doors. He held them open so Alexei could get into the treatment area. Wordlessly, her bodyguard pointed out the exam room where Shay waited. Judging by the stony expression on Stas's face, the enforcer wasn't happy. Whatever had pissed him off would have to wait.

Hoping he had the right room, Alexei pulled the curtain aside only a few inches to check. Shay sat on a hospital bed, her legs dangling over the side and her arm resting on a tray. Her injured palm and fingers were covered by a blue surgical towel. Head drooping, she looked utterly exhausted.

He stepped into the room. "Shay?"

Her head snapped up, but instead of greeting him with a relieved smile or happiness, she scowled. "What are you doing here? I told Stas not to call you."

"Of course he's going to call me, Shay." He walked closer and stopped in front of her. "I belong right here with you if you've been hurt."

When he tried to brush a few strands of hair behind her ear, she pulled her head away from him with a harshly hissed, "Don't."

Surprised by her reaction, he dropped his hand. "I'm sorry."

"Whatever." She wouldn't meet his confused gaze and seemed thoroughly pissed off by his presence.

Alexei tried not to let her behavior bother him. She was obviously in pain and tired. He vividly remembered the many times he had been in emergency rooms because of injuries sustained on the streets or fighting in cages. He had always been irritated and frustrated and a right bastard.

"Are you thirsty? Hungry? I can send Stas for something." He wanted to make her comfortable while they waited.

"Stas took care of me already." She gestured to the bottle of water and empty candy bar wrapper on the counter. "I don't need anything from you."

In all the time he had known her, Alexei had never glimpsed this side of Shay. It convinced him that she was in an intense amount of discomfort. Otherwise she never would have been so cross. Wanting her to know that he didn't intend for this to ever happen again, he apologized. "I'm sorry that I missed your call earlier and that I didn't get here sooner. You needed me, and I wasn't there for you. It won't happen again."

Shay lifted her tired head and stared at him. Her expression turned dark. "How was your business meeting?"

He might have imagined it, but her tone sounded accusatory. "It was fine. I had dinner with Mueller. We ironed things out between us over steak."

"And your other meeting?"

He frowned. "Other meeting?"

She made a disgusted sound and rolled her eyes. "Are you seriously going to stand right there in front of me and fucking lie?"

Thrown by her statement, he asked, "Lie about what?"

"I saw you!"

"Saw me where?"

"At the penthouse!"

"What were you doing at the penthouse?"

"*That's* the question you ask?"

Suddenly, he was very glad for the tray between them.

Shay looked as if she wanted to punch him right in the face. "What other question am I supposed to ask?"

"Apparently, this is the point where men like you ask what bright, shiny, expensive thing I want to make up for the other woman you're sleeping with behind my back," she shot back nastily.

"Men like me? The other woman? What are you—?" And then it hit him. She must have seen him with Marissa. "Shay, I don't know what you *think* you saw—"

"All right, Miss Sandoval," a doctor interrupted and pulled back the curtain, "let's take a look at that hand."

Alexei stepped aside so Shay could receive the care she needed. As he watched the doctor examine the nasty burns on her fingers and palm, Alexei tried to control the panic building inside him. His meeting with Marissa had been completely innocent, but he could imagine what it must have looked like to Shay. She knew why he had that penthouse. She knew his history. She was already feeling vulnerable after his morning blunder in bed. Finding him with Marissa must have been shocking and upsetting to her.

I should have told her I was meeting Marissa. It seemed so obvious now, but at the time, it hadn't even occurred to him. *Because you aren't treating her like your partner.* No, he was still treating her like a pretty piece of arm candy. She deserved better and more from him.

"You did a number on these fingers," the doctor said. "I want to have a plastic surgeon consult on this. She may have a different idea for treatment."

"Um…I don't know think my insurance—"

"I'll handle it," Alexei insisted. "I don't care who you have to call or what it costs. I want her to get the best treatment."

"That's all I want for any of my patients," the doctor said before leaving the room.

Assured of a few private moments with Shay, he stepped back in front of her and moved the tray out of the way. He supported her wrist with his left hand and cupped her face with the right. "Shay, please look at me."

She reluctantly lifted her gaze. "I don't want to hear it, Alexei. Maybe it's good that this happened now. I realize that I'm not cut out for this. You want something I can't give you."

"Stop," he ordered gently. "You are all I want." She started to protest, but he pleaded for a moment. "Please let me explain."

She exhaled slowly. "Fine."

"Yes, I did meet with Marissa today. I did *not* sleep with her. In fact, I made it very clear to her that I'm serious about you."

Shay's eyes glimmered with hope. She wanted to believe him, but the childhood she had suffered had left her wounded and vulnerable and unable to trust. He had abused her trust this afternoon by not being honest with her. "Are you going to Vegas this weekend?"

"How did you—?"

"I saw your redhead—Marissa—at the salon. She was telling her stylist about her plans to meetup with her ex in Vegas. When I saw you with her—"

He couldn't even begin to imagine how betrayed she must have felt when she had seen him with Marissa after having to listen to her talk about Vegas and her plans. "I was going to Vegas, Shay. I've done it for years to celebrate my birthday. It's a boys-only trip with my friends. If she was going, it was on her dime and without an invitation from me."

Standing in front of her, caressing her cheek, he finally realized what a colossal asshole he had been. "I can't believe I was stupid enough to think I would be able to enjoy Vegas without you. I think my days of boys-only trips are behind me."

"There's nothing wrong with you going on trips with your friends."

"I should have told you I was planning to go. I should have told you about my meeting with Marissa."

"Why did you meet with her today?"

"She's a very good real estate agent. I'm selling the penthouse."

"What? When did you decide—?"

"This morning," he said, stroking her cheek. "I don't need that place anymore." He kissed her forehead. "I have you, and we have our house."

Her surprised gaze flicked to his. "*Our* house?"

Teasing his mouth against hers, he whispered, "Ours."

"Knock knock." A surgeon in scrubs poked her head into the room. "Oops! Sorry to interrupt."

Shay smiled up at him and then at the surgeon. "It's fine."

Alexei stepped aside as the surgeon and a nurse walked into the small room. The surgeon washed her hands in the sink and slipped into a pair of gloves before sliding the tray back under Shay's hand to examine it. He moved behind Shay and put a comforting, soothing hand on her shoulder.

Shay winced and hissed as the surgeon probed her burned skin. Seeing her in pain was almost too much for him to handle. He listened intently as the surgeon decided on a plan of treatment. When the nurse stepped out to get the necessary supplies, the surgeon assured Shay the injury looked much worse than it was.

"We'll watch for contracture as the wounds heal. If you scar badly, I can revise them. We'll make sure you get the number for my office so you can schedule an appointment next week. I see no reason to be overly concerned. The biggest risk right now is infection. In a month, you'll be fully healed. But maybe we'll be more careful with our tools?"

Shay smiled sheepishly. "Yes. Definitely."

Half an hour later, Shay held her freshly bandaged hand close to her chest. Each finger had been slathered in antibiotic ointment and wrapped individually. Her palm had also been treated and bandaged.

"Have you had a tetanus booster?" the surgeon asked as she washed her hands.

"Um…"

The surgeon laughed. "I'll see if we can get you one tonight."

"Great," Shay answered sarcastically.

"Better safe than sorry," the surgeon said and patted Shay's arm. "I'll see you next week in my office. Okay?"

"Yes. Thank you."

It was another hour before Shay had her tetanus booster and discharge instructions. Feeling terrible for her, he draped his jacket around her shoulders and curved his arm around her back as he walked her out of the emergency room. She stopped to thank each nurse and technician who had helped her tonight, even the harried triage nurse who had made her wait so long for her turn.

"It's not her fault that this place is so busy," Shay said when she saw his face. "You know how emergency rooms are," she said with a shrug. "If you can't afford insurance or if your copays are too high, you put things off until they become serious."

"That doesn't mean I have to be happy that you were made to wait while you were in pain." He spotted Stas and Boychenko as they came through the double doors. Both men had their gazes fixed on something across the room. They reminded him of a pair of watchdogs with their hackles raised. When he realized what they were staring at, he understood why.

Eric Santos and two police officers stood on either side of a handcuffed man with a bloody face and even bloodier shirt. Another line of officers stood in front of the entrance to the emergency room. Alexei didn't have to think too hard to come up with possible explanations for the police presence. Even from here, he could see the Hermanos tattoos on the bloody man's arms and neck and the sides of his shaved head. With what Nikolai had told him earlier, he would put his money on retribution.

Stas stood up. Voice lowered, he said, "We need to get the hell out of here right now."

"Shay?" Eric called out to her, and Alexei quietly cursed under his breath. There would be no quick escape now. "Shay?"

"Hi, Eric." She flashed the detective a smile as he approached. Stas and Boychenko stepped up behind her, forming a human wall of support.

Eric's gaze slid to the men flanking Shay before it moved

to her bandaged hand. "Are you okay?"

"I got a little careless with my tools and burned my hand. I'll be fine in a few weeks."

"That's good to hear." Eric glanced around the busy waiting room. He motioned toward the nearest corner. "Can we talk?"

Alexei caught Shay's questioning gaze and shook his head. "It's late, Eric. She's tired, and she's in pain. Whatever it is can wait until morning."

"No, it can't." Eric stepped forward and lowered his voice. "We found Ruben's Escalade this afternoon. There was enough evidence in the vehicle to confirm that someone was killed in it."

Shay's face went slack with shock. "He's dead?"

"Yes—and that's not all." Eric glanced left and right before stepping closer and lowering his voice to a barely audible level. "We identified that body from the motel. It's Lalo. Before all this shit," he glanced back at the bloody man, "blew up tonight, the biggest news on the street was about your sister. Everyone thinks she iced Lalo *and* Ruben. There's a bounty on her head, and a lot of people will want to collect. One of my informants mentioned your name as part of that bounty."

"What the hell is your problem, Eric?" Alexei snarled at the detective as Shay went white next to him. "Why the hell would you say something like that to her?"

"Because it's the truth," Eric snapped. "She needs to know. If she's going to be safe—"

"She's perfectly safe. Nikolai has given his word, and you know what that's worth. If you're not clear on that, maybe you should ask your cousin to give you a reminder."

Eric narrowed his eyes. "Let's leave Vivian out of this. I'm just trying to keep Shay safe."

Stas stepped forward. "She is safe."

Eric sized up Stas. "And when you're not with her and when Alexei isn't with her?"

"Then I'm with her," Boychenko said.

The bloodied man on the other side of the waiting room started to shout and kick. Eric looked back and frowned before returning his attention to them. Locking eyes with Alexei, he said, "Get Shay out of here. Take that hall. Make a left and then a right. Go out the side exit. Nikolai may have vouched for Shay, but there are a lot of hotheaded soldiers with itchy trigger fingers hanging around this place." He expelled a tired breath. "And I'm tired of cleaning up blood tonight."

Alexei took Eric's advice and escorted Shay out of the building using the side exit. Boychenko took his valet ticket while he stayed behind with Stas and Shay. She burrowed into him for warmth as they waited. Stas pinned him in place with an aggravated look when he kissed her temple and embraced her.

Shay must have seen the look because she reached out and touched Stas's arm. "We're fine. It was a misunderstanding. She's a real estate agent."

Stas grunted and looked down the street. "If you say so…"

Alexei didn't blame Stas for being skeptical. Stroking Shay's hair and her back, he thought about how damn lucky he was that she had listened to his explanation and trusted that he was telling her the truth about Marissa. She could have made him grovel and beg and buy her forgiveness but she had given it freely. He wouldn't abuse her kindness by putting her in this position again.

When Boychenko arrived, Alexei helped Shay into the passenger seat. He offered to drive the two guards to the valet stand to retrieve Stas's vehicle, but they both declined.

"Do you have a list of supplies she needs?" Stas asked. "We can stop at one of the drug stores and pick them up."

He handed Stas the list he had scribbled down in the emergency room. "It's mostly bandages. They called in her prescription to CVS. The one on Kirby. It's on the way home."

Stas pocketed the list. "I'll take care of it."

"Thank you." Alexei slid behind the wheel and buckled his seatbelt. He touched Shay's good hand. "Are you hungry? Do you want me to stop somewhere?"

"I really just want to go home."

He brushed his knuckles along her cheek. She sagged in the seat, and he didn't think she would make it home still awake.

He was right. Shay nodded off before they reached the house. When he pulled into the garage, she woke up and smiled sleepily. He parked and got out, walking around the vehicle to her side and opening her door. He reached in and unbuckled her belt. "I'll help you get undressed when we get upstairs."

"You would try to get me out of my clothes even with twenty yards of gauze wrapped around my hand," she teased.

He laughed and kissed her. "I promise I won't try anything. Come on. Let's get you in the house."

When they reached the door, he paused to turn off the alarm but noticed it hadn't been set. "Did you or Stas turn on the alarm when you left?"

"I don't remember," she admitted. "Probably not. We were in a rush."

"It's fine. I just wanted to be sure that someone else hadn't turned it off." He unlocked the door and led her into the house. He turned on the lights in the kitchen. "Do you want me to make you something to eat? You need to stay up long enough to get your medicine from Stas. It might be easier on your stomach if you have something in it."

"Nothing too heavy," she said.

"Toast? Juice?"

"That works." She settled into one of the seats at the smaller breakfast table. He made quick work of toasting bread and pouring juice. He scraped a thin layer of butter and another layer of blueberry preserves onto the toast before bringing it to her. Before she took the first bite, she said, "I kind of left a mess in your office. I'll clean it up in the morning."

"Don't worry about it." He kissed the top of her head. "I'll handle it." He gestured to her plate. "Eat."

He left her in the kitchen and made his way across the house. He had just stepped into his office when he felt the unmistakable presence of another person. The hair on his arms stood on edge as he took a step back and then another.

But it was too late.

"Stop right there," a shaky female voice ordered. "Or I'll blow a hole right through you."

Raising his hands, Alexei did as instructed. From the shadows of his office, Shannon stepped into view. Her face was a mess of bruises and scrapes. The men's clothing she wore looked as if it had been stolen from a hobo. Looking at the stains and wear, he decided it probably had been. Her sunken eyes were bloodshot. The white residue around her nose was impossible to miss.

High as a kite and pushed to the edge, she held a piece of shit pistol in her trembling hand. The Lorcin .380 was a true Saturday Night Special and it made him nervous. This one even had athletic tape wrapped around the grip to prevent print transfer. Whoever had sold it to her had known that she wanted a cheap piece to use and toss. Having it pointed at his face with her shaky hand at the trigger didn't sit well with him. One wrong move, and he was going to eat a bullet.

Hands in the air, he said, "Shannon, please put that gun down. It's not safe."

"Don't tell me what to do," she snarled. "I'm fucking sick of men telling me what to do."

"Shannon, I'm not trying to upset you. I just want to keep both of us safe. That gun is a throwaway piece for a reason. If it fires—"

"I know what I'm doing. Ruben taught me how to shoot." She swallowed hard and then pointed the gun at his chest. "From this distance, I won't miss."

He gritted his teeth. "Shannon, Shay is in the kitchen right now. If you hurt me, you'll hurt her."

"Fuck Shay," Shannon snapped. "She betrayed me. She told Lalo where to find me. He nearly killed me in that motel."

"Nearly killed you? He nearly killed Shay *and* Kylee *and* me that night when we all ended up at that shithole where you were hiding. Shay didn't betray you. She went there to save you. She was willing to let Lalo take her—to rape and abuse her—to save you and Kylee and me"

"Bullshit!" Shannon shouted angrily. "She was the only

430 | ROXIE RIVERA

one who knew where I was hiding!"

"Really? What about Ruben? He knew where you were hiding."

Shannon roughly wiped her nose, smearing fresh blood across her upper lip and cheek. "He wouldn't do that. He wouldn't betray me. He loves me."

"Shay loves you."

"Oh, yeah. She loves me so much that instead of coming to look for me she decided to shack up with you like some sugar baby." Waving the gun at him, she said, "I always used to think that she was so stupid holding onto her virginity like that. Now I see why." Gesturing around his office with the gun, she laughed. "Look at what she bought with her golden pussy."

Alexei frowned with distaste at Shannon's remark. "Your sister is not a whore."

"You sure about that? What did she trade for all of this? For the cars? For the money? For the house? For your protection?"

"I'm not going to stand here and listen to you talk about your sister like that in her own fucking house." Lowering his hands, he shook his head with disgust. "If you had come here for help and asked properly, respectfully, I would have given it to you with no questions asked. Breaking into our house? Putting a gun in my face? Talking shit about your sister? About the woman I plan to marry? You know what, Shannon? You can go fuck yourself."

"Fuck me?" she screamed shrilly and gestured angrily with the gun. "Fuck you!"

Alexei saw the muzzle flash before he heard the crack of the gunshot. It echoed in the house like a thunderclap.

Something hot and sharp burned through his arm. He stumbled back into a wall and tried to stay on his feet as Shay's panicked voice rang through the house.

Ptichka, he thought with frustration. *Run. Run.*

But she was running toward him instead of to safety…

CHAPTER TWENTY-FOUR

I HAD JUST bent down to put my plate and cup in the dishwasher when I heard Alexei yelling. It surprised me because we were the only people in the house.

The alarm!

The alarm hadn't been set which meant anyone could have gotten into the house while we were away.

Oh no. No. No. No.

Thinking only of him, I ran out of the kitchen. I gasped with shock at the gunshot that blasted my eardrums. "Alexei!"

It was stupid. It was dangerous. But I ran toward across the house toward him, desperate to find him. He wouldn't have left me behind to bleed to death. I wasn't about to abandon him.

I rounded the corner of the arched doorway that led from the main living area. I spotted Alexei against the wall, crumpled forward, blood spilling down his arm and onto the floor.

He looked at me and mouthed one word, "Run."

But a second later, Shannon stepped into the hallway. I almost didn't recognize her at first. She looked like hell. Strung out and bruised, she was dressed in an outfit that had to have been stolen from a homeless shelter. When she noticed me, she raised the gun in my direction and I flinched, fully expecting her to shoot me.

The bullet never came. I opened my eyes and found her staring at me. Just standing there with the gun pointed in my face as if wasn't sure whether to shoot me or not.

"Shannon?" I said her name quietly. "Shannon, what are you doing?"

She lowered the gun by a few inches. "What are *you* doing?"

She seemed confused and scared. Trying to talk her down, I stated the obvious. "I'm standing here. I'm waiting for you to tell me what you need."

"What I need?" she repeated angrily. "What I need is help, but everyone abandoned me. Ruben left me. You left me. I'm all alone and everyone is trying to kill me."

"I'm not trying to kill you. I'm trying to save your life. Everything I've done since that night at the Arena has been to keep you safe."

"Fucking this guy is supposed to keep me safe? Is that what you're telling me? That you bartered your body for me?"

"No, that's not what I'm saying. Everything Alexei has given me, everything he's done for me and for you, was given freely."

She wavered with uncertainty. Her lower lip wobbled as she asked, "Why didn't you come for me at the motel?"

"I *did* come for you. Kylee and I both came for you. We had to get money first. I went to see Abby to get her to cash a check. I took the ten grand to the motel, but you were gone. Lalo was waiting. He was so angry. He tried to…" My voice drifted off, and I gulped. "I killed him, Shannon. He's dead. He can't touch you or me or anyone else we love anymore."

Her face slackened. The gun drifted even lower. "You killed him?"

"We were fighting. He had a gun pointed at me. I shoved it toward his face, and Kylee hit him. The gun fired—and he died."

"How are you still alive?"

"Alexei took care of it." I stared back at her, and her eyes widened. She understood what that meant.

"Took care of *you*, you mean," she corrected. "Something tells me that he and that mob boss friend of his pinned all this shit on me and Ruben."

Not wanting her anger to turn on Alexei, I glanced at him. Still holding his bloody arm, he leaned against the wall and watched us with intense focus. I was afraid he would go for the gun and end up hurting Shannon or getting himself killed.

Desperate to save the man I loved *and* my sister, I started walking toward Shannon. "You are not safe here in Houston, Shannon. We have to get you out of the city. We have to get you some place safe." I moved closer and closer to her, approaching her like a wounded animal that might lash out at any moment. "If you want my help, you have to give me the gun, Shannon. I love you, and I want to save you, but I can't do that if you're trying to kill me or Alexei."

We were so close now that I could smell the cigarette smoke and something far worse clinging to the clothing she had borrowed or stolen. I could see the vein in her neck jumping as her heart raced. Whether it was from fear or adrenaline or the drugs in her system I couldn't say. She was lost and afraid—and I had to save her.

The door alarm chimed. I knew it was only a matter of

time before Stas and Boychenko found us. There was a risk they would overreact and hurt her. I couldn't let that happen.

Bravely—and stupidly—I gripped the muzzle of the gun and slowly pushed it toward the ground. When she didn't fight me, I took the pistol out of her hand, tugging gently until she let go. Alexei stepped forward and snatched it away from me. He removed the magazine and cleared the chamber all while scowling at my sister.

Still holding the gun and magazine, Alexei glanced down the hallway just as Stas came into view. My bodyguard skidded to a halt. His shocked expression was almost comical. He looked at me and then Alexei and then my sister. "What the fuck happened here?"

"Shay's sister dropped her gun, and it went off accidentally," Alexei lied without missing a beat.

Stas didn't believe him for one second, but he didn't question it. Glaring at Shannon, he said, "Sounds like she needs to be more careful with guns."

"Stas, will you please get Alexei a towel?" I noticed Boychenko lingering behind Stas. He had a weapon in his hand and seemed uncertain about whether or not he should holster it. "Please put that away and help me get this mess cleaned up." I glanced at Shannon. "Go sit in the office and wait for me."

With trembling hands, I cupped Alexei's face and gazed up at him. In that moment, my love for this man overwhelmed me. I could have lost him because of my sister's carelessness. Choking back a sob, I asked, "Are you okay?"

He nodded stoically. "I think it was just a graze."

That was just like him to minimize his injury. I pressed a

lingering kiss to his mouth. "Let me look."

Alexei nodded his permission. I managed to rip open his torn shirt sleeve and uncover the wound. It was a bloody, nasty mess, but it wasn't as bad I had feared. It really was a graze, but the skin was torn open and needed suturing or strips. "You need to go to the hospital."

"That's not happening." His hard expression reminded me of the night he had come to my rescue with that bat. This was the version of himself that he tried to keep hidden from me and everyone else. This was the cold-eyed man who could separate himself from pain and fear and do the terrible things that had helped him survive in prison and on the dangerous streets of Moscow and Houston. "If I go to the ER, they'll report the gunshot. Eric will come sniffing around and then we'll have a real problem."

"Here." Stas brought some of the medical supplies that he had picked up for me at the drug store. "I'll bandage it for you, but you'll need some antibiotics and butterfly closures. I'll have to make a trip to see our doctor."

"It can wait until I've dealt with Shannon."

I wanted to be the one who treated Alexei's wound, but with a bandaged hand of my own, it wasn't possible. Stas, Alexei and I entered the office and found Shannon sitting in one of the chairs by the fireplace. She had her head in her hands and sobbed quietly. Torn between comforting my sister and the man I loved, I hesitated. Alexei made the decision for me when he walked away and dropped into his desk chair. I tried not to let his sudden change in demeanor upset me. He'd just been shot, after all.

Kneeling down in front of Shannon, I wrapped my arms

around her. Despite my anger with her for shooting Alexei, I was relieved that she was alive. "It's going to be okay. I promise. We'll find a way to make it right."

Alexei hissed as Stas cleaned his wound. He met my gaze across the room. "We have to get her out of the country."

"How?" I didn't know the first thing about something like that. "If she goes to Mexico, she's walking right into cartel territory. There's no way we can get her to Canada. I'm sure Eric has her ID and passport flagged."

"I know someone who can help." Alexei winced as Stas applied pressure to his wound. "Shay, go upstairs to our bedroom and open the bottom drawer in my dresser. There are some burner phones there. Grab one. Then go to the closet and open the drawer where I keep my ties. Lift the tray and pick up the leather jewelry case there. Bring them to me."

I nodded dutifully and hurried upstairs to do as he instructed. Burner phones weren't the only things I found in that bottom drawer. There were loaded weapons, extra boxes of ammunition, two knives and rolls of cash. When I went to his tie drawer, I found the jewelry case. It was stamped with the logo of a high-end jewelry store that I had only ever dreamed of visiting. I ignored the urge to open the case to see what was inside, grabbed a clean shirt for him and hurried back downstairs to the office.

Boychenko was wiping down the floor when I walked by him. "I'll come by in the morning to repair the drywall."

I stopped and looked back at the wall and noticed the hole for the first time. Boychenko stood up and held out his hand. The round he had recovered rested on his palm. "Give this to Alexei."

"What? Why would he—?"

"Trust me." Boychenko pressed it into my good hand. "He'll want it."

I brought everything Alexei had requested to him and placed them on the desk. I started to walk back to Shannon, but Alexei grasped my hand and kept me from leaving. He rubbed his thumb in slow circles over the back of my hand. I understood this was his way of telling me that we were going to be okay. Leaning down, I kissed his forehead and whispered, "I know."

"Open the jewelry case," he ordered gently. "I need you to see it."

I did as he asked and nearly fainted when I uncovered the incredible necklace and earrings. Brilliant diamonds, some white and others canary yellow, glimmered inside the case. "What is this?"

"I bought this for you. I bought it the morning after I saved you in that alley." Alexei traced the stones with his finger. "I wanted you to have these. I wanted to use these to show you how much you mean to me."

Not caring that my sister or two enforcers were watching us, I caressed his jaw. "I don't need diamonds to know how much you care about me."

Alexei turned his head and kissed my palm. He smiled sadly. "That's a good thing because I'm going to have to use these to buy your sister's safety. I don't keep enough cash in my safe, and we can't wait for the banks to open. We have to get her out of the city tonight."

"I'm sorry," I whispered, feeling so much guilt at the situation we were in now. "I'm so sorry."

"Hush." He kissed my palm again. "I'd spend every fuck-ing penny I have to make you happy. Saving your sister will make you happy. That's all that matters."

"I have something that might help you spend a little less money," Shannon interjected in a ragged voice. "Well—I mean, I did have something that might help. I'm not sure where it is now."

"What do you mean?" I asked.

"Our house is empty. All of our shit is gone."

"It's not gone. It's here."

"I figured as much. That's why I broke in here." She made an apologetic face. "You're going to need a new window in your pool room. Your alarm isn't working either."

"You're lucky I forgot to turn on the alarm when we left for the ER," I said, lifting my hand. "Otherwise, you'd be in the back of a police car right now."

As if she hadn't even noticed my hurt hand, her eyes wid-ened. "What happened to you?"

"I burned myself."

"With those stupid wood burning tools? I told you those things are dangerous! I warned you that those cords were going to get tangled up and that you were going to knock something over and hurt yourself."

I rolled my eyes. "It was an accident."

"Why did you break into the house?" Alexei interrupted our sisterly spat. "What did you hope to find here?"

"There was a box in my bedroom. The little jewelry box with the ballerina," Shannon clarified. "It has something in it that I need."

"I saw it when the delivery came," Stas said and pushed off

the wall he had been leaning against. "I dropped a box and it fell out. I'll go get it."

"What is it?" Alexei asked. "And don't lie to me, Shannon. The man I'm going to call is not someone who tolerates lies."

Shannon swallowed anxiously. "Earlier this year, Ruben and I started thinking about getting out of the life. We were tired of it. He was sick of the drugs and the guns and the gambling. He felt like Lalo was never going to let him have his own crew or grow his territory." She rubbed her face between her grubby hands. "One of his friends from high school—Edgar—came to him with this scheme. He'd been running it small time by himself, but he needed money to get it off the ground and he needed access to computers and businesses."

"Like mine," Alexei interrupted with irritation.

Shannon nodded reluctantly. "Like yours. We came up with a plan, and we started small with companies that had little or no security. I would plug in a flash drive, hit a few keys and then let the program run while I cleaned. I would grab them when I was done, hide them in my smock and go to the next job." She gave a little shrug. "It was easier than we thought it would be."

"But what was the plan?" Alexei touched his injured arm. "Who was going to buy this information you were stealing?"

"Edgar put a listing on some deep web site. There were a few offers, and he accepted one. We were getting ready to package it and sell it. Edgar was going to Belize. Ruben and I were planning to run away to some place like Thailand."

"Were you going to tell me before you left?" It was impossible to keep the hurt out of my voice.

Shannon met my gaze. Quietly, she said, "No."

"No? You were just…what? Going to leave and hope I didn't notice? You were going to leave me here to clean up your mess?"

"I was going to tell you when we were some place safe," she insisted. "I wasn't worried about you. I knew that you'd land on your feet like you always do." She glanced at Alexei. "I knew that he would come running the second I was gone. He's been watching you for months. You were blind to it, but I wasn't. I knew that the moment I was out of the picture, you were finally going to get your chance at happily ever after."

While I was trying to process all of that, Stas returned with the jewelry box. He handed it to Shannon who opened it and produced a handful of flash drives. "These are the originals. I kept them. All of them. It was the way Ruben and Edgar decided to keep things fair. Edgar couldn't sell the information behind our backs, and we couldn't sell it behind his. I don't have the decryption key that Edgar kept, but I have everything else."

"Who was your buyer?" Alexei asked.

"I don't know. It was anonymous."

"Maybe not so anonymous," he grumbled. Picking up the burner phone, he turned it on and waited for it to find service. He dialed a number and left a cryptic message with an answering service along with the number for the burner he held. Putting the phone down, he sighed. "And now we wait."

"For?"

"For me to make a deal with the devil." Alexei held my hand a little tighter. "It's going to be a long night. You should get your sister cleaned up. If she's hungry, feed her." He kissed my fingertips. "You need to take your medicine, too."

I had a feeling Alexei wanted us out of the office so he could make other phone calls. There were things I didn't need or want to know. I did as he asked and took Shannon upstairs to shower. We didn't say a word, not even when I handed her some of my clothing. She got dressed quickly and swirled her hair into a loose bun.

"Shannon?" I didn't want to tell her, but she needed to know what Eric had told me earlier.

"Yeah?"

"Shannon…it's about Ruben."

"I already know." She didn't look away from the mirror. Her voice was calm and detached. "I knew as soon as he didn't come back to the motel for me."

"I'm so sorry, Shannon."

Silent and serious, she turned away from the mirror and walked toward me. She put both hands on my shoulders and gazed down at me. "Shay, I never meant for any of this to happen. I need you to know that."

"I do know that."

"I love you, and I'm sorry that I screwed everything up for us."

"I love you, and we're going to be okay. You made some mistakes. You've paid for them. You don't have to keep apologizing to me." Shannon had lost everything trying to run this scheme—her man, her freedom and nearly her life. There was no reason for me to try to punish her further. She would be doing that to herself for the rest of her life.

After grabbing a hoodie for her and a jacket for me, I took her downstairs and let her make a sandwich. Feeling fatigued, I fixed a cup of coffee and took the medicine Stas had picked up for me. I was halfway through my coffee when Alexei walked into the kitchen with the clean shirt draped over his good arm.

"We need to go," he announced. "Zec can't keep his plane waiting very long."

Leaving my cup of coffee on the table, I crossed the kitchen and helped him out of his ruined shirt and into the clean one. He handled the buttons himself because the fingers on my right hand were still too painful to move. I didn't like it when Stas produced a shoulder holster for Alexei to wear, but I accepted that it was a necessity.

I picked up Alexei's suit jacket from the back of the chair where I had left it earlier and helped him slide his arms through it. Behind me, Shannon finished her quick meal and put on the hoodie I had given her. Stas handed me the jacket I had brought down for myself.

Ten minutes later, we were driving to a private airport I hadn't even known existed. I sat in the middle row of the SUV next to Shannon and held her hand as we made a drive that was going to forever change our lives. Alexei remained tight-lipped so I had no idea what was going to happen to Shannon once we reached the airport. Who was taking her? Would they treat her well? Was she going somewhere even more dangerous?

When we arrived at the airport, Alexei's burner phone rang. He gave Stas directions in Russian. The SUV pulled into an open hangar. Boychenko followed close behind in his car. The doors closed behind our vehicles. I could see two men standing near a private jet. One of them I recognized as Besian. The other was a stranger to me.

Alexei turned in his seat. "Shay, stay here. I'll come get you when it's time to say goodbye. You," he pointed at Shannon, "get out of the car and come with me."

Shannon nodded and gave my hand a squeeze. My heart hammered in my chest as I watched my sister climb out of the SUV and follow Alexei. Stas trailed them with a duffel bag stuffed with cash and the jewelry.

Face taut with fear, Shannon glanced back at the SUV. In that moment, our entire life together flashed before my eyes. For better or worse and despite all her mistakes, she was my sister, and I loved her. Tears burned my eyes as I began to accept that I might never see her again.

To save her life and mine, she had to make a choice. She could disappear—or die.

CHAPTER TWENTY-FIVE

"KEEP YOUR MOUTH shut," Alexei warned as he came around the SUV to escort Shannon. His arm throbbed incessantly, and it left him feeling irritated and short-tempered. "Don't say a word unless you're specifically asked something."

Shannon's face contorted with distaste. "Are you always this controlling and rude with my sister?"

He scowled at the woman who would one day be his sister-in-law. "I love Shay, and I'll do anything for her—but you have pushed me right to the fucking edge tonight, Shannon. You need to remember that I'm the only thing standing between you and a bullet."

"I'm sorry," she said quickly. "I really didn't mean to shoot you. I was mad and my hands are shaky. I haven't been eating, and I was using a little bump here and there to stay awake. It was an accident. I mean it."

He didn't doubt that it had been an accident, but he wasn't about to cut her any slack. "You could have killed me or Shay tonight. We're family, Shannon, but that doesn't mean I have to like you."

"Since when are we family? And that goes both ways. I don't have to like you either."

"I'm going to marry your sister. That makes you my fami-ly."

"Does she know that?"

Alexei glanced at the SUV where she waited. "She will soon."

"You better treat her right, Alexei."

"Does she look unhappy to you? She's living in a beautiful home. She has her pick of a fleet of luxury vehicles. She doesn't have to worry about money anymore and can focus on her handbags."

"That's not what I meant," Shannon argued. "I mean that you better love her right. She's soft inside and good. She needs someone who appreciates that. She needs a man who will make her feel special. She needs a man who can be her rock."

"I do love her. She means more to me than you can ever imagine or understand." Alexei couldn't believe he was talking about his relationship with Shay with her sister. This night was getting crazier and weirder by the minute. "I'll make sure that Shay never wants for anything."

"All she's ever wanted is to be part of a family."

"I'll build a family with her," he promised.

"Are we going to make this deal or what?" Zec called out in Albanian. "Some of us have schedules we're trying to keep."

"Remember what I said," Alexei warned. "These men are a different breed, especially Zec. He's the most dangerous man you'll ever meet."

Shannon nodded to assure him she understood. He led her across the hangar to where the two Albanians waited. Besian she was probably familiar with because of Ruben's involve-ment in the underworld, but he noticed the way she stiffened at the sight of Zec. He didn't blame her for that reaction. Even after all these years of doing business with the smuggler, Alexei still felt uneasy around him.

Wealthy and powerful, Zec had built a legitimate import and export business based out of the Balkans. He used it to hide his illicit activities. There were few things he wouldn't smuggle from country to another. As far as Alexei knew, Zec drew his only line at human trafficking. Everything else was fair game.

Intensely private and secretive, he was a difficult man to pin down, and other than Besian, Alexei didn't know if he had any true friends. The scar across his throat from the razor that had slashed him open served as a reminder that this was a man who had cheated death and feared nothing. In the past, he had done some huge deals with Zec. He liked to think they had a good working relationship, but he never took it for granted. Zec was the kind of man who would think nothing of cutting his throat over a perceived slight.

"Let's see it," Zec rasped in that destroyed voice of his.

Shannon held out the small jewelry box filled with flash drives. Nervously, she admitted, "I don't have the decryption key. Edgar was the only one who had it, and he's dead."

"That's what happens to people who try to double cross me." Zec showed little emotion as he admitted to having ordered the hacker's death.

"You were the buyer all along." Alexei had suspected as much, especially after Besian was so helpful. Pinning Besian in place with a look, he said, "And that's why you were so happy to run interference for Shay."

Besian smiled and shrugged carelessly. "It's easier to ask

Nikolai for forgiveness than permission. He'll be angry tomorrow when he realizes that we caused this mess. He might even thank me for helping solve the Lalo Contreras problem without any of us having to lift a finger. He'll get over it when he gets his cut. He's going to be a father soon. That son of his needs a college fund."

"Speaking of sons," Alexei said, "I want to talk to you about Zel's debt."

"There's nothing to talk about," Besian replied. "He fights on Saturday night. If he wins, the debt is settled. If he loses, he still owes me."

"Send me that bill."

"You're the second person to ask me that today."

Alexei assumed Ivan was the other one. "Zel's had enough, Besian."

"As touching as your concern is," Zec interrupted, "I don't have time to stand here and listen to you two negotiate an old debt. I'm here to finish my deal."

He stared at Shannon, and she shrank back as if struck. "I'm not paying you a single penny for those. You and your boyfriend and that scam artist hacker tried to fuck me with this deal. First, you agreed to sell this information exclusively to me. Second, you tried to sell another copy to Lalo. Third, you found out that you had something Mueller wanted and gave him the chance to buy the information back."

Alexei struggled with the shock that tore at him as Zec described Shannon's brazen double and triple dealing. Was she stupid or just that greedy?

Zec's lip curled as he slashed his hand through the air. "This should have been a clean transaction. No blood. No deaths. You three set the city on fire with your greed and your lies, and you've forced my man here," he gestured to Besian, "and this man," he gestured to Alexei, "and all the other bosses to put out the flames. So you don't get shit."

"That's not fair!" Shannon snapped. "I worked hard to get these!"

"Fair?" Zec laughed right in her face. "Do you know what fair is where we come from? Fair is killing you and your sister and your sister's friend and Alexei for your betrayal. So—I'll give you a choice. I can treat you fairly." He pulled aside his jacket to reveal two holstered weapons. "Or I can teach you a hard lesson about liars and thieves."

Shannon gulped and licked her lips. "I'll take the hard lesson."

"Good choice." Zec let his jacket fall closed. Glancing at Alexei, he said, "You know the terms."

Relieved that Shannon hadn't stupidly called his bluff, Alexei nodded. "It's all in the bag."

"It will be three to five days before she'll contact you. You know the rules about phone and internet use." Zec paused. "Do you have any location requests?"

"It needs to be some place that Shay can visit easily." He remembered what Shannon had said in his office about running away with Ruben to Thailand. That dream had died with her lover, but that didn't mean he couldn't still give her some part of it. "Some place warm," he added. "With beaches and low living costs."

Shannon glanced at him in surprise. He wasn't an ogre. Yes, she'd shot him and put Shay in danger again and again, but he wasn't going to punish her for the rest of her life by asking Zec to drop her in some shithole.

"Beaches and low cost of living?" Zec repeated. "I can make that happen."

Alexei signaled Stas to hand over the duffel bag. "Get Shay."

After giving one of Zec's men the bag, Stas lumbered away, and Alexei turned to Shannon. He reached into his jacket and produced four thick envelopes of cash. "These are for you. It's all you're going to get for a while so make it count."

Seemingly surprised by his generosity, Shannon accepted the money from him. "Thank you, Alexei. For everything," she added sincerely. "I know you didn't have to help me, but you did and I'm grateful for that."

"Be careful, Shannon. Be *smart*. This has to be the last time you get in trouble like this. I won't allow Shay to be put in danger again."

"I understand," she promised. Then, sheepishly, she added, "I'm really sorry about your arm."

Besian frowned. "What happened to your arm?"

Unhappily, he grumbled, "She shot me."

Besian's eyes widened fractionally. "When? Tonight?"

"Yes." Alexei motioned toward his injured arm.

Besian chuckled darkly. "Hell, you and Ivan really know to pick sisters, huh?"

Alexei grunted in agreement, all the while thinking of Ivan's advice about the dangers of dating sisters. He'd have to remember to buy Ivan a beer the next time they were out and ask him for advice. He hoped that Shannon would learn from this experience and go straight, but he was a realistic man. He had to prepare for either outcome.

Shay approached their small group. When Besian spotted her bandaged hand, he asked, "Did your sister shoot you, too?"

Shay frowned at him. "No, I burned myself."

Besian glanced at Alexei. "All this time and all those women and you still haven't found one who can cook?"

Shay rolled her eyes. "I burned myself on a pyrography pen. I'm fully capable of cooking a meal without setting a kitchen on fire."

"You'll have to prove that by cooking dinner for me," Besian teased.

"Fat chance," Shay shot back rudely.

Alexei watched Besian to see how he would respond to Shay. The loan shark surprised him by offering an olive branch.

"And would my chances improve if I arranged a sit-down with your friend and made things right for her?"

Shay hesitated. "I'm not sure that's possible. She's carrying around a lot of hurt and anger over the way that all went down. It isn't just taking her horse and humiliating her father that she holds against you. Her mom died in that awful homeless shelter. Kylee couldn't even scrape together the money for her mother to have a proper burial. They forced her to cremate her mom and put her in that terrible pauper's field. She doesn't even have a real grave or a place to mourn her mother."

Besian's face darkened. "That wasn't all my fault."

"I know that. Deep down inside, I'm sure Kylee knows it. You're just an easier target to hate than the banks and the SEC and everyone else who ruined her life."

Looking at Besian, Alexei wondered if this was the first

452 | ROXIE RIVERA

time he had ever considered what really happened to the families connected to the debts he collected. Or maybe it was the first time someone had ever laid it out so plainly to him. Judging by the change in his demeanor, Besian was troubled by the facts that had been presented to him. Alexei was left to wonder what his friend would do about it.

Standing back, he gave Shay and her sister some space as they hugged and cried. He hated to see Shay so upset, but there was no other way to help her sister. Hector wouldn't be able to keep the local boys from going after Shannon now that the body in the morgue had been identified as Lalo's. Mueller would want revenge once Zec used that information he had just obtained to blackmail him.

With his trademark coldness, Zec rasped, "It's time to go."

Shay and Shannon reluctantly separated. They whispered and smiled one last time before Shannon turned her back and headed straight for the stairs leading up into the jet.

Zec eyed Shay with some interest. "So you're the girl who stood up to Lalo and then killed him, huh?"

Shay didn't correct him, and Alexei was glad for it. Sometimes it was better to be the star of an underworld legend.

Nodding with approval, Zec addressed him in Russian, "This one will do, Lyosha."

Confused, Shay looked to him for an explanation but he simply shook his head. Later, if she asked again, he would tell her. Taking her hand, he tugged gently and coaxed her to follow him back to the SUV.

Besian fell into step beside him. "Are you headed home?"

Home sounded so good right now. He wanted to drop into bed with Shay and sleep for the next twenty-four hours—but it had finally occurred to him that he and Shay needed to have a real discussion about their future. Tonight had changed everything. "I need to make a stop first. Why?"

"I can send my doctor to visit you. He can get you patched up if you need it."

"I do." Alexei could feel the bandage on his arm growing wet. "Send him in an hour?"

"Sure." Besian broke away toward his own idling car.

Alexei wiped the tears off Shay's cheeks and kissed her before helping her into the SUV. The heartache of sending her sister away wouldn't leave her anytime soon. She needed time to grieve, and he needed to remember that. He'd promised Shannon that he would be good to Shay. He was determined to keep that vow.

"Where are we going?" Stas asked after sliding behind the wheel.

He rattled off the address as he buckled his seatbelt. Shay kept her gaze glued to her window as they backed out of the hangar and then twisted to look out the rear window. She seemed unable to tear her gaze away from the plane that would carry her sister away.

"She'll be fine, Shay." He didn't want her worrying unnecessarily.

"Are you sure?" She bit her lower lip with concern. "That guy with the scar on his throat looked really dangerous."

"He is dangerous," Alexei confirmed. "But he won't hurt your sister. We made a deal. He is duty bound to honor it. In a few days, Shannon will call you and you'll see that everything is fine."

"I hope so," she answered softly.

The drive across the sleepy city was quiet and uneventful. They rode in silence, each of them mired in their own thoughts. Alexei suspected Stas was thinking of all the ways he could get out of bodyguard duty as quickly as possible. In the last week, Stas had been through a baptism by fire. He'd gained a better understanding of the city's underbelly and the players and the loyalties and grudges that would always complicate things.

Alexei smiled ruefully as it finally dawned on him that Nikolai had planned this from the beginning. He now suspected Nikolai had known all along that Besian and Zec were scheming to pull off that massive identity theft. Assigning Stas to Shay had been the boss's way of ensuring he had an inside man to report back with information and that Stas got a much-needed introduction to the city. Before he could turn Stas loose on the streets, Nikolai had to test him and be sure that he was trustworthy and loyal. If this week with Shay hadn't proved that, nothing would.

Nikolai truly was a master when it came to the game of surviving in the underworld…

"Pull in there," Alexei instructed when they reached the half-completed retail center. Stas stopped in the parking space Alexei had indicated. He glanced at the hulking enforcer. "Wait here. We won't be long."

Alexei grabbed the envelope holding the legal paperwork before getting out of the SUV and walking around to Shay's door. She eyed him with confusion as he took her hand and led her to the dark and unfinished building. He hadn't been to the building in a few weeks, but the lockbox combination on the sealed door was the same. He punched in the code, retrieved the keys and opened the door.

"What are we doing here?" Shay followed close behind him and latched onto the back of his jacket so she wouldn't get lost in the dark.

"We're going to talk about our future." He found a light switch. Only one side of the room was illuminated but it was enough for them to see each other.

"Our future? Here?" She glanced around the unfinished building. "In this abandoned place?"

"It doesn't look like much right now, but it will. Give me some time."

"And what will it look like when you're done?"

"Read this." He handed her the envelope. "You'll understand."

Gawking at him as if he were crazy, she took the envelope. "You realize it's almost two in the morning, right?"

"Humor me, *ptichka*."

"All right." Shay opened the envelope and removed the papers inside. She scanned the first document, and her eyes widened. She glanced up at him as if unsure that she was actually understanding them and then started reading each one. "Alexei, what is this?"

"The paperwork for incorporating your business is straight-forward, but you'll need an attorney to review them and make recommendations. I have the names of a handful that I trust."

She flashed a page at him. "And this?"

"Nikolai and I have decided to turn this into a high-end shopping destination. Vivian will have a gallery of her very own down on the other end. Kazimir and Zoya will move their jewelry store into the larger center space. And this space," he gestured around them, "will be your handbag shop. Maybe you can let Kylee share the space with you."

"My own shop?" she asked in shock.

"I spoke to An Trinh a few days ago. She knows people in the fashion production industry here. I'm going to get some quotes from her so we can figure out a way to increase your production while still keeping your designs handmade and unique."

"Employees? Me? A boss?"

"You'll be good at it," he assured her. "You have what it takes to build something truly special here, Shay." Pointing to the real estate paperwork, he said, "After you sign those, you'll own this building. Forever," he added. "It's yours."

"Mine? Forever?" she repeated in disbelief.

"Whatever you decide about me, this place will be yours irrevocably."

"Whatever I decide about you? What does that mean?"

"It means that we can't go on as we are, Shay." Even before Shannon had shot him, even before the misunderstanding with Marissa, he had come to accept that as fact.

Visibly crushed, she asked, "Are you breaking up with me? Is this your parting gift? Is this supposed to make up for not having you? Because if that's the case, I don't want it. I only want you. Just you. Always."

"Shay," he said with a tired laugh, "of course not. You and I are so tangled up in each other we can never be separated. The only way I'm walking away from you is if you walk out the door first and leave me behind."

"That's impossible," she said simply. "I don't ever want to let you go."

"Good." His heart thudded powerfully in his chest. "Because I love you, Shay."

She burst into tears. Taken aback, he wasn't sure if they were tears of joy or sadness. Crossing the distance between them, he embraced her with his uninjured arm and kissed her cheek. "Shay, talk to me."

She wound her arms around his neck and kissed him hard. Rising on tiptoes, she deepened their kiss to one of such passion that it left him throbbing and lightheaded. "I love you, Alexei," she whispered as she gazed adoringly up at him. "I love you so much."

"Then there's only one thing for us to do," he said firmly.

"And what's that?"

"Tomorrow, we both fly to Vegas to celebrate my birthday. We'll bring Stas and Kylee with us."

"And then?" she asked breathlessly, her eyes alight with hope and excitement.

"And then we get married," he said matter-of-factly. "We make it official. You and me." He kissed her until she started laughing. Pulling back, he smiled at her and brushed his fingers down her cheek. "What?"

"Is this really a proposal?"

"Do you want me to kneel? I will." He started to slide down to one knee but she stopped him.

"Don't be silly!"

With a mischievous grin, he reminded her, "You enjoyed yourself the last time I was kneeling in front of you."

"Alexei!" A blush darkened her cheeks and ears.

Laughing, he kissed her again. More serious, he traced her lower lip and asked properly, "Will you marry me, Shay?"

Her lip trembled beneath his thumb. "Yes, Alexei. I'll marry you."

This time their kiss seemed never-ending. Neither wanted it to end as they celebrated their decision to spend their lives together and to build a family.

"Are we really going to do this?" she asked as he combed his fingers though her beautiful hair. "Just run away to Vegas and get married?"

"It's the most obvious thing, isn't it? You love me. I love you. It's what people do when they love each other the way we do. I didn't know it was possible to love like this until you, Shay." He took her hand and put it over his heart. "I didn't know it was possible to feel like this."

"Neither did I," she admitted. Lightening the mood, she pointed out, "We won't have much of a honeymoon. You're probably going to end up with stitches tonight, and I have a gauze paw complicating things."

"Shay, you underestimate me." He let his hand ride the curve of her back right down to her plump bottom. "I can think of twenty different ways to have you that won't hurt either of us."

She arched her brow. "Only twenty?"

"Careful," he warned. "Twenty-one includes leather cuffs and silk rope."

"And twenty-two?" she asked with a playful smile.

Alexei laughed and kissed her again. He loved her so

much. After everything they had survived in the last week, there was nothing they couldn't face now. Hand in hand, side by side, they would create a new life together, one filled with love and passion and happiness

And nothing in this whole wide world would stop them.

The End.

For Free Reads that continue each couple's story and for new release and sales announcements, please sign up for

my newsletter.

http://eepurl.com/sX-z1

Also by Roxie Rivera

Her Russian Protector
Ivan

Dimitri

Yuri

Nikolai

Sergei

Sergei 2

Nikolai 2

Alexei

Kostya – Coming 2016

Ivan 2 – 2016

Danila – 2016

Fighting Connollys
In Kelly's Corner

In Jack's Arms

In Finn's Heart

Debt Collection
Collateral

Collateral 2 – Coming 2016

Past Due – Coming 2016

Paid in Full – 2017

Down Payment – 2017

Final Installment – 2017

About the Author

A *New York Times* and *USA Today* bestselling author, I like to write super sexy romances and scorching hot erotica. I live in Texas on five acres with my red-bearded Viking husband, our sweet, mischievous little girl and two crazy Great Danes.

You can find me online at www.roxierivera.com.

www.ingramcontent.com/pod-product-compliance
Lightning Source LLC
Chambersburg PA
CBHW071634260626
47170CB00001B/92